ALSO BY STINA LINDENBLATT

CONTEMPORARY ROMANCES

Carson Brothers Series

One More Chance

One More Secret

One More Betrayal

One More Truth

One More Heartbeat

Pushing Limits Series

This One Moment

My Song For You

I Need You Tonight

ROMANTIC COMEDY NOVELS

By The Bay Series

Decidedly Off Limits

Decidedly with Baby

Decidedly with Love

Decidedly with Mistletoe

Decidedly by Chance

Decidedly with Luck

Decidedly with Wishes

Visit stinalindenblattauthor.com for more books

ONE MORE HEARTBEAT

A CARSON BROTHERS NOVEL

STINA LINDENBLATT

To Ralph, you were my real-life book boyfriend,
my soul mate, my best friend, my husband, my forever.
Not a day goes by that I don't miss you. XOX

ONE MORE HEARTBEAT

1

GARRETT

I reread the text while I wait in line at Picnic & Treats for my turn at the counter. The last time I'd received a text like this from Maxwell Rodgers, my literary agent, was never.

> Maxwell: When I call you in forty minutes,
> ANSWER THE GODDAMN PHONE!!!

Some of his clients had warned me, years ago, if he ever used all-caps and exclamations in a text, I'd better be worried. And I am. What if my sales dropped? Would my publisher drop me?

Maxwell didn't even give me a hint as to why he needs to talk to me. No email. No voice mail. Nothing.

I check the clock on my phone. I still have thirty minutes. Plenty of time to get my lunch and drive the short distance to meet my brother before Maxwell calls me. But it just means we have to delay our run.

Loud conversation and laughter from the tables behind me yank my thoughts back to Picnic & Treats. My best friend's blood and sweat, ambitions and dreams, have been poured into the café. Her grand vision. A vision my stomach always appreciates.

It rumbles at the mouthwatering smells. Smells that only come from my kitchen when Zara visits my house and cooks. For fun. For our friends. For me.

Unfortunately for my stomach, I don't get to enjoy my lunch until after my run.

It's not even noon, and the café is swarming with local customers. We're in the final week of April, the end of off-season in Maple Ridge, Oregon. Tourist season, in the small mountainous town, starts soon.

And then Picnic & Treats will have a line out the door.

Zara is behind the counter, chatting to a mother with a baby in a car seat. Zara's wearing the café's white T-shirt with the P&T logo on the chest, and purple pants. Her violet scarf holds back a halo of black coils that brushes all the way past her shoulders.

With her stunning hair, copper-brown skin, and sparkling chocolate-brown eyes, my best friend is fucking gorgeous. A fact I'm sure her boyfriend—what's-his-name—appreciates.

The scrawny little girl who'd waved her fists in the face of the kid who'd bullied me has long since grown up. But she's still as fierce and loyal as she was in elementary school. A true warrior.

She also might be the inspiration for the love interest in the psychological thriller I'm writing. Not that I would ever admit that to her. Or anyone else.

It's my turn to step up to the counter.

"Hey." Zara's usual smile could light up a room during a power outage. It makes you feel like you belong here, whether you're a regular or a tourist visiting the mountains for the day. But that smile is nothing compared to the one she gives me now.

This one is several hundred watts brighter.

"The usual? Or are you gonna try something different this time?" The equivalent of a smirk slides into her tone. She already knows the answer. I'm that predictable when it comes to her cooking.

"Nope. The usual." I can't get enough of her African curry —*kuku paka*—and rice.

Zara's gaze travels over my sneakers, running shorts, and sweatshirt. "You meeting up with Kellan?"

"Yep." I flash her a one-sided grin. "You wanna join us? We're running on one of the trails near the Warrior cabins."

Zara shakes her head, giving me a comical cross-eyed expression. "Do I look certifiable? Running with you and Kellan—or Troy and Lucas—would be the death of me. I'll pass, thanks." As I knew she would. Running has never been Zara's thing.

I fold my arms on the high countertop and lean forward, closing the distance between us. "If you change your mind, Golden Girl, you know where to find me."

Zara releases a low, throaty laugh. "Trust me, Garrett, it'll be a rainy day in Hell before I work out with you."

"How do you know it doesn't usually rain in hell? Heavy rain sounds hellish to me."

Zara snorts. "Even in heavy rain, I bet you two would still go running."

I puff up my chest, smiling. "You don't get to skip your run while in the Marines just 'cause it's raining hard."

"True...but all that rain would extinguish the flames of Hell."

I chuckle. "Good point."

Zara gives my arms a playful shove, hinting for me to remove them from the counter. "I'll be right back with your order."

She disappears through the door to the kitchen and returns with my takeout lunch and hands it to me. "Have a good run."

I drive to the Wilderness Warriors property on the outskirts of town. The land, which covers fifty acres, is mostly open meadow and a forest of maple trees, with the local mountain range beyond.

I park the Explorer next to Kellan's Trailblazer on the gravel driveway in front of the main building. It resembles a large log cabin with a wheelchair ramp on one side. The driveway is scheduled to be paved in two weeks. One more thing on my to-do list that has nothing to do with my writing, which pays my bills. But since I've got seven more months until my manuscript is due to my editor, it'll be fine.

Time to make a video for social media. Gotta nurture my connections with my readers.

I shoot a video of the landscape that was buried under a thick layer of snow last month. "Hey, everyone," I say, the camera still on the meadow. "About to go running with one of my brothers, to help get those creative juices flowing." I move the camera up. "Check out these snow-covered mountains. Another week or two and everything here will be green, as far as the trees are concerned. Beautiful. What does it look like where you live? Comment below."

I tap the Stop button.

"Thought your readers prefer seeing your ugly face."

Kellan's shoes crunch across the gravel, and I turn to greet him. He has on the same running gear as me, minus the hoodie. "Hey."

When most people see us together, they assume we're biological brothers. Maybe even fraternal twins, given we're the same age and our hair is the same shade of dark brown. We're both in great shape from working out daily, a way to deal with the demons we don't like to talk about. His eye color is the only obvious difference that separates him from Lucas, Troy, our parents, and me. My adopted brother's eyes are blue; ours are brown.

"Maybe they would like to see me, but after what happened with the Annie Wilkes clone three years ago, I keep my face out of my social media posts whenever I can."

"At least she wasn't as crazy as that character in Stephen King's *Misery*."

"Yeah, Annie Wilkes 2.0 didn't lock me in her house and demand I resurrect a character I'd killed off. But remember, she did stalk me and send insane messages, outlining our happily ever after together. She even showed up at all my book signings that year—including the ones overseas."

Kellan grunts. "The beautiful ones are always the most dangerous."

A laugh erupts from me. "I doubt Lucas and Troy would agree. Simone and Jessica are beautiful, and they're far from dangerous."

Even so, I know what my brother means. I'm not the only one who discovered the hard way that beauty doesn't always reflect what's beneath the surface. In Kellan's case, the beautiful demon from his past cost him three years in prison.

"Anyway, most of my readers don't give a damn what I look like. As long as the stories are exciting and well written, they're happy." Stories that I need at least nine months to write so the characters and plots are gripping and the books are impossible to put down.

My phone rings, and I glance at it. Maxwell.

"I've got to get this," I tell Kellan, tossing him an apologetic look. "Hopefully it will be quick." I accept the call, and Kellan begins stretching his legs, lunging his right foot forward. "Hey, Maxwell. What's up?"

"I've got some great news...and some not-so-great news."

"Okay. Hit me with the not-so-great news first."

"You don't get a say in the order." If his tone could take human form, it would guffaw and slap me on the back.

"Okay, just tell me however you'd like."

"I just got off the phone with Bethany. She sold the movie rights to your next book."

Surprise sends my stomach into a backward flip. "Holy shit. She sold the rights to *Unfallen*?"

This isn't the first time movie rights have been sold for one of my books. But none of the sold rights have resulted in actual movies. It's just been extra income. Nice extra income. Still, I've learned not to get overly excited whenever Max tells me news about movie rights.

"Not exactly." His barely held-back excitement vibrates through the phone line, the emotion straining on an invisible leash.

"What exactly did she sell the rights to, then?"

"*Untold Mercy*."

"The book I haven't finished writing?"

"That would be the one."

"Okay, so what's the not-so-great news?"

"Because of this movie deal, your publisher moved up the deadline for the book. They need the manuscript months sooner than what was originally agreed on."

Months? Is this deal for real?

I always have words. But now? I can't think over the explosive pounding in my ears.

Maxwell's talking, but I don't even try to listen. I'm only a third of the way done with the book. My synopsis is completed. I know where the plot's going. But writing fast? Never done it.

I cut Maxwell off mid-monologue. "What did you say?"

"They have several actors in mind for William and Safina." The excitement in Max's voice is amped up, like a cheerleader on amphetamines. He throws out a few names I recognize, including two previous Academy Award nominees.

And it feels like I've walked into the path of a grizzly bear. That oh-shit moment when you haven't had a chance to process the danger. Only this, what Maxwell just told me, isn't dangerous. No, I must have misheard him. Misunderstood what he just said.

Because...what he's saying...is big. Holy-fucking-shit big.

None of my other books have resulted in actual movies. But this deal? It's the real freaking thing.

My book will be a movie.

With big names playing my characters.

HOLY. MOTHER-OF-GOD. SHIT.

I want to run and scream and jump up and down and hug Kellan, like I've just shot the winning goal during the final game of the Stanley Cup playoffs. In overtime. And the whole crowd is cheering for me, chanting my name.

"Bethany has also included in the contract that you'll be involved with writing the script."

Wait, what? My excitement screeches to a standstill. "I know nothing about script writing."

Kellan pauses in his calf stretch and glances at me, one eyebrow cocked.

I mouth the word *later* and turn the other way. I don't want to be distracted right now.

"You learned how to write novels; you can learn how to write scripts. You won't be the only writer working on it. Plus, it's a bigger deal when an author is involved in writing a movie script. More money. Bigger name recognition."

I can do this. I know I can. Right? "Okay. I'm in. First, I'll finish the book, then worry about my script-writing skills. Exactly when is it due?"

"August fifteenth."

Shit. "What? Like...in four months?"

"Three months and three weeks, to be exact. That won't be a problem, will it?" He isn't really asking if it's possible. Not when he's using the tone that says, *Sorry, not sorry, but this is the way it is.*

I don't have a fucking choice. Not unless I want to turn

down this career-changing opportunity. And I'd be an idiot to do that. A mountain-sized idiot.

"What about my contract? Can the publisher legally move up the date?"

"Do you really want to quibble over the due date when your book is being made into a big-ass movie? A movie that will be shown in theaters all over the world?" He releases a long breath, his patience with me clearly teetering on a super-sharp edge. "Or do you want Bethany to tell them you're not interested?" Now his tone implies he'll hop on the next flight from New York to Oregon and strangle me if I say yes.

"No, I'll do it, but it'll be tight, what with Wilderness Warriors starting for the summer again soon. As long as nothing else unexpected pops up, I should be able to finish it before August fifteenth."

"Should?" His voice has an eyebrow-lifted tone. A challenge.

"Will. I *will* finish it by then." Who needs sleep anyway?

"That's what I needed to hear. It's a good thing you're a free agent. Because your partner and kids wouldn't get to see you for the next four or so months."

"Yep, no worries about that here."

"I'll let you go now, Garrett. And I'll send you the contracts this afternoon." Maxwell ends the call.

"What's going on?" Cautious curiosity hangs on Kellan's question. He's not one for prying, but even he can't ignore my reaction to Maxwell's news.

"My subagent sold the movie rights to the book I'm currently writing." I give him the short version of what Maxwell just told me. Of my three brothers, Kellan is the reserved one. The brother who usually keeps his emotions locked away. But even he can't keep his excitement at the news off his face—in the subtle rise of his eyebrows.

Or at least it's there until I tell him the catch...that my deadline has been moved forward.

"How long do you have to write it?" Kellan continues stretching.

"Three months and three weeks."

"You think you can finish it?"

"I can do it. I think. It's not ideal, what with the release of *Unfallen*. I'll be ramping up my presence on social media over the next four and a half months as I build up buzz for the book."

"You're gonna be busy."

"It will be tough to get the book done in time but not impossible. Most of my interviews and public appearances have been scheduled for late August and early September, after *Untold Mercy* is now due to my editor."

I yank off my hoodie, toss it onto the front passenger seat of the Explorer, and nod at Kellan to indicate I'm ready. I'll have to stretch later due to lack of time now.

We run along the dirt trail that meanders through the meadow and disappears into the trees. The temperature is perfect for running, the sun peeking from behind the clouds and the cool spring breeze. I barely notice it with the shock of Maxwell's news sinking in.

This soon changes as the rugged terrain becomes tougher, requiring my full attention if I don't want to trip on a stone or exposed root. The route is one of Kellan's favorites, because it deters us from talking while we run.

And talking is something he prefers to avoid if possible.

By the time we have finished, Kellan and I are breathing hard and our T-shirts are sticking to our sweat-drenched bodies. We each disappear into separate cabins and have a quick shower. I emerge soon after, wearing clean sweatpants and a dark-green Henley, my hair damp.

The clouds grew steadily heavier with rain during our run.

The first drops begin to fall as we drive to my house. We have Wilderness Warriors business regarding the upcoming season the two of us want to discuss before Kellan is due back at his office.

Now that I'm not navigating the challenging trail, the excitement and shock at Maxwell's news return, as well as a heavy dose of anxiety at having to finish the manuscript in such a short time.

Holy shit. I still can't believe it.

I pull into my driveway, the rain coming down harder now. A garden of trees, bushes, and flower beds creates a private oasis between my sprawling single-story house and my neighbors'. And that's even before the spring leaves are fully out.

I reach up to press the garage door opener on my visor, but movement on the front stoop catches my attention. A woman who looks to be in her late twenties is sitting on the top step with a toddler on her lap.

What the heck? Who are they?

There's no other vehicle in the driveway, nor is there any parked near my house on the street. I don't recognize them, and I'm not expecting anyone.

They're lucky where they're sitting is sheltered from the rain. Otherwise, they might have been drenched, depending on how long they've been there. Neither of them has on a jacket—and...are they reading a book?

Damn, they must be cold. The temperature has dropped over the past few minutes. It's about fifty degrees.

I park near the garage door, kill the engine, and slide out of the driver's seat. Kellan stops behind me. I have no idea if he's seen the two individuals, who are no longer visible from where I'm standing.

I walk around the corner to the path leading to my front door. Neither the woman nor the toddler looks up. Their attention is still on the book. The woman's skin is pale, and her long strawberry-blond hair is tied back in a ponytail. The toddler's dark hair is pulled up in some sort of bun on top of her head, and her skin is a shade lighter than Zara's golden-copper coloring. Wearing only jeans and T-shirts, they aren't dressed for being out in the rain.

"Hi? Is there something I can help you with?" I ask, raindrops soaking through my Henley.

The woman's and the girl's heads snap up, surprise rounding their eyes. The toddler whimpers. Probably because she's damn cold.

Kellan's Trailblazer door slams shut. At the noise, the toddler releases a shriek and presses herself farther into the woman's side, as if trying to hide or stay warm. She's clutching a stuffed animal to her body, its black-and-white shape pinned under her arm.

"Sorry, I didn't mean to startle you," I tell them. "I thought you heard me pull up to the house. Is there something I can help you with?"

The woman closes the book and pushes to her feet, the toddler cradled against her body. The little girl buries her face into the woman's chest and keeps it there.

"Is she okay?" I take inventory of the woman's features, but nothing about her is familiar. She's not a neighbor. Door-to-door canvassers don't usually bring small children with them when they knock on doors, especially not when it's raining heavily. And they don't usually wait for people to come home, nor do they read on the homeowner's porch.

The woman's gaze darts to something over my shoulder, possibly Kellan. She shifts on her feet, as if she'd rather be anywhere but here, her attention returning to me.

"She's your..." She adjusts the girl a little higher on her waist, her eyes never leaving me, her skin a little paler than before. "She's your daughter."

I stare at the pair for a fraction of a second, positive I've misheard her, the heavy rain drowning out her words.

Like I thought I'd misheard Maxwell when he'd told me about the movie deal?

Anger flares in me. Why would someone think it's okay to accuse me of being a father—and think I won't call bullshit on their lie? This is *my* house. Is she some hyper fan who found out where I live and is trying to infiltrate my life? "She's absolutely, definitely, *not* mine."

2

ZARA

I shift on the couch in the empty staff room, trying to get comfortable. On the wall is a poster of New Orleans at night that showcases one of my favorite places. I was there five months ago for my grandmother's funeral. Five months and the grief from losing Mimi hasn't dimmed.

I rub the achy spot in the back of my neck and then the one in my shoulder. The pain started in my neck five years ago and hasn't gotten better. "Lord, I'm only thirty-five," I mutter. Just how long will it take to heal from whatever I'd done to it?

I pick up the bottle of ibuprofen from the coffee table and swallow a capsule with a glass of water. Initially, I hadn't needed the medication on a regular basis. But after the pain in my body increased five months ago, my physician told me to start taking the medication again until things got better.

She figured it might be an overuse injury, the result of my job. I'm careful while working in the kitchen and when lifting heavy things, but even then, I must have pulled a muscle or something.

My knees twinge in agreement, the ache in them also

flaring up lately, but not enough to keep me from doing the job I love.

I hide the ibuprofen in my desk drawer and return to the couch to do the payroll paperwork.

As I hit submit, the staff-room door opens, and Keshia walks in. The Keshia I saw twenty minutes ago, after the lunch rush was over, is not the same one taking her break. The Keshia from twenty minutes ago was smiling and joking with a customer. Now she looks like someone's kidnapped her puppy. If she had a puppy.

"What happened?" I ask as her friend and not as her boss.

She sinks into an armchair and removes her scarf, her box braids tied up in a top-knot bun. Gold flower earrings dangle against her bronze skin. "Tyler and I were supposed to get together tonight. Just the two of us. But he canceled a few minutes ago, claiming something came up and he's not gonna make it."

"Claiming? You don't sound like you believe him."

She lets out a sigh, like a bicycle tire with a rapid leak. "I would if his buddies hadn't been laughing and joking in the background. He probably bailed on me to hang out with them." I didn't think the curve of her mouth could deflate any lower. I was wrong.

What she's saying doesn't surprise me. If Tyler were listed on Yelp as boyfriend material, he would barely scrape by with a 2.5-star rating. This isn't the first time he's pulled this crap with Keshia. Nothing I say will change anything, so I zip my mouth and let her rant.

"I love him, but I wish he was more attentive, you know?"

I nod. "I do."

"It drives me nuts that he would rather be with his friends than with me. It's not like I'm some controlling girlfriend who never lets them hang out together."

I nod once more. She has a point. Keshia is sweet and kind

and considerate. She's also an incredible singer and cake decorator. Tyler is lucky to have a wonderful, talented girlfriend like her. Too bad he's not smart enough to appreciate it.

"What you need is a boyfriend like Joseph." *My boyfriend.* The words slip out easily, but there's something frail about them, like dry crumbs falling on the floor.

Keshia stares at me for a beat, then bursts out laughing. "You mean boring?"

"Joseph isn't boring." Much.

"Oh, please. Last week I heard him going on and on and on about one of his client's accounting errors that took him forever to fix." She flashes me a pitying glance that has me grimacing on the inside. "Don't tell me you don't remember that. He came here during his lunch break to spend time with you. And complained when you told him you were extremely busy with customers."

I can't deny it. He did complain, and when I took him into the staff room to eat, because there were no available seats in the café, he couldn't stop talking about the accounting errors. "So he gets a little overexcited about his job. That's not a bad thing."

Keshia huffs a muffled laugh. "What you need is a boyfriend like Garrett."

True.

Wait. What?

I thought we were talking about her boyfriend and not my hopeless crush on my best friend. The crush she doesn't know about.

"You and Garrett are so good together; you'd make a great couple." Pride at the suggestion beams on her face. "I'm surprised you haven't already gotten together in that way." She tilts her head, knowing eyes assessing me. "Or have you?"

I choke out a strangled laugh and cough to cover it. She doesn't need to know the truth. That I've been in love with

Garrett since college. I'd spent a year flip-flopping between deciding to tell him how I felt about him...and deciding that would be a terrible, *What-were-you-thinking?* catastrophic idea.

Then one day during my junior year, I got up the courage to tell him. I'd just received my midterm grade in the class I'd been struggling with. I'd gotten an A...and had thought it was a sign from the universe to let the chicken out of the bag, so to speak.

I mentally scoff at that naïve thinking.

I found Garrett where I'd predicted he would be—under a tree in the grassy common area. He was wearing a gray T-shirt that deliciously fit his tanned hockey-honed body. His trademark messy brown hair was even messier—as if someone had run her fingers through it during a heated make-out session.

The way I'd imagined it looking after I kissed him.

He wasn't alone. He was staring into the eyes of a girl—and it was clear from his expression he was lost for her.

But it wasn't just any girl. I recognized the bright floral head wrap tied around her coily hair. The floral head wrap I had given her for Christmas. It was Kenda.

My best friend.

The girl who'd strode into my freshman psychology class on the first day, surveyed the other students, and taken the empty seat next to mine. We'd instantly become friends.

She was my best friend, but I didn't tell her when my feelings for Garrett had gone from him being my childhood best friend to something more. And she didn't tell me...she didn't tell me she had fallen for him.

"Have you?" Keshia asks, yanking me back to the present. She's looking at me expectantly, her eyes flaring with meaning.

"Have I, what?"

"Ever been with him that way?"

"Definitely not." The words rush out a little too quickly. "It's not like that between us." *And never will be.*

Garrett had been so in love with Kenda. And I was the best friend he'd come to for advice about their relationship.

I was the friend who'd smiled at every seemingly innocuous question. Questions that left my heart feeling like it had been tossed into a meat grinder. But I couldn't complain. They were perfect together.

The happily-ever-after kind of perfect.

Heck, I'm waiting for her to realize she still loves Garrett. I know he would get back together with her in a heartbeat. I don't think, deep down, the man has ever really gotten over her, and he probably never will.

Keshia purses her lips, unconvinced at my answer.

"I want to be with a man who looks at me like I am his world." The way Garrett was looking at Kenda the day I stumbled across them together. "Garrett definitely doesn't look at me that way."

"Does Joseph look at you like you're his world?" Keshia flashes a warning glance that says: *Don't even try BS-ing your way out of answering the question, Z.*

She already knows the answer.

"Hey, we're not talking about *my* boyfriend. We're talking about yours." Praying the ibuprofen kicks in soon, I shift on the couch, my hips and lower back now grouchy. My mouth curves into a wide smile, hopefully hiding my physical discomfort.

I put my laptop on the coffee table and push to my feet. I need to get moving, and then I'll be fine. "I'm going to check on things out front. Enjoy your break."

I hurry from the room before she can say anything more about Joseph or Garrett.

It's midafternoon, and the café is still busy. And once tourist season is in full force, Picnic & Treats will only get that much crazier—the ultimate dream of every small-business owner.

The tables along one wall have been rearranged for the weekly book club meeting currently underway. But the group of ten women has grown steadily in the past few months, resulting in the noise level, with everyone in the café competing to be heard, increasing exponentially.

What I need is a separate room for small groups like the book club, but there's no space for one.

I walk to the tables by the window to see how Rose, Delores, and Samantha are doing. They like to sit near the book club to listen in, even though they aren't members of it. I've known the three women for most of my life, and they are regular fixtures here. Rose is the grandmother of one of my closest female friends, and she's currently wearing a hot-pink T-shirt proclaiming that she's The Hot Grandmother.

Mimi would have loved the three women if she had ever ventured to Oregon. She'd preferred life in New Orleans and Louisiana, even after Katrina's devastation. "Nothin' like the vengeance of an angry woman to put a man in his place," she would frequently say.

I chuckle to myself at the memory. A woman walks past the window, her red umbrella protecting her from the light rain. She's probably happy Mother Nature isn't being vengeful right now.

"How's it going?" I ask Rose, Delores, and Samantha. My voice is loud enough to be heard over the book club's discussion, the pitch suitably low for the women's age-diminished hearing.

Mischief sparkles in their eyes, and I brace myself for whatever they're going to say. You never know with them. "Have you read the book they're talking about? *Before I Let Go* by Kennedy Ryan." Rose directs the question to me, referring to the novel the book club is discussing.

"Yes. I love anything by Kennedy." No one knows how to write spicy scenes like she does. Her stories are Kahlua in hot chocolate, like cozying up under a blanket on a rainy day.

"So you know Yasmen, the heroine, does yoga?" Delores pipes in.

I nod, unsure where any of this is going.

"Did you know yoga is great for improving your sex life?" Rose's eyebrows bounce up her forehead.

"Er...sure," is all I can think to say. Joseph and I haven't had sex yet. He told me he's waiting for the right time; he's old-fashioned that way.

Keshia's words from the staff room flash in my head like a flickering neon sign. *Boring.* That's what she'd called him.

Oh, Lord, please tell me he's not that way in bed.

I pick up Rose's empty coffee mug. "Are you telling me I should practice yoga?"

Rose flashes me a sassy grin. "Do you want to have a great sex life?"

A hearty laugh erupts over my lips. "I'll take that into consideration. You make a compelling argument for slotting it into my schedule. Yoga, I mean." My busy schedule doesn't exactly have time for things like yoga.

Or sex, apparently.

I return to the kitchen with their empty mugs and place them in the dishwasher. Two years ago. That was the last time I had sex, if I don't count the vibrator stored in my bedside drawer, which died a year ago. I can't even remember the last time I had an orgasm.

Joesph and I have been dating for two months now. How much longer will we have to wait for the perfect time? Surely he can find the romance in consummating our relationship if he can find excitement in fixing accounting errors.

Maybe it's time we move things up a notch—starting tonight. Maybe it's time the drought finally comes to an end.

3

GARRETT

"**S**he's absolutely, definitely, *not* mine." Anger and annoyance heat my words, bring them to a boil.

The toddler whimpers, her eyes round, and she buries her face in the woman's chest again.

Shit. I hadn't meant to scare her.

I take a step back, giving the little girl space so she doesn't feel threatened.

The rain picks up intensity, soaking through my Henley. The front stoop shelters the woman and the toddler from the rain and the wind, but not the spring chill. The girl must be cold.

I rein in my emotions at the woman's outrageous claim. "There's been a mistake. You have the wrong house." Because I know for certain the toddler is *not* my daughter.

The woman shakes her head, her strawberry-blond ponytail slicing the air. "There's no mistake. You're Garrett Carson."

Shit. Shit-Shit-Shit. Annie Wilkes 3.0. Is that what this is?

At least the last obsessed fan hadn't tried to foist a child on me and pretend it was mine.

"I can guarantee she's not my daughter. For one, I've never

seen you before. And you might not know anything about genetics, but I do. You and I are both white. The little girl isn't. One of us needs to be Black for her to be biologically ours."

Kellan moves up beside me, and the toddler lets out another whimper. Her fear-widened eyes dart between Kellan and me.

I pull out my phone from my pocket, ready to call the cops. It was bad enough being stalked, but for a child to be dragged into this woman's delusions...

And how did she end up with the little girl? Yes, she might be the girl's mother. But it's also possible a family somewhere is desperately searching for their missing toddler. Like in *Untold Mercy*.

Shit, is that what this is about?

No, that can't be it. The blurb for the book hasn't been revealed yet. She might be imitating something she's read in a novel, but it isn't the one sitting on my laptop.

A flush spreads up the woman's neck and cheeks, drowning out the freckles splattered across her face. "Oh, cats in a flying saucepan." Her hand goes to the oval pendant around her neck, and she rubs it between her fingers. "I didn't mean *I'm* her mother. Kenda is her mother. *Was* her mother." Pain twists on her face, the final three words hovering on a silent sob.

The words—spoken so softly I almost missed them—roar in my head like a tornado tearing through a small town, turning my thoughts to dust. "What do you mean *was*?"

"She-she's dead." The woman hugs the little girl closer as if protecting her from the truth.

A cold chill numbs my body more than the rain ever could, and my voice comes out like a shard of rough ice. "Dead? How?" *She's lying. She has to be lying.*

I may not be in love with Kenda anymore, but she will always hold a space in my heart. She can't be dead—I'd know if she was.

The woman straightens her shoulders. The flush on her face has faded, and her skin is once again pale. "She-she was shopping and-and was caught in the crossfire. A mass shooting. Several people died."

"Maybe we should continue this inside." Kellan eyes the pair with an unsettled interest. He doesn't look like he believes anything she's just told us any more than I do, but he's obviously willing to hear what she has to say.

Maybe because he's thinking the same thing I am—the toddler has possibly been abducted to be used in this woman's charade.

The woman shoots him a grateful, if not somewhat uncertain, glance and nods. "We're going into your daddy's house." The words are spoken softly to the toddler like a lullaby.

She picks up the bag by her feet. I open the door, and they follow me into the foyer.

The woman scans the space, no doubt taking in the dark colors and the simple, masculine interior design. The same masculine theme can be found in the rest of the house—a fact Zara loves to tease me about.

Zara.

Shit. Kenda was one of her closest friends in college, and as far as I knew, they kept in contact. If Kenda had been pregnant, surely, she would've told Zara. Zara never mentioned Kenda had a baby. Why not? To spare my feelings, knowing I was once in love with her? That was a long time ago. Things change. People change.

People change, but Kenda knew me. She knew I would accept responsibility for my child if I'd accidentally knocked her up. She'd had no reason to keep the truth from me.

Kenda. Dead.

The woman's lying about that too. This is nothing more than a twisted stolen-identity scam.

I should just call the cops and turn her in, but something

has me stalling. Curiosity, maybe. Curiosity about what other lies the woman has planned. I point toward the living room, indicating for us to continue the discussion in there.

She toes off her sneakers and carries the toddler to where I pointed. Kellan and I hang back in the foyer.

"There's no chance you could be that little girl's father, is there?" he asks.

"Kenda would've told me if she was pregnant."

He regards me for a beat. "You're saying there *is* a chance? You and Kenda had sex two or so years ago?"

I shove my fingers through my wet hair, pushing the longer strands off my forehead. "Yes. We bumped into each other in New York City. I was there to meet up with my agent and editor. Kenda and I got together afterward for drinks, and well..." I leave the rest hanging. He'll fill in the blanks. "We used protection, if that's what you're wondering." But even that's not infallible.

"You never heard from her after that?"

I shake my head, though that's not entirely true. She texted me a month or two later, but I was pissed at her and ignored her text.

Fuuuuck.

No, it can't be that. If she was pregnant, she wouldn't have sent me the single text and kept quiet when I didn't reply. She would have tried again. Plus, if it was true, she knew where I lived. She would have told me the news to my face.

Kellan looks over his shoulder, toward the living room. "Guess we'd better find out what this woman wants."

I glance down at my phone. "I should call Noah. We don't know where the toddler came from—and if someone is searching for her. Or if Kenda *is* dead."

"Let's talk to her first and then decide on the police front. That little girl is scared as it is, without us making things worse by bringing the cops in just yet."

I release a hard breath that does nothing to settle the tangle of emotions. "Okay." He's right. Whoever that little girl is, she's terrified. But she seems to trust the woman. Stockholm Syndrome, perhaps?

"Stay here," I say to Kellan. "I'll grab you a towel." *Stay here and make sure the woman isn't up to no good.*

I return to the foyer in dry clothes and toss him a towel and spare T-shirt. I towel-dry my hair while he quickly changes into the top.

The woman and toddler are sitting in the middle of the large sectional couch when we walk into the living room. The woman is reading to the girl, the light from the huge picturesque windows falling softly on them.

The woman points to a picture in the children's book. "Do you think the tiger eats butterflies for lunch?" Her voice is soft, sweet, but there's also a touch of hardness beneath the surface. As if she wouldn't hesitate to reveal her claws should someone threaten the girl.

The little girl rapidly shakes her head, a smile breaking out on her small mouth. It vanishes as soon as she spots Kellan and me. Her bottom lip pushes out, and she shrinks back against the woman.

I flick on the gas fireplace. What the hell was the woman thinking? She could have at least put a jacket on the toddler before they sat outside to wait for me.

I sit on the end of the sectional.

Kellan takes the armchair, his posture deceptively laid-back. "Do you two have names?"

"I'm Athena, and this is Peony." The woman nods at the girl.

The girl—Peony—looks up again from the book and her smile returns once more for Athena's benefit.

She has Kenda's mouth.

I push the thought away. Until I know if she is Kenda's daughter or not, I can't think of Peony in those terms.

Peony.

Kenda's favorite flower. Or it was when we were a couple. I'd given her a bouquet of them on more than one occasion while we were dating.

"Athena what?" The casualness in Kellan's voice is fake, but Athena won't know that. "Do you have a last name?"

"Williams." She unzips the large bag by her side, searches through it, and pulls out an envelope. "This is for you, Garrett."

I reach across the coffee table and take it from her. My name is written on the front in Kenda's loopy handwriting.

"Kenda told me if anything should happen to her, I was to give that to you."

I rip open the sealed envelope and pull out two folded pieces of paper. One is a letter. The second is a birth certificate. Kenda's name is listed as the mother, and I am listed as the father. The birth certificate is from Louisiana. I flip it over. Is it possible the document is fake?

Dear Garrett,

If you're reading this, it means one thing. I'm dead. And if that's true, I'm so sorry. So sorry for not telling you sooner you have a daughter. In my defense, I did try to tell you once I realized our one night together in New York was going to result in a baby. You never returned my text.

I can't pretend not to know why. I shouldn't have slipped out of the hotel room while you were sleeping without saying good-bye or without leaving you a note. I hurt you. We were once close friends and a couple, and I couldn't even treat you with more respect than a one-night stand who couldn't get away fast enough.

I could say it was complicated, but that sounds like a cop-out, even if it is true. The same with why I didn't contact you again. It was complicated.

I've asked Athena to bring Peony to you should something happen to me before I can tell you about your daughter. My father doesn't know about her, and I would prefer it stays that way. I've told you enough about him for you to understand my decision.

Kenda didn't talk a lot about her parents while we were together, and I never met them. I knew her father could get mean when he was having a bad day. From the sounds of it, that was often. Her mother had died of breast cancer the year before Kenda and I'd bumped into each other in New York.

Peony points at the picture in her book. Now that my initial shock and defensiveness has somewhat dissipated, I can see she has her mother's mouth and pretty nose.

I know you will love Peony as much as I do. She's my world. She's also extremely shy and it takes her a while to warm up to people. It's for that reason I implore you to keep Athena on as Peony's nanny. Our daughter has known Athena since the day Peony was born and sees her almost as a mother. Athena will help make Peony's transition into being part of your family smoother. She will make things easier for you when it comes to your career. Please, I beg that you let her stay with Peony. She loves our little girl so much and is used to moving to new places for work.

Again, I'm so sorry for everything, Garrett. I wish, if you are reading this letter, things had gone down so differently. I wish I had lived to see our daughter grow into the beautiful and intelligent woman I know she will be one day. Please tell her often that I love her. I beg you. I want her to know without doubt that she was my absolute world.

Love,

Kenda

I reread the letter. "This is it?" I ask Athena. "This is her version of a will?"

Athena lifts her shoulders in a jerky shrug and fidgets with her pendant again. "She kept saying she would get a will but never got around to it. Her...her work kept her busy."

"Was she still working as a journalist?"

"Yes. She was...a freelance journalist and was working undercover at the time...at the time she was killed."

"Undercover on what?"

"It wasn't something she discussed with me." Athena's gaze flicks between Kellan and me, her chin slightly raised, almost in challenge. But something about the way she's sitting, her expression, tells me she's as leery of us as Peony is. "She did tell me she loved you and knew you would do what was best for your daughter. She trusted you would be the father Peony deserves."

"Did she tell you she asked me to keep you on as Peony's nanny?"

"She did mention something about it." What could be cautious hope shines in Athena's eyes.

"How did the two of you meet?"

"Through...through a mutual acquaintance. It was before she became pregnant with this little sweetheart." Athena kisses the top of Peony's head. "What animal is that?" She points to a picture in the book.

"Gi-af." Peony grins up at her. And that curve of her lips, filled with pride and innocence, worms its way in past my ribs.

I lean forward and put the letter on the coffee table. "How old is she?"

"Eighteen months." Athena points to something else in the book, not bothering to look at me.

I do the math in my head. It's possible Peony is my daughter. The numbers add up. "I want a paternity test done. Just to make sure." I don't believe Kenda would lie. The Kenda I knew was focused on exposing the inequalities and injustices faced by the most vulnerable of society. And she certainly wouldn't have forged a birth certificate, listing me as the father. But Athena is the wildcard. I need to make sure she isn't trying to scam me.

I need to make sure another man isn't searching for his missing daughter.

Athena's shoulders deflate, but her mouth twists into a small smile. "Oh, okay. That's as understandable as a fox in a henhouse."

Odd thing to say, but okay.

"Do you have somewhere to stay in the meantime?" Kellan's

tone gives nothing away as to what he's thinking, but it's also not the equivalent of wide, welcoming arms.

That's hardly surprising. It takes a lot to gain my brother's trust—and Athena is starting at the bottom of a steep mountainous incline.

She shakes her head, the downward curve of her mouth making me somewhat sympathetic to her situation. Assuming she's who she says she is.

She has a letter from Kenda. It's possible she forged Kenda's handwriting, but that seems like a rather elaborate scheme. It would be one thing if she was on her own, but she's got the welfare of a child to consider.

The welfare of a child who needs somewhere to stay while I figure this all out.

My phone pings on the coffee table with a message from Maxwell. The draft for the studio's contract is in my inbox.

A message indirectly reminding me that not only do I possibly have a daughter, I have a book due in three months and three weeks.

"It's a good thing you're a free agent. Because your partner and kids wouldn't get to see you for the next four or so months."

Shit. If Peony really is my daughter, how the hell am I supposed to deal with all this drama and finish the book on time?

How the hell am I supposed to not screw everything up?

4

———

ZARA

Jessica walks into the kitchen as I'm dicing a tomato. Her golden-brown hair is pulled up under a hairnet, and her mouth curves into a crooked smile. The thick, diagonal scar from the corner of her mouth to her jaw fights a full smile, but it doesn't distract from the happy glow in her eyes.

"Looks like someone recently got some." Keshia chuckles, measuring flour and pouring it into the industrial mixer.

"Maybe I'm just having a great day," Jess singsongs.

I laugh, the sound a low rumble in my throat. "No, you definitely had a little action before coming here. And I bet if I visited Troy, I'd find him humming."

Jess grabs an apron from the hook on the wall and loops it over her head. "*Hmm.* I don't think I've ever heard him hum."

"She's deflecting." Keshia puts her hands on her hips, her smug look almost comical.

"Yep. She definitely is." I grin at my friend who has lived in Maple Ridge for a little more than a year. When I first met Jess, she was struggling with complex PTSD. She's far from fully healed yet, but she is doing a lot better. Thanks to Troy—one of Garrett's brothers.

30

"That boyfriend of yours must be doing something right." Keshia laughs, a wistfulness in her expression I don't want to examine given my own sorry sex life.

"I just spoke with Sabrina Duncan," Jess tells us, clearly wanting to change the direction of our conversation. "Did you know she's selling her store?"

"She is? Why?" I put my knife on the butcher block.

"She wants to move to Texas, where her grandbabies live."

"I do know she misses seeing them every day." Speaking with them on Zoom is just not the same as doing so in person. "I wonder if she has anyone interested in the store?"

Jess walks to the island counter. "We didn't exactly get into that. She started showing me photos of her adorable grandkids."

The square footage of Mountain Lore would be perfect for Picnic & Treats. Lord, the things I would do if I could expand the café. But for that to happen, it means the space has to become available for lease. And that won't happen if someone buys the business from Sabrina.

I tap my finger on my leg as I contemplate the possibilities. "I think I'll ask Sabrina before I go home about her plans. I'm curious what they are."

"Curious for any reason?" Jess scoops the steamed jasmine rice into a bowl for the order she's working on.

Eyebrows raised, Keshia looks over her shoulder at me, the same question echoed in her delicate features.

"I might have been thinking lately about what I would do if I could expand Picnic & Treats."

Jess stops ladling the rice into the bowl and turns to me. "You have?"

"Yes. Hypothetically."

"The café certainly is busy enough for you to expand."

"I agree. But like I said, it's all hypothetical. First, the store next door needs to be vacant. If someone buys Sabrina's business, the dream of expanding will remain just that. A dream."

"If no one buys it, would you then go ahead with your goal?"

"If the hypothetical became reality? Possibly. It depends on what expenses the building's landlord would cover. He might not want to deal with the hassle of converting the two business spaces into one—unless the business owner pays out of pocket for the renovations."

I would need to review my contract for starters. There might also be a clause that prevents me from knocking down walls. "But if I could make my dream a reality, I would do some of the renovations myself." To save money.

The ever-present pain in my neck and shoulder hollers, *The hell with that.* I ignore it, like I do most of the time. Thanks to the ibuprofen I took two hours ago, the pain isn't screaming as loudly as it might have been. It's currently a dull roar.

I pick up my knife and resume dicing tomatoes to keep from rubbing my aching joints. That would only draw Keshia's and Jess's attention to the pain, which I'd rather avoid.

If I could grow Picnic & Treats, however, I could earn more money and maybe even take on more staff. Then I'd have more time to focus on my health since I'd have more people to cover me when I wasn't at the café. Plus, I could do more for this community—especially the women-owned businesses in the area.

Excitement buzzes beneath my skin the more I think about the idea of expanding P&T. "Of course, this is all hypothetical," I remind Keshia and Jess. I need to talk to Sabrina first, before I get too ahead of myself.

Anastasia rushes into the kitchen a short time later. "Zara!"

A man's loud voice follows my head server through the open door, the heat in it enough to scorch anyone in his path. "I work my ass off all day while you sit around doing nothin'."

Shit. I race into the main part of the café, Anastasia right behind me, and stop at the counter.

The usually noisy café is unnaturally quiet, everyone's attention turned to a man standing next to a table by the windows. He's towering over a seventeen-year-old girl, her eyes wide, face pale. Her two friends appear equally terrified, ready to bolt, yet unwilling to abandon her.

"Get your ass out of here." Spittle flies from his mouth and hits her face.

She recoils as if the droplets sizzled through her skin but doesn't say anything or make an attempt to stand. The friend next to her moves her hand under the table—possibly in a gesture of support. I can't see it from where I'm standing.

No one else moves or speaks. Worried gazes dart to the exit.

It's not unusual to see men in the café at this time of day, grabbing food here with their friends instead of at Barside Brewery. But right now, the only males present are a group of teenage boys who don't look any older than fifteen. Too young to stand up to the man. Too young to protect the girl.

"*Get up.*" The man sways on his feet, alcohol no doubt pumping through his veins.

"Call nine-one-one." My words are spoken softly so only Anastasia can hear them. "Tell them we have a potentially violent customer."

Hopefully, there's a cop nearby who can get here before things escalate. Before the girl or someone else gets hurt.

In the meantime...

I rush past stunned customers sitting at the other tables. All seem frozen, unsure how to proceed.

"Hi, is there something I can do to help?" My voice is surprisingly calm, the direct opposite of the fast-thumping pulse in my ears. My gaze rests briefly on the girl, hopefully making it clear to her that I'm on her side.

"This is none of your business." The man's voice is a sharp whip, and he straightens to his full height. He's a good four inches taller than me. Slightly intimidating? Yes. But his height doesn't completely faze me.

Garrett insisted a few years ago that I learn self-defense. I haven't practiced the moves in a while, but I'm sure they'll come to me if I'm pushed too far.

"Actually, it *is* my business. The café's my business. Ensuring my customers' safety is my business." I'm standing a few feet from him, but the reek of booze on his breath rolls over me in nauseating waves. "I could get you a coffee. And maybe we can sit down and talk." A large thermos of coffee wouldn't be enough to sober him, but it would buy me time until the cops arrive.

Please be on the way.

"I don't need coffee. And she doesn't need to be here." He points to the girl with a mean jab of his finger. "She needs to be home, cookin' dinner and cleanin' the house."

The girl picks up her backpack from the floor, her hands shaking. The leather is well-worn, the bag once expensive and stylish. The fabric of her top and jeans are also well-worn, but not in the intentional way designers charge a lot for. Nor are her clothes, from the looks of it, a cheap brand.

Stall them. Stall them till the cops get here.

I casually step between the man and the girl. In my periphery, I note several phone cameras directed our way. I release a slow, steadying breath. Hopefully, he won't try anything foolish, knowing his every action is being recorded.

The man snatches up the chair next to him, holding it up like a baseball bat.

And a sharp, collective gasp falls over the room.

Air leaves my lungs in quick, shallow breaths, and my heartbeat is a loud, rhythmic *boom-boom-boom* in my chest.

I slowly shake my head, warning the man not to do something stupid. Careful not to make a sudden move and risk him lashing out at me or someone else.

He leans past me. "Sarah. Now."

"Yes, Papa." Held-back tears quiver her voice, the volume barely louder than a whisper. "I'm sorry, Papa."

Shit. What do I do? I shift to the side, blocking her again from his view. "You're not sober. And you're not in the right state of mind for her to go anywhere with you." I bolster the words with a bravery I don't feel. A bravery I hope he's too inebriated to see through.

"You don't get a say in what I can and can't do. I'm her father." He slams the chair on the edge of the table. Large pieces of the chair go flying, and several people shriek.

The ceramic vase on the table topples onto its side. I don't try to save it, and the vase rolls off the edge and smashes on the floor.

I avoid glancing down to check the damage. I'm focused on the man in front of me, who is now holding what looks like a deadly weapon. A stake.

The sound of rustling clothes, clicking of shoes against tile, jingling of bells above the door hints that some customers are escaping to safety. I don't turn to see how many remain.

My body is shaking—either from fear or the surge of adrenaline—but hopefully not hard enough for him to notice. I refuse to let him think he has the upper hand or for him to believe I'm easily intimidated.

"You don't want to hurt anyone," I say, praying it's true. Praying the alcohol is dictating his actions, and I can talk sense into him before it's too late.

Shit. Where are the cops?

Not a single siren breaks through the fear in the café, letting us know help is on the way. The sour taste of dismay and concern sits in the back of my throat.

Someone behind me whimpers. Possibly one of the girl's friends.

"Move it, Sarah!"

Spittle hits the side of my face. I don't so much as flinch, my body rigid, muscles taut.

"No—you can't go with him." The faux bravery in my voice softens to a plea. "Whatever you do, don't leave with him." *I can't protect you if you do.* "He's in no state to drive." My next words are directed at the man, gentled so as not to anger him further. "You could get in an accident and get you both killed. You don't want that, do you?" *Please tell me you're not suicidal.*

"I'm fine," he snaps.

"No, you're not. You're barely standing upright. You're drunk." My tone remains steady, designed to lull him into compliance. Or ideally lull him to sleep.

"I'm not drunk. I only had one beer."

A keg of beer, more like it.

"Please, if you leave like this, you might end up doing something you'll later regret."

He lifts the splintered piece of wood, as if to strike me over the head. I step out of his reach. The edge of the table behind me lightly presses into the backs of my thighs.

He mutters something I can't make out, the red of his face darkening.

Jess. Is she still in the kitchen? She spent five years married to an abusive husband—a marriage that left her struggling with complex PTSD. What if seeing this triggers a flashback, which she gets from time to time?

Sirens wail from down the street. *Thank God.*

I almost slump in relief, but now's not the time to let my guard drop.

The man doesn't seem to notice the sirens or doesn't care. He remains in front of me, the anger in his face going nowhere.

The sirens stop with a half-gurgled *yip* outside Picnic & Treats. I don't dare shift my attention from the assailant to glance out the window. Don't dare to check if the cops are here responding to Anastasia's 9-1-1 call, or if they're outside the building for some other reason.

Murmured voices surround me, but I can't hear what's being said. The tapping of fingers on phone screens accompanies the voices—the soft music before all hell breaks loose in a movie.

The door chime jingles again, and two officers enter the café. The man turns to them, his makeshift weapon drawn and ready.

I briefly register one of the cops is Noah, a friend of mine. Then I turn to the girls and gesture for them to get down. The four of us duck under the table. We aren't the only ones. Chairs scrape across the floor as people scramble to get out of the way.

Lord, please tell me we'll make it out of here unharmed.

5

GARRETT

My living room was designed for the comforts of a grown-ass man and not a toddler. Many of the ornaments—like the ceramic vases and glass candleholders—decorating the built-in bookshelves on either side of the fireplace are easily broken. The houseplants are potentially poisonous to a curious child.

And the rest of the house isn't much better.

"I'll put you up in one of the hotels in town for the next few days," I tell Athena. "If she is my daughter—"

"She is," Athena says softly. "She's your daughter."

"If she is my daughter, I'll need to childproof the house and buy supplies." I unfold from my end of the sectional and stand. "Does she sleep in a crib? Or a bed?"

"A crib." Athena's face pales as I draw closer to where she and Peony are sitting on the couch. The freckles on her nose and cheeks become more noticeable, and her hand returns to her pendant. "But she'll be ready to switch to a toddler bed soon."

Peony glances up from her picture book to where I'm standing. Fear widens her eyes, and she whimpers, burying her face into Athena's side.

I crouch, making myself smaller and hopefully less intimidating. "I'm not gonna hurt you." I lower the pitch of my voice, hoping my tone is a soothing lullaby.

My words don't seem to make a difference. Her little body trembles, and her face remains buried against Athena.

At a loss for what to do, I turn my head to Athena for suggestions. If I am Peony's father but she's scared of me, it will only make things more challenging. Perhaps if I knew what I was doing, it would help. But I don't. Raising a kid isn't something they prepare you for in the Marines.

Athena releases the pendant and drops her hand to her lap. "She's shy around most people, but more so with men."

Shy? If her reaction to Kellan and me is any indication, she's a helluva lot more than shy.

"She just needs a little time to get to know you." Athena's gaze slides to Kellan. "To get to know both of you. You're one of her uncles, right?"

He gives her a stiff nod.

"He's Kellan," I tell her.

"And Lucas and Troy are your other two brothers. Kenda told me about them. You all joined the Marines after college. And you will do everything to protect those you love." She kisses the top of Peony's head. "It's gonna be okay, baby girl. You're safe. Those bad men won't hurt you." The words are softly spoken on Peony's temple, but loud enough that Kellan and I can hear them.

"Bad men?" I share a confused frown with Kellan.

"The two men who sent Kenda to heaven." Athena's voice catches, and she hangs her head, her shoulders slumping.

"She witnessed what happened?" My gaze falls on Peony so Athena knows which *she* I'm referring to.

"We both did." She drags in a stuttering breath. "The three

of us had left a clothing store when Peony realized she'd dropped Poppy somewhere inside it. Kenda had to make a call, so Peony and I returned to the store...and then..."

Athena squeezes her eyes shut, and her hand goes to the pendant again.

She reopens her eyes. Tears wet her cheeks. "We came out of the store just as everything went down. The first shooter. Kenda..." She sniffs and scrubs her hand over her wet cheeks.

Maybe she's a talented actress, but something in my gut tells me she's telling the truth. Peony's and her reactions make sense. If Peony saw two men shoot her mother, of course it would affect her.

Which means once I get confirmation she is my daughter, I'll make sure she receives all the support she needs. I might not know much about children, but I do understand how something like this can mess up a kid, the impact often far reaching.

I steal a quick glance at Kellan; he's a prime example of that.

"Which mall was this?" Kellan's tone isn't exactly unfriendly, he just isn't as accepting of her story as I am. That doesn't surprise me, given his past relationship with his late biological mother. And then with the woman he cared deeply for who ended up double-crossing him. He approaches every female with a heavy dose of skepticism and distrust.

Athena tells us the mall in North Carolina. It doesn't sound familiar, but with the high volume of mass shootings these days, they tend not to get much, if any, coverage on the national news unless the casualty count is high.

But that doesn't mean we can't look up the shooting to check if she's telling the truth. Another reason I'm leaning more toward believing her. Why lie about the shooting and the victims if we could easily discredit her?

"You were living in Louisiana and visiting North Carolina?" I had no idea Kenda had been living in Louisiana. Come to think of it, she'd never really answered the question about where she was living when I bumped into her in New York City.

Athena shakes her head, the movement adamantly quick. "No. We were living in North Carolina."

"But you had been living in Louisiana at one point." I lift Peony's birth certificate to show her the state listed on it.

Athena shakes her head again. "No. We were visiting the place when Kenda went into labor. We never lived there."

Fair enough. I glance down at Peony. Her face is still smooshed into Athena's side. "What is Poppy?" I ask her and touch what could be a stuffed panda clutched under her arm. "Is this Poppy?"

She doesn't reply, but Athena gives a small nod.

"He's a handsome panda. Is it a he or she or gender neutral?"

"She. She's a girl panda. Isn't that right, Peony?" Athena gently strokes Peony's neck.

Kellan remains quiet, his expression impassive. He's no doubt taking in the whole scene, drawing his own conclusions. Determining the next steps in validating or discrediting her story.

"How 'bout I make us lunch, then see about getting you two a hotel room. We'll go from there once we've got some things straightened out." Like confirmation I really am Peony's father and after childproofing my house. I unfold to my full height. "I'll be right back."

I make eye contact with Kellan, and he follows me outside onto the front stoop. The rain isn't falling as hard now. It's mostly just drizzle.

I close the door behind me. "Looks like we'll have to discuss the excursion ideas another time."

Kellan frowns, but I sense it has nothing to do with our delayed plans. "Do you believe any of what she's told you?"

"It's hard to know for sure until I get the paternity results. It wouldn't be like Kenda to claim I was the father of her child if I wasn't, and then go to the extreme of forging a birth certificate."

He scoffs, the grumbled sound cutting. "People change."

"True. Our careers have caused her and me to see and do things over the years that altered us." I'm certainly not the same man I was prior to my last deployment. "But if she lied about me being Peony's father, she did it for a reason." I shrug. "Who knows? Maybe I'm not her father, and her biological father's a real asshole. Kenda wouldn't want to risk her daughter's well-being with someone like that." Not after having a father like that herself. So maybe it is possible that she would do whatever she could to protect her daughter—including getting faked documents.

"You think she'd fabricate the story to keep her daughter safe?"

"It's possible. Her own father was an asshole. The Kenda I knew"—and loved—"would want to protect her daughter from the same nightmare she grew up with."

"Even if it meant lying to you?"

I don't have an answer for that. I have no clue what was going through Kenda's head once she found out she was pregnant. It's possible she knew Peony wasn't mine and decided not to tell me the truth. And that could be the reason she never contacted me after the initial text.

But if that's true, what changed her mind and caused her to write the letter, claiming Peony is my daughter?

Kellan folds his arms across his chest. "I'll see what I can find out about the nanny."

"Check if she has a police record, but that's it. Whoever she is, she hasn't done anything yet to warrant me snooping into her life without her permission. Kenda trusted her with her daughter. She wouldn't have done that if she had any doubts about the woman." Kenda might have changed over the years, but her fierce protectiveness for those she loved wouldn't have.

"Of course, if Athena gives us any reason to not trust her, I give you permission to do a more thorough background check."

Kellan isn't police or FBI or with any other government agency like that, but he has connections that go deeper than anything I have as a thriller author. Connections our family and friends aren't allowed to ask him about.

I doubt even Emily—our close friend and his office assistant—knows the full extent of his connections.

Kellan gives me an on-it nod, and we walk toward his Trailblazer in the driveway. "What about Zara? You think she knows about Peony?"

"She might. But if she did, she only would have known Kenda was pregnant. She would've told me if she suspected I was the baby's father."

I pull out my phone as Kellan drives away. *Fuck.* Three months and three weeks. That's all the time I have left until *Untold Mercy* is due to my editor. The time frame was tight before finding out I might be the father of an eighteen-month-old, but now...

How the hell am I supposed to juggle both the deadline and being a father—a dad to a toddler who's scared of me?

I google information on paternity tests. There are two types. One requires a blood sample. The other involves swabbing of the inside of the mouth.

The first test is recommended for legal purposes and is done in a medical office. The second test will be useless if I want to challenge Athena's claim in court, but it will also be less stressful for Peony.

If the swab test results are negative, but Athena wants to still argue I'm Peony's father, I'll have to go through the hassle of getting blood work done. But for now, the swab test is enough.

I order the test online. The kit will arrive in a few days. It will take up to a week to get the results.

Next, I call one of the hotels in town. "Hi, I need a room for an adult and toddler for..." What—a week? Until I get the results? Or two weeks, so if Peony is my daughter, I have time to get her bedroom ready?

In the meantime, am I banishing Athena and Peony to a hotel room and letting them fend for themselves? That would be the simplest thing to do with my looming deadline.

Shit. I spend long hours on the computer when writing—especially when I have a fast-approaching deadline. So how exactly will this work? Kenda urged me to keep Athena on as Peony's nanny. Did she mean as a live-in nanny, or would Athena rather live somewhere else and show up during regular work hours?

"Hello?" a female on the other end of the line asks. "Are you still there?"

"Sorry. I need the room for three nights. But I might need to extend it." Three days should give Kellan enough time to see if Athena has a police record or any outstanding warrants.

"Will you need a crib or a cot?"

"A crib." I give the woman the necessary information and my credit card number. She confirms the room will be ready in an hour.

With those two essential to-do items checked off, I rejoin Peony and Athena in the living room.

The container of kuku paka still sits on the island counter that separates the living room from the kitchen. My taste buds beg for a mouthful of the spicy food, a lick of the spoon.

"I've booked a hotel room for three nights for you and Peony. I can drive you there after lunch." I remove an open jar of Alfredo sauce and a block of white cheddar from the fridge. "Does Peony like macaroni and cheese?"

"Yes. It's one of her favorite dishes."

"I'm not big on cooking," I warn Athena. Usually I just whip up something quick for myself or grab food from Picnic &

Treats. "This will probably be nothing like the mac and cheese she eats."

"I'm sure it'll be fine." Athena winces as if not believing her own words. "And I can cook. Nothing fancy, 'cause I'll be taking care of Peony. I mean, assuming you keep me on as her nanny."

I take in the way Peony is clutching her panda and clinging to Athena, wide, frightened eyes trailing my every move.

"Once I have the paternity results, I'll draw up an employee contract for you." After everything Peony has been through, it doesn't make sense to take away the one person who knows her best. Plus, I don't have time to interview for a new nanny. I need to focus on my manuscript. Fortunately, I'm currently in the right place to handle the expense of a nanny. I've made some smart investments over the past few years. For now, I'm in a good financial position to hire someone to look after a kid of mine. That might change if I don't get the book finished in time.

I pull out a bag of macaroni from the pantry. "Do you want to work as a live-in nanny? Or will you be looking for somewhere else to stay?"

"Live-in nanny."

Thank Christ for that. I'm not ready to be thrown headfirst into being a single parent without a safety net. Especially not with a child I've known less than an hour and who looks like she's on the verge of a panic attack every time I get close to her.

"What does the paternity test involve?" Athena asks, carrying Peony into the kitchen.

I explain the process and how things will go for the next few days. "You and Peony showing up on my doorstep couldn't have come at a worse time. I have a book deadline coming up soon."

Athena rolls her eyes. "Zeus on a cracker. Too bad the shooter wasn't more considerate."

I huff out a humorless laugh. "Yeah—in so many ways. So how did you get here? To Maple Ridge."

"We took a bus. Several buses. There's no direct bus here from Greensboro."

"You traveled all that way with a toddler?" That couldn't have been easy.

"She slept most of the trip. The vibration of the bus kept lulling her to sleep." She kisses Peony on the cheek. "Isn't that right, baby girl?"

"Where's the rest of your stuff?" I point to the oversized bag next to the couch.

"Er, that's all we have. We-we were living in an apartment, but-but there was a fire. We weren't in the building at the time. Thank all the kittens in the world for that." She makes a comical wide-eyed expression. "But we lost everything. That's why we were at the mall. To replace some of our things."

"Shit. I'm sorry." I wish I had known sooner—like right after it happened. Kenda deserved a lot better than the shitstorm she found herself in. Peony deserves better.

Athena shrugs, her sigh long and hard. "Guess the Fates were bored and decided to spice things up a little."

"The Fates?"

"The three old crones in Greek mythology who decide one's future."

I pour the dry macaroni into the boiling water. "I take it you enjoy Greek mythology. Because of your name?"

"That might have something to do with it. Er...can I use your washroom? Her diaper needs changing."

"Sure, go ahead. It's the second door on the right." I point in the direction of the closest bathroom, thankful I'm not being thrown into the deep end and expected to change Peony's diaper.

I'm as knowledgeable on that topic as I am when it comes to cooking.

Shit, is Peony really my daughter?

6

———

ZARA

"**P**ut down the weapon," Noah commands in a tone I'm not used to from him. He's usually smiling adoringly at his girlfriend, Avery. He's normally friendly and easygoing. None of that describes the police officer standing inside Picnic & Treats, his gun pointed at the drunk, hell-raising father.

From my vantage spot on the floor, half-covered by the table I'm hiding under, I scan the area, making sure everyone seems to be okay. We're crouched under the tables, and I'm praying this will all end soon, preferably with no bloodshed.

Shards of what was once a ceramic vase lie a few feet from me, the tulips broken and torn.

The man lets go of the broken piece of chair in his hand. It lands in front of me with a *bang*, and I jolt as if hit by lightning.

My heart rate eases off the gas pedal, and I blow out a hard breath. I'm alive. I'm alive and unhurt. As is everyone else, which is more important.

Slowly inhaling and exhaling, I give myself several seconds to recover from the shock and uncertainty of the last five

48

minutes. Then I stagger to my feet as the other officer hand-cuffs the man.

I walk to Noah, my legs shaky from the adrenaline after-math, and proceed to tell him what happened. "I need to check on Jess," I say once I'm finished. "She was in the kitchen when the man started causing trouble. I don't know how much she witnessed."

Noah is fully aware of her past. "Go ahead. I'll be out here, speaking with the other witnesses, if you need anything."

I turn to leave but pause. "What about the girl? Sarah? I have a feeling it's not the first time she's dealt with him like that. And her mother...what about her?" Her mother could be like Jess once was—trapped in an abusive marriage.

"That will be part of our investigation. We'll do what we can to make sure all parties are safe."

From what Jess told me about her past, "do what we can" often doesn't mean much. If the wife chooses not to press charges, there's not much the police can do about the home situation.

I hurry toward the kitchen, checking on each of my customers on the way, seeing if they need anything. Some had left after talking to Noah and Officer Hunter. The remaining customers are sharing notes as to what happened.

The rain outside the windows has slowed to a light shower, as if relieved the nightmare is over, and the weather is shedding a few tears for Sarah and her family. For all those impacted by what happened. For Jess.

Mrs. Seger gives me a hug. "How are you doing, Zara? You were so brave, standing up to that man."

I smile at the woman who recently retired from teaching high school math. "I'm not so sure about being brave."

"You definitely were," her friend says, her hair covered under a coral hijab.

"Thank you."

I grab the broom and dustpan, sweep up the broken vase, and toss the damaged tulips into the compost bin.

Keshia and Anastasia are at the counter, talking, as I approach. Anastasia is pouring hot water into a tea pot. Steam unfurls from the ceramic container.

"Did Jess see any of that?" I ask.

Anastasia puts the pot onto a tray. "She did. She came out of the kitchen at the same time we did and is pretty shaken. She's in the staff room with Troy."

"She called him?" The dull ache in my shoulders has intensified over the last few minutes, and the base of my spine, my hips, and my knees aren't fairing much better.

"No, I texted him," Keshia replies. "Like he asked me to do if Jess has a flashback at work."

Of course, he did. He'd asked me to do the same when Jess returned to work part time at P&T. I should've known he would make the same request to the rest of the staff.

"I'm going to check on her. Could you two get everyone anything they need—on the house?" Still lightly massaging my shoulder, I walk down the hallway to the staff room. At the doorway, I stop kneading the muscle and stride into the room.

Jess and Troy are sitting on the couch. Troy's talking to her in a low, soothing voice, one hand on the curve of her spine. The other is holding her hand. Bailey, Jess's golden retriever, is lying on the floor by her feet. She has on her *Service Dog in Training* vest, indicating she's on duty.

Jess smiles softly at Troy, and my insides go unexpectedly warm. I don't remember having a boyfriend as attentive as Troy is with Jess. They are the perfect couple, so sweet and loving after all they've been through, together and separately.

They gaze lovingly at each other, and a small amount of jealousy for what they share wiggles into my belly. There's a silent communication between them, as history has taught me well, that often shortly proceeds Troy and Jess kissing.

I clear my throat, causing them to tear their gazes from each other. "Sorry to interrupt. I wanted to make sure you're okay, Jess."

Her smile returns, brighter this time. "I am."

Troy opens his mouth to speak, but Jess's hand squeezes his thigh, and his mouth snaps shut, trapping whatever he was going to say.

She snuggles farther into Troy's side. "What about you? You were the one risking your life."

I scoff out a half laugh. "I would hardly call what I did risking my life." Hopefully she didn't catch everything that went down...specifically the part where the man broke the chair. "Is there anything I can get you?"

"No, I'm fine. Thanks."

"I'm taking her home, if that's okay with you?" Troy's tone carries a featherlight warning. He plans to take Jess home early, no matter what I have to say.

"I was going to suggest she bails as soon as she has her legs back under her. I've got everything under control. And if you need a few days off," I tell Jess, "that's fine too." She's scheduled tomorrow, but I'll come in early to cover her shift.

Relief smooths out Troy's brow. "Thanks, Z."

I walk over to my friend and hug her. "Let me know if you need anything."

"Have fun on your date tonight." She flashes me an easy smile. "Make sure Joseph takes good care of you." Her eyes flick to Troy for a fleeting moment, her message clear: *Make sure your boyfriend takes good care of you the way Troy takes care of me.*

Lord, I'd forgotten about my date. Do I even want to go anymore after what happened?

The rest of the afternoon is a whirlwind of activity. I barely have a second to catch my breath.

"Do you have everything you need?" I ask Anastasia at the end of my shift. She and Clara are here until closing.

"I do. Have a good night with your man."

"Thanks." I decided two hours ago that a date with my boyfriend is exactly what I need after the day I've had. My eyes jerk to where the drama occurred several hours ago. To the empty spot where the broken chair once stood. I'll need to find a replacement for it. ASAP. I'm hoping to expand Picnic & Treats—not *lose* available seating.

It helps the chair wasn't part of a matched set. That's one advantage of P&T's eclectic aesthetic. I found most of the furniture at garage sales and in flea markets. I then sanded and whitewashed the individual pieces.

There's so much to do between cleaning up this mess—and thinking about the expansion, if I want to make it happen.

And I do.

I grab my things from the staff room and change into my bootie-hugging jeans, tank top, and cardigan. Sabrina is at the counter, assisting a customer, when I walk into Mountain Lore. I casually study the space, as if I'm not drooling over the possibility of it one day being part of Picnic & Treats. The interior is dark, a contrast to the café's light and airy feel.

I wander through the store, checking out the merchandise. Sabrina approaches several minutes later as I'm examining a jar of preserves from a local small business.

"Hi, Zara. I heard about what happened earlier next door. How are you doing?" Her mouth tilts up, but it's worry that reaches her eyes and not her smile.

"Better now." I return the smile, mine a lot brighter. "Jess mentioned you're planning to move to Texas."

"That's right." Excitement slips into her voice. "I figured now's a good time to retire and be closer to my grandbabies. They'll only stay little for so long. I'm in the process of selling the business to a couple of sisters."

"That's great." I infuse my tone with a happiness I don't entirely feel. I'm happy for her, since this is what she wants. But I guess it means I won't be expanding Picnic & Treats after all.

"It is. They're just deciding if they're going to keep the business in Maple Ridge or move it to Spring Falls, where they live."

Hope pops up its head, but I keep it reined in. The emotion has burned me on more than one occasion. "They might move the business?" The space next door to P&T might be up for lease?

"The last I heard, they're figuring out the numbers and pros and cons of staying here versus moving it to their town. They've got a month to make a decision." Sabrina is practically vibrating with joy, her smile wide.

The sun is low in the sky, casting long shadows on the quiet sidewalk as I walk to my car. The soothing pine-scented breeze clears my head of what happened a few hours ago.

Call him now.

The silent words float on the breeze, insistent. Nudging. Powerful.

Why wait for the future when the moment is in front of you, biding time until you grasp hold of it? Mimi's favorite saying.

She didn't believe in procrastination. She felt it was nothing more than fear of facing the unknown. A wilted excuse.

I dial Mr. Cartwright's number. The least I could do is tell him I'm interested in taking over the lease should the sisters choose to move Mountain Lore elsewhere.

The line rings several times before he picks up. "Hello?" The voice of my fourth and fifth grade teacher has the low, gruff edge I've known most of my life. He was the man who got me excited about science. He wasn't the teacher who taught me to believe in myself, but pretty damn close.

"Hello, Mr. Cartwright. It's Zara Thompson."

"Hello, Zara." The gruff tone switches to his exuberant voice that he used for all things science. "What can I do for you this fine evening?"

"Sabrina Duncan mentioned she's selling Mountain Lore. And the new owners might not be taking over her lease."

"That's right. I'm waiting to hear back from them on their decision."

"Do you have anyone else interested in the property?"

"Not yet. I haven't told anyone the property might be available. I'm waiting to see what the sisters decide. Why? You know someone who wants to lease it?"

I click on the key fob, unlocking my car door. "Yes. Me. I've been thinking about expanding Picnic & Treats. I only found out this afternoon Sabrina is selling her business, so I haven't looked into the numbers yet. But I'm interested in talking to you about the possibility."

"How 'bout you look into the numbers. Create a proposal. And we can discuss it in a few days."

"Thank you. I'll do that."

AN OUT OF ORDER SIGN THAT WASN'T THERE THIS MORNING NOW glares at me from the closed elevator door of my apartment building. *Great.* Not at all what I needed or expected.

Wishing the day hadn't been quite so prickly, I trudge up the four flights of stairs to my floor and walk down the nondescript hall to my apartment. The steady ache in my joints slows my pace.

I enter the apartment and flick on the light. The warm glow highlights the series of framed photos on the wall, taken by my super-sweet, super-talented sister-in-law, Kim.

Most of them are nature photos of the area. But my favorite one was taken at Windermere Lake, just outside of town. I was standing in the water, wearing a simple black bikini, streaks of gold paint adorning my body.

Golden Girl.

The second Garrett saw the photo, his nickname for me stuck. It's the name he likes to tease me with.

But in that brief moment, when he'd first called me Golden Girl, I'd felt special. Seen.

Like he finally saw me as something more than just his close friend.

From my bedroom closet, I remove my black silk pantsuit. Paired with my black silk camisole, the outfit is the essence of sexy. Perfect for seducing my boyfriend into taking our relationship to the next level.

I grab a pair of lacy black panties and a bra from my dresser. In the bathroom, I hang the clothes on the back of the door and run water into the bath. The sweet scent of jasmine fills the room.

The opening bars of "Listen" float from the small speakers on the counter, and I step into the tub. The hot water laps over my calf muscles, and I sink into the scented water.

Beyoncé's strong, energized voice wraps me in bliss, and I recline on the gentle slope of the tub, my eyes closing. Heat soaks into my body, easing the unrelenting ache in my hips and shoulders. The unrelenting ache that worsened following the afternoon I had.

Exhaustion ripples through me, taking me deeper and deeper into a dreamlike state. But I know I'm awake. Beyoncé's voice still echoes off the bathroom tiles.

My thoughts drift to my conversation this afternoon with Keshia. About Garrett and Joseph. About how Joseph is boring.

He's not boring. He's just enthusiastic about numbers. As a small-business owner, it's something I can appreciate.

With his broad shoulders, narrow waist, and short black

hair, he's a fine specimen of a man. A man who I hope will make me feel equally fine between the sheets tonight.

The image of Garrett pops into my head. His shoulders are slightly broader than Joseph's, and he stands a few inches taller. His lightly tanned skin will darken during the summer—mostly from running shirtless with Kellan.

No, no, no, no. Stop thinking about Garrett. Think about your fine boyfriend.

The fine boyfriend I have a date with soon.

7

ZARA

Goose bumps prickle my skin, the once hot bath water rapidly cooling. A telling silence replaces the playlist I was listening to when I stepped into the water.

Oh. Shit. I fell asleep, and now I'll be late for my date with Joseph unless I haul ass.

I awkwardly push to my feet, my muscles stiff from the cooling water. Droplets slide down my body, stumbling over goose bumps and making things worse.

I shouldn't have had the bath. I should have stuck with a shower.

Shivering, I climb out of the tub, towel-dry, and moisturize my body. Then I slip on the silk pants, cami, and shirt. The dip of the neckline reveals the teasing mounds of my breasts.

I'm a goddess. No man can resist me.

No man other than Garrett. But it's not Garrett I plan to seduce tonight.

I wipe the condensation from the mirror and apply my eye makeup with a smoky touch. To top it off, my lipstick sparkles with hints of gold.

Hey, Golden Girl.

Garrett's deep voice rumbles in my head. *Nope. Not happen-*

ing. Now's not the time to think about my best friend. Joseph—that's who I need to focus on. My boyfriend. The man I have a chance at a future with. A future with happy kids and a loving husband.

It's not that I'm looking for a husband or to have kids yet. I have a few more years until my biological clock is a concern. My main focus now is my business. My main focus is how I can benefit the community to make it a better place for the children I'll have one day.

I check the time on my phone. I'm running a few minutes late, but I'm sure Joseph won't be too annoyed. He'll probably be on his phone, too busy to even notice my tardiness.

I slip on a pair of glittery-black stilettos and confidently stride to the elevator...only to remember it's out of order.

Dammit.

I head for the stairs and descend them as quickly as possible in four-inch heels. But even then, it takes me longer than I had allowed for. I send Joseph a text.

> Me: On my way. Running a few minutes behind.

I arrive at the restaurant five minutes late. Joseph hasn't responded to my text.

La Brezza Ristorante is the fanciest restaurant Maple Ridge has to offer. It's a pale comparison to what you find in large cities, but maybe that's why I love it so much. The food is delicious and the ambiance is cozy and quaint, like a courtyard restaurant in Italy or Spain. The exposed brick walls only add to the sentiment.

The hostess is my age with curly auburn hair and an easy smile. "Hi, Zara. He's already at your table."

"Thanks, Aria." As predicted, he's on his phone, his back to the entrance. He's wearing a light-blue dress shirt that fits his broad shoulders just right. "I see him."

"I heard about what happened at Picnic & Treats this afternoon. Are you okay?"

"I am, thanks." I hope what happened is the first step for the man and his family to get help. I don't know him. Perhaps he is a decent, loving person when he's sober. The key word being *when*.

A subtle, clean floral scent wafts in the air, just noticeable among the delicious food aromas. The scent is coming from...

"Are you wearing perfume?" I ask Aria. "I like it. It's really pretty."

"Thank you. I made it myself. I recently started my own home business and make various perfumes and scented products."

We talk for another minute about her new enterprise, then I make my way to Joseph's table. The restaurant is busy for a Thursday night during offseason, with most of the tables occupied.

"The woman claims she has chronic pain," he says into his phone. "Fibromyo-something-or-other. It's all in her head. She just doesn't want to do the work, so the rest of us have to pick up her slack. And she takes off more sick days than all of us combined. Hell, I should be paid extra for doing her work..." There's a pause as he no doubt listens to whatever the other person has to say, then he chuckles. "You have that right."

Despite the pain meds I took before coming here, the dull, lingering ache intensifies a notch, and a flare of outrage at his words cuts through me.

I've never mentioned the pain to Joseph. Other than when I told my physician several months ago, no one else knows. If I told Joseph, would he claim the pain is all in my head? Or would his opinion be different because he cares about me?

Of course it would. He's never given you a reason to believe he would be anything but supportive.

The conversation I overheard is a good reason for keeping

the pain to myself. Things will improve. All I need to do is take it a little easier. Soak in the bathtub more. Take care when I lift heavy objects at work.

I sit on the chair across from his and mouth, *Sorry I'm late.*

He gives me an acknowledging nod, his serious expression all business. "Gotta go. See you at work tomorrow." He ends the call and flashes me a quick smile. A quick smile I'm not usually on the receiving end of. Usually, his smiles are all sexy and alluringly sweet. "Hey. Got your text."

The waitress fills my water glass. "What can I get you to drink?"

I request a glass of Chardonnay. Joseph already has a pint of beer on the table.

"Do you know what you want to order? Or do you need a few more minutes?" she asks.

Joseph and I place our orders, and she leaves. I put my hands in front of me on the table, waiting for him to take them like he did on our last date, but his hands stay wrapped around his beer. *Okay, then.*

That's all right. I've got other ways to seduce him into my bed tonight. "How was your day?"

"It was good. Yours?"

I tell him what happened, minimizing the part where I stepped between the man and his daughter. A frown crinkles across his forehead. The more I tell him, the deeper the crease gets. If he were Garrett, he would give me the caveman speech about putting myself at risk. How I wasn't a Marine. And it was the job of men like him to keep women safe. Yada, yada, yada.

Joseph's callous words about his coworker's chronic pain lurch into my thoughts. Would he have stepped in to protect me? Would he have stepped in to protect the girl?

I brush the doubt aside. Of course he would have. You don't have to be a Marine to do something like that, as I've proved. It's just human decency.

"Was anyone hurt?" His frown eases.

"Just a chair. The police came before things could get uglier." *Thank the Lord for that.*

Joseph releases a hard breath. "That's good."

The waitress puts my wineglass on the table.

Joseph picks up his beer. "So…"

Uncertainty rubs along my flesh at the odd way the word trails off. I don't respond, waiting to see where the sentence meanders to. It's not like Joseph to be without words.

Don't jump to conclusions. You don't know what's going on in his head.

It could be he's still processing what happened to me this afternoon. Lord knows I'm reliving the moment in my head, thinking of better ways I could have dealt with the situation. Wondering what will become of the girl and her family.

"So," he repeats, tone more determined this time, and something about his voice has my heart sinking. "I've been thinking about us. You and Me. And where I see us going…"

Freaking wonderful. This conversation could go one of two ways. He's on the same wavelength as me and thinks we should get down and dirty.

Or…

"It's been fun. But this thing between us has been moving too fast. I think we need to end it."

Too fast? If we went any slower, we'd be going backward.

"Too fast? I'm a little lost here. Is this because I want to have…" I glance to the nearest table, gauging how much the man and woman seated at it can hear. "Sex?"

The word is whispered but at the same time it feels like I've screamed it. The attention of the older woman sitting near Joseph darts my way. Her eyebrows disappear behind black-rim glasses and gray-curtain bangs.

Absolutely freaking wonderful. I'm about to be dumped in a restaurant in front of witnesses. Couldn't he have just dumped me via text? Crass? Yes. But a lot less humiliating than this.

He clears his throat and shifts on his chair. "No. Not at all. It's just I bumped into my ex-wife the other day..."

I blink, positive I'm in a twisted, modern-day episode of *The Twilight Zone*. "Ex. Wife? What ex-wife? You never mentioned you used to be married." Hell, he didn't even have a tan line on his finger from his wedding band.

"We've been divorced two years." There's a sadness about him I hadn't noticed until now.

"But you've never gotten over her," I finish for him, kicking myself for not seeing it sooner.

Shit, why do I fall for emotionally unavailable men...the ones still in love with their exes?

I hadn't fallen yet for Joseph, but the reality of what he just told me still stings. Stings with the force of a dozen wasp bites.

After what I overheard him say about his colleague, I shouldn't be all that disappointed. Maybe he did me a favor, saving me from greater heartbreak when he tells me the pain in my body is all in my head.

The woman at the next table sends me a look of pity, getting a side order of entertainment with her pasta dish.

Right. I fan out my options. I can sit here and eat dinner as if I don't have a care in the world. I can storm out, cursing men. Not a bad option given the day I've had.

Or I can...

I catch our waitress's eye and wave her over. "Hi. I'm not staying after all. So please pack my dinner to go. And add a slice of the chocolate ganache cake to my order. Thanks." I point to Joseph. "But he's paying for it." It's the least he can do.

This time the other woman seems to be on the verge of giving me a standing ovation.

If the waitress's sympathetic expression is any indication, she must have also sensed my date didn't go as planned. "I'll bring it right away." She turns her attention to Joseph. "Are you eating here, or did you also want to take your food to go?"

"I'll stay." Only a small amount of regret weighs down his tone. Or maybe it's just relief.

Either way, I don't care. I push to my feet. "I'll be waiting by the hostess stand," I tell her.

After the day I've had, I don't feel like making small talk with Joseph while I wait for my food. Because that's all it will be. I don't need to hear about the woman he's still in love with. I don't need to hear why they got divorced. It has nothing to do with me.

I pick up my glass of wine and toss back the contents. Then I walk to the front entrance, my head held beauty-pageant high. On my way there, I deliberate if I should update Simone, Emily, and Jess via our group chat about what happened. Or text Keshia. Or Garrett.

I stomp on the last thought. I don't feel like discussing with him what happened when I'm positive he's still in love with Kenda.

In truth, I don't want to talk about it with anyone. I want to watch some good TV and eat my dinner.

I want to spend the evening doing self-care...and drinking more wine.

But tomorrow. Tomorrow I'll tell my friends about my night and how I didn't realize Joseph was married. I doubt Keshia or Garrett will be too disappointed by my news. Neither seemed to be a fan of his. Garrett always rolls his eyes at the mention of the man, as if he thought Joseph was an idiot.

He might have had a point there.

Lord, how did I not see it coming that Joseph was planning to dump me?

Am I really that clueless when it comes to men?

8

GARRETT

I stare at the blank page on my laptop screen. The early morning sunlight streams through my office window, painting the armchair I'm sitting on in a soft glow. The sun has moved position in the past thirty minutes, but I can't say the same for the cursor.

Fuck. The words didn't come any easier last night, after I dropped Athena and Peony off at the hotel. I had hoped whatever blocked the words would disintegrate by morning, and they would flow better today.

I let out a hard breath, push to my feet, and pace. With all the pacing I do while working on a book, it's surprising a threadbare path hasn't been worn into the blue rug.

Birds chirp from the tree outside the window, obviously not dealing with a crisis like I am. Maybe they have a point. I should be outside, dealing with my frustrations another way.

I power off my laptop and go outside and weed the flower bed near the house. I cleared away the winter debris a few weeks ago. That's more than I can say for the tangled thoughts now suffocating my creative flow.

I should check on Athena and Peony, since Athena

doesn't have a phone. Or I could just phone the hotel and get the call transferred to her room. That would save me from going there. I told her last night they could order room service or go to the hotel café and charge the food to the room.

Kellan called after I got back and told me Athena doesn't have a police record and there are no warrants for her arrest. There are also no missing girls matching Peony's description.

He also confirmed Kenda died just as Athena had told us—which I already knew. I googled the shooting. Police are investigating what happened, so there wasn't much information, other than the suspected shooters were dead.

Dead. They deserved a lot more than that after leaving a little girl motherless.

And now I'll have to tell my parents what happened to Kenda—who they had loved—and how her daughter is quite possibly also *my* daughter. I scrub my hand down my face. I'm not looking forward to telling them any of that.

I also need to tell Zara. Soon. I'm not ready to tell her just yet though.

I dig up a few more weeds, but the usually calming activity does little to stop my growing restlessness. *Shit.*

I need to get out of Maple Ridge for a few hours. To burn away that gnawing edge.

Knowing I won't get any writing done until I've talked to Clarke, I decide to head out of town. But first, I drive to the hotel where Peony and Athena are staying and park the Explorer on the street.

The girl working behind the reception desk has a reputation of being a gossip. Christ knows what rumors she might spread if she spots me, especially if she realizes who I'm here to see.

To avoid the risk of that, I walk to the hotel café and the small gift shop in case Athena and Peony are there. They aren't.

I dial the hotel's number and request the call be transferred to their room.

"One moment, please," the woman on the other end of the line says.

The phone rings three times, then a tentative voice answers, "Hello?"

"Hi, Athena. It's Garrett. Just checking if you need anything. I'm in the lobby."

"You wanna come up and see your daughter?" Athena's voice is less tentative this time, more hopeful.

"Sure. I'll be right there." I would run up the stairs to burn off the restlessness, but I need a key card to get into the staircase. I didn't think of that yesterday when I checked them into their room.

I walk to the elevator as I type a text for Kellan.

> Me: Need to cancel run. Heading out of
> town for a few hours. Back later.

I pressed the elevator button. Dots pop up on my phone, indicating Kellan is replying to my text.

> Kellan: Does this have to do with your
> unexpected news yesterday?

> Me: Yes.

I leave it at that. Kellan won't push for more information. And I'm not interested in sharing the truth about my plans.

> Me: I'm at the hotel, checking on Peony
> and Athena first.

> Me: Will let Mom and Dad know what's
> going on once I get back.

They need to find out from me before I tell anyone else—

other than Clarke. And they need to hear it from me before the news of Peony becomes local gossip.

> Me: And will let Lucas and Troy and the
> others know tonight. Please don't
> mention Peony and Athena to anyone
> until then.

The elevator door pings open. I step inside and push the button for the third floor.

> Kellan: I won't say anything.

I knew he wouldn't, but I had to say it for my own peace of mind.

I tuck my phone into my jeans pocket and pace the small confines of the elevator. It ambles its way to the third floor, in no particular rush to get there.

I'm not sure what I plan to do when I get to the room. I'm not used to interacting with kids Peony's age. My child-related experience is mostly with older kids, like the ones I play street hockey with. Older kids are less scary than their smaller counterparts.

The elevator door opens, and I walk along the corridor toward Athena and Peony's room. The risk of changing my mind and fleeing—or of someone recognizing me—quickens my pace. I knock on their door.

The door slowly opens, and Athena waves me in. She's wearing the same clothes she had on yesterday, the light pink T-shirt slightly more wrinkled than it was last night.

The room is decent-sized, with a king-sized bed and plenty of room for a toddler to move around. There's also a love seat and coffee table, but nothing to keep a toddler busy. Unless climbing on the furniture and hiding behind the curtains is all a toddler needs to be happy.

"Ni-na." A tiny voice calls out from the playpen in the

corner of the room. Small fingers and a head poke up. Peony's hair isn't tied up this time. Her textured curls resemble her mother's while we were dating. My heart tightens at how she looks so much like Kenda.

I swallow the heartache and focus on the name Peony just used. "Nina?"

"She has trouble saying Athena, so it comes out sounding like Nina." Athena walks to Peony and picks her up.

Peony's wearing what looks like the same jeans as she had on yesterday but paired with a different T-shirt. This one is bright-pink with white polka dots.

Peony points at the playpen. "Poppy."

"I'll get that," I tell them. Athena's arms are full with Peony, making it awkward for her to reach down and grab the stuffed panda.

I retrieve the toy and hold it out to Peony. Her bottom lip wobbles, tears filling her eyes, and a burst of cold panic shoots through my veins. I've never done well with tears—especially from someone so little.

I fail to retreat in enough time, and a high-pitched scream explodes from her lungs, the noise surprisingly loud from such a small body.

The sound triggers something inside me, and the panic coursing through me flares to full-out fear. Even while deployed in enemy territory, I'd never felt this helpless, this out of my league.

My gut tightens, and I reverse a step, giving her space. That seems like a sensible course of action.

Athena gently rocks Peony. "Hey, sweet girl. It's okay. Your daddy isn't gonna hurt you. He just wants to give you Poppy."

I tentatively hold the panda out to her again.

Still wailing, Peony snatches it out of my hand and buries her face in Athena's chest.

Helplessness and panic refuse to loosen their grip on me,

their talons digging into my flesh. I need to get out of here. To regroup. To get my mind back in the game so I can finish *Untold Mercy*.

"I have to leave town for a few hours. I'll swing by a mall in Eugene and pick up some things for the two of you while I'm there. Maybe some clothes. Diapers. Toddler food. Can you make a list for me?"

Athena stares at me for a beat, as if I've just told her to run down Main Street in her underwear. "It's...it's not like that. I...I just want to take care of Peony and earn a paycheck as her nanny."

"Right. We established that yesterday with Kenda's final letter. But you and Peony can't keep wearing the same clothes. You lost everything in the apartment fire. The least I could do is help you out while you wait for the insurance money."

Her eyes widen a minuscule amount but enough for me to notice.

"You and Kenda didn't have renters insurance?"

"We, um, we never got around to it. We had...we had just moved in."

Shit. They really don't have anything. "Look, I get it you're not thrilled asking for my help, but if Peony is my daughter, it's my responsibility to make sure she's clothed, fed, happy, and safe. So the least I can do in the meantime is also get *you* any essentials you need while I'm at the mall."

"Okay." A smile eases across Athena's face, and she suddenly appears so much younger than her late twenties that I'd originally assumed her to be. As if the weight of the world had been placed on her shoulders, and I just knocked some of it off.

I study the back of Peony's head and her small body pressed against Athena. "What are you planning to do if the paternity test proves I'm not her father?"

"You *are* her father. Kenda didn't lie. And I'm hoping once you see the truth for yourself, you can love Peony the way her mama did."

I reach out to touch Peony's shoulder, an act of reassurance, but catch myself. Father or not, I need to gain her trust before I can touch her without causing a meltdown. I drop my hand to my side. "The list?"

Athena finds a few sheets of blank paper in the desk drawer, writes a short list of items, and hands it to me. Peony's wails have quieted to a hiccupping sob, and she watches me take the list from Athena, her eyes wide with unconcealed distrust.

I scan over the list. It's all for Peony. Athena has written nothing for herself.

"Thanks. I'll be back later this afternoon." I can't afford to take that much time off with my rapidly approaching deadline, but until I've talked through everything with my old friend, I won't be able to focus on the story.

"Bye, Peony." My voice is kept light and friendly, even though she makes me feel like I'm dangling from the edge of a cliff, my fingers barely gripping hold of the ledge.

She doesn't respond, but she also doesn't scream again, so I count that as a win. I leave the room and jog to where I parked the Explorer. I didn't have sex with Athena, and no one witnessed me leave the hotel...but it still feels like I'm doing the walk of shame.

Shame for how I didn't know about Peony before yesterday.

Shame for how I scared her. It hadn't been my intent.

Shame for how I have no idea how to chase away her fears or how to calm her.

Shame for how she could be my daughter, but hell if I deserve her—something so sweet and innocent. Not after what happened...

I swallow the memory and box up the emotion long enough for the two-hour drive to Roseburg. Bruised clouds hang low in the sky with the promise of late morning rain. I didn't bring a jacket. If I get soaked, it'll be the least I deserve.

I pull up to the National Cemetery and park in a spot farthest from the gates. Then I walk to where Sergeant Joshua Clarke is buried. I keep a lookout for signs of his parents, siblings, or wife and children. The oldest child was three years old when Clarke died. Her brother was barely more than five months. Too young to remember their father, to remember how much he loved them.

No one is at his grave, but the fresh-cut mixed flowers suggest he had visitors not long ago. Maybe this morning. Maybe yesterday. *His wife.* I've learned over the past few years it's her signature bouquet.

I crouch in front of his plot and place my hand on the patchy spring grass. "I see Aurora was here. Does she still blame me as much as I blame myself for what happened?" Do his kids hate me for failing to save their father?

Silence sits like a lead weight on my back. Not even a bird responds to my question.

I lower my ass to the ground and remember the laughter and jokes and sharing of stories during our last deployment. Clarke and Cooper were two of my closest friends in the Marines. My brothers. The men who stuck with me during our darkest days.

"Remember Kenda, the woman I told you about?" I ask Clarke's grave.

"How come you never put a ring on her finger?" Clarke had teased when he first saw the photo of her. Kenda and I had long since broken up, but I kept a laminated photo of Kenda, Zara, and me in my duffel bag at the base. He had seen it in the bag and snatched it out before I could stop him.

"Because she's got big ambitions that don't include being tied to my sorry ass." I grabbed the photo from him, my gaze grazing over the two gorgeous women smiling up at me. It had been taken during our junior year of college. A fuchsia scarf secured Zara's hair, a few coils teasing the sides of her face. Kenda's medium-length Afro showed off her high cheekbones.

Clarke laughed. "So, she's as smart as she is pretty."

The photo was whipped from my hand. I spun around to find Tyson staring down at it, a hungry gleam in his eyes. "Who's the other hot one?"

His expression gave away the dirty thoughts crossing his mind, and a protectiveness reared up in me. *The hell.* "Zara. But don't even think what I know you're thinking. She's a good friend of mine who deserves better than the likes of you." A low snarl brushed my tone. Not exactly what I was aiming for.

A burst of laughter boomed in the room from the two men, along with Cooper.

"Possessive, huh?" Cooper chuckled. "You sure you don't have something going with that hot piece of meat?"

"She's a woman. She's not a chuck roast."

"Oooh, someone is possessive."

"Not possessive. It's just my mother taught me to respect women."

Clarke snickered. "Someone's protesting a little too much."

"Agreed." Tyson's smirk was too wide for my liking.

I rolled my eyes. "Zara's been my best friend since elementary school. So it's definitely not like that between us."

Cooper's snorted laugh almost had me rolling my eyes again. "According to my sister, who reads, lives, and breathes romance books, those are the ones who make the best lovers. The best friends to lovers."

Yeah, Emily—one of my other childhood friends—had said something like that a few months ago. But I don't think she was referring to the same sort of lover Cooper was.

"Whatever," I grumbled. "Anyway, Zara is off-limits to you." The words had been directed at Tyson. The other two men had wives back home.

A crow caws somewhere nearby, snapping me to the present. "Anyway," I tell Clarke's grave, "I hooked up with Kenda over two years ago...and I might have knocked her up." I tell him the rest of the story. "Peony is the sweetest thing, pretty like her mother. But she's also scared of me, which makes getting to know her more challenging. If she is my kid."

Water droplets hit the exposed skin on my arms. I glance up at the darkening sky. "Do I think she's my daughter? Now that I'm coming to terms with everything, I do. It's not—wasn't like Kenda to lie about something like that. But I need to be positive she's mine. Otherwise, there's another man who's being denied the chance to get to know his daughter."

What if another man is Peony's father, but there's a reason Kenda told me in the letter that Peony is my daughter? Did she tell me that so I could protect Peony? And if that's the case, why did she believe her daughter needs protecting?

Now that I've had time to absorb the news, I'm fairly certain Peony is my daughter. But even so, I can't ignore the other scenario is possible. Hence the need for the paternity test.

"You want to know the weirdest part?" The wind picks up, ruffling the flower petals. "For a second, I felt a flicker of joy at the news that I could have a daughter." I laugh, the sound harsher than the deep howl of the wind. "How crazy is that? But how can I be a father? What if I fail Peony like I failed you and Cooper? Like I failed Kenda?"

Peony deserves someone better than me for a father. Someone who won't let her down.

As if in agreement, the sky opens up in a deluge of rain.

9

GARRETT

I stay at the National Cemetery for more than an hour in the rain, then drive to Eugene. After failing my two close friends and their families, standing in the heavy downpour didn't come close to what I deserve.

The rain has stopped by the time I arrive at River Run Center—the mall where I'm hoping to get most of the things on Athena's list. I remove my phone from the Explorer's console and send Zara a text.

> Me: Can you come over after work?
> There's something I need to talk to you
> about before everyone else shows up.

It's our weekly Friday Game Night with my brothers, Zara, Simone, Jess, and Emily. And while I'm in no rush to tell Zara what happened to Kenda, I can't put it off any longer. I plan to tell my brothers tonight about Peony. Zara deserves to hear the news about Kenda's death and about Peony from me first.

I climb out of the Explorer and shove my phone into my damp jeans pocket. My sweatshirt isn't doing much better, but

74

my clothes and sneakers are somewhat dry from the hour drive with the heater on.

I wander through the busy mall, searching for the stores I need. A small group of young mothers pushing strollers walks past me, chatting and laughing.

"I love that dress you bought Casey," one of them says. "It's adorable."

I turn my head in the direction they came from and spot a kids' clothing store—if the pint-sized clothes on the pint-sized mannequin out front are any indication.

I step into the store and feel as comfortable here as I did at the hotel when Peony started screaming. I quickly survey the area, a Marine in unfamiliar territory, getting the lay of the land, preparing for the worst, and knowing I'll never be ready enough. One half of the store is a sea of pink, orange, and yellow. The other is a sea of green and blue. But that's all I know.

If Peony wasn't in desperate need of clothes and supplies, if Zara wasn't at work, and if I hadn't wanted to visit the National Cemetery on my own, I could have brought Zara here. She'd have a better idea of what the heck I'm looking for.

I'm the only man in the store. Probably also the only clueless person here when it comes to kids' clothing—especially clothes for a little girl.

"Can I help you find something?" a woman asks from behind me.

I turn to her, checking her name tag as I do—Daphne. The petite, blond woman eyes me with sympathy, as if she knows this is all foreign to me—like I've gotten lost in the tampon aisle. *Am I that obvious?* "Where's the toddler section?"

"Boy or girl? Or are you looking for something gender neutral?"

"Girl and gender neutral."

She leads me to the pink-clothing side of the store. "These

are our girls' clothes." She points to a section amongst the sea of pink, yellow, and orange. "Those are our gender-neutral clothes for younger kids." She waves at the circular rack in the middle of the store. "What size are you looking for?"

"Size?" I shove my hand into my front pocket and pull out the list. The paper is damp and torn, the ink faded. I can't make out much of what Athena wrote. *Great.* Guess I'll be winging it after all.

"How old is the toddler?"

"Eighteen months."

"I take it this is for a gift?"

"No. It's for...for my daughter." The moment the words are out, I want to snatch them back. Niece. I should have said they were for my niece in case she recognizes me...or in case Daphne recognizes my name when I pay for the clothes. I don't need news I have a daughter being leaked on social media. It's my choice if I reveal my fatherhood status and the time frame for doing that.

A smile twitches on the corners of her mouth, then smooths into a full out grin. "I take it your wife usually buys the clothes." There's a not-quite-there question in her tone.

"Yeah, something like that."

"So, you're looking for something your daughter can grow into....Is she big or small for her age?"

I shrug. *Hell if I know.* "She's about this big." I demonstrate with my hands, but it's hard to say for sure. I mostly have only seen Peony when she's sitting or on Athena's hip.

"It depends on if she's potty training. Size twenty-four months fits diapers better. Size two if she's potty training." Daphne looks at me expectantly, like she's waiting for me to answer the question I have no idea how to answer. I do know Peony is still in diapers.

"Is there specific clothing you're looking for?" Daphne asks, seemingly unaware of my internal debate.

"Everything. All her clothes were lost in a fire."

Sympathy flashes on Daphne's face. "I'm so sorry. Did you lose everything in the fire?"

I shrug once more. "It changed my life completely." That's the partial truth. It was the mall shooting that turned my life upside down.

Thirty minutes later, I leave the store, carrying way more items than I'd intended to buy. Pink unicorn PJs, as well as tops, skirts, and pants in a variety of colors and styles, fill my arms.

Hopefully, Peony likes something in the pile.

I drop off the clothes in the Explorer and head to the bookstore in the mall, like I do whenever I'm in the city. It's one of the places where I'm most comfortable, along with the library. Both of which might seem odd, given I was a reluctant reader and struggled with the skill in my early years. It was Zara who taught me the power of getting lost in a story. Who got me addicted to books.

And who inspired me to one day become an author.

Now, reading all genres—but especially thrillers—is part of the job. A very enjoyable part of the job.

I walk past the tables at the front of the store that hold the latest new releases and Booktok bestsellers and head to the children's section. It's a section I haven't been to since I was a kid, when it brought me comfort, when it brought me joy. Here, in this store, they've gone all out to entice kids into the space, with the bright-colored rugs and kid-sized furniture.

I pick up a board book with a pigeon on the cover from the display of colorfully illustrated picture books.

"Hi, Garrett." Camila's faded English accent curls around her vowels. If Zara is the inspiration for my protagonist's love interest, Camila is the inspiration for the antagonist's wife. She's tall and willowy, but unlike the villain's partner, she has a big heart. "Are you here to sign our recent shipment of your last release?"

"I was in the area. Thought I'd drop by."

Camila peers at the book in my hand, and the thin dark line of her eyebrows lifts.

"I also need to get a few kids' books. For toddlers. Any recommendations?"

"Absolutely." She rattles off a few titles, grabbing two of them from the table where I got the pigeon book, and hands them to me.

The illustrations are eye-catching—not that I know anything about what toddlers like. "These look good. I'll take them. Where are the books you'd like me to sign?"

I sign the twenty copies they have in stock, pay for the kids' books, and enter a store farther down the mall that sells toys and furniture for babies and small children.

A toddler not much older than Peony climbs onto a kid-sized armchair and sets it off rocking. She giggles and beams up at her parents.

Her father crouches next to her. "Do you like this chair? Or would you prefer that one over there?" He points to the other option, but I can tell from the way she clutches the arms of her seat, and her grin, the chair she's on is the clear winner. Can't say I blame her. The other chair doesn't rock.

"Chair!" She taps her palms on the armrests, her grin widening.

I pretend to examine a squirrel-shaped pillow and covertly watch the family checking out the rest of the toddler furniture. I take mental note of what items the little girl approves of, which seems to be a fair amount, and what items barely get a passing glance.

"Is there something I can help you with?" a man wearing a blue store vest asks.

"Yes, I need to order some furniture. For my niece. Do you ship to Maple Ridge?"

"We do."

We walk around the section, with me pointing out the things I want to order. The toddler bed. The rocking armchair. A little bookshelf that goes with the other two items. A rug that also got the little girl's stamp of approval. And finally, neutral-colored bedding with cute woodland critters on it...but no pandas. Hopefully that's okay with Peony. If not, I'll find something else she likes more.

I also grab toddler-appropriate wooden puzzles and stacking toys, along with a few other toys Charles recommends for Peony's age.

"Your niece is a lucky girl to have an uncle like you," he says, surveying the toys and squirrel pillow on the counter. He checks the computer. "They can deliver the furniture next Tuesday."

I agree to the delivery-time window, pay for everything, and leave the store with the bedding, the pillow, and the toys.

I might have been a little too enthusiastic with everything, given I don't have the paternity test results. And I'm positive once Zara gets over her shock and grief about Kenda's death, she'll be highly amused at just how overboard I went with my purchases.

As I walk to the mall entrance near where I'm parked, I pass a women's clothing store with a Taylor Swift song playing in the background. Unlike the other stores I passed earlier, this one seems to cater to women Athena's age.

I double back and stare at the store. Yes, Athena was offended when I offered to buy some essentials for her, but she has nothing left after the apartment fire. The least I can do after everything she's been through—with the fire and witnessing the murder of her former employer—is to get her some clothes.

Thoughts of Kenda bleeding out in the Greensboro mall tighten my throat, and I have to stop to catch my breath. Much like I did a number of times last night, staring at my computer screen, the words failing to come.

Dead. It still doesn't feel real. Being a single father to a toddler feels more real than knowing I will never see Kenda's smile again. Never hear her view on issues that are important to her.

My phone pings in my pocket, and I pull it out.

> Zara: I can be there around 5:30 ish.

> Zara: Can you give me a hint what it is?

> Zara: Or is this your way of getting me to make the game night snacks?

> Zara: *snickers*

I close my eyes, composing my response in my head. But all I can see is Kenda standing in the mall, blood spreading across her chest. Her image is quickly replaced with Cooper and Clarke, gaping wounds in their bodies spilling blood.

I open my eyes, banishing the image that has haunted me for the past seven years.

Breathe in. Breathe out.

I repeat the words several times. The action helps. A little.

"Tell me five things you see," a voice in my head prompts. A voice that sounds suspiciously like the therapist I saw for a few sessions after retiring from the Marines. I quit seeing him soon after, figuring therapy wasn't for me. I'd started to write my first novel after that, which did more for me than therapy ever could.

"Tell me five things you see," the voice in my head repeats, more insistently this time.

I roll my eyes but go with my subconscious's prodding. "Trash can. Kids. Mall cop. Stores. Benches."

Christ, this is so stupid.

"Tell me five things you hear..."

"Laughter. Talking."

I ignore the rest of the exercise and walk into the store. *You've got this under control, soldier.*

If I'd felt lost in the kids' stores, that's nothing compared to this place. I don't know what Athena likes to wear—other than the jeans and T-shirt she had on.

A young woman approaches, wearing a short flowery dress and a store-employee smile. "You look lost? Is there something I can help you with?"

"I, er...I need help finding a pair of sweatpants and some T-shirts. She's about your size."

"A girlfriend?"

"No...just a friend. It's a birthday present." Because buying clothes for your kid's nanny is probably frowned upon.

Maybe I could put William Lockheart, the male protagonist of *Untold Mercy*, in the same awkward situation. Of course, he would handle it better than I am.

The woman shows me the section I need. I put the bag I'm carrying down and pick up a light-blue T-shirt from the table.

I hold the T-shirt up, checking what's on the front, but quickly realize it isn't long enough to cover Athena's stomach. I grip the back of my neck, deliberating the sexual harassment suit I'll be liable for if I give her this.

"Do you have anything longer?"

The woman shows me several tops that are much more suitable. I grab two of them. Maybe Zara, Simone, and Emily have clothes Athena can borrow.

"Um, she'll also need underwear." I inwardly groan at how that sounded. What guy buys underwear for a female friend? It's not like I've ever bought any for Zara.

Face burning hot, I tell the salesclerk to pick something. She must sense my discomfort. She doesn't show me what she selected and escorts me to the register.

Zara, Simone, and Emily will never let me hear the end of

this...once they've stopped laughing their asses off. That's assuming I tell them.

Christ, if Cooper and Clarke were alive, they'd mock me about it until we were old men in wheelchairs. And even then, that wouldn't end their ribbing.

Next, I pick up the rest of the items on Athena's list—diapers, finger foods for toddlers, fruit—as well as a few more toys, and head back to Maple Ridge.

The rain from earlier picks up again as I drive on the highway, large drops hammering my windshield.

And coming along for the ride is dread. It escorts me home, sings to the song on the radio.

Dread about the next part of my day. Dread at telling my parents about Peony.

10

ZARA

I sketch on my iPad three different design options for the potential expansion of Picnic & Treats. The winning design will depend on several factors—one being Mr. Cartwright's approval. If there's even the opportunity to lease the space, that is. And I need to get renovation quotes from Troy. I'll ask him tonight.

I wiggle my butt on the staff-room couch, doing what I can to relieve the growing ache in my hips and the base of my spine. Doing what I can to distract myself from the fact I got dumped last night by a boyfriend who was still in love with his ex-wife.

When that doesn't work, I stand and walk around the room. That does the trick. For the ache.

I frown at the seemingly offending couch as if it was the one that dumped me. It's only a few years old. It shouldn't need replacing yet. No one else has complained it's uncomfortable. Just the opposite.

The staff-room door opens, and Keshia walks in. She throws me a sympathetic smile. The same smile she's been giving me every time she sees me, ever since this morning after I told her what happened last night.

"Boring *and* an idiot," she mutters to herself, as if I'm not in the room. She puts a steaming mug of hot chocolate on the coffee table. "Figured you could use this."

A smooth chuckle rolls from between my lips. "I guess you were right about him being boring. I just didn't want to see it. And thank you for the hot chocolate." My favorite comfort drink.

"And what about how he is an idiot?" She lifts her eyebrows in an encouraging question.

"Yep. He's definitely that too." I return to the couch, sit, and take a sip of the hot chocolate. It's Mimi's recipe. And pure magic.

Someone knocks on the door.

"Come in," I call out, putting the mug on the coffee table.

The door opens once more, and Mr. Cartwright strolls in, smiling. "Hello, Zara. Keshia. I was just in the neighborhood and thought I would tell you the news in person."

My heart stammers at his words, then screeches to a halt in anticipation of his next ones.

"Hey, Mr. Cartwright." Keshia shares a glance between my former teacher and me. "I have to get back to the kitchen. Let me know if you need anything."

After he tells her he's good, she hurries off, leaving me to mentally kick-start my heart again.

"The sisters won't be renewing Mountain Lore's lease," he tells me, jumping right to it. "So I'm officially looking for a new tenant to take over the space."

Yes. I somehow keep my arms from shooting up in a praise-the-Lord gesture.

"Will your proposal be ready by Tuesday? Wednesday at the latest?"

I nod, trying to keep from betraying how fast my excited heart is thumping. "Yes. Tuesday will be fine."

"Sounds good. Would it work for you if I came over around, say, three, to discuss your proposal?"

When I'd originally approached Mr. Cartwright about opening Picnic & Treats, there hadn't been any competing bids for the retail space. Which had been a good thing. I didn't know much at the time about running a café. I didn't have a business degree. I had a chemistry degree—because at one point I'd thought I would follow in my father's and oldest brother's footsteps and become a physician.

But then I changed my mind after spending the summer with Mimi in New Orleans. I saw how good food, comfort food, makes people happy. And as much as I loved science, the idea of dealing with the frustrations of the medical system didn't appeal to me.

My business skills have grown since I opened Picnic & Treats, like bread dough in a hot, humid oven. And Mr. Cartwright is a regular customer, frequenting the café often enough to know I'm good at what I do. That must count for something.

"I look forward to hearing what you have in mind for the place," Mr. Cartwright says, smiling. "I want to see what you plan to do with the space before I make a decision of leasing it to you or leasing it to another potential business in Maple Ridge."

"Is it possible to send me the floor plans for next door so I can show them to Troy?" Troy was also a student of his, so Mr. Cartwright knows about Troy's successful construction business.

"I can drop a copy off tomorrow. Does that work for you?"

"Thank you!"

He leaves, and I check the time. Two more hours until I told

Garrett I would show up at his house. Two more hours until I find out what he needs to talk to me about.

And yes—I am curious what he has to tell me.

More than likely, his text was nothing more than a ploy to get me to help him with the Game Night snacks.

This wouldn't be the first time he's done that.

I doubt he's heard yet the news about Joseph, and that's why he wants to talk to me.

Or maybe he has.

Maybe he wants me to come over earlier so he can tell me that he told me so, he always thought something was off about Joseph.

11

———

GARRETT

The first summer Kenda and I were a couple, I brought her to my parents' house, eager for her to meet Mom and Dad. Naturally, they loved her. How could they not?

She spent the next two Christmases staying with me there, because she didn't want to spend the holidays with her parents. She hadn't told me much about them, but I got the idea her father was an asshole. Of course, Mom had been adamant—even if I was twenty at the time—Kenda and I would sleep in separate rooms. Right—as if that had stopped us from hooking up while under my parents' roof.

We had snuggled on the porch love seat, our bodies buried under a pile of blankets, talking about our futures. I would attend law school after the Marines. She was going to be a great journalist, traveling war-torn countries. Right, I hadn't exactly been thrilled with that. We had argued, heatedly, before I finally understood why she had to pursue her world-changing goal.

The love I felt for Kenda has faded, but the pain in my heart that she's gone from this world is very real.

And now I have a daughter. A daughter who will grow up without her mother.

Each step toward my childhood home is like trudging through wet mud, my newly appointed single-father status and the looming book deadline sucking me down.

The front door swings open, and Mom's smiling face meets mine. The once-brown waves of her shoulder-length hair are now gray, but despite that, she still resembles the woman who raised me. And that includes the jeans and light-blue T-shirt dusted with flour.

"Garrett, I wasn't expecting you today." She steps back, letting me into the house. "You're just in time for your favorite double-chocolate cookies. They're fresh from the oven."

The smell of chocolate reaches me as I step onto the stoop, and I'm returned to a time when she made them whenever I'd had a bad day. I didn't have to tell her something was upsetting me. She always knew.

I flash her a wan smile and step inside my childhood home. Memories of Kenda in this house make it difficult to fasten on a more convincing upward curve of my mouth.

A few specific memories sneak in, and a small, silent laugh fills my heart. Of her making out with me in the old treehouse that used to be in the backyard. It had been damn cold, but Kenda hadn't cared. Of her unabashedly throwing her arms around my neck in front of my family after she opened her Christmas present from me. I had given her some pretty journals Zara had told me Kenda had been eyeing in a store.

Of her tiptoeing into my room late at night, looking adorably sleep ruffled, after having a bad dream.

I had kissed the memory of it out of her until she fell asleep in my arms.

Worry creases Mom's brow. "Is something wrong, sweetheart?" She sweeps me into a hug, the top of her head barely meeting my shoulders.

I hug her back, relieved and happy this woman, who'd put up with my dumb ass growing up, is still part of my life. She has always been there for my brothers and me. Attended all our hockey games and practices. Supported all our decisions, including those I'm sure deep down she cringed at. The only exception was when she had temporarily, last year, disagreed with Troy's choice of girlfriend, Jess, because of her past.

She releases me, the frown on her face still there. "What's wrong?"

"Is Dad here? There's something I need to talk to you both about."

"He's working in his study. Has some numbers he needed to crunch for a client and decided to do that here instead of at the office."

"I can come back later." After I attempt to put words on the page.

"No, no. He shouldn't be much longer. You can sit and have cookies while you wait."

"Did someone say cookies?" My father's wide shoulders fill the doorway, and a grin breaks out on his lined face. "Hey, son. Are you the reason your mom was busy baking cookies this afternoon? And here I thought she was baking them for me." He's not wearing the button-up shirt and trousers he would've worn to the office. He's wearing jeans and a T-shirt that reveals arm muscles that only come from hitting the weights.

Mom laughs the familiar sound of my childhood. "Of course I was making them for you, dear. Garrett dropping by to talk to us is an added bonus."

I follow the pair into the kitchen and sit at the table. The kitchen cabinets were recently repainted to a gray-blue, but the rest of the room hasn't changed much since Kenda was last here. Back when I wouldn't think twice about scaling the tree outside the guest room, just to spend the night with my girlfriend without Mom being wise to what I was up to.

"You want coffee or milk with your cookies, Garrett?"

After the past twenty-four hours, I need something stronger than coffee or milk, but I doubt Mom would go for that. "Coffee, please."

While Mom brews it, the three of us make small talk about the upcoming Wilderness Warriors season. She places the mugs and a plate of cookies on the table and sits on her chair.

The late afternoon sunbathes the table in a warm glowing light but does nothing to soothe me like it did when I was a kid. If anything, it just highlights the empty seat Kenda had sat on.

But while that might have been Kenda's chair, the cookie plate with the hand-painted, cute chubby bird on it was a gift from Zara. Over twenty years ago.

Mom loves that plate.

And I secretly love it too.

"So, what's up, son?" My father asks once we're settled.

I pick up my mug and take a sip of the hot drink. "I..." I put the mug down and rake my fingers through my hair. Rub the back of my neck. "I came home yesterday after my run with Kellan and found a woman and a toddler on my front stoop. I've never seen either of them before, but the woman had a letter from Kenda. The toddler is my daughter. Kenda's and my daughter."

"Your daughter?" Mom says at the same time my father splutters, "What kind of scam does this woman think she's pulling?"

"I'm pretty sure it's not a scam. She told me Kenda was killed in a mall shooting last week. I looked it up. Kenda was listed as one of the deceased."

Mom gasps, her shock reverberating throughout the room. Her hand flies to her mouth, shaky fingers pressing against her lips.

"And this woman just showed up out of nowhere to tell you

that you have a daughter?" Dad sounds as convinced that Athena is telling the truth as he is the tooth fairy is real.

"That's right."

"But if the toddler is your daughter, Kenda would have told you she was pregnant." The shock on Mom's face has morphed into a battle of emotions, with hope and longing sitting on top of the pile. "She knows you wouldn't turn your back on your child. *We* wouldn't turn our backs on your child."

I can only shrug. I have no idea why Kenda thought she couldn't tell me. Fuck, why had I acted like a sulking asshole and ignored her text?

Yes, she'd left while I was sleeping and hadn't bothered leaving a note. But we'd both agreed it was only one night. No strings attached.

Had she really believed I'd want nothing to do with my daughter because of that agreement? I hadn't planned to become a father due to a one-night stand with a former love, but it is what it is.

Of course, I'm not about to tell my parents this. They don't need to know I was the idiot who never returned her text asking me to call her. And besides...she could have tried again —but she didn't.

That's all in the past. I need to focus on the future. With my daughter.

"Are you sure she's your daughter?" My father leans back in his chair, his expression that of a man who has seen and done things he's not proud of—which has made him leery of other people's actions and motives.

"I've ordered a paternity test to find out for sure, but Kenda had no reason to lie to me. Or no reason I can think of." Other than the possibility the father was an asshole and she didn't want Peony anywhere near him.

But she'd have known I would do a paternity test. I wouldn't take things at face value.

"Where is she? Your daughter?" Mom's face is soft with that dreamy look she always gets when talking about her friends' grandkids.

"I put Peony and her nanny up in a hotel for the next few days."

"Her name...my granddaughter's name is Peony?" Mom smiles, her face further softening. Any softer, and it would drip onto the kitchen floor.

Dad takes Mom's hand. "Jo, maybe you shouldn't think of her as your granddaughter. Not yet. Not until Garrett sees the paternity results."

Mom's shoulders sag. She then pushes them back, her expression taking on a determined tilt. "How long will that take?"

"I ordered the test online yesterday. So about two weeks."

She huffs out a sigh, tearing her hand from Dad's. "Two weeks?" She snatches a cookie from the plate. "Please tell me I don't have to wait two weeks to meet my granddaughter." She waves the cookie in my face, as if tempting me with a treat will get me to change my mind.

"Jo," Dad drawls, his tone a sympathetic warning. He picks up his mug, peers inside, and shakes his head at it—though I suspect his reaction has nothing to do with the contents and more to do with Mom's response to my news.

She snaps the cookie in half and waves his warning aside. Flying crumbs hit Dad in the chest. "Oh, hush. I'm not waiting that long to meet her."

Dad grunts and straightens his spine, his tell that he's about to hunker down for a storm with Mom. "And what if she isn't your granddaughter?" His tone is no longer sympathetic. It's commander stern. "Are you sure you're willing to risk that disappointment after getting your hopes up? She could be trying to scam Garrett."

Mom lifts her chin, unfazed by his tone. "Yes. I am. And if

Kenda was positive Peony is Garrett's daughter, so am I. You're worried the nanny is scamming Garret. I'm worried about that little girl who has no mother."

I stare at my parents. I knew they wouldn't lecture me about not practicing safe sex and getting my ex-girlfriend knocked up. But I also hadn't expected Mom to accept Peony as her granddaughter so easily—not without proof.

Really? You hadn't expected the woman who has been dying to have a grandchild for years to get excited at the possibility now?

Mom might be done with the topic, but Dad isn't. I can see it in his expression. "How do we know the nanny isn't actually the girl's mother? Or the little girl isn't someone else's child who was abducted for this farce?" He leans forward on his chair, his concerned eyes on Mom. "Your son's a famous author."

"I'm not that famous." Just famous enough to end up with a stalker one time. "And Kellan checked the database to make sure there are no missing children fitting Peony's description."

"Okay, she wasn't kidnapped from another family, but that doesn't mean she's Kenda's child."

"She looks nothing like the nanny. She does look like Kenda though." I take a sip of my coffee, wishing it were something stronger.

"Why are Peony and her nanny at the hotel?" Mom asks.

Dad makes a sound that's somewhere between a grunt and a huff. The sound of surrender. He knows he's lost this battle. Until the paternity results are in and they prove otherwise, Mom's stance won't be swayed.

"My home isn't toddler proofed, and I didn't have anything for Peony to sleep on."

"Didn't?" Of course Mom would pick up on the past tense.

"I was in Eugene this afternoon and bought a few things. Including, er, furniture for her. It arrives on Tuesday." Which means I need to empty one of the rooms to use as Peony's room.

And redecorate it so it's little-girl friendly. The voice in my head belongs to Zara.

Dad scoffs a laugh. "Sounds to me like you don't care what the paternity test has to say. You've already made up your mind she's your daughter."

"Kenda had her reasons for finally telling me Peony is ours." I'm glad she did, though I would've preferred she hadn't waited until she died to tell me. "And given I seem to be the only thing she has left in this world, other than the stuffed panda she showed up with—"

"What do you mean 'the only thing she has left'?"

"There was a fire at the apartment where Kenda, Peony, and the nanny were living. They lost everything."

Mom gasps. "The poor dears."

I explain to them about Kenda's request in her letter and about Peony and Athena. "As soon as I have Peony's and Athena's rooms set up, I'll move them into the house. And then you can meet your granddaughter."

Dad looks like he's going to argue again, but Mom gives him a quelling glance, and he shuts his mouth.

Mom's lips push out in a pout. "Do I really have to wait till Tuesday? Couldn't you arrange for Athena to take Peony to a playground, and we meet them there? That way it might not be so overwhelming for Peony, especially if she's as shy as you say she is."

Mom makes a valid point. Things might go better if I can ease Peony in when it comes to meeting my parents.

"Alright." I place my hand over Mom's. "I'll see what I can do."

12

———

GARRETT

The hotel room door opens, revealing Athena with Peony on her hip.

At seeing me, fear rounds Peony's eyes, and she buries her face in Athena's chest, like she does every time I come too close to her.

"The rest of the stuff's in my vehicle." I smile at Peony, my arms filled with bags. She can't see the reassuring gesture, but maybe she can hear it in my voice.

I slip off my shoes and put the groceries next to the TV on the dresser. The dreary, late afternoon sunlight fills the room from the partially opened curtains. The room seems colder than it did this morning, though the temperature is the same.

"That's the food you asked for. And I bought board books for Peony that someone at the bookstore recommended." I set them on the bed. "I'll be right back with everything else."

When I return to the room, my arms are even more weighed down than last time. "I ordered some furniture for Peony. It'll be delivered Tuesday to my house." I put the bags in the center of the bed. "That will give me time to decorate her

95

room. You can take the room next to hers." Luckily, the guest room is furnished.

"I also got her some clothes. The woman in the store told me to get a larger size, so Peony has room to grow into them."

Why the hell am I telling her this? Athena would already know that. She's a nanny. She knows way more about little kids than I do.

"So...you've accepted she's your daughter?"

I open the first bag and pull out an orange pair of pants. "I've accepted Kenda would never lie to me about something like that. But I'm still having the paternity test done." I hold the pants up for Peony's approval. She doesn't say anything, but she also doesn't start crying, so I figure she's okay with them.

"That's fine. I mean..." Athena cringes, and her hand goes to her pendant. "Froggies...you—you make me as nervous as a chicken sitting next to a fox sharpening his teeth."

An unexpected, barked laugh erupts from deep in my chest. Living with Athena will be interesting if that's a sample of things she'll be saying.

I fold the pants and put them in the top dresser drawer. "Sorry." I press my lips together, but the betrayal of a smile twitches on my mouth. "I don't mean to make you nervous. Anyway, my mom's happy to also help out with Peony"—understatement of the year—"since I'll be busy with my book. It's due to my editor in three and a half months." One hundred and eleven days, to be exact. "Plus, I'm away on the weekends until the end of October."

I remove from the bag a white top with bees embroidered on it. Zara would think it was adorable. Peony doesn't react to that one either. I fold it and put it in the drawer.

Athena gently rubs Peony's back, as if Peony's a magic lamp with a genie inside. "That's probably not a good idea. Your mom. Peony's shy around strangers."

I continue to fold and put away the clothes, but now

without bothering to get Peony's feedback. I just need something to keep me busy, so she doesn't sense how out of my element I am. And it goes well beyond picking out clothes for a little girl. "My parents won't be strangers for long. They're excited to meet their granddaughter." Well, Mom is. Dad is being cautious on her and my behalf.

Athena doesn't say anything. She just keeps rubbing Peony's back, her forehead wrinkled with fine lines.

"They're hoping to meet Peony Tuesday evening." Mom suggested this weekend, but given Athena's reaction to the news, Tuesday evening will give Peony a chance to get used to me first—before she meets my parents. "My mother thought you could take Peony to a playground, and they can see her there. She figured that might be easier for Peony." I move on to the bags with the toys.

I pick up the squirrel pillow. "Hi, Peony," I say, distorting my voice into a comical, squeaky sound. I jiggle the pillow so it looks like the squirrel is dancing on the bed. "Have you seen my nuts?"

Peony blinks at me, as if she thinks I'm ten nuts short of a full brain.

"I don't think that's a good idea." Athena shifts her body slightly, putting more space between Peony and me. I assume she's referring to my parents and not the talking pillow.

I open the bag of cartoonish plastic animals and remove the purple hippo. "What do you say, Peony?" The hippo's voice is much lower than the squirrel's, but no less comical. "Do you want to meet your grandparents?"

Still nothing, other than the tilt of her head. One by one, I remove the animals from the bag and line them up on the bed to face her.

Peony squirms in Athena's arms and reaches for them.

"You wanna play with the animals?" Athena asks.

Peony nods with a level of enthusiasm I haven't witnessed

from her yet. She's not smiling, but she's definitely interested in the toys.

I'm one tiny step closer to gaining her trust, although that has more to do with the gifts than her wanting to get to know me.

Athena puts Peony on the bed. Peony picks up the hippo, crawls over to the bag containing the blocks, and bangs her palms on it.

I slowly pick the bag up, so as not to frighten her with any sudden moves. "How about I open this for you?"

Peony watches me, fear and shyness and curiosity flip-flopping in her expression. The curiosity seems to win out. She doesn't shrink from me, but I bet if I tried to pick her up, she'd let her opinion be known to everyone on this floor of the hotel.

Even so, a flicker of hope sparks inside me that we're on the path—long and winding as it might be—to her accepting me in her life. That she isn't about to have another meltdown because I'm here.

Hopefully.

I pour the blocks onto the bed, the pile separating her side of the mattress from mine. Then I kneel on the floor, to make myself smaller, less intimidating.

Remaining motionless, as if I'm a big bad wolf, ready to strike if she makes a sudden move, Peony keeps watching me as I build a house.

"I also picked up some clothes for you, Athena." I indicate with a wave to a bag on the bed. "Plus, there's some underwear," I mumble, my face heating up like I'm a goddamn virgin. My attention remains on the house I'm building. "I had the saleswoman pick them out."

Peony picks up two blocks and puts them together.

"What are you building?" I point at her blocks, desperate to change topic. "Is that a house?"

"Thank you." Athena's words are spoken slowly, softly, like she's trying them on for the first time.

She sits next to Peony on the bed and works on her own construction project.

While the three of us play with the blocks, Athena talks with some prompting about Kenda and Peony. But I can't get her to open up about herself. She's like Troy's girlfriend, Jessica, when she first moved to Maple Ridge. But Jess had a good reason for not being talkative. She hadn't wanted anyone to know she'd spent the past five years in prison for killing her abusive husband. She was later found innocent of the crime but feared people's reactions if they knew her real name.

Jess had a reason for not talking about herself. What's Athena's deal?

Athena and Peony remain on their side of the bed as we play with the blocks. It's like a deep chasm is stretching between their side and mine, and I'm the stranger, the unwanted intruder on the connection they have between them.

Peony occasionally flicks a puzzled glance at me, as if she can't figure out why I'm still here, but she makes no attempt to interact with me beyond that.

"I have to get going now," I tell them. "Is there anything else you need for tonight?"

Athena shakes her head. Peony doesn't comment.

I push to my feet. "I'll drop by around noon tomorrow to see how you're doing." Before my run with Kellan.

"O-okay."

"Bye, Peony. Bye, Poppy." I wave at my daughter and her panda and memorize her features. Memorize those parts of her that remind me of Kenda. Remind me of the woman who is dead, and now I have to tell my best friend that. Kenda might have confided in Zara about Peony but not about who her father is.

And I have no idea how to tell Zara the news about Kenda —not without breaking my best friend's heart.

13

─────

ZARA

The irritating noise of my alarm clock echoes off the bathroom tiles, and I startle awake.

The bath water temperature has dramatically cooled, and goose bumps prickle my skin. Exhaustion still drapes my body like a soggy blanket, partly due to my inability to sleep through the night lately.

My shoulders and hips and the base of my spine twinge, reminding me why I keep waking up and have trouble falling asleep.

Maybe I need a new mattress.

Groaning, I push to my feet. Only to groan again as my muscles protest the movement. Cold water streams down my body, making things worse.

Shivering, I grab my towel and quickly get ready, dressing in the black silk pantsuit I wore for less than an hour last night. I then put the same effort into my appearance as I did for my date. Only, this time I'm not doing it for a man to appreciate.

I'm doing it for myself.

Doing it so my friends don't notice my fatigue.

I'm only running a few minutes late by the time I arrive at

101

Garrett's house. I gather up the groceries I bought after work and walk to his front door. I don't bother ringing his doorbell. Garrett leaves the door unlocked when he knows I'm coming over.

I step inside the home that was decorated with a bachelor in mind. The rich brown colors are like creamy hot chocolate on a cold winter day, with splashes of bright color scattered throughout the space. Color mostly in the form of the framed landscape photos on the hallway and living room walls. Photos of the local mountains and Windermere Lake. Photos taken by Kim, my sister-in-law. They're a nod to Garrett's love of nature.

"Hey, Golden Girl." Garrett walks toward me, a towel wrapped low on his hips. "I thought I heard the door." Water droplets trickle down his muscular body, and my mouth goes desert dry.

I've seen Garrett shirtless plenty of times, but like a sunset, his chiseled chest doesn't grow any less spectacular each time I see it. The scattering of shrapnel scars on his side does nothing to mar the perfection. They beckon me to kiss them, to let him know I'm glad they didn't steal him from me.

A handful of tattoos decorate his fine body. Beautiful tattoos that also pay homage to his love of nature. My favorite is the scripted words along his side: "Courage is found in unlikely places."

The quote is from *Lord of the Rings*, a book we read together when we were teens.

Garrett stops in front of me, close enough to watch a droplet succumb to gravity and caress his lightly tanned skin. *Lucky droplet.*

I force my eyes to find his, but his gaze isn't on my face. It's on the soft mounds of flesh peeking above my cami's plunging neckline.

A smug smile tugs at the corner of my mouth. I'm tempted

to adjust the top, pulling it down an inch, to flash more of my skin. To remind him that I am all woman.

His eyes linger on my breasts for a fraction of a second more, then slide down my body. Under the stroke of his gaze, my body heats, my breath stumbles, and my heart rate tumbles out in a rapid *pitta-patter-pitta-patter.*

Why does he have to have this effect on me?

Garrett clears his throat, and his eyes move up to mine. Any hint of what he might have been thinking is gone. "New outfit?"

I nod, unable to find my voice with him standing there in nothing but a towel. I'm pretty sure my brain cells are fried from this whole interaction.

"It looks nice." He slowly reaches toward the opening of my shirt, then seems to catch himself and drops his hand to his side.

"Thank you." The words push past my dry mouth, my voice catching-my-breath husky.

"Let me get changed first. Then we need to talk."

His spell on me breaks, and those three dreaded words pound in my head on an echo.

Need to talk?

He smiles, as if trying to lessen the impact of his words, but the sadness in his tone, missing a moment ago, snuffs out all hope of that. I knew he wanted to tell me something. I just didn't realize it wouldn't be something good.

We're not dating, so at least I don't have to worry he's dumping me.

I'm not looking at a repeat of what happened with Joseph. Heck, whatever it is Garrett wants to tell me, I have a feeling it has nothing to do with my ex-boyfriend. Perhaps it has something to do with his book that releases in September. Or his most recent book deal.

Lord, I hope it has nothing to do with his parents—like one of them is sick.

I lift the cloth bags I'm carrying. "I'll put these things away for now. I didn't have a chance to whip up anything. I'll do that after we talk."

I walk past him and put the bags on the counter.

I stroke the cool granite surface, wishing for the hundredth time my kitchen looked like this. The room is both beautiful and a masterpiece, like the mountains Garrett loves to hike and climb. This room is meant to be cooked in every night, to be loved and respected. The endless counter and storage space are a cook's wet dream.

Storage space that makes my small kitchen look so sad and inadequate.

While I wait for Garrett to get changed, I organize the food supplies I brought with me. We've got two hours until everyone shows up. Plenty of time for me to make the guacamole and tapas.

I don't hear Garrett come into the kitchen as much as sense him. The fresh outdoors scent he wears so well wraps me in a loving embrace. Nope, I don't imagine him—now that I'm single again—hugging me from behind. I definitely don't imagine him kissing the side of my neck. And I absolutely don't imagine him humming his satisfaction on my skin.

It's been more than fifteen years since he fell in love with one of my friends. Aren't I supposed to be over him by now?

Correction, I wasn't supposed to fall in love with him to begin with. I knew it was a mistake the second my feelings for him altered their trajectory. I hadn't wanted to risk our friendship. And yet, I still fell.

I turn, the curve of my spine against the counter grounding me. It's not the teasing Garrett whose eyes are locked with mine. It's the sad Garrett. The his-heart-has-been-ripped-out-of-his-chest Garrett.

And it's suddenly as if the ground is shifting under my feet. That brief moment just prior to an earthquake, when birds and animals get the spine-tingling sense to take cover. That brief moment before the surrounding world crumples and nothing is the same again.

"Are you gonna tell me now what's going on? And why you wanna talk to me before everyone else gets here?" My voice comes out strong, the opposite of the shaking of the foundation inside me.

"Let's go sit down." He points to the large sectional couch, and a thousand moths go berserk in my belly. I don't think he could make me any more nervous than this.

Garrett sits next to me and releases a never-ending breath, his gaze on his long, strong fingers resting on his thighs. The jeans he changed into lightly hug the hard contours of his leg muscles.

I wait for him to collect his thoughts, to speak, to break my world apart. Because that's exactly what I sense will happen. Whatever he has to tell me will impact me in ways both of us have yet to realize. I just can't imagine what it could be.

And that's making me more lip-biting, leg-bouncing, thought-spiraling jittery.

I can't even wipe my sweat-slickened palms against my silk pants. The fabric won't appreciate it.

With each tick of the mantel clock, my unease grows steadily thicker, denser.

"I'm not sure how to tell you this…"

I wait for the rest of what he wants to tell me, but the words seem to fail him. I lean forward and lace our fingers together.

He holds my hand securely in his. "There was…there was a mall shooting last week. In North Carolina. Kenda was at the mall."

The pain in his eyes tells me everything I need to know. I jerk my hand from his, as if that's all it will take for him to yank back the words and tell me he made a mistake. He meant someone else.

No, no, no. It's not true. She can't be dead. Not Kenda. She was going to make a difference in the world. Bring awareness to the injustices marginalized women face.

How...how can she be dead? Where's the justice in that?

Random memories replay in my mind. Memories of Kenda and I pulling all-nighters and studying for our exams together. Of dancing at nightclubs and borrowing each other's clothes. Of talking late into the night about all kinds of things.

Of sharing our secrets, other than my biggest secret of all.

The one dealing with Garrett—of how we had both fallen for him.

A harsh sob builds in my chest, and my lungs burn from within—a flash fire ready to devastate me. Ready to burn my world to a crisp.

Garrett gathers me in his arms. I rest my forehead on his shoulder, and the dam crumples under the weight of my tears. Of all the things that cycled through my mind as to why he'd wanted to talk to me, Kenda's death hadn't been one of them.

Why? Why? Why? Why would anyone shoot her?

Everything I'm feeling—the loss of a friend, the exhaustion, the constant ache in my muscles and joints—pours out of me and onto Garrett's shoulder in body-shaking sobs. He rubs soothing circles on the base of my spine, but it's not enough to slow the tears.

All I can do is cry and cry and cry, the broken dam unfixable.

It's only when there are no more tears left, when the sobbing has lulled to a watery hiccup, when shame and guilt and dismay turn to lead in my belly—because he's consoling me even though she was once the love of his life—it's only then, after all those things, I finally sit up. A damp patch stains his T-shirt, a combination of tears and streaked mascara.

Sniffing, I trace my finger over the black smears on the light-gray cotton, as if that's all it will take to make them vanish.

As if that will bring Kenda back to life and make everything right in the world. "I'm sorry. I didn't mean to make a mess of your T-shirt."

"It's okay." He brushes his thumbs under my eyes, wiping away the wetness.

I lean into his hand, absorbing his strength and hating myself for it. I was supposed to be the one sharing my strength with him, helping him deal with his heartache. He loved Kenda. She was the woman he was destined to spend the rest of his life with.

"There's more I have to tell you." The pain in his eyes strengthens, and his heartbroken voice reaches inside me and clenches my stomach in a tight vise.

He leans back on the sectional, his gaze on the ceiling, like we used to do as kids when he wanted to tell me something but wasn't sure how. Sometimes we would sit on his parents' deck and stare at the stars for what felt like hours before he found the words he was looking for.

I sniff and lean back too, resting my head on the couch, and ease out a bracing breath. It does nothing to relax me.

"I came home yesterday after my run with Kellan. There was a woman sitting on my front stoop. With a toddler."

I ready myself for what's coming next but don't say anything. I have no idea where this conversation is headed.

"The woman—Athena—is the one who told me Kenda is dead."

The finality of the word sets off a new round of tears pricking my eyes. I close my eyelids against the picture in my head.

"The toddler...she's Kenda's daughter," Garrett explains, the heartache in his voice softening slightly. I open my eyes but keep them directed on the ceiling.

The poor little girl. I can't even imagine...

His last words sink in deeper, kick-starting the brain cells that must have shorted with the first part of his news. *Daughter?* "Kenda doesn't have a daughter. She would've told me if she was pregnant. She would've told me if she'd met someone." Sure, we hadn't been as close as we were in college, but we talked from time to time. And maybe I hadn't heard from her in more than two years, but she certainly would have told me if she was pregnant.

Wouldn't she have?

I continue staring at the ceiling as if the answer is scrawled across it. And if I look long enough I'm bound to find it.

"She definitely had a daughter." The pain in Garrett's voice intensifies, laced with another emotion.

"And the father?" Is that what the pain in his voice is about? She had a baby with another man? "Where does he fit into all of this?" If she never told me about him, maybe he's no longer in the picture. *Lord, did he die too?*

A cavernous silence settles over us. The weighted silence prior to the drop of a bomb. It takes a moment for my brain to move the pieces of the puzzle around, slot them into position. Then with the final piece falling into place...*boom.*

The hard truth stares me in the face and my heart stalls and my lungs collapse, like an imploding building, the air all sucked out.

No, no, no. It can't be true. Please tell me I've got it wrong.

"The little girl is mine," Garrett says, confirming exactly what I feared. "She's my daughter."

The last two words are whispered, but the outcome is no less staggering.

My world shatters into a thousand pieces, each one raining on me. Cutting into my flesh.

Kenda and Garrett had a baby. A daughter. Together.

I jerk up and turn to face him, wincing at the sharp stab in the lower curve of my spine. "How? I didn't know you and

Kenda..." Hooked up? Got back together and forgot to mention that to me?

"Kenda and I bumped into each other in New York City. When I was there to meet my editor and agent. And, well..."

"You hooked up? When did this happen?" The casual, unconcerned tone of my voice sounds genuine, even to my ears. But in my head...in my head it's a disbelieving, high-pitched wail.

A daughter. They had a daughter together.

One more thing that binds Garrett and Kenda, that makes me the outsider once more as I try to keep the broken pieces of my heart taped together. One more reminder Garrett is hers... even in death. They had a daughter to forever cement that bond. I can't compete with that.

Not that I would've been able to, even without the little girl in his life. Garrett has never seen me the same way he saw Kenda, his once-upon-a-time girlfriend.

"Just over two years ago," Garrett replies.

Sure, it would have hurt even if his daughter was the result of a one-night stand who he had barely known at the time, but nowhere near as much as when the one-night stand was Kenda.

"And you never told me about her?" I slip a teasing quality into my tone, the further breaking of my heart only loud enough for *my* ears. Sure, I'd always thought those two would eventually find each other again and have a second chance at their happily ever after, like Simone and Lucas.

But believing and finding out it had happened aren't even... I can't wrap my head around it.

A daughter. They have a daughter together.

"There wasn't anything to tell you. We both agreed it was a one-time thing."

That might be true, but...

I sit up straighter and gape at him for a flutter of a heartbeat. "Are you telling me you had sex with Kenda but didn't know you'd knocked her up?" Because the Garrett I know would not ignore his responsibilities, including if a one-night stand had resulted in a child.

And he certainly wouldn't keep her a secret from his family and close friends.

"She might have tried telling me when she first found out, but I never called her after she texted me. And she never reached out again."

That's weird—that doesn't sound like Kenda.

The Kenda I was friends with in college wouldn't have done that, but the world-weary Kenda...well, who knows what she was thinking.

"Why didn't you return her call?" Because that doesn't sound like Garrett either.

Regardless, I can't believe this is happening. The man I've been in love with for most of my life is a father—and one of my closest friends in college is the little girl's mama.

14

———

ZARA

"I didn't return Kenda's call because..." Garrett winces next to me on the large sectional couch, his gaze on the ceiling. "Because it's complicated."

Right. Complicated. The code word for "I fucked up" or "I don't want to talk about it."

Despite my curiosity and so many unspoken questions, I respect his wishes and push up from the couch. "I need to get to work on the snacks."

A daughter. He and Kenda had a daughter. Together.

A hot urge to chop something, anything, thrums through my veins, and I head for Garrett's kitchen. My thoughts are a train wreck, and the cars keep piling up. Even the idea of working in my dream kitchen doesn't put them back on the track.

Being dumped by a boyfriend who was still in love with his ex-wife doesn't seem so big anymore. Not in comparison to finding out Kenda is dead and she left behind a daughter who belongs to Garrett. And given what Garrett is currently going through, it's hardly the time to bring up what happened between Joseph and me.

III

I remove a knife from Garrett's knife block and begin chopping the onions I brought with me. Now all the tears can be blamed on the onions and not on how the truth—Kenda is dead and Garrett has a daughter—has left me gutted, bleeding out across the floor.

He joins me in the kitchen. "What can I do to help?"

I point the knife at the carrots. "They need peeling and chopping." *Sniff.* "Where's your daughter right now?" I look around the kitchen as if that will make her magically appear. *Sniff.*

"She's staying in the hotel with her nanny."

"Nanny?"

"Athena. The woman who brought Peony here."

I guess that would make sense. Kenda needed someone to look after her daughter while she was making a difference in the world. But why not bring the little girl home to stay with her father while she did that? Garrett's mother would've been overjoyed to help out and look after her granddaughter.

But instead of saying any of that, I splutter, "Your daughter's name is Peony?"

He nods, and I smile at him through a new round of tears. "That's a pretty name. When do I get to meet her?" When do I get to meet the little girl who is breaking my heart for so many reasons?

"Tomorrow? Will that work for you?"

"It does. I can't wait to see her." A picture of what she'll look like pops in my head. An adorable little girl with Garrett's brown eyes and Kenda's coils. In my mind, she's a sweet combination of the two people who once were everything to me.

Garrett pours me a glass of Shiraz, grabs a beer for himself, and helps me prepare the snacks for tonight. While we work, he tells me about his daughter and how she's super shy with him. About his parents' reaction to the news they're now grandparents. About Kenda's letter. About how he bought furniture and supplies for Peony, even though he's waiting for the paternity results.

I can't imagine what Peony's going through after losing everything she owned in a fire and violently losing her mother. And then to find out she has a father...and an entire family she didn't know about.

It's no wonder she's so shy with Garrett. All of it must be so overwhelming.

Simone, Jess, Emily, and Garrett's brothers arrive at his house an hour later for Game Night, and I listen as he explains it all again for their benefit. Not once does the tightness in my chest ease even a tiny amount at the senselessness of Kenda's death. Or at the news about Peony—and how her existence means Garrett and I can definitely never be together.

"Wow, that's a lot to process." Emily takes a sip of her Chardonnay.

Garrett slouches back on the couch. "It is a lot. I've known about it for just over twenty-four hours, and I'm still processing."

"I can imagine," Troy says, his arm protectively around Jess. She's leaning into him, her head on his broad shoulder. "So, you're positive she's your daughter?"

"I won't know for sure until I get the paternity results, but I have accepted there's a good chance she is my daughter."

Garrett doesn't say it to our friends, but he has told me his other concerns. If he isn't Peony's father, Kenda had a good reason for not telling him the truth. She knew he would do the paternity test. Just to be certain.

But he didn't tell me what he will do if the results are negative, and I didn't push the issue.

Simone, Jess, and Em watch me, sympathy shaping the curve of their mouths. Silently asking me how I'm doing now that Garrett is a father and Kenda is dead. Silently asking me how I'm doing, given I've been in love with Garrett forever.

I flash them a smile I hope they translate for what it is—a surrendering of my heart to this new reality.

"How's Joseph doing?" Simone asks once there's a lull in the conversation. She's curled into Lucas's side, the two of them cozy together on the far end of the couch.

"We broke up last night."

Garrett gives me a double take. "You never mentioned you guys broke up?" There's almost an accusation in his tone, the brush of surprise.

I shrug, the movement coming so casually. "It didn't seem important after what you had to tell me." That, combined with what happened yesterday afternoon at P&T with the drunk father, made my breakup seem insignificant. Not worth mentioning.

"How come you broke up?" Emily's eyes widen, doing nothing to hide her devastation on my behalf.

"Turns out, he was once married and is still in love with his ex-wife." The words burn my throat on the way out, not so much because I'm truly broken over what happened, but because I feel like an idiot for being blindsided by the news.

Just...not as blindsided as I was by Garrett's life update.

A daughter. He and Kenda have a daughter together.

No matter how many times I say the words in my head, the truth isn't any easier to swallow.

"Damn," Troy mutters.

Garrett's forehead puckers into a frown. "What? The asshole never told you he'd been married?"

"That's right. Let's just say the past twenty-four hours have been nothing but an oil slick of secrets." I look up at the ceiling. "Lord, please tell me that's the end of them for a while."

"I can't believe the day you had yesterday," Jess says to me. Troy tenderly kisses her temple. "Between that and the violent drunk in P&T—"

"Wait, what?" Concern creases deeper grooves across Garrett's forehead, and his eyes pivot my way. "What drunk?"

A flush spreads up Jess's pale cheeks. "Sorry, was that supposed to be a secret too?" She leans down to stroke Bailey, who is lying by her feet in her *Service Dog in Training* vest.

I wince at how I had kept that information from Garrett. But it hadn't been anything he needed to worry about. Nor is there anything he can do about it. And he clearly has other much bigger things to worry about.

I get Garrett and the others up to speed on what happened yesterday. "It's not that big a deal." The lie burns on my tongue like acid. "Everything worked out fine in the end. The cops were called, and they dealt with it."

"Except the man broke your chair," Em points out.

"I can replace it," I hurry to reassure. "No one was hurt; that's the important thing." Garrett opens his mouth to no doubt argue this, so I rush to add, "But that reminds me." I tell them my plans to expand P&T and how the place next door is available for lease, skillfully diverting the discussion in a new direction. I'd rather not relive yesterday's events. It's enough I did that in my dreams last night.

"Would you be able to give me an estimate for the renovations I'm looking at doing?" I ask Troy. "In case I get the lease approved on the space."

"Sure. I can come over tomorrow afternoon. Say around one?" He grabs one of the cheesy Creole shrimp toasts from the plate on the coffee table and takes a bite.

"That would be great. Thanks, Troy." I turn to Garrett, who still looks a little unsettled by everything that has happened in the past twenty-four hours. "Does that time work for you with me meeting Peony?"

"It should. We can go to the hotel at eleven. I'll check with Athena if that works with Peony's schedule."

"And then the four of us can go to P&T for lunch. I bet after you give her one of my desserts, your daughter will be less shy with you." I flash him a grin and give his hand a quick squeeze. "So...does anyone else have any secrets they should share with us before we find out the hard way?" My question rolls out on a chuckle, and my gaze lands on each of my friends in turn.

Simone and Lucas exchange a knowing glance. That gets us all sitting up a little straighter, anticipation for their news an electrical current in the air.

An easy smile spreads across Lucas's face. "We found out this afternoon, we've been approved to be foster parents. We'll be getting the two girls next week."

Emily and I shriek, our grins uncontained. They've been discussing becoming foster parents for the past year, after Lucas learned about the car accident more than ten years ago that robbed them of their unborn child and resulted in Simone having an emergency hysterectomy.

"Congratulations," I tell them, my grin still in place.

"Two? And I thought I'd be busy with a toddler." Garrett laughs, the rough, rumbled sound that hits me straight between the legs like the stroke of a finger along my pussy.

I shift, attempting to ease the effect that sound has on me.

"The youngest is two and a half," Simone explains, "so maybe we can have playdates with your daughter, once she gets more settled."

"That doesn't sound like a bad idea. Then you can help me figure out what the hell I'm doing."

Lucas snorts a laugh. "I think we'll be figuring this all out together. Simone and I have taken the required foster care classes, but we're also new to this parenting thing."

I nudge Garrett in the side with my elbow. "If you need help with Peony...I might not know a lot about being a parent, but I do know about being an aunt to a young toddler."

"I'm also available if you need any pointers," Jess adds. "I had two glorious years with my daughter until I had to give her up. I remember a thing or two about that age." Troy presses another kiss to her temple, knowing Jess still hurts from what happened in her life prior to moving to Maple Ridge.

"Thanks. I'll take any help I can get. I've already faced my first toddler meltdown, and something tells me it won't get any easier."

In all the years I've known Garrett, this is the first time I've seen him look so beautifully, heartbreakingly lost. A tugging in my gut warns me there's more to it than just Kenda's death and finding out he's a father.

It's the same unexplainable tugging I have felt for several years now, ever since he retired from the Marines. Every time I bring up his time in the military, he changes the topic, shuts me down.

Or acts like I'm imagining things.

But I know the truth. Something happened while Garrett was overseas, something that made him feel adrift—and one day, I hope he tells me what that was.

15

ZARA

The next morning, I'm making jambalaya, the international special of the day, when Clara pokes her head through the kitchen doorway. "Hey, Zara. Garrett's here."

"Thanks. I'll be right out."

The door closes behind her as she goes off to presumably relay my message.

I untie my apron. "Everything's good to go," I tell Abby, who is taking over for me in the kitchen. "Text me if anything comes up before I get back."

She walks to the stove where the jambalaya is cooking. "Go! Enjoy the rest of your day, and don't worry about this place."

Ha! As if that's possible. The place is part of me, like my bones are part of my body. Even when Picnic & Treats is closed, I'm thinking about it. Thinking about what new things I can try with the menu. What I can post on social media. What I can do to make my customers, who are like family to me, happy.

I hang my apron on the hook by the door and enter the main part of the café. Garrett is standing near the counter, worry crinkling his brow.

He's looking at his phone, but as soon as he sees me, the frown vanishes, replaced with a not-quite-so-easy smile. Strain lightly creases the corners of his eyes.

"I just have to quickly get changed. I'll only be a second." I wasn't expecting him for another five minutes; otherwise, I'd have been changed and ready to go.

I disappear down the hallway, my heart rate fluttering into overdrive. *It's gonna be okay. She's a toddler. There's nothing scary about that. You'll be fine.*

It's not like I haven't been around little kids before. But this is Garrett's and Kenda's daughter. What if she doesn't like me? What if she reminds me too much of Kenda and I can't stop crying? Crying because a beautiful soul has been stolen from this world.

I grab my jeans and top from my locker and take them into the washroom.

Humming to myself, I lock the door and check my face in the mirror. My eyes are a little puffy from last night. I couldn't sleep and kept alternating between sobbing and trying to get comfortable on my mattress.

My eyes aren't as red as they were this morning, so I consider that a win.

I change, the ibuprofen I took earlier still doing its job. I check my reflection one more time, making sure my makeup isn't smudged or smeared. "You've got this."

I join Garrett outside and find him pacing on the sidewalk. It's a beautiful spring day. The sun is warm, and so is the gentle breeze blowing a wayward strand of hair in his face. Storm clouds are gathering along the horizon, but they aren't expected in Maple Ridge until this evening.

"You trying to solve a plot problem?" I ask. Whenever he's stuck on something that has to do with a book he's working on, he paces or gardens.

"Hell if I know if I've got a plot problem." He rakes his hand through his hair, pushing the longish strands out of his face. "I haven't written much in the past two days. Since Peony showed up."

Oh. Damn. No wonder he looks so stressed. His publisher bumped up his deadline, and then Peony fell into his lap. Add to that, the love of his life died in a mall shooting. How would anyone get anything done under those circumstances?

"Hey, Garrett. This is me," I say as we walk down the sidewalk to the hotel farther down Main Street. "What do you need?"

"A miracle," he mutters.

"Unfortunately, I'm no voodoo priestess, so I can't help you there." Not even Mimi, who claimed to be a priestess, could have given him the miracle he's looking for. Not at this level. "But I can help in more practical ways. And you have a nanny who'll take good care of Peony while you work. Kenda trusted her, so you know you can trust...what was her name again?" Apollo? Aphrodite? I remember it had something to do with Greek mythology.

"Athena."

"Right. Athena. Which Greek goddess was she?"

"The goddess of wisdom."

"Ah. So she's a wise nanny. That's good."

"Compared to what I know about kids Peony's age, she's freaking the Einstein of kids as far as I'm concerned."

I stop walking and touch his arm. His biceps are warm and taut under my fingertips. "You're gonna be a great father, Garrett. You just need to give Peony time to get to know you. She's been through so much." I wrap him in a tight hug. "And you're already proving you're a fantastic father."

Garrett's arms go around my waist. I close my eyes, breathing in the scent of pine and leather and the mountain sunshine, a scent that's all Garrett.

"You haven't done the paternity test yet, but you're making

sure your home is her home." I step away from our hug, even though I would be happy to stay in it for another lifetime or so.

I wish I could reassure him about his book and the deadline, but it would just be empty platitudes. "If you need someone to brainstorm with or rant to about the book, I'm your woman." That much I can do.

"Thanks." He gifts me one of his smiles that never fail to make me warm and tingly on the inside.

GARRETT QUIETLY KNOCKS ON THE HOTEL ROOM DOOR.

"Who-who's there?" The female voice on the other side is soft, almost timid, but there's also a strength buried just beneath the surface.

"It's Garrett."

The door opens, revealing a woman in her mid-twenties. Forget the goddess of wisdom. This woman could double for the goddess of love, but instead of a toga, she's wearing jeans, a shell-pink T-shirt, and has bare feet.

My heart drops like an elevator, its cables severed. *This* is Peony's nanny?

I hadn't thought to ask Garrett what Athena looks like. Maybe I should have so I would've been more prepared.

Her strawberry-blond hair falls in loose waves past her shoulders and brushes the tops of her perky breasts. Her mouth is a perfect bow shape. And her eyes. Her doe-like hazel eyes would cause plenty of men to fall to their knees. The splattering of freckles across her pale, creamy skin also adds to the Greek goddess persona that goes with her name.

How many romances have I read where the hero falls in love with the nanny? The woman who is like a mother to his child?

I don't know if I made a noise of dismay—or something a little less noteworthy—but Athena's gaze slides from Garrett to me, and her eyes go wide.

"Hi, Athena," Garrett says, clearly oblivious to my messy thoughts. "I hope it's all right with you, but I brought my friend with me. Zara knew Kenda."

"We were close friends in college and kept in contact over the years." My voice comes out rough, the knowledge burning my throat that I will never see Kenda again.

It might be my imagination, but I swear Athena's eyes marginally narrow. I can only imagine what she's thinking. If Kenda and I were so close, why didn't Garrett know he was a father? If Kenda and I were so close, why didn't she tell me she was pregnant?

Unless Kenda pays me a visit from the other side, it's an answer we'll never get.

"Nina," a small singsong voice says from inside the room. It's followed by a giggle.

"Is that her? Peony?" My voice staggers out in an awed whisper. I don't bother asking why Peony referred to Athena as Nina. Athena is probably hard to pronounce for an eighteen-month-old.

Athena steps aside to let us in. Garrett enters the room, and I follow behind him, conscious of Athena's eyes watching me, judging me. And for whatever reason, I'm coming up plenty short.

The large hotel room Garrett scored came well-furnished but nothing about it reminds me of Kenda. She was all about colors, big and vibrant, much like her personality. The bedding, the love seat, and the dresser in here have a down-to-earth, mountain-cabin vibe. It's a nice room.

A tourist pleaser.

But it isn't the room's aesthetic that has my heart limping into my throat. An adorable little girl is standing next to the couch, her textured curls scooped up in two high pigtails on either side of her head. She has on the cutest outfit, orange pants and a long-sleeved white top with a giant sunflower on it. An outfit Garrett no doubt bought. But it's the bend of her lips, the way she tilts her head as she plays with the colorful blocks on the coffee table, that screams Kenda. This is her daughter. Her rip-my-heart-out and put-me-back-together-again daughter.

"Hi, Peony." Garrett says her name with the caution of someone approaching a small animal they're worried might bite them out of fear.

The little girl stops what she's doing, a block in her hand, and her scared, wide eyes fix on him. Tucked under her arm is what could either be a panda or a black-and-white dog. She shifts it in front of her body like a shield. Or a cross to ward off evil.

Garrett sits on the floor near where she's playing, positioning himself so the coffee table is between them. My heart squeezes at the picture the pair make, at how he's trying to come off as less intimidating. And I swear my ovaries weep at just how amazing a father he already is, even though he doesn't realize it yet.

For the longest moment, I can only stare at Peony, a new round of tears pricking my eyes. "She's beautiful," I whisper.

Beautiful like her mother.

Beautiful like her father.

There's no doubt in my mind this is their daughter. I've seen Garrett's pictures from when he was a toddler. She has his eyes.

Peony's attention shifts from Garrett to me. The fear she has for her father isn't directed my way. Curiosity takes its place.

"This is my friend, Zara." Garrett points up at me.

"Hi, Peony." I smile at her, the curve of my lips gentle but genuine, and I take a tiny step forward. "I was friends with your mother." Another slow step forward.

She doesn't balk at my approach, and I lower myself to the floor on the opposite side of the table to her.

"What's your friend's name?" I point to the stuffed toy once again wedged between her arm and her body.

"Pop-py." She holds it out for me to see. Ah, so it's a panda, not a dog.

"Well, hello, Poppy." I wave at it. "What are you two building?" I point at the multicolored structure on the table.

"We're making a house," Athena says, the smile in her voice clearly directed at Peony and not me.

"It's nice out." Garrett's gaze remains on his daughter. "I thought maybe you and Athena would like to go for a walk. We could get some lunch at Zara's café."

Athena crosses her arms, her stance giving off a caged-animal vibe. But I can't tell if we're making her feel caged or if it's the hotel room.

Garrett gracefully pushes to his feet like a sleek panther unfolding from a nap. My muscles have stiffened in the short time I've been sitting on the floor, and my attempt to stand will be nowhere near as graceful. I stumble up and put my hand on the edge of the table for balance. No one seems to notice my momentary clumsiness.

"I-er-didn't pick up a stroller when I was ordering the furniture." Garrett shares an uncertain glance between Peony and Athena. "I wasn't sure if she wanted one."

"That's okay. She will want to walk," Athena tells him. "And I can carry her the rest of the way."

"I can carry her if that's too much."

"No, that's fine. She'll probably be happier if I carry her. She's...she's still..." Athena picks up a block from the coffee table, avoiding eye contact with both of us.

"Nervous around me," Garrett fills in, the words falling on a hard sigh.

I rub his arm. "Give her time." I turn my head to Athena,

hoping she'll support me on this. But it's not support I see in her expression. It's the tail end of a scowl directed at my hand on his arm.

Without meaning to, I let my hand drop away and take a step back.

I've read this book before. Looks like the nanny's going after the single dad.

16

GARRETT

Athena crouches to Peony's level. "Hey, baby girl. You wanna go for a walk?"

The grin my daughter gives her is wide enough to melt the heart of the grumpiest of grumps. "Walk!"

She toddles past the end of the coffee table as if I'm not kneeling next to it and walks over to Athena.

Athena scoops her up. Giggling, Peony loops her thin arms around Athena's neck, trapping Poppy between her body and Athena.

At Peony's reaction, jealousy strikes me like an arrow to the chest, nicking my heart. Which is ridiculous. I only found out less than forty-eight hours ago I have a daughter. Of course she'd pick Athena instead of me.

Less than forty-eight hours ago, I was questioning if she even is my daughter.

Athena removes a small coat, the hood trimmed with pink faux fur, from the closet. "You wanna wear the coat your daddy bought you?"

"That's a pretty coat," Zara tells Peony. "Your daddy has fine taste."

126

I snort a laugh. Zara twists to me, her eyebrows lifted in a wordless question.

"It was on the *end-of-season* clearance rack. I was lucky to find something in her size." Well, almost her size.

Athena helps Peony put on the coat. The hem falls to her knees and swamps her small body. To her credit, Zara doesn't laugh at my lack of ability to guess a kid's size.

We walk along the sidewalk, stopping every few feet so Peony can inspect each distraction. An abandoned dime that Athena stops her from picking up. An empty concrete planter. A bird singing in a tree. A squirrel darting across the road.

She squats next to a beetle and watches it scuttle over the ground.

I crouch on the other side of it while respecting Peony's personal boundaries. "That's a beetle."

She points at it. "Bee-el."

"That's right. Beetle." I beam at Zara and catch Athena glancing up and down the street like a rabbit on the lookout for a coyote. I can't tell if she's searching for something specific or just memorizing landmarks.

She turns back to us, her freckles more noticeable against her pale skin than they were a moment ago, and flashes Peony a bright smile. "That's right, baby girl. It's a beetle."

Picnic & Treats is crowded when we enter it a few minutes later, the place noisier than normal. The only empty table available is next to the window and behind a group of rowdy teenage boys, who are laughing and mocking each other.

Peony covers her ears with her hands and presses her face into Athena's shoulder.

Athena murmurs something on her temple, then her gaze swings to me. "Maybe we could go someplace quiet. Without so many people."

Good idea. Preferably where no one recognizes me. I want to give Peony a chance to get to know me before it gets out she's my daughter, especially should the paternity test prove otherwise.

"We can go to the staff room," Zara suggests. "No one is scheduled to take their break just yet."

We follow her down the corridor. I sneak a glance at Peony; she's not paying attention to me. Her face is still pressed against Athena's shoulder. Zara opens the door to let us into the room. I take the armchair. Athena sits on the super-comfy couch. Peony scrambles onto her lap, clutching Poppy tightly to her body.

Zara grabs menus from the white-washed cabinet and hands them to us. "This is our regular menu," she explains to Athena. "The kids' menu is listed at the bottom. We also have international dishes I rotate daily. Today's specials are jambalaya and Thai green curry with tofu."

Athena reads the menu and points at something for Peony to see. "Look, they have macaroni and cheese. Would you like that?"

"It's really yummy," I tell Peony. Zara makes a mean baked macaroni and cheese, although I'm not sure if the one I love is the same as the one listed on the kids' menu. But I am certain the one listed is still better than the macaroni and cheese I made Peony yesterday with the jarred Alfredo sauce. Mine isn't even in the same stratosphere as Zara's. Anything I cook isn't in the same stratosphere as hers.

Peony glances briefly at me, as if not sure if she should trust my recommendation. Or me.

"That sounds good, doesn't it?" Athena prompts with a nod. "Would you like macaroni and cheese and apple juice?"

Peony looks up at her with a big grin, and my heart squeezes at how I haven't earned that smile of hers yet. "Yes!"

Get over yourself, man. Give her time.

Athena and I place our orders, and Zara leaves to get the food and drinks. Part of me wants to go with her since I'm at a loss for what else to do to gain Peony's trust. Maybe someone could write a book on the topic. *How to Gain Your Child's Trust After Not Knowing They Existed Their Entire Young Life.*

This isn't how I had envisioned things while dating Kenda, during those infrequent times when I'd thought about us one day being married and having a family. I had envisioned the 2.3 kids. Had envisioned attending their hockey games like my parents had done for my brothers and me. Had envisioned helping them with their homework and cuddling with my wife in front of the fireplace. The latter would always lead to hot sex.

I rest my forearms on my thighs. "Is there anything you would like to do after lunch?" Not that I have time to take them anywhere, what with my ticking deadline. *Shit.* How the hell am I supposed to balance all this? A book on that topic would be helpful too.

"I was going to take Peony to a playground." Athena glances around the room. "This seems like a nice place."

"It is. Zara's done an incredible job with the café." Pride shines in my tone, hugs each syllable. "Assuming the paternity test proves she is my daughter, I'll need your banking info so I can direct deposit your salary. And I'll need your Social Security Number." As much as I don't want to discuss the business side of this arrangement, I can't ignore it.

"I, er, don't have a bank account."

"You don't?"

"I was always paid in cash."

"What? You don't trust banks?" I know a few people who are paranoid about the banking institution, but they still have bank accounts.

She shrugs.

"You can set one up in Maple Ridge. It's easy enough to do."

She strokes her pendant like it's a lucky charm. "Hot sauce in a hen house, I can't do that. I lost my ID, and the bank will need to see it to set up an account. But not to worry—I'll apply for a replacement. Same with my Social Security Number." Her hand drops to her lap. "In the meantime, just pay me in cash."

"Okay, I can do that for now. And I'll get my lawyer to draft an employment contract. Once I have the paternity test results."

She nods and pets Poppy on the head.

Clearly bored with the conversation, Peony squirms and twists onto her stomach. She slides off Athena's lap and onto the couch cushion next to her and glances around.

"I'll need extra help with Peony while I'm working on my book. But I'll pay you overtime."

"Did you hear that, Peony?" A rush of excitement practically does cartwheels in Athena's tone. "I'll get to spend more time playing with you and reading your favorite story."

Peony grins at her, then wiggles backward on her stomach until her feet are dangling above the floor. Athena helps her down.

A look of uncertain mischief lightens Peony's expression as she takes in the room from her new vantage point. A room that wasn't designed with young kids in mind. And I'm sure if given a chance, Peony could get into all kinds of curiosity-motivated trouble. Especially if she's anything like I was as a kid.

"Do you like to draw?" I remove several sheets of blank paper and a container of crayons from the side cabinet and put them on the coffee table. I grab a page and a green crayon and kneel on the floor, close enough to Peony so she can see what I'm doing, but far enough away so as not to scare her.

I start drawing a friendly dragon. Or a winged horse that looks slightly ill.

Peony studies the crayons for a beat and selects a red one.

Athena points at it. "What color is that?"

Peony lifts the crayon, showing it to her. "Red!"

"Very good. Should I draw something too?"

Peony hands Athena a blue crayon, and Athena begins

drawing, the tip of the crayon effortlessly gliding across the page.

Peony scribbles on the paper in front of her.

"What are you drawing?" I ask her.

She doesn't reply or acknowledge me. She just keeps making patterns and squiggles.

The door opens, and Zara enters carrying a tray filled with our food.

She peers down at my paper. "That looks great, Garrett. Um, what's it supposed to be?" She tilts her head to the side as if that will help her figure it out.

"A dragon. A friendly one." I grab a red crayon and draw flames shooting from its mouth.

Zara chuckles, the rich, throaty sound pouring over me like sweet molasses, soothing my dented self-esteem at my sad artistic abilities. "Yes, the flames make it look very friendly."

I grin at her. "Right?"

She puts the tray on the other side of the coffee table, avoiding Peony's picture. "That's pretty, Peony. And wow, that's amazing, Athena."

The image of a young girl's face stares at me from Athena's paper. It's only partially finished, but what she has done is impressive. The fact she drew it with a crayon makes it more so.

"You're an artist?" I'm unable to tear my gaze from the two soulful eyes. The soulful eyes and side-swept bangs and the bridge of the girl's nose are the only things Athena has drawn, but they're mesmerizing. Deep-to-your-soul mesmerizing.

Athena shrugs, her expression neutral, if not a little sad—much like the girl on the paper.

I expect Athena to keep working on the picture, to bring the girl's face fully into view, but she returns the crayon to the container and pushes the page aside. "Where did you learn to draw like that?" I ask.

Another shrug. "Here and there."

"I would love to be able to draw like that," Zara tells her.

"You draw?" In all the years I've known Zara, I don't remember seeing anything she's drawn, other than when we were in elementary school.

She snicker-snorts. "I haven't drawn since Mrs. Dixon's sixth-grade art class. Her reaction whenever she saw my projects was enough to tell me I should find something else to focus my energy on. Anyway, I'll be right back with the drinks."

She leaves, and the awkwardness I feel around Peony and Athena presses down on me again. Usually I don't have trouble talking to women. Usually I don't find myself in this situation. "So, you were living in North Carolina?"

Athena isn't paying attention to me. She's drawing something new. "That's right. Where mermaids like to gather and lure sailors to their demise." She says it so casually, like it's an everyday fact.

Or at least I assume she doesn't actually believe mermaids exist. "Did you grow up there?"

"Sure." Her answer is half-hearted at best. A non-real answer. She removes three crayons from the container and holds them out to Peony. "Which color should I use next?"

Message received. The topic isn't up for discussion.

But why? Why is Athena's past not something she wants to discuss?

17

GARRETT

"I'm gonna paint your room, Peony," I tell her once she's finished eating her lunch. "But I need your help picking a color for the walls." I reach over the staff-room coffee table, holding my phone out for Peony to see. "Which of these is your favorite?"

Athena takes the phone and shows her the five color swatches.

"We'll narrow it down once we know the color family she likes." No point looking at different shades of pinks if she prefers green or purple or orange.

The colors swatches are the popular kid-friendly choices. Soft shades that go well with Peony's new furniture.

"Which of these pretty colors do you want on your bedroom wall?" Athena asks her.

Peony examines the screen, though I'm not sure if she understands what Athena is asking. But Athena will have a good idea what colors my daughter is drawn to.

Peony points to the pink, the green, and then the purple.

"The green would look great in your room." I pull up several additional green options, and she swiftly picks one. It

133

happens to be my favorite, but I don't tell her that. I doubt she gives a damn what I like.

Peony cuddles closer to Athena, her attention on anything but me. Unlike before, she doesn't seem completely terrified. Now it's more like she's extremely shy toward me. But that doesn't mean the fear isn't still there, lingering beneath the surface, waiting to let me know it hasn't gone anywhere.

"Can I see what color you picked, Peony?" Zara joins her on the couch, leaving several inches between Peony and herself.

Peony flashes Zara a tentative smile. Shyness still cloaks her, but less so with Zara.

I hand Athena my phone to pass to Zara. Zara taps in my code and shows the phone to Peony. Peony points at the screen.

"Oh, that's pretty. Your..." Zara looks at me, and I know what she's silently asking.

I nod. Athena has referred to me as Peony's father, and I've accepted she's my daughter. Maybe it's time Peony thinks of me that way too.

And what if she isn't your daughter?

I ignore the voice. Even Zara seems convinced Peony is the result of my swimmer who went rogue.

"Your daddy and I are painting your bedroom tomorrow. And you'll have the best room in the house. It overlooks the backyard, where all kinds of magical things happen while you sleep. *Shhh.*" Zara presses her finger to her lips. "But you can't tell anyone about the magic." The pitch of her voice drops to a near whisper. "It's a secret."

I laugh softly, the sound vibrating low in my throat. "Some things never changed from when you were a kid."

I might be a fiction author, but of the two of us growing up, Zara had the brightest imagination. When we played make-believe during recess and after school, she was the one who came up with the best ideas, whether we were pirates, or knights fighting dragons, or on an Indiana Jones adventure.

I swipe to another set of colors and hand the phone to Athena. "What color would you like for your bedroom walls?"

She stares at me for a beat. "My-my walls?"

"As you might have noticed, I didn't exactly decorate my house with a woman in mind. As Zara keeps pointing out." I flash Zara a quick grin. "I thought you might like a different color on your walls. Something less..."

"Masculine?" Zara pipes in on a chuckle.

Athena takes my phone and studies the choices.

"Sorry they're not as colorful as the ones for Peony. Zara thought the neutral shades would look good in the guest bedroom."

"No, these are perfect. Thank you...thank you for giving me a choice." Athena points to the blush beige and hands me the phone. "We should get back to the hotel now."

"Oh, okay," I reply, torn between wanting to spend more time watching my best friend interact with Peony, and knowing I don't have time for that. I need to drive to Eugene to pick up the paint for tomorrow. And I need to get in my word count for today if I plan to make my deadline. Besides, we'll have plenty of time to spend hanging out with Peony once she and Athena move into my house.

Athena hoists Peony onto her hip. "Thank you for lunch." She glances down at my daughter and waves at me. "Say bye-bye to your daddy, Peony."

"Bye-bye." Peony's words are soft and tentative, her tone innocently sweet. She waves at me, her hand movement mirroring the flapping of a baby bird.

And I feel like I've just won a trillion dollars.

I wave and stand. "I'll walk you two to the hotel. Or if you want, I can drop you off. My SUV is parked around the corner from here."

"Do you have a car seat for Peony?" Athena asks.

I cringe. I hadn't thought to pick one up in Eugene yesterday. Guess I can add that to the list of things I'll need to pick up in the city tomorrow.

"It's nice out. Peony and I can walk. We'll see you tomorrow." Athena turns to Zara. "Thank you for the food. It was delicious." She starts toward the door.

"I'll walk you to the hotel."

"That's okay," Athena tosses over her shoulder to me, her tone bordering on dismissive. "We'll be fine."

Peony peers around Athena's arm, her lips pressed in a little pout. I get one last glance at the combination of Kenda's and my features, and then she and Athena disappear into the hallway.

I drop my ass into the armchair. "I can't believe I forgot to get a car seat," I mumble to myself, dropping my head on the back of the chair. I rub my hand down my face.

Zara sits on the armrest and drapes her denim-clad legs over my thighs. "Don't be hard on yourself. You're doing great." She brushes aside a strand of hair on my forehead and winces.

"You sure about that?"

"Absolutely."

I raise a challenging eyebrow. "Is that why you just winced when you said I was doing great?"

Confused divots form between her eyes. "I didn't just wince."

"Yes, you did."

Zara's features twist into an expression I recognize. She's replaying in her head the last few minutes of our conversation, trying to figure out what the heck I'm talking about. "That wasn't why I was wincing."

"Then why did you make that face if you weren't cringing at how bad a job I'm doing?"

"It's nothing. I hurt my shoulders a few months ago, and they still bother me from time to time."

I frown. "How come this is the first I'm hearing of this?"

"Because it's no big deal."

"If it's no big deal, you wouldn't have winced when you moved your shoulders." I spread my legs apart and pat the spot between them. "C'mon, Golden Girl. Sit here and I'll massage them. See if I can get the knots out." Or whatever it is that has caused her discomfort.

"That might work." She shifts to sit between my legs. Her ass lightly touches my package, and I have the sudden need to adjust myself.

She undoes the buttons of her cardigan and lets the top slide down her arms, leaving her shoulders bare under the thin strap of her tank top.

Blowing out a steadying breath, I push her hair aside, exposing her neck and shoulders, and gently massage her tight muscles, working out the knots.

This isn't the first time I've massaged Zara's shoulders, but something...I don't know what...something feels...different... this time. There's a fluttering in my chest, a breathlessness I can't explain.

Zara drops her head forward, and a soft moan escapes her. The sound goes straight to my cock. *Dammit, it's not that way between us*, I remind it. *We're friends.*

The kind without benefits.

I blow out another slow breath. *Mind back in the game, soldier.*

I study the elegant length and beautiful copper skin of her neck and lean in ever so slightly, catching her sweet jasmine scent. A craving to trace my lips along her silky skin thrusts through me. A craving to see if she tastes as sweet as she smells.

I close my eyes, but it only boldens the craving. Heightens the way she penetrates my senses.

A memory taunts me of a time in college when Zara, Kenda, and I went dancing with our friends. It was before Kenda and I became an item. Zara had dragged me onto the dance floor, and her favorite song came on. She'd started to dance...

I swallow at the memory. She had turned her back to me and was dancing in a way that was so seductive, so hot, I was sure every guy watching her had cursed me for being the lucky bastard who got to be pressed against her like that.

I wanted Zara, my best friend, that night in a way I hadn't wanted before. In a way that violated my *No hooking up with friends* rule.

A rule I later ignored when Kenda and I became involved. But that...that was different. If things had gone sour between us, it wouldn't have been as bad as compared to if I lost Zara from my life.

Still kneading her muscles, I open my eyes and lean away. It doesn't make a difference. My body still wants her. I clear my throat. Swallow harder. "Have you talked to Lucas? About your shoulders?"

"No. I talked to my physician a few months ago. She told me to take an NSAID, like ibuprofen, daily until it's better."

My hands stop moving but remain on her shoulders. "Have you been taking it regularly since she told you that?"

Zara nods, her coils brushing my hands.

"And it hasn't improved?" I trace my finger along her shoulder, then catch myself. I jerk my hands away from her skin.

"Yes and no. It's still there—so I probably did something again without realizing it. I've been careful not to aggravate it, but apparently not careful enough."

"You should talk to your physician. Make sure it's nothing serious."

Zara straightens and turns to look over her shoulder. She winces once more.

"Dammit, Zara, talk to your physician."

Zara goddamn freaking chuckles. "You're gonna make a great father, Garrett. Always worrying...even when there's nothing to worry about." An emotion crosses her face, but it's gone too quickly to pinpoint what it was.

"I just don't like seeing you in pain."

"I'll be fine. I'm sure it will go away soon. It just means I can't go running with you." She snickers. "Oh, wait. I wasn't going to anyway." She shifts between my legs, her ass rubbing against my package once more, making it jerk in response. *Down, boy.*

She unfolds from the chair, using the armrests to help her to her feet.

I frown at the way she seems to need assistance to stand. "Well, in the meantime, I don't think you should help me with painting Peony's room tomorrow. It won't do your shoulders any favors. And talk to Lucas. He might—"

The staff-room door opens, and Troy enters, smiling like he and Jess had a great fuck before he came here. Which they probably did. "Ready to talk renovations?"

At least he's getting some—one of the perks of being in a long-term relationship. The last time I saw any action was several months ago.

No wonder my cock came to life while I was massaging Zara's shoulders. My reaction to her was nothing more than basic male instinct after going without for so long. A reminder my cock is tired of surviving on nothing but a hand job in the shower.

Now that I'm a father, and my daughter—plus, her nanny— will be moving in with me soon, jerking off in the shower will have to suffice. Screwing one-night stands at their houses or in hotel rooms isn't possible when I have to hammer out words the next day. And flings are no longer an option.

Or they won't be for the immediate future.

Not until I've sent *Untold Mercy* to my editor.

Thoughts of abstaining for a while might be circling in my brain, but that doesn't stop the craving to touch Zara's soft skin again.

18

___

ZARA

Mr. Cartwright studies the proposal in front of him on my laptop. I try not to wipe my clammy palms on the fabric of my work pants.

The Tuesday lunch rush is over, and we're sitting in the staff room. Mugs of half-empty coffee are on the coffee table, along with pictures and a mood board to give him a visual of what I'm thinking of for the expansion.

None of my plans will be cheap, but Troy promised I could keep the costs down if I did some of the work myself.

I would normally have asked if Garrett could help me, but between his deadline and Peony, he won't have time. Nor do I intend to mention it to him. If I so much as breathe Troy's suggestion, Garrett will pull on his superhero cape and jump in to do the work. That won't help him with his book deadline. That won't help him be a father to Peony.

"These plans are impressive, Zara. Especially your projected numbers." Mr. Cartwright picks up his coffee mug. "I heard you're planning to help promote women-owned businesses in the area."

"That's right. I would like to include various products for

140

sale at Picnic & Treats. Products like jellies and handmade soaps." That would be plan A. "And I would also like to host various small events throughout the year. These will hopefully help increase awareness of the different products and services offered by the women-owned businesses. For example, Aria Johnson, who works as a hostess at La Brezza Ristorante, has created a line of perfumes. Maybe she would be interested in talking about how to pick a scent that works with your individual body chemistry."

"That sounds great." Mr. Cartwright scans the summary of my presentation in his hand. "I reviewed your lease contract and spoke with my lawyer. As it stands, you're responsible for the cost of all renovations."

I swallow hard, trying to squeeze air past the proposed cost wedged in my throat. I can arrange the money to do plan B, but it will be tight. If I want to do plan A, I'll have to contribute a fair chunk of my rainy-day savings set aside for emergencies. "That's right. But I was hoping you might be interested in taking on some of the cost, like some commercial business owners do."

He nods, rubbing his thumb across his bottom lip, and looks down at the proposal summary again. His mouth quirks into a smile. "I figured you might ask me that, and I talked to my lawyer and my banker and my wife about it. If you do plan A, I could cover forty percent of the costs."

With Mr. Cartwright's offer to cover forty percent of the expense, my cost will now be in line with what I'd budgeted for with plan B. The plan that hadn't allowed me to promote the women-owned small businesses in the area as much as I would like. Plan A will let me do so much more—especially since he will be covering forty percent of the renovation costs.

I clench my hands together to stop them from shaking with excitement. If he's asked his lawyer and banker and wife about this...does that mean he's leaning toward giving me the lease?

Hot excitement sweeps through me, engulfing all other emotions—fear, doubt, shock—until I'm surfing on a rainbow of hope. Hope everything will go according to plan. Hope this will be the start to the even brighter future I'd dreamed about when I'd first gotten the idea five years ago for Picnic & Treats.

"It looks like we've got a deal, then. Congratulations, Zara."

"Thank you!" If I wasn't trying to be professional about this, I'd hug him. And then rush over to his house and hug his wife. Oh, who am I kidding? I'll probably do that anyway.

He laughs. "Don't thank me, Zara. You did all the work. I knew from the first time I saw you sitting in my class, you were destined for great things. What you want to do for this community and what you've accomplished so far proves I was right."

Picnic & Treats and being a strong voice within the local business community are Phase II of my dreams. Dreams that blossomed while Mimi was teaching me to be a great cook like she'd been. Prior to that, I'd been floundering, trying to find my true self.

In college, I loved Kenda's drive to be a voice for those who felt they didn't have one. It was the motivation behind everything she did. Every course she took. Every term paper she wrote. Maybe I'd had the same spark all along, but it had been buried deep, waiting for Kenda's fire to light it.

But it wasn't until I dreamed up Picnic & Treats that everything came together.

"I'll call my lawyer tomorrow and get everything in motion." Mr. Cartwright pushes to his feet. "In the meantime, consider yourself the new lease holder for next door, starting the middle of next month." Tomorrow is the first day of the new month. May 1st. "As soon as we get everything legalized, you and Troy can start on the renovations." He holds out his hand for me to shake. His grip is firm and warm. "And I won't charge you for next month's lease, 'cause this is all rather last minute.

The women who bought Sabrina's business will be packing up everything over the next two days."

"Thank you. For everything. You always were my favorite teacher." I flash him a grin.

He laughs, and I walk him to the main entrance of the café. As soon as he is out the door, I turn and give Keshia and Jess a big nod, a huge-ass smile spreading across my face. "He went with plan A and will be helping me with forty percent of the renovation costs."

They squeal and rush around the counter to hug me. My vision goes blurry with happy tears. They really are my second family. Everyone working at Picnic & Treats is my second family.

The bell above the door jingles, and a group of people enter. Jess and Keshia return to the kitchen. I trail behind them as I send Troy a text.

Me: I got the lease! And plan A is on.

I type the same text to Garrett, and I don't think about the feel of his hands on my body, when he massaged my shoulders three days ago.

The same way I spent the weekend not thinking of how my body responded to his touch. How I didn't fantasize about how his strong, heavenly hands would feel exploring every inch of me, bringing me to orgasm.

NoNoNoNo. It was a friendly massage between friends. Nothing more.

Now, if only my body would agree with me on that.

19

GARRETT

Athena straps Peony into the child car seat I installed yesterday in the Explorer. "Isn't this exciting? We're gonna live with your daddy. And you get your own bedroom, which your daddy decorated. Just." Athena pokes her in the stomach. Peony giggles. "For." Another poke. More giggling. "You."

Peony beams at Athena, her bright smile mirroring the one I'd witnessed so many times on her mother. My heart squeezes, but not as hard as it once would have. It's the reaction felt for a lost friend instead of for a lost love.

Athena kisses her forehead. Peony holds up Poppy, and Athena pretends to kiss the stuffed panda's head. "Ready for this new adventure?"

Peony throws her arms up, jerking Poppy above her head and almost whacking Athena in the face. "Yes!" Not once does her gaze fall on me. As far as she's concerned, I'm not here.

I place the last of their things from the hotel room in the trunk and close it. In the short time they've stayed here, they've accumulated quite a few belongings—a lot of which I bought for Peony. Emily, Zara, Simone, and Avery also contributed to

Athena's wardrobe, which she didn't protest over, unlike when I offered to buy her some clothes.

I drive us to my neighborhood. It's midafternoon and the sun is shining, as if welcoming Peony home. One more week and the paternity results will prove what I already know. The test arrived yesterday morning, and I fired it back to the testing facility soon after, with the swabs containing Peony's and my DNA.

Both Peony and Athena are quiet, looking out the windows of the Explorer as we pass the neighborhood houses. Elementary-school-aged kids run and skip and chase each other on the sidewalk.

Peony's holding her stuffed panda tightly, her eyes wide with wonder. "Doggie." She points at a small dog walking alongside its owner on the sidewalk.

I return my attention to the road. "You like dogs?"

A silence heavy with indifference meets my question, drowns out the children's song playing through the speakers.

A quick glance in the rearview mirror is met with a wobbly-lip expression. A wobbly-lip expression I can't help but feel is the result of me asking Peony the question. Of me acknowledging her presence.

Of her having to acknowledge mine.

"She...she doesn't have much experience with dogs," Athena says after a long beat, "other than in her favorite picture book."

"One of your uncles has a little dog like that." My gaze flicks briefly to Peony. She continues looking out the window. "His name is Butterscotch. And his girlfriend has a golden retriever named Bailey. She's training to be a psychiatric service dog for Jess, so you won't get to stroke Bailey unless she's off duty. And Uncle Lucas and Auntie Simone have a large golden Labradoodle." I have no idea if Peony understands anything I'm saying. I'm just scrambling for common ground between us.

No matter how tiny.

"You don't like dogs?" Athena asks.

I turn my head, catching the same assessing expression on her face I've witnessed a few times in the past six days. "No, I like 'em."

"But you don't have one."

"My schedule doesn't allow for one. Between being a full-time author and being away on Wilderness Warriors excursions, I don't have time for pets." Not even a pet goldfish.

"That's sad." Athena's tone is soft, almost a whisper. "What is Wilderness Warriors?"

"My brothers and I created an outdoor recreational program for military veterans. Of all abilities and disabilities. Right now they're weekend trips, like hiking, canoeing, camping, climbing. But we're planning to start doing week-long programs next year."

We'll be hiring summer staff to help with that. Lucas, Troy, Kellan, and I have full-time careers we love. But Warriors is a way for us to give back to those who served our country, fighting for the freedoms we hold dear.

"What about you. Do you like dogs?"

"Can't say I've ever had one." Her voice is dreamy, almost... nostalgic? "Kenda wanted a dog."

"She did? I find that hard to believe given her career goal. She just wanted to move from one journalism assignment to the next."

"Priorities change. Especially when you become a parent." Athena glances over her shoulder to where Peony is sitting behind me.

I can't tell if she's hinting my priorities will need to change now that I have a daughter. Or if she's talking about Kenda and how her priorities veered off their original path.

At least in my case, I'm not moving from one place to the

next with no permanent address. I can give Peony stability, a chance to make long-term friends.

I turn onto my driveway and park in the garage. Athena helps Peony out of her car seat while I remove the bags from the trunk.

We enter the silent house through the laundry room. A silence I prefer when I'm writing. A silence that will be a thing of the past with a toddler now living here. I can't expect her to be quiet while I write—nor do I intend to demand she keeps the noise down while I'm getting words on the page.

I'm not that man. I'm not the military man who needs to be in control and for everything to be orderly.

A few of my routines will need to change. I won't be able to write in the garden anymore, like I enjoy doing when the weather is warmer. Or rather, I won't be able to write in the backyard when Peony is playing there. She'll be a distraction I don't need, especially now, when my book is due to my editor in three months, two weeks, and two days. When I'm lost in my story world, the words flowing like nobody's business, the last thing I need or want is a distraction yanking me out of the story. Although the last time I was lost in the story was almost a week ago. I barely remember what that's like.

Athena takes the hand of my new pint-sized distraction, and they tentatively walk into the hallway as if unsure what to do next.

I put the first of their bags in the laundry room and lead them to the guest bedroom. I point to the open door. "This is your room, Athena."

We step into a room that looks nothing like it did a week ago. The walls have been repainted a soft blush beige. Off-white bedding has replaced the old navy sheets and comforter.

"Wow." Athena runs her hand along the lace edging of the bedding. "It's nothing like I was expecting."

"You can thank Zara. She figured you'd prefer this over the previous man-cave look."

Athena picks up Peony and carries her to the window. The blinds are open, providing a great view of the garden. "Jesus," she blurts, a Texan drawl that wasn't there before now reshaping her vowels.

Her face flushes, and she clears her throat. "I mean, it's like an enchanted garden." The Texan drawl is gone from her tone. "Do you think there are fairies and woodland creatures out there?" She tickles Peony, who giggles.

Athena slowly walks around the room, checking out the previously sparsely decorated space. Zara added a few extra feminine touches throughout the bookshelf. Mostly small bouquets of silk flowers and wicker baskets.

"It's as beautiful as morning dew sparkling on a spiderweb." Athena smiles, and it's brighter than anything I've witnessed from her yet. It takes years off her age. Like she's momentarily free of everything that's been weighing her down. Her employer's death and the apartment fire and taking care of Peony while they traveled across the country to get here. "I've never stayed in a room like it before."

"Just wait till you see Peony's room."

The furniture arrived this morning, and I spent the next few hours setting up the room...with Zara's guidance. She FaceTimed me from work.

I open the door and let them go in ahead of me.

Uncertainty laps over me like a rogue wave at the possibility Peony might not like the room. My gaze jerks to the ceiling in a silent prayer to Clarke. A prayer that I can be the type of father he was to his little girl...until I failed to save him.

A prayer I won't fail my daughter.

I walk into the bedroom in time to see Athena's wide-eyed expression as she takes in the pale-green walls. Framed woodland-critter posters hang on the wall above Peony's new bed.

Peony toddles to the low bookshelf and grabs the wooden shape-sorting toy. She drops her butt onto the new rug and starts playing, oblivious to Athena's reaction to the room.

I kneel next to the toddler bed, protecting her personal space.

My movement snares Peony's attention from the toy, and her curiosity-widened eyes watch me. But it's the other emotion, the one hovering in her features like a storm cloud passing in front of the sun, that has a dejected huff coasting my lips.

In her mind, I'm the boogeyman, scheming to haunt her dreams.

Give it time.

The voice in my head isn't my own. It's Zara. The woman who has an endless supply of patience. Who volunteered in a program during college that helped young kids in crisis.

"I know you're used to sleeping in a crib," I say to Peony, "but I thought maybe you would like to start sleeping in a big girl's bed."

Peony's bottom lip wobbles and tears fill her eyes.

And it's like a grenade once the pin has been yanked. Panic tightens the vise around my chest, and my heart rate kicks up. I can almost hear the robotic voice in my head, counting down the seconds until her meltdown begins.

Ten.

Nine.

Eight.

The ticking of another clock echoes in the back of my mind, reminding me I'm wasting time I don't have while I try to get her to accept me as part of her life.

Panic at the prospect of Peony having a meltdown is greeted by self-doubt. It slithers in, wraps me in a knot, squeezes my chest tighter and tighter. What if she hasn't accepted me because deep down she knows I'm not her father?

No, no. It's not that. She is my daughter. I'm positive of it. She would just prefer I wasn't.

"I'll...er...I'll give you two space while you get settled. And if she would rather have a crib...well, let me know. I'll be in my office if you need anything." I push to my feet and practically sprint to the door, needing to leave before it's too late.

Seven.

Six.

Five.

"Garrett." My name rides on a rushed breath. "Thank you. Thank you for everything you've done for us so far. You didn't need to do any of this"—Athena gestures to the room with her hand—"but you did. You've given Peony something she hasn't had..." The last word seems to fade before it's fully formed. Like there's more to the sentence but it never comes.

"And what's that exactly?"

A flush spreads across Athena's cheeks. Her mouth opens and closes several times as if she's scrambling to find the right words.

Peony's sudden high-pitched wail rips through the room like a tornado siren, yanking my attention back to her. Tears stream down her face, and the familiar helplessness kicks me in the ass again.

"Hey, sweet girl, it's gonna be okay." Athena picks her up and carries her to the window. The view is the same as from Athena's room. "Should we see if we can spot any fairies?"

"I'll get the rest of your stuff." My words are barely heard over Peony's wails.

I hurry to the door, unable to get out of the room fast enough, and grab the bags from the Explorer. I leave them outside Peony's room for Athena to put away. By the time I'm finished, Peony's meltdown has petered out, and I can hear Athena's gentle voice reading to her.

I retreat to my office and sit in the wingback chair overlooking the backyard. Instead of writing, like I should be doing, I get up and remove from the bookshelf the framed photo of Kenda, Zara, and me. The picture was taken during our junior year in college. All three of us are smiling at the camera.

"Why is she so scared of me?" I'm not sure who I'm asking: Kenda or Zara. Or maybe them both. "How am I supposed to be her father if she looks at me like I'm the Big Bad Wolf getting ready to eat her?"

THE TIMER GOES OFF, PULLING ME OUT OF MY STORY, AND THE sound of giggling draws my attention from the laptop screen to the window. I remove my reading glasses and place them on the side table next to the wingback chair. Relief flows through me, leaves me feeling lighter than normal, at how many pages I've written since sitting down at the computer. It's the most I've written since Peony came into my life.

I was so engrossed in the story, I hadn't noticed Peony and Athena outside. Athena is blowing bubbles, and Peony is trying to catch them.

She toddles as fast as she can around the small patch of grass, tripping a few times, but keeps missing the bubbles as they float away.

I would go out there and lift her so she can pop them, but I doubt she would appreciate that. So I just watch Peony and Athena for a few minutes laughing and having fun.

My phone pings with a text.

> Mom: Just checking that I'm still getting
> to meet my granddaughter after dinner.
> [smiling emoji]

> Me: Yes, that's the plan.

Me: Remember, she's nervous with strangers.

Me: Don't rush her.

Mom: [sad emoji] I'll do my best to curtail my excitement.

A delicious smell greets me as I walk to the kitchen. I noticed it from the office but thought it was my stomach playing tricks on me, hinting I needed to make something for dinner soon.

I enter the kitchen to find several pots on the stove. Two of the gas burners are off, but the third one is set at simmer. Athena had agreed to make dinners for us, but I hadn't expected her to cook on her first day here. Guess I'd forgotten to mention that to her.

Relieved I don't have to disappoint them with my unimpressive cooking skills, I slip on my sneakers and join Peony and Athena outside. They're still running on the grass, laughing. Neither of them seems to have noticed me keeping to the shadows of the house, and I watch them for a minute.

"What should I be now?" Athena asks her.

"Ti-ger." Peony growls, the sound more like that of a tiger cub.

"The tiger is coming to eat you!" Athena's voice is the low purr of a large feline, her throat sounding slightly strained. She stalks toward Peony, her movements graceful.

Peony giggles and tries to run away. She trips and falls onto the grass.

Athena scoops her up. "Gotcha."

Peony squeals. Athena blows a raspberry on her stomach, and Peony giggles uncontrollably.

Athena says something to her that I don't hear and puts Peony on the grass. They both turn to the door and, at seeing me, startle.

Athena's eyebrows disappear under her bangs, and her freckles become even more noticeable against her suddenly paler-than-normal skin. "How long have you been standing there?"

I take a casual step forward but maintain my distance so as not to upset Peony. "Not long. You two were having so much fun, I didn't want to interrupt. I came out to thank you for making dinner."

"You're welcome." Athena's gaze roams down my body and up to my face. The color has returned to her cheeks by the time she's finished her perusal. "You're a Marine. Can you teach me self-defense?"

"Sure. I can do that." Kellan and I taught Zara and Emily self-defense two or three years ago. "We can use the training mats in the main Wilderness Warriors building."

Athena catches her bottom lip between her teeth, and something sparks in her eyes. "Can you teach me how to shoot a gun?"

Her question has me mentally stumbling back, although it probably shouldn't. She survived a mall shooting. Like other people who have been in her situation, she's thinking of arming herself with a handgun in case something like that happens again.

"No. I'm not a licensed gun instructor. Also, I don't allow guns in the house." Gun accidents happen all the time. Deadly accidents. Accidents often involving children.

Athena nods, and I can't help but wonder if I've just passed some sort of test I didn't know about.

The three of us go into the house and get ready for dinner.

"Can I put you in the booster seat?" I ask Peony as Athena spoons the rice and sauce onto the plates.

Athena smiles encouragingly at her. "That's a good idea. Let your daddy put you in the seat. I bet he would like that."

Peony eyes me like I'm an insect she's not too sure about,

but there's no hint in her expression that we're heading for another crying fit. She lifts her arms up but doesn't close the distance between us.

I take three slow steps toward her, careful not to spook her, and cautiously pick her up as if she's a live explosive.

I grimace, waiting for the worst to happen. But there are no tears, no wobbling lips, no warning signs she's about to detonate.

And I ease out a long, relieved breath.

20

GARRETT

The early-evening spring breeze is cool against my cheek as Athena and I walk to the neighborhood park. But as cool as the temperature might be, it isn't cold enough for me to wear a jacket. I only have on a hoody.

Athena is carrying Peony, who is bundled in her coat. She's babbling in a toddler language, and hell, she has a lot to say. To Athena.

Not to me.

"Peony seems happier now," I point out.

"She had a nap." Athena smiles fondly at my daughter.

"When does she usually nap?"

Athena shrugs. "Whenever she needs one."

I might not know much about young kids, but even I know they have regular naptimes. As someone who thrives on keeping to a routine, I can appreciate that. "She doesn't have a regular naptime?"

"Nothing specific."

"So, what? You wait until she's cranky before putting her down?" There's no judgment in my tone. I'm just trying to

155

understand Peony's schedule...and possible triggers for her meltdowns.

Another shrug of Athena's narrow shoulders. "Pretty much."

"What time's her bedtime?"

"Whenever she gets tired."

That sounds...not right. "So she doesn't have a regular bedtime either?"

"No," Athena snaps, startling me. "She doesn't."

I stop walking and gently grab her arm, forcing her to look at me. The glare she hurls my way is hot enough to scorch me to the ground.

I drop my hand away from her. "I'm not judging you or Kenda." Even if it might sound like I am. "But Kenda isn't here, and maybe it wouldn't hurt to put Peony on some sort of routine. For her benefit."

Athena's scowl doesn't soften. If anything, it deepens. "What kind of routine?"

"She eats and sleeps on a regular schedule. Maybe you can take her to the playground at a set time too, so she knows she can look forward to that each day and knows what to expect."

Peony squirms in Athena's arms, her attention on something behind Athena. "Doggie." She points to the small white dog. Her face is glowing, an adorable toothy grin spreading across it.

I step onto the road, giving the older woman and her dog room to get past.

The woman stops and beams at Peony. "Well, aren't you as cute as a fluffy baby duckling?"

"Doggie."

The dog peers up at us, its tail wagging at supersonic speed.

"You can stroke her if you'd like." The woman splits a knowing look between Athena and me. "Lucy's good with young kids. I have a granddaughter your daughter's age, and Lucy is always happy when the little girl fusses over her."

I glance at Athena. She knows a helluva lot more about Peony and little kids in general than I do—other than the part about kids needing a routine. Maybe she won't think it's a good idea.

"Would you like to pet the dog?" she asks Peony.

Peony nods, her head moving faster than Lucy's tail.

"Sit, Lucy," the woman says, delight smoothing the edges of the command. "The little girl is going to stroke you."

Lucy drops her ass on the sidewalk, her tail still wagging at high speed. I don't know who's more excited about Peony getting to pet the dog—Peony or Lucy.

Athena demonstrates how to stroke Lucy. Peony squats next to the dog and lets Athena guide her hand over the dog's curly hair.

"Looks like your mommy and daddy need to get you a puppy." The woman winks at me, and I try not to groan. A dog is not what I need. Especially not now. Not when I have a rapidly approaching deadline, a book that is a long way from being completed, and a toddler I'm learning to navigate my life around.

Adding a dog to my chaotic life will be the iceberg that sunk Titanic.

I smile at the woman, hoping Peony didn't understand her and get ideas of her own. Her stuffed panda is more our speed. Besides, she'll have plenty of time to hang out with Jasper and Butterscotch once I introduce her to my brothers.

I check the time on my phone. "Time to go to the playground, Peony." *To meet your grandparents.* "Say goodbye to Lucy."

"Bye-bye." She waves to the dog and raises her hands above her head, gesturing for Athena to pick her up.

Mom and Dad are already at the playground when we arrive. They're on a bench, watching a boy who looks to be about three years old climb up the slide ladder. A little girl is waiting at the bottom of the ladder for her turn.

They are the only kids here. Two sets of parents are standing off to the side, talking and keeping an eye on their kids.

I recognize the parents. Both sets live on my street, and I've said hi to them plenty of times. They know I'm single—or I assume they know I'm single. It's not like my relationship status has come up in conversation.

I inwardly cringe. While I might be ready to admit to myself Peony is my daughter, I'm not ready to admit it to anyone who isn't part of my inner circle until I have the paternity test results.

And even then, it's no one's business.

But it might be tricky to avoid the truth coming out if they come to talk to me. The two men are fans of my books. And because they are fans, I can't be rude and brush off their questions or lie to them, only for the lie to later slap me in the face.

Christ, please don't come over.

Athena takes Peony to the toddler swing, and I walk to where my parents are sitting. Mom is practically vibrating as I draw closer, her gaze darting between me and Peony.

Dad has on his skeptical face. He's missing the facts he needs to draw a valid conclusion, and it's not sitting right with him. But skepticism isn't the only emotion in the tilt of his head, the purse of his lips, the lift of his brow. A slim ray of hope shines through the small cracks in his expression.

His eyes remain on me, as if commanding himself not to look at the little girl who could be his granddaughter. As if afraid of falling in love with her before we have the lab results —in case he ends up with a broken heart.

"Hi, Mom. Dad. Sorry we're late." I hug Mom.

"You're not late, son." Dad gives me a one-armed hug. "Your mom was getting a little impatient waiting at home."

A nervous chuckle escapes me. "How long have you been here?"

Mom flicks the air with her hand, waving off the question. "Just a few minutes."

Dad huffs out an eye roll of a laugh. "More like twenty."

She scoffs and tosses him a cross glance. "Don't exaggerate." Her attention shifts to Peony, and she misses his expression that almost has me snickering. It's his *Really?* expression. His I'm-not-wrong face. "So that's her? Peony? My granddaughter?"

"Your potential granddaughter," Dad mutters. His comment lands him an elbow in the stomach.

I ignore their amusing bickering. I'm used to it. "Yes, that's her."

Mom starts to walk toward the swings. I hook my hand on her arm, keeping her from advancing more than three steps. "Maybe wait a minute." My voice is kept low so as not to reach curious ears.

Mom pats my hand like I'm a little kid who needs placating. "I'm just going to say hi to her and her nanny and see how things go. Her nanny is very pretty, by the way. And I'm guessing single?" Mom's eyes gleam with matchmaking mischief, and I barely keep in a groan.

"Don't even go there." The pitch of my growled voice is so low, it almost scrapes the artificial grass covering the playground surface.

"Well, you are single, Garrett. And now you're a single father. Not to mention a great catch."

I huff out a grunt. "I'm not a trout."

Mom snickers. "No, you're not. But that doesn't mean you're not allowed to fall in love. I can't remember the last time you were in love...after you and Kenda broke up." Pain flashes on

Mom's face, the reality of Kenda's death no doubt sitting heavily on her too.

She pats my hand again and makes her way to the swings.

I don't try to stop her this time. I just brace myself for the next part of her plan...whatever that might be.

Athena is gently pushing Peony on the toddler swing and talking to her. She doesn't seem to notice my mother heading their way. Her attention is solely focused on Peony, who is hugging Poppy and grinning at Athena.

Sighing at how everything could go south in the next few minutes, I walk over to join them. I reach them in time to hear Mom introduce herself to Athena.

I'm not sure what I expected Athena's reaction to be, especially when she was leery about my parents meeting Peony. What I hadn't expected was her warm, welcoming smile directed at my mother.

What the hell did Mom say to her?

The two women shake hands, the smile never leaving Athena's face.

Athena stops the swing's motion. "Peony, this is your grandmother." She points to my mother.

Mom looks at Peony and makes a funny, strangled sound. Her hands fly to her mouth. "Oh." The word releases on a muffled sob. "You have his eyes." She turns to me. Her eyes glisten in the setting angle of the sun. "She has your eyes."

She turns back to Peony. "You, sweet little one, can call me Granny. And who's that?" Mom points to Poppy.

Peony gifts her one of her shy smiles and cuddles her panda. "Poppy."

"That's a lovely name. And I love your name too. It's so pretty."

Peony's smile widens, revealing tiny teeth.

Mom releases a small noise. A noise that says: *Oh, aren't you just the cutest?* "I'm so happy to finally meet you. Is it...can I help swing you?"

Peony pumps her legs, the action lacking the coordination needed to get the swing moving again.

Athena nods at my mother, telling her without words to go ahead, and steps to the side. Mom takes her place, and I watch the three of them interact. Peony doesn't show any signs of being scared of my mother. Just the opposite.

In less than thirty seconds, Mom has won her over. Why is it Peony seems to be accepting of everyone else but still uncertain about me? What have I done to make her treat me like I'm a leper?

Feeling like they're better off without me standing there, I walk to the bench where Dad is sitting.

He shakes his head in resignation as I sit next to him. "God, I hope your mother's heart won't be broken. She was devastated enough when she found out about Lily and about Simone's hysterectomy."

I wasn't there when Simone and Lucas explained to my parents how Simone had been pregnant with Lucas's baby over eleven years ago—something none of us, including Lucas, had known about at the time. A drunk driver resulted in her losing the baby, and Simone needed an emergency hysterectomy to save her life. I wasn't there when they told Mom, but I heard afterward how devastated she'd been at losing her only grandchild.

"Mom seems convinced Peony is my daughter."

Dad blows out a short laugh. "Of course she does. She desperately wants this to be true. But most of all, she wants you to be happy. Are you happy?"

Happy? I'm not sure that describes how I feel. I have a daughter I didn't know about until recently. A daughter who isn't particularly fond of me. She's only eighteen months old—what will she be like when she's sixteen? Will she resent me more than she does now because I wasn't in her life from day one?

I rub my neck, trying to ease the growing knot.

"Are you happy?" Dad repeats.

"Ask me that once my current project is in my editor's hands." Better yet, once my editor tells me he loves the story and confirms massive rewrites won't be necessary.

"Like that, huh?"

Screams of laughter come from the slide, the two other kids running around it, arms up like they're airplanes.

"I don't know how single parents manage. At least I have Athena to help me muddle through it. But it's not making things easy for hitting my deadline."

"I wish I could say I know what you mean, but I can't. I missed those early years when you and your brothers were that age." He dips his head toward Peony. "You won't miss those precious years like I did with you and your brothers. And the mother of your children won't have to worry about you dying in action, leaving her with young kids to raise without a father."

His words, spoken without malice, are a grenade to my heart, shrapnel shredding my insides. Yes, Peony won't have to worry about her father dying in action. But Clarke's and Cooper's children can't say the same...because I couldn't save my friends.

Memories flash in my mind. Memories of the day I lost them both.

SWEAT DUE TO THE HEAT FROM THE AFGHAN DESERT SUN HAD dampened my hair and dripped down my back. The sweltering temperature had been the least of my problems, what with the recent Taliban activity. My M27 was in position, the butt against my shoulder, as I slowly reversed into the old stone building.

I focused on the dry terrain surrounding the entrance. Cooper and Clarke had been the first to enter the building as we worked to secure it. I was watching their backs. The rest of our unit was in position, ensuring we weren't ambushed from outside.

I searched around the room, and an unease stirred in my gut. *Something's not right.*

An explosion at the back of the house shook the building, shattered the windows. I dropped to the ground, covering my head and neck with my arms. Dust and debris landed on me. Something sharp sliced into me just below my ribs.

It took a moment to regain my senses. All I could hear was the loud ringing in my ears. The explosion hadn't been big enough to level the house, but a thick layer of dust covered the front room.

Coughing, I pushed to my knees and gasped at the pain in my side. Blood soaked through my cammies, but the amount seeping through wasn't enough to worry about yet. "Cooper? Clarke?" I yelled.

The ringing in my ears drowned out their replies. *Please let them be okay.* I staggered forward, calling out their names again, using the wall to keep me upright.

I entered the hallway. Clarke was on the floor, unmoving, face down.

I hurried toward him, my breath labored, and dropped to my knees next to him. "Hey, buddy. Hold on. I've got you. Cooper?" I yelled out his name, my voice hoarse, in case he could hear me. I didn't have a visual on him. He wasn't in the hallway.

The ringing in my ears began to settle into a dull background noise.

Clarke groaned and moved his leg a fraction of an inch. *Thank Christ.* He was alive.

"I'm just going to roll you over," I told him, "so I can see what we're dealing with."

Shouted voices came from the front door.

I rolled Clarke over carefully. His groan squeezed something inside me, the resulting pain worse than the physical one from my injury.

Blood flowed from the open wound in his belly. *Fuck. Fuck. Fuck.* I covered it with my hands, attempting to stop the flow of blood. "It's gonna be okay. You're gonna be okay." The lie tasted sour in my mouth.

Agony contorted his face, and my insides crumpled. It should have been me. I didn't have a wife and kids waiting for me at home—but Clarke did.

"You're gonna be okay," I had told him again and again and again, but I didn't know if the words were for him or for me or for his family.

I WHITE-KNUCKLE THE EDGE OF THE PARK BENCH WITH BOTH hands, fighting to suck air into my lungs, fighting to keep the memory of that day from my face.

What do you see? my old therapist's voice says in my head.

Peony on the swing. Her sweet smile. My mother. Poppy…

"You okay, son?"

I drag my gaze to Dad, abruptly ending the therapy exercise I didn't want to do anyway. "Yeah, I'm good." I reluctantly release my grip on the weathered wood of the bench.

"How is the book going?"

"It's going. It'll probably be a struggle for a few days. Peony, Athena, and I need to come up with a schedule that works for all of us. But at least the plot isn't giving me any problems." *For now.*

"She's a pretty thing. The nanny." He doesn't say it in a leering sort of way. It's more like he has correctly guessed Mom's matchmaking thoughts.

I roll my eyes. I've been so overwhelmed with everything, I haven't paid attention to what Athena looks like, beyond my initial impression when I found her and Peony on my doorstep. "I'm just happy to have her around to help make everything smoother for Peony."

"How's that going so far?"

"As well as can be expected, given she's lost her mother." And she had no idea I existed until five days ago.

Dad winces. "That rough, huh?"

"With me, she's nothing like she is with Mom." I nod toward where Peony is giggling at Mom from the swing and Mom is playing peekaboo. "She's scared of me when I haven't given her a reason to be. She was the same way with Kellan."

"*Hmm.* Well, your mother has already fallen in love with her." He eases out a heavy, despite-my-warnings sigh and unfolds from the bench. "You might as well introduce me."

We walk to the swings. The two fathers on the other side of the playground glance my way. I pretend not to notice them. Hopefully that will be enough to keep them from coming over to chat.

"Peony." I keep my voice soft and even, hoping that will be enough to ward off any potential problems.

She squeezes Poppy to her body, a shield against perceived evil, and rounded eyes dart between Dad and me.

"This is your grandfather," I tell her, a bad feeling settling over me. The same feeling that had hit a second before the explosive that killed my friends detonated. That seemingly elongated period when no amount of hoping will prevent the sequence of events from unfolding.

Peony stretches her arms to Athena. "Nina!"

The high-pitched wail of her voice is a hook in my chest, yanking my heart out, dragging it across the artificial turf.

"Hey, baby girl. It's okay." Athena lifts Peony from the swing, but her foot gets caught on it.

I lunge forward and gently untangle it, taking care not to further upset Peony. "No one will hurt you, little flower. I'll make sure of that." I put my fingers on her shoulder. "I'm your daddy, and it's my job to make sure you're safe and loved."

Her small body trembles under my touch, but she doesn't pull away. She stares at me, perhaps processing my words. Or willing me to vanish in a puff of fairy dust.

Her trembling eases after a beat, but she continues to stare at me with uncertain eyes.

Dad looks no less uncertain than Peony. "It was nice to meet you, Peony. Joanne, we should go and give her a little space for now."

Mom's gaze moves between Dad and Peony. She's clearly torn between leaving with Dad and staying with her granddaughter.

"Okay," she replies on a sigh. "But let me know when I can see this little angel again. Or when you need someone to look after her."

Athena's body goes rigid, her shoulders pulled back. "*I'm* looking after her." There's a possessiveness to her tone, the extending of claws. "I mean, I'm the live-in nanny. I can look after her." The possessiveness dulls only a fraction. The claws remain fully extended.

My brow furrows, and a spark of anger flares in me at her reaction. I open my mouth to...I don't know what I plan to say.

But Mom cuts me off before the words can form. "And you've done a great job taking care of my granddaughter." Mom smiles patiently at her, not at all put off by Athena's reaction. "But you're not her mother."

Athena's eyes widen, and she jerks back a step as if Mom

has just slapped her, though upsetting her would never have been Mom's intent.

"You get to have time off from the job," Mom continues, undaunted by Athena's reaction. "That's the law. And during your off hours, when you get to take a break and enjoy your downtime, I'm happy to step in and help out."

Athena looks like she wants to argue, hurt burning in her eyes, but she just nods, her jaw tight.

What the hell was that—Athena's reaction—all about?

21

ZARA

Thursday after work, I let myself into Garrett's house and follow the sound of Peony and Athena playing in the living room. Poppy and several other stuffed animals and a large squirrel pillow are lying in a row on the floor in front of Peony.

"Hey there, Peony. Hi, Athena." I give them a friendly wave.

Peony waves back. A small smile bends the corners of Athena's mouth, but there's something half-hearted about it. "Hi."

I crouch next to them. My hips and the base of my spine grumble, waiting for the recent dose of ibuprofen to kick in. "What are you two playing?"

Peony grins up at me and picks up Poppy. "Dac-ter."

Athena strokes Peony's back, the adoring smile on her face solely for the little girl. It's the same smile Mama often has for my brothers and me. The smile that tells us we're loved. We're her sun and her universe.

An image of Athena as Garrett's wife and Peony's mother slithers into my head and takes root. My chest constricts, my stomach drops, and my limbs feel like dead trees during the winter freeze. That's it. No more reading romances in which the single father falls for the nanny. I don't need the trope fueling my imagination more than it already is.

True, Garrett and Athena would make a beautiful couple and produce beautiful babies. But they would be nowhere near as beautiful as the little girl I get to spend the next two hours with while Garrett teaches Athena self-defense.

"Da-ter?" I ask the nymphlike nanny. Her strawberry-blond hair is secured in a messily sexy ponytail. Peony's coils are tied up in two cute little buns on top of her head, decorated with red bows.

"Doctor. We're playing doctor." Athena looks at me—*really* looks at me—as if trying to get a solid read on me. Her head then turns to where Garrett is standing in the entranceway to the living room, near the huge screen TV. "Maybe we should bring Peony with us. She can watch."

"No, it's better she stays here with Zara. It will be hard to teach you self-defense if we're distracted, keeping an eye on her. But we can always delay the lessons a few weeks if you want."

"No!" The word flies from the usually soft-spoken Athena, its edges whip sharp. "I mean...I want to learn some moves. So I can protect Peony. Just in case."

O-kay. I can understand that. The odds of someone attempting to hurt or kidnap Peony while she's with Athena are low in Maple Ridge, but it doesn't mean it can't happen. Athena is thin, like a dancer, but without the muscles that come from training. She'll need any advantage she can get, whether or not she is Peony's nanny.

"Peony and I will be fine while you're learning to be a bad" —I glance at Peony, catching myself in time—"a bad-antelope."

Athena's brow scrunches, and she straightens to a stand. "Bad-antelope? Is that Oregon slang for something?"

Garrett laughs, the sound abrupt. "I think Zara was sparing

Peony from learning a word you don't want her repeating." He spells out badass.

That gets a grin out of Athena. "Yes, I would love to be a bad-antelope," she tells him. To me she says, "Are you sure you'll be okay looking after Peony?" She bites her lip, looking far from convinced.

"I love kids. And I have a niece who's a little younger than Peony." Well, more like five months younger. "We'll be fine. Go!"

Athena touches Peony's arm, distracting Peony from her game of putting colorful Band-Aids on the stuffed animals' legs. "I'm going somewhere with your daddy for a little bit, and Zara"—she points at me—"will play with you while I'm gone." She strokes Peony's head. "You be good for her, okay?"

The adorable toothy smile Peony flashes her makes my heart go a little gooey.

Athena kneels next to Peony. "Do I get a bye-bye hug?"

Peony scrambles to her feet and gives Athena a big hug, almost knocking her off-balance.

Athena kisses her on the crown of her head. "Give your daddy a bye-bye hug?"

Without looking at Garrett, Peony shakes her head, her declaration firm, and returns to playing with the stuffed animals.

A flare of hurt clouds his expression, and I ache to reassure him things will be okay. After everything he's done for her so far, she's got to see just how wonderful the man standing in front of us is. He's not a man to fear. He's a man to respect. To appreciate. To love.

Oh, screw it.

I push to my feet, my back and hips grumbling a little louder this time. Kids learn by example, so...

I throw my arms around Garrett, hugging him like I've done so many times. His arms, thick with muscle, strong with heart, embrace me. And like every other time I've hugged him, his arms feel like home.

"Thanks," he murmurs in my ear, his deep voice igniting a round of fireworks throughout my body. "I needed that."

"You're welcome," I murmur, holding on to him for a beat longer than is probably necessary to prove my point. Afraid to meet his eyes and risk him seeing how I really feel about him.

I step away and glance down at Peony. She's not paying attention to us, engrossed with putting each of her stuffed animals on the couch, one by one. So much for that idea.

"Bye-bye, Peony," Athena says, moving away from the couch.

Peony turns long enough to wave and grin at her, seemingly not at all worried that Athena's leaving her with me.

The garage door clicks shut behind Athena and Garrett, and I lower to the floor to play with Kenda's daughter. I have so many questions I want to ask her about her mama. So many things I want to know about Kenda's final days.

But even if I did dare ask Peony, she's only eighteen months old. She doesn't have the communication skills to tell me everything I want to know.

Only Athena can tell me, but there's something about her I can't put my finger on. Something I can't quite puzzle out. It's like there's a wall between us. A wall that is completely her doing, but I don't know what's compelled her to erect it.

Oh, I don't know, maybe it has something to do with her moving to a small town where she doesn't know anyone?

Or maybe it has something to do with her losing her employer and friend to the senselessness of gun violence.

BEYONCÉ'S RICH VOICE FLOWS FROM THE SPEAKERS AS PEONY AND I dance to "Spirit." My body is less stiff now than it was while I was reading to her on the couch. My hips and lower-back muscles were so tight, I could barely push to a stand without wincing.

Peony giggles and bounces on the spot, Poppy tucked in the crook of her arm. My feet and arms move in time to the beat, the words and music reaching down to my soul. The low light streaming through the windows wraps me in nature's spotlight. I laugh.

I close my eyes, embracing the First Lady of Music's lyrics, and lift my arms above my head. A sharp pain slams my shoulders at the movement, and I grimace, dropping my arms to my sides.

"Nina!" Peony rushes toward the entrance to the living room.

Athena scoops her up, and Peony loops her arms around her neck, almost strangling her. Athena laughs and kisses her cheek. Not once does Peony acknowledge her father, who walked into the living room behind Athena.

"How did it go?" Garrett asks me, smiling as if Peony's snub doesn't hurt, but his eyes tell me otherwise. The bruise of emotion is slight, the wisp of a cloud. Recognizable only to those who know him well.

Lie to him. Reassure him Peony reacts to you the same way she does him.

But I can't lie to him. He needs my help with her so he can focus on his book when Athena is off duty. During those times his mother can't help out. And I love spending time with Peony. Love spending time with the only link I have left to Kenda.

I pick up my phone from the coffee table and stop Beyoncé midsong. "It went great. We had a lot of fun. Didn't we, Peony?"

At her name, she turns in Athena's arms and grins at me. I

take a step forward. The urge to kiss her on the forehead, like Mama did when I was little, flickers in my chest.

I then catch the look in Athena's eyes—a look heavily laced with jealousy or annoyance or resentment—and it's enough to snuff out the urge.

Or maybe her reaction is just my imagination, triggered by grief. And at knowing that Kenda had kept Peony's existence a secret from both Garrett and me.

"How did the self-defense lesson go?" Or am I better off not knowing?

Athena's hair is messier than it was when she left. An I've-been-freshly-fucked messy. It's also damp around her hairline.

"It was good. Garrett didn't go easy on me, which was great."

"You're a fast learner." Garrett smiles at her like she's his prized student. *Oh, God, did they make out?*

Please tell me they didn't make out.

"Yeah, he's not known for going easy. My body was sore for a week after he taught me moves." I was also highly turned-on during our lessons, which had left me wanting to dry-hump him while he was on top of me, my body pressed into the mat.

Needing to get out of here before I can torture myself any further, I say goodbye to Peony and Athena and walk to the front door. Garrett comes with me.

"You want to tell me your secret?" he asks, escorting me to my car. The golden sunlight bathes the driveway and a narrow strip of the flower bed alongside it in a warm glow. The trees and bushes create shadows over the rest of the ground.

"My secret?" The question comes out on a choked squeak. Which secret? The one where I've been secretly in love with him since college?

"Yes. Your secret. How did you get Peony to accept you? It's obvious she'd prefer it if I disappeared." His tone isn't bitter or sad. It's hopeful. Hopeful I have the magic equation he's searching for.

"I don't think there is any secret to it. You told me she's scared of your brothers and father. One of my employees adopted a kitten last year who was scared of men. It had been abandoned in a dumpster, and the vet figured a man may have dumped her in there, and that's why she was scared of men."

The corner of Garrett's mouth tilts up. "So you think a man dumped my daughter in a dumpster, and that's why she's scared of me?"

I playfully punch him in his rock-hard stomach. "No, silly. But the explanation makes sense. A man killed her mama. Maybe she generalized that to mean all men are dangerous. They're all someone to fear."

"That's what I thought, but...I don't know." He rubs his neck. He's a man who's often in motion when he's stressed, who paces, who gardens, who moves. It speaks volumes about our friendship—I try not to resent the word too much—that he's okay being still with me. "Did your employee's kitten ever get over her fear of men?"

"Eventually. But I don't think Peony is scared of you. Not anymore. She didn't seem scared this time. Just...um..."

"Indifferent?"

I nod. "Which is good. It means she's progressing. I'm positive things will improve soon." I reach for his hand and lightly squeeze it. "Keep making her feel loved and protected, and you'll get there, Garrett."

I press my front teeth into my bottom lip, wondering if I have the right to ask the next question. I probably don't, but I have to know. "Is there something going on between you and Athena?" Dread splits the words down the middle, a flash of lightning ready to ignite everything in its path. To burn me with the truth.

Garrett chuckles. "Odd thing to say."

"I know. I'm just...curious."

"What exactly are you asking?" His raised eyebrow tells me he isn't all that clueless of the implication behind my question.

"Are you hooking up with her?"

A laugh rumbles low in his chest. Our bodies aren't touching, but that doesn't prevent the sound from vibrating through my body. "There's nothing to be curious—or jealous—about." A teasing smirk tilts the corner of his mouth.

"I'm not jealous." I roll my eyes as if the idea of me being jealous is preposterous.

"She's my daughter's nanny. An employee. Nothing more."

It's on the tip of my tongue to mention the single-father-nanny romance trope, but I think I'll save myself from having that embarrassing conversation. "Okay. Not that it's any of my business if you two hook up." *Shut up, Zara.*

I open my car door. "Peony is going to realize soon just how incredible you are, Garrett. You have to keep believing that." I reach up to give him a friendly peck on the cheek.

Except Garrett turns his head at that precise second, and my lips accidentally brush his. His subtle mountain-fresh scent lassoes me, keeps me from pulling away.

I stay motionless for a beat, breathing him in, stunned at how soft his lips are. Stunned at how my lips tingle from the touch, how my heart beats faster than hummingbird wings.

A bird caws loudly from somewhere nearby, sending a wave of reality crashing over me, endlessly questioning what the hell I'm doing. I jerk away. "Oops. Sorry. Didn't mean to do that."

I duck into the driver's seat before he can ask me why the fuck I kissed him. Or before he lets me know how he's not into me like that.

I turn over the engine and reverse out of the driveway, not once daring to meet his eyes.

22

ZARA

M y phone alarm chirps from the bedside table, cheerfully telling me to get my ass out of bed. I will myself to move and turn off the noise, but my arm is now heavy, immovable concrete. And it aches.

Fuck, my entire body aches.

That's nothing new. But the intensity of the pain is stronger than usual, as if I had traveled at high speed and slammed into a brick wall. The flu? No, it doesn't feel like the flu. I just don't feel...right. It's like fog has rolled into my head overnight. The fog of exhaustion that hits after I've spent the night tossing and turning, trying to get comfortable.

Chirp. Chirp-chirp-chirp. Chirp.

Someone...anyone...please turn off my alarm.

No magical beings heed my wish, and I inch my arm from under the cover, kill the noise with the tap of a finger. But that's as far as things progress in terms of getting up.

I lie motionless in bed, like roadkill, eyes closed, waiting for my mental cheerleader to wave her pompoms in my face. To *rah-rah* at me to get going. But she's having a nap, and I can't find it in me to move even a fraction of an inch.

My thoughts drift to five days ago, to last Thursday, and the kiss with Garrett that wasn't a kiss. I can't stop thinking about it.

I can guarantee, though, Garrett hasn't replayed it like I have. Why would he?

He certainly didn't bring it up Friday night—thank the Lord —when he showed up for Game Night. He seemed his usual self—other than being a little stressed. But that wasn't surprising with everything he has on his plate. He didn't stay long. Forty minutes at most.

No, Garrett hasn't given the kiss a second thought.

Now, if only *I* could stop thinking about it.

A hot shower. That's what I need. A hot shower and ibuprofen and then I'll be fine. I have lots to do today, including getting the space that was formerly Mountain Lore ready for the renovation. That's why my body aches so much. I hung brown paper on the windows and the entrance to the store last night, so people can't see the work being done before I'm ready to reveal it.

And now my body is paying the price.

Are you positive that's what it is?

Ignoring the whispered voice in my head, I focus on the large painting on the wall of five women, dancing in brightly-colored traditional dress, and draw strength from it. I push up to sit and slowly swing my legs over the side of the bed.

I sit like that for a moment, searching for the additional inner strength needed to get up. Once I find what I'm looking for, I shift my body weight forward until I'm on my feet and slowly unfold to my full height, my joints moving like rusty metal. My hips, the base of my spine, and my shoulders are stiffer than normal. Even my neck and knees seem more pissed off at me than usual.

Ibuprofen. Hot shower. In that order.

I shuffle to the bathroom, the stiffness easing slightly, like it does every morning. But usually, I'm a lot less stiff by the time I get there.

Why the hell does my body feel like it belongs to someone twice my age?

Dr. Cole initially mentioned, if the symptoms didn't disappear in three months, I should schedule another appointment with her. It's been a lot longer than that since I last saw her. Maybe...maybe the ache has nothing to do with an overuse injury like I've been assuming.

I fill the glass on the counter with cold water, swallow the ibuprofen, and switch my bonnet for the shower cap. Once the shower water is hot enough, I carefully climb into the bathtub. Then I stand under the stream of hot water and wait for the benefits to kick in.

SITTING ON THE MEDICAL-EXAM TABLE, I CHECK THE SOCIAL media accounts for Picnic & Treats while I wait for Dr. Edwards to enter the room. Dr. Cole, my usual family physician, is away for the week due to a family emergency, but the clinic was able to fit me in today with her temporary replacement. I remember Dr. Evelyn Edwards from the last time I saw her. I liked her, so I'm good with seeing her instead of Dr. Cole—who I also like and admire.

Someone knocks on the closed door. It opens before I can say, "Come in."

But it's not Dr. Evelyn Edwards who steps into the small room. It's a man whose skin is a shade darker than skim milk. He looks to be in his early sixties, his tall frame less muscle than mass. His thinning gray hair is short on the sides and missing on top of his head, which shines in the stark overhead lighting.

"Hello, Ms..." He types on the computer keyboard next to the exam table. "Thompson. I'm Dr. Shane Edwards." He looks back at the computer screen. "It says you're dealing with pain that hasn't gone away since it started five months ago." He slides the rolling stool away from the exam table and sits facing me.

"That's right." I describe the shoulder pain that has been coming and going over the past five years, and how I started to have pain in the base of my spine and my hips and knees at the beginning of the year. How the pain has its ups and downs, but it was especially bad this morning when I woke up. "I thought it was the result of my job, but I've been careful with how I lift heavy objects. Now I'm not so sure it's an overuse injury."

"I agree. At this point, I question if it is one, especially because it involves more than one joint." He spends the next few minutes examining me, checking for swelling, redness, and warmth around the affected joints—signs of inflammation—as well as testing my reflexes and muscle strength. "It's possible you're dealing with early symptoms of rheumatoid arthritis," he says once he's finished the examination and his questions.

I stare at him blankly. *Arthritis?*

"I'll make a referral for you to see a rheumatologist to confirm things and to decide the next course of action. Their office will contact you shortly with the appointment. For now, take things easy, rest as much as possible, and continue taking the ibuprofen. I can prescribe a stronger painkiller if you'd like."

Dr. Edwards's words repeat in my brain like a loud, never-ending echo. *Arthritis. I might have rheumatoid arthritis.* "That's okay. I'll manage." The pain and stiffness isn't as bad as it was this morning. And I'd rather not rely on stronger painkillers. I don't like how they make me feel.

I focus on his recommendations. Rest? Take things easy? How the hell am I supposed to do that now that I'm renovating the space next door? The expansion—it's my dream. I can't give up on that now. But I also don't have the luxury of spending more money on the renovations to get someone else to do the tasks I'd planned to do.

I thank him, pay for the visit, and return to Picnic & Treats, my thoughts on his recommendations.

"Anything happen while I was away?" I ask Keshia, not alluding to where I just came from. She's measuring flour into the industrial mixer.

I didn't tell anyone I had a doctor's appointment. Everyone is like family here, but that doesn't mean I want to dump my health problems on them.

Arthritis. I might have rheumatoid arthritis. I don't know a whole lot about the disease, other than the few things I've heard—mostly that you don't want to get it. The disease is a nightmare.

"Nope. Everything's been good. I'm just making another batch of caramel brownies. The first batch went so quickly, and the girls out front are getting lots of requests for them." She's practically bouncing on the spot at this news.

I smile, the movement genuine and effortless despite what Dr. Edwards told me a short time ago.

I can't tell her that I'm getting a referral to a rheumatologist. I don't want anyone to know what's going on with my body. The brain fog from this morning has disappeared. The achiness and stiffness have returned to their normal daytime level.

And I have way too much to do to waste time taking a break.

"That's great. We'll have to add them to the regular offerings. I'll let you get back to it. If you need anything, I'll be next door, dismantling the shelves," I tell her and head for the staff room. I have jeans and a T-shirt on, so I lock my purse in my desk drawer and get to work.

I step into the old store. The wall that divides this space with P&T will eventually be torn down, but not until most of the other renovations have been completed. Otherwise, I'd have to close P&T for longer than I want while the renovations are being done.

My phone vibrates in my pocket, and I check who's texted.

> Garrett: Want to come over this evening?
> And go with Peony and me to the
> playground?

> Garrett: I told Athena that she's taking the
> evening off. No arguments.

I smile, typing out my reply.

> Me: And you need someone to go with
> you who Peony trusts? [smiley face
> emoji]

My smile fades, the truth of the words squeezing my heart like a chew toy being mauled. Peony showed up in Maple Ridge almost two weeks ago, and she still hasn't warmed up to Garrett. And neither has Athena when it comes to me. It's not like she's being cold to me. She comes off friendlier than that. Friendly enough that Garrett doesn't seem to notice anything is off.

> Garrett: That's partly it. And I haven't
> seen you since Friday.

> Me: That's only because you and your
> brothers were away.

On their first Wilderness Warriors excursion of the season.

> Me: What time are you taking her to the
> playground?

I've missed both him and Peony, so there's no question about me joining them. They're the distraction I need from Dr.

Edwards's earlier words about my possible rheumatoid arthritis diagnosis.

Garrett: 6 p.m.

Me: Okay. I'll drop by your house then. Now get back to work. No more using me for procrastination. [silly face emoji]

Garrett: Yes, ma'am.

I snicker, and my thoughts shift in a new direction. To the accidental kiss. *Nope. Nope-nope-nope. Not happening.* With a *not-going-there* huff, I get to work removing the shelves from the walls...while not thinking about Garrett's lips on mine.

While not thinking about the way my body tingled in response to the kiss.

While not thinking about what it would feel like to kiss him once more but longer. Harder. Deeper.

Because what happened five days ago, when my lips accidentally touched his, can't happen again. He doesn't feel that way about me.

But what if he does?

I push the thought aside. He hasn't given me any reason to think there's anything else between us. And the last thing I want is to read into something that doesn't exist.

So. No more kissing Garrett.

Even if I want to.

23

GARRETT

My inbox pings with a new email notification. Zara is due here any minute, and I'm more than ready to take a short break from writing. The chapter I'm working on is an emotional, heart-stopping, breath-stealing rollercoaster.

Now that I have a daughter, who I already love and would do anything for, writing about a kidnapped child is emotionally draining. The story hits too close to home.

How would I feel if Peony were kidnapped? She might be indifferent toward me, but enough of her pieces have woven into my heart, if something happened to her, the organ would unravel, cease beating, turn to dust.

I shake my head, clearing the thought away, and check the inbox. My gut clenches. The email is from the lab that runs the paternity tests.

I take a deep breath and hover the mouse over the subject heading, my clicking finger suddenly paralyzed. *Are you ready to see what it says?*

Am I ready to find out if the girl who doesn't want to be my daughter really *is* my daughter? Or maybe the testing facility will make my life easier and tell me someone else is her father.

Then I can ship her and Athena off, and Peony and her distrust of me will no longer be my problem.

Except, what will happen to them? Does Athena have the name of another man whose doorstep she and Peony can show up on? Do they have a place they can call home? Hopefully if there is another guy, Peony accepts him, even though she hasn't accepted me.

Are you ready to know the truth?

Peony's giggles outside my office window tear my attention from the inbox. She and Athena are leaping from one stepping stone to the next, along the path weaving between the trees. Peony's coordination isn't there yet, and her leaping is more like stepping. But she doesn't seem to care. She loves the game, which they frequently play.

She steps onto the next stone and giggles again.

Am I ready?

I power off the laptop. I'll wait until I'm with Zara at the playground. For better or for worse, no matter what the results say, I need my best friend by my side when I read them.

My gaze returns to Peony, but my brain is no longer interested in dwelling on what the email might say. It revisits the same memory that has plagued me for the past five days.

Zara's kiss.

It happened so quickly, and it was an accident. I know that. But I can't stop thinking about it. Can't stop dwelling on the feel of Zara's lips on mine. I thought about it all weekend, when my focus was supposed to be on the veterans participating in the Wilderness Warriors camping trip.

I thought about it yesterday and today, when my focus was supposed to be on the damn book that's due to my editor in three months and eight days.

If I don't get the kiss out of my thoughts soon, I'll never finish the story.

I shove the air out of my lungs in a frustrated breath and push to my feet.

The doorbell rings, and I go answer it. I unlocked the door earlier, knowing Zara was coming over, but Athena must have relocked it.

Zara is standing on my front stoop in body-hugging black jeans and a bright-pink cardigan. The cardigan's neckline reveals the ripe, copper-brown swell of her breasts, and my mouth waters at the thought of running my tongue over them, tasting them.

Whoa. Where did that come from?

Eyes up, soldier. You're not supposed to be looking at her breasts.

"C'mon in. She's outside playing with Athena." I step aside to let Zara in. "I'll round her up." Whether Peony wants to listen to me is something else entirely.

She and Athena are making their way back to the house as Zara and I join them outside.

"Hey, little flower." The nickname slips out so easily. I have no idea if Peony hates it or not. She reacts the same way regardless of what name I use.

She looks up, and her face brightens. For a millisecond, I allow myself to believe the reaction is directed my way. "Za-wa." She doesn't give me another glance, doesn't notice the bubble of hope pop in my chest.

I should be used to it by now, but her reaction is a knee to the gut, a slap to the face. I have no clue how to gain her trust, how to get her to accept me. Sure, she no longer screams when I'm around, but it's hardly a ringing endorsement.

Peony rushes over to us, her little legs covering a surprising distance in such a short time.

She flings her arms around Zara's leg, and Zara laughs that rich sound that reaches into my soul. Just hearing it soothes some of the lacerations from Peony's indifference toward me. It's a kiss to the...

Goddammit, stop thinking about Zara's kiss.

It can't happen again.

Zara crouches next to Peony and strokes her cheek, brushing off a bit of smudged dirt. "I heard you and your daddy are going to the playground. Can I come too?"

Peony leans over Zara's thigh and wiggles as if to pull herself onto Zara's lap.

The sudden movement knocks Zara off balance, and she falls backward onto her ass, laughing. "I hope that's a yes."

"I think she wants you to carry her there." My words are strung together from a guess rather than actual knowledge of what Peony wants.

I look to Athena for conformation, but she doesn't notice. She's watching Zara and Peony, her face paler than normal. I shrug it off. It must be my imagination, brought on by stress, that she looks like she's seen a ghost from her past.

"I can do that." Zara adjusts Peony to straddle her hip and starts to stand, using her free hand for balance. But it's as if her legs refuse to cooperate, and she can't quite push herself to her feet as she staggers upright.

My arm goes around her waist, keeping her steady, and I help her stand. "You okay?" I don't let go of her, the solid warmth of her in my arms tugging back the memories of her lips on mine.

"Yeah, I'm fine. Just a little stiff from removing the shelves this afternoon."

I frown. "Your shoulders are hurting again?" If you ask me, her shoulders aren't the only things that are causing her problems if she's having trouble standing.

"They're not bad."

"Which means they *are* hurting." I look at Peony, who's watching me with wide eyes, but I have no idea what she's thinking. She doesn't seem scared of me this time, but I can't be sure. Her opinion of me changes so frequently. "Maybe I should carry her to the playground."

Zara's gaze flicks briefly to Athena, then to me. The tiniest frown divots between her eyebrows, but it's probably only noticeable to me. "I really will be fine, Garrett. Promise."

"I can carry her," Athena offers, her words coming out in a rush.

"No, you're off for the rest of the evening," I remind her. "Other than to help me get Peony to bed."

I've made progress establishing a regular routine for Peony over the past few days, but I rely on Athena to put her to bed. We're nowhere near the point where Peony will let me do it.

"Can I carry you, Peony?" I hold out my arms to her.

Peony buries her face into the side of Zara's breast, which is answer enough.

Athena hands me Peony's cardigan with tiny daisies embroidered on it that was hanging on the back of the wrought-iron chair. "In case she gets cold." She chews on the inside of her bottom lip. "Are you sure I can't come with you? I don't have to come as the nanny. I could come as a family friend."

"You're with Peony pretty much all day. You need a break."

She rapidly shakes her head. "I honestly don't need a break. I enjoy spending time with her."

"Maybe it would be good for Peony to have a break from you for a little bit," Zara says, not at all unkindly. "It will give her a chance to get to know her father without using you as her security blanket to avoid him."

From the way Athena's eyes widen, it's obvious she heard something different in Zara's words than I did. But what Zara said makes sense.

Athena's gaze implores me not to side with Zara, begs me in a thousand different ways to let her join us.

But I won't be swayed. I trust Athena with Peony—she hasn't given me a reason not to—but I trust Zara's instincts more. She might not be a mother, yet, or work with kids, but that doesn't matter. "Zara's right. Peony needs to learn she can rely on me and I will never hurt her."

Just a few more minutes. A few more minutes and I'll finally know the truth about my role in her creation.

My phone grows heavy in my pocket, the email holding the test results weighing it down.

Athena slowly nods. "Alright. I'll stay here." But she still doesn't seem convinced our going without her is a good idea.

Zara and I walk toward the playground Athena takes Peony to almost daily.

"You sure you're okay carrying her?" I ask Zara once we've walked past several houses. "She's not too much for your shoulder?"

"She's featherlight. Aren't you, Peony?" She bounces Peony in her arms.

Peony grins at her and reaches for the tree charm dangling from the chain around Zara's neck. She inspects it and says something in toddler talk.

"My grandmother gave it to me," Zara explains, as if answering a question I missed. Or maybe she understood Peony and it's only me who can't understand toddler talk.

Peony releases the charm and points to a ginger cat lounging on a nearby driveway. "Kitty!"

We stop walking. The cat slowly stretches to its paws, as if it has all day, and plods over to us. It curls its chubby body around Zara's leg.

"See kitty." Peony points at the cat again.

Zara lowers Peony to the ground. The cat meows and lets me stroke it, greedily soaking up the attention.

Peony crouches next to the cat and clumsily pats it. The cat purrs and rubs against her side.

Peony giggles and has what sounds like an animated conversation with the cat. I have no idea what she's saying, but her enthusiasm has me grinning.

Peony looks my way, and I pretend for a beat that her bright smile is directed at me. That she's happy to see me and not just delighted the cat's super friendly.

I expect her smile to vanish once she realizes I'm the recipient. But it doesn't. She says something I can't decipher and goes back to stroking the cat.

Her smile sends a shot of warmth winding through me. "I'll have to take you to visit Uncle Lucas and Auntie Simone soon. They have a cat named Snowball and a dog named Jasper."

Peony doesn't respond. She's too busy playing with her new friend.

After a minute or two, the cat loses interest and trots up the driveway to the house.

I'm tempted to see if Peony is okay with me carrying her the rest of the way to the playground, to give Zara's shoulders a longer rest. But in the end, I don't push my luck, even though I'm worried about Zara's shoulders. Toddler steps. That's what I need to do to win Peony's trust. But first...

"The lab sent me the paternity results," I tell Zara as she picks up Peony.

I help her stand, my arm around her waist...and for a second, the test results are forgotten and the memory of Zara's lips on mine floods in. My body pleads for me to kiss her again, to taste her once more, only this time for longer than a brief touch of our lips.

"So you're her father?" Zara starts walking, snapping my thoughts back to the email. "It's confirmed?"

I walk alongside her, positioning myself between Peony and the road. "I don't know. I haven't looked yet."

"What do you mean you haven't looked yet?" Skepticism draws out her vowels, surprise the *pièce de résistance* on top.

"I was waiting until you got here. I guess I...Kenda was your friend. And well, I didn't want to face the results on my own."

"Are you hoping she's your daughter?" Zara's words are spoken so softly I barely catch them.

"I'm hoping if she is my daughter, she'll give me a chance to be her father."

"And if she isn't? Then what? Hypothetically."

I shrug. Something tells me things will be complex even if the results are negative. Sure, I won't have to deal with Peony's indifference anymore, but it will leave the question of who her real father is and why Kenda lied. "I'll figure that out once I know for sure." That's as honest as I'm willing to be with myself and Zara.

We arrive to an empty playground. Zara slips Peony into the swing and gently pushes her.

Staring at my phone's Home screen, I pace on the artificial grass behind Zara. Do I look at the results now? Or wait until we're ready to go home?

She's my daughter. I know in my gut she's mine. So what's the problem?

Read. The. Email.

Zara glances at me over her shoulder. "Are you figuring out a plot problem or getting the courage to look at the results?"

Christ. I don't even want to think about the book. Not right now.

"I'm just warming up my clicking finger." I flick my index finger up and down, up and down, making a show of it.

Peony giggles and pumps her legs in the swing, but it looks more like she's running in the air. Usually, I find it funny when she does that, but now I can't even crack the smallest smile.

My mind flashes back to thoughts of Peony being kidnapped. *Shit.* Why did I think it was a great idea to write a thriller about a child kidnapping?

I stop pacing and push a hard breath from my lungs. Okay. Enough with the stalling.

Peony deserves to know the truth.

I walk to where Zara is still pushing her in the swing. Peony is chatting to Zara in toddler talk. My best friend answers as if she knows what the heck Peony is saying.

Zara takes my hand and gives it a light squeeze. Her fingers are soft against my calloused skin. "No matter what it says, I'm here for you, Garrett. In whatever way you need me to be."

I squeeze her hand in thanks and click open the email from the testing center.

The email contains a website link for the paternity results. I hover my finger over it. My palms grow slippery; my heart rate kicks up a notch, telling me not to be a chickenshit.

I click on the link, sign into my account, and skim to what I'm looking for. "She's definitely my daughter."

White-cold fear shoots through my veins, turning my legs boneless. *Christ*, how the hell can I be her father? I don't mean the mechanics of it. I know damn well *how* I knocked up Kenda the last time I saw her. But if I couldn't keep Cooper and Clarke alive, if I couldn't protect them, how am I supposed to keep a child happy and safe?

I shove the phone into my pocket and swallow down the fear, panic, helplessness in my throat. They don't budge. They cling like a cancerous growth. "I don't know the first thing about being a father."

"You'll learn." Zara's tone is the calm of a lighthouse beacon during a storm. "You're gonna be a great father. You *are* a great father." Her arms go around my shoulders, and she hugs me tight.

I loop her waist with my arms, pulling her close. Holding her like this feels so good but also so wrong. She's my best friend, and I can't afford to screw things up between us. Not now, when I need her the most. Not ever.

I release her and step away, ignoring my body's indignant rant to the tune of *What the hell is wrong with you?*

The toddler swing's momentum has slowed, and Peony is watching Zara and me with an expression I can't read. An expression beyond the frustrated crease of her brow at how the swing is no longer moving.

"Can I swing you?"

She doesn't reply, and I give the chair enough of a push to get it going again.

The frustration falls from her face, replaced with a smile. I don't kid myself this time into believing her toothy grin is directed at me.

Zara pats my arm in support. "Your daddy is great at pushing the swing, isn't he?"

A self-depreciating laugh rumbles from me. At least someone appreciates the skill I'm rocking. "Maybe this is my new superpower."

Zara chuckles. "Maybe. But I seem to remember you were good at pushing me on the swing when I couldn't figure out how to coordinate my body to get the swing moving."

She was seven at the time, and I could barely push her without landing on my ass every time.

"I was good at that, wasn't I, Golden Girl?" I gently shove her arm.

Her answering throaty laugh sends a rush of heat to my groin, and I silently curse my idiotic body.

24

———

GARRETT

Small, staccato barks come from one of the nearby houses. Three little kids under the age of five, who showed up at the playground a short time ago with their parents, run around the artificial grass, shouting and pretending to be airplanes.

Peony squats at the top of the little kids slide and drops onto her ass. Zara is up there with her, like she has been for the past seven times Peony slid down. The warm May breeze kisses the exposed skin on my arms and brushes a coil of Zara's hair against her cheek. *Lucky coil.*

Before Zara can get into position, with Peony on her lap, Peony twists so she's on her stomach. Like she saw one of the other kids do a few minutes ago.

"Wait a second, Peony," Zara says as she lowers her ass onto the slide platform.

But Peony doesn't wait. She wiggles her body far enough onto the slide for gravity to take over, and slowly slides, giggling, feet first. Her arms are stretched in front of her, pointing up the slide.

Unlike the previous seven times, when she slid down the

slide with Zara, I catch her as she gets to the bottom. I don't have a choice.

I hold my breath, bracing for her reaction. Hoping for the best. I'm pushing her boundaries just a little, testing if it will take us a step closer to her accepting me.

Taking care not to scare her, I scoop her up under the arms and swing her high in the air. Her resulting laughter is the sweetest thing.

Pride swells through me, temporarily replacing my earlier fear. She's my daughter. Really my daughter. She doesn't belong to some guy Kenda didn't want to see again or didn't want to be the father of her child. She's mine, and I plan to do everything in my power to be all she could ask for in a father.

Even though I have no clue what I'm doing.

"You ready to go home?" I ask Peony. "It's almost your bedtime." Right after Athena gives her a bath.

I lower her to the ground. I may have made some headway, but I can't assume she's fine with me carrying her yet. That won't help me gain her much-needed trust. She needs to be the one who chooses who carries her home.

Zara slowly slides down next, arms raised like she's on a roller coaster. "Wheeeeee!"

The earlier pride in me twists into something entirely new. For Zara. Her animated expression. The way she looks so free and joyful, her inner child coming out to play. All this combined...there's something just so freaking adorable and sexy about her like this.

And super comical.

Peony and I burst out laughing. Peony lifts her arms, mimicking Zara. "Wheeeeeee!" The action is made even cuter with her tiny, high-pitched voice.

Zara stands up at the bottom of the slide, her movements slightly halted, like it's taking her more effort than normal to straighten.

Shit. I'm not sure she can carry Peony all the way back.

I squat in front of my daughter. "Can I carry you home?" I hold my hands out to her, hoping she'll say yes, for Zara's sake.

She tentatively steps forward, possibly thinking through her options or trying to figure out what I asked her.

She takes another tentative step, and another, until she's standing in the space between my hands. Seeing that as a positive sign, I slowly close my hands around her waist, giving her a chance to change her mind. Watching her body language for any indication things are about to go south.

I ease out a relieved breath when she doesn't put up a fuss, and I carefully pick her up. Her legs straddle my waist, and I keep my arms protectively around her small frame. Holding her—my own flesh and blood—feels so right. So perfect.

Zara beams at us, as if Peony and I just won a gold medal in pairs skating.

I feel like I've won an Olympic gold medal. Or a Noble Peace Prize.

Only better.

"Have you talked to your physician or your father or Samuel about your shoulder pain?" I ask Zara as we walk to my house. I don't want her to ignore the pain any longer. Samuel, an ER physician, and her father aren't allowed to treat family members, but can't she check to see what they recommend she should do?

"I had a medical appointment this afternoon."

"And?"

Zara looks to the driveway where the ginger cat was earlier. It's not there now. "He said it's nothing to worry about. It will get better. I just need to give it more time."

A comfortable silence joins us on the walk, but it's not alone. An odd tension crackles in the air, whips around Zara and me, bringing with it the memory of her lips on mine.

Kiss her, a voice in my head commands, conveniently forgetting I'm carrying Peony.

No, I can't kiss Zara. She's my best friend. You don't kiss your best friend 'cause you get the urge to.

Besides, what happened the other day was an accident. Neither of us planned for it to occur. She leaned in to kiss my cheek as I happened to turn my head. It was the accidental brushing of lips. Nothing more.

Get over it.

A bird tweets from a branch in a nearby tree, as if agreeing with my assessment.

Peony points up at the branches. "Bird."

"That's right, a bird." A smile nestles in my tone.

"Fly!" Peony holds her arms out like wings preparing to take flight, her face bright with a toothy grin. The grin tugs on my heart, yanks at my soul. I honestly wasn't sure if I would ever see that smile of hers intentionally directed my way. And now I'm not sure I can look away. Afraid if I do, I'll never see that smile specifically for me again.

"Fly!" she repeats.

"You want to fly again?"

She bops her head, the toothy grin in full force.

"Okay." I adjust my hold on her and lift her above my head, then swoop her through the air as if she's flying.

She shrieks with delight, and her infectious giggles have Zara and me laughing alongside her. Christ, this moment is better than a golden sunrise after a cold and wet stormy night.

I carry her like this all the way to my driveway, my arms trembling slightly by the time we get there. My old CO would be disappointed. Clearly, I've been "slacking" on those killer runs with Kellan compared to when we were in the Marines.

I lower Peony to my waist. Her legs clamp around me with surprising strength, and the three of us stop next to the driver's door of Zara's car.

"So, you're happy with the test results?" Zara's eyes remain on mine, but she nods at Peony.

"Well, I'm glad I didn't buy her all that stuff only to find out Kenda lied. Am I scared stiff I'm now a single father?" I nod. "Whenever I thought about Kenda and I one day having babies together, not once did I imagine going it alone." Not once did I imagine her never getting to see them grow up.

"You don't have to go it alone," Zara says, the compassion in her eyes making it a little easier to breathe. "You've got your family, you've got me, and you've got Athena to help you out. Kenda might not be here anymore, but you aren't alone." Her gaze drops to my lips, and I feel myself lean in a minuscule amount.

Peony squirms in my arms, her interest in this conversation nonexistent, and points to the ground.

"I'd better let you two go." Zara waves goodbye to her. "Bye, Peony. Thank you for letting me play with you and your daddy." She climbs into her car.

I step away and watch her reverse out of the driveway.

I walk toward the front door, Peony in my arms. She's happily chatting again in the toddler language I haven't learned to decipher. Yet.

The door opens, and Athena steps out of the house, desperation wild in her eyes. "Oh, there you two are." A weak smile curves across her face, the panic in her eyes unwavering.

What exactly did she think would happen while we were gone? Sure, if I had taken Peony to the playground on my own, Athena would have had a reason to worry. But I wasn't alone. I was with Zara.

Peony stretches her arms out to her. "Nina!"

Athena doesn't wait for me to pass my daughter to her. She's removing her from my grasp before I realize what she's doing.

As soon as Peony is securely in her arms, the panic quickly

smooths from Athena's expression. "You ready for your bath and bedtime story?"

They step into the house, leaving me on the stoop wondering if I should join them for this part of the bedtime ritual.

Toddler steps.

Athena doesn't ask me to join them, so I head to my bedroom, change into sweatpants and a T-shirt, and return to my office to work for a bit while she gets Peony ready for bed. I'll say good night to her once they're finished. That's more than I've done since they moved in with me.

I settle in the wingback chair, reread where I last left off in the story, and type. But the words don't flow like I'd hoped they would. The endless memory of the kiss with Zara is blocking them.

Focus.

The next few paragraphs flow like I'm milking frozen blood from a rock. By the time I stop to check on Peony, I've barely typed out a page...double-spaced.

The memory of the kiss, Zara's soft lips against mine, has yet to let me go.

Heaving out a disgruntled breath because I'm getting nowhere with the chapter, I put my laptop on the desk and walk down the hallway to Peony's room. Peony is in bed, hugging Poppy and listening to Athena read Peony's favorite book to her.

I lean on the doorjamb, waiting for them to finish. Peony's animated expression while she listens to the story has me smiling. She really does love that book.

Athena closes it and sets it on the bedside table. The book is the same one they were reading the day I found them on my doorstep almost two weeks ago. The same one I've seen Athena read to her so many times, I'm surprised the board book hasn't fallen apart.

Athena kisses Peony on the forehead. "Sweet dreams."

I want to let Peony know with more than just words she's my daughter, but we're a long way from that point. One day. Maybe one day she'll let me kiss her forehead too.

I walk to Peony's bed and pat her panda on the head, a little at a loss at what to do. I'm not the one who puts her to bed every night. I'm not the one who reads her a bedtime story. I'm not the one who tucks her in and checks under her bed for monsters. And I'm not the one who says good night to her and kisses her on the forehead. For the past two weeks, I've simply let Athena do those things. It was easier that way, given Peony's opinion of me.

But maybe that needs to change. Maybe I need to be the one who does all those things for my daughter.

Soon. Once I'm positive she has accepted me and what happened this evening, at the playground, wasn't a one-time thing. Then I can fully jump into my role as her father.

"Good night, Poppy. Good night, little flower." I wave to them.

A shy smile sneaks into Peony's expression, and she buries her face in Poppy's fur.

She turns her head a fraction, peering at me with those big, pretty brown eyes, her smile still in place.

A small amount of relief rushes through me, bringing with it a rainbow of hope. Her new opinion of me hasn't slipped down the drain in the short time we've been home. We have a chance of being the family Kenda had wished for—minus the part about Kenda being in it.

I leave the bedroom but wait in the hallway for Athena.

She says good night one more time to Peony, turns off the bedroom light, and steps out of the room. She doesn't close the door fully, even though a baby monitor sits in the room in case Peony calls out in the middle of the night.

Athena startles, clearly not expecting to find me waiting for her.

"That book? Any reason she keeps asking for it?" I've seen Athena read to her the other picture books, but nowhere near as often as that one.

"It reminds her of her mama. Kenda read the story to her whenever...she just read it a lot."

Fair enough.

My thoughts slip back to the high I'd felt when Peony let me carry her at the playground. They then flip to the kiss with Zara. It's no wonder my words are coming out sluggishly. I'm too distracted to write. My thoughts are everywhere, other than where they need to be: on the book.

I need to take a break and go see Zara. Just for a few minutes.

That should straighten my mind out.

"I'm going out. I won't be long," I tell Athena. "Then I'll be up late working. Do you need anything before I head out?"

"No, I'm good. Let me know if you want me to make you a late-night snack. I can do that."

"Unless Peony needs you, you're off duty for the rest of the night."

The only time Peony has needed Athena during the night is when Peony wakes up from a nightmare. I doubt we're near the point yet where she'll let me comfort her after she wakes from a bad dream.

I add *Find a child psychologist* to my mental to-do list. It doesn't take a genius to figure that the nightmares are the result of seeing her mother shot. But I have no idea where to find someone qualified in that department. I can't ask for recommendations at the Veterans Center.

I grab my wallet and keys on my way to the garage and head to Zara's building. I park in Visitor Parking and walk to the main entrance. One of the residents who knows I'm a friend of

Zara is leaving the building, and he holds the door open for me.

"Thanks," I tell him and head for the staircase. The elevator was recently repaired, but I prefer taking the stairs, especially when restlessness plagues me, like now.

I jog up to the fourth floor. But as I pull open the door, a craving to kiss Zara hits. And it grows stronger the closer I get to her apartment.

Is that the real reason I wanted to come here tonight? Because I need to get the craving out of my system, otherwise I won't be able to focus on the book?

I stop at her door and knock.

Christ, I hope she's home.

25

ZARA

I step out of the hot shower, my body less achy now than after I got home from the playground.

A cold shower might have been better—what with how I can't stop thinking about how much I want to kiss Garrett. Even after I'd come to terms with how Kenda and Garrett were a couple, I had never fully moved on. My feelings for him have dialed up a notch over the past few years.

And then Garrett and I accidentally kissed.

Ugh. Stop thinking about it.

I wipe away the steam on the mirror, revealing my makeup-free face. "Garrett isn't interested in you that way," I tell the reflection. "He's not interested in kissing you. We're just friends." That's all.

I remove the shower cap and pull on my sleep shorts and T-shirt.

Yes, my body might have almost convinced me at his house that he was interested in me in the same way I want him. I'd thought he was leaning in for another kiss, and my body had been on board for that.

But my brain? My brain knew better. This is Garrett we're

202

talking about. He wasn't jealous I was dating Joseph. If he feels the same way toward me that I feel for him, wouldn't he have been jealous? Even a little?

Heaving out a you've-got-to-get-over-Garrett huff, I walk out the bathroom and head for the living room. The world outside the window is dark now, but the tall lamp by the wall casts the space in a cozy glow. Since my apartment faces the mountains and not another building, I leave the curtains open and pick up my book from the coffee table.

I make myself comfy on the couch and start reading the romance novel from where I left off.

A rapping on my apartment door startles me during a particularly spicy scene in the book. No one buzzed to get into the building, so it's probably sweet Mrs. Lindsay from down the hall. I'm not exactly dressed for visitors, but she won't care. It's not the first time she has come to my apartment because she was lonely and wanted someone to talk to.

I unfold from the couch, my body having grown stiff again, the benefit of the hot shower diminishing.

The stiffness loosens a little by the time I make it to the door. The rapping comes once more, and I open the door without looking through the peephole first.

I *really* should have looked through the peephole first.

The last person I expected to see is standing in my doorway, looking breath-stealing as always. He has changed into a pair of gray sweatpants and one of his old Marine T-shirts that show off his very fine specimen of a body.

I try not to drool—because that would be awkward.

"Hi?" I reverse a step into the apartment, letting Garrett in. He shuts the door behind him.

Something is slightly off about him. It's the look I've seen in his eyes when he's feeling unsettled, moments before he starts pacing. "I think we need to kiss again." He says it so straightforwardly, like it's a fact. Like the moon orbits the Earth; the Earth revolves around the sun.

"Er..." is the only answer I can formulate.

I'm not sure kissing again is a good idea. My heart might not be able to come back from that.

I might be thinking those things, but my mouth doesn't want to put voice to the words. My heart stutters and my lips part a fraction of an inch.

Without meaning to, I close the gap between us. The heat of his body, the scent of his soap, caress me with a whisper. Encourage me. Beckon me. Plead for me not to walk away.

I lean in a little more, until there's hardly space between us, and lick my suddenly dry lips. I should pull away, shouldn't give in to my body's craving.

Garrett's eyes track the movement, the rich brown of his irises growing darker. It feels like he's reaching inside me, searching for secrets hidden within my soul. Sifting through the debris left after he picked one of my close friends instead of me.

My breath shudders and stumbles; my breasts heave. The tips of my nipples graze Garrett's chest, the touch light but enough to cause them to sensually tighten. I bite back a moan.

We still for a heartbeat, and I absorb every second of this moment. Then Garrett erases the remaining distance, and his lips meet mine.

The kiss lasts longer than the accidental brushing of lips, but he pulls away before I can let him in.

I really want to let him in.

He stares at me for a beat, and his gaze drops to my T-shirt. The T-shirt I forgot I was wearing...without a bra. The T-shirt that is thinner than the ones I wear outside my apartment—and is showing off my now taut nipples.

A light blush creeps across Garrett's face, and he reverses a step, his eyes flicking up to mine. "I...I should go." He gropes for the doorknob and yanks the door open.

I fold my arms across my chest, praying this moment can't get any more awkward. Clearly, Garrett didn't enjoy the kiss. As far as he's concerned, it was a mistake and he can't get away fast enough.

But while he might have thought it was a mistake, my body has a different opinion. Every inch of my skin tingles with unleashed electricity. Every inch of my skin craves to be touched the way my lips were. A slow exploration. A lit match to the fuse.

"It was nice seeing you again," I say lamely and watch him disappear into the stairwell.

26

ZARA

Ten days after the kiss Garrett couldn't escape fast enough from, I'm sitting fully clothed on the exam table and waiting for the rheumatologist to return.

Ten days of Garrett and me pretending he didn't drive to my apartment and kiss me. Pretending the three times we saw each other—which was never just the two of us alone—I wasn't disappointed the kiss hadn't been more than the brushing of lips. That our tongues hadn't become intimately acquainted.

My brain is still spinning from Dr. Holmes's barrage of questions about the pain and other symptoms, like if I have abdominal pain or psoriasis or tenderness over my joints. So many questions. Questions I hope result in an answer as to what is causing my body to be bitchy.

The door opens, and the rheumatologist walks into the room. He looks to be in his early sixties, with the remanence of a faded tan. He parks himself on the rolling stool, his face giving nothing away. I could be dying of a terminal disease and wouldn't know it based on his expression.

I don't say anything. I just wait for the ax to fall. Or not fall.

"Zara, the results are nonconclusive. You are negative for

206

HLA-B27, so you don't have Ankylosis Spondylitis. I didn't think that would be the case. You said you first felt the pain in your shoulders. AS focuses on the spine, and there was no sign of it in your X-rays. There are several other disorders that could be causing the pain, but at this point, we don't have any definitive answers. Your symptoms could be the result of rheumatoid arthritis, as Dr. Edwards suggested. It's too early to know with certainty."

Wonderful. I drove all the way to Eugene and still don't have any answers. The only thing I have accomplished from this trip is getting farther behind on my to-do list.

"I recommend increasing the daily dose of the NSAID you're taking or alternating between NSAIDs, so the pain doesn't interfere too much with your quality of life." He goes on to explain how best to go about this. "Make a follow-up appointment for six months on your way out, and we'll check where things are progressing at that point. We'll redo the X-rays and blood work to see if anything has changed in the meantime. How does that sound to you?"

"Okay," I reply, biting back my growing frustration at the grumbling pain and the increasing discomfort from sitting on the exam table. I just want to get off the damn thing.

"Most importantly," he continues, "listen to your body. If it tells you to rest, then do. If things progress in a way that interferes with your daily activities, you can talk to an occupational therapist for ways to better cope."

Interferes with my daily activities? An occupational therapist?

Just how much of my life and business is this *whatever I've got* going to disrupt? I shift, desperate to relieve the pain in my back and hips and shoulders. Desperate to return to Picnic & Treats.

I make an appointment with the receptionist and head out to my car. The drive to Eugene and sitting in the medical office increased the stiffness in my body. It's the same as it was when I got up this morning.

I groan at the idea of driving home to Maple Ridge, but I don't have a choice.

An hour. That's how long the drive is. I can survive that. I have to survive it. I've got a café and renovations to return to. I can't take the entire day off. I've wasted enough time here as it is.

Rest? That was what Dr. Edwards and Dr. Holmes told me I need to do during those times my body is having a fit. How the hell am I supposed to rest? I have too much to do.

On the drive to Maple Ridge, I focus on the mountains ahead, using them as the marker for my progress instead of the mileage on my odometer. Green fields stretch out in all directions on either side of the highway.

Twenty minutes into the drive, I approach the tail end of what appears to be barely-moving traffic. *Fuck. Fuck. Fudgedy-cake. Fuck.* There wasn't construction on the highway during the drive to Eugene, which means there's been an accident.

If I'm lucky, it isn't too far ahead, and it won't take long to pass it.

If I'm lucky—but that doesn't seem to be the case. The traffic inches along, which is better than us not moving at all. But the longer we inch at a sloth's pace, the more my previous hope that this won't take long sinks, and the more I shift in my seat, trying to get comfortable.

I haven't had issues with the car seat until now. The discomfort must be due to the rheumatoid arthritis or whatever is causing my body to fail me.

Megan Thee Stallion comes up next on my playlist. I crank up the volume. If I'm going to be squirming to get comfortable, might as well do it to the beat of "HISS."

I dance to the song, rapping the lyrics along with her, not

caring what the people in the car behind me or beside me think.

I might be seated, but that doesn't stop me from using my whole body as I dance, swaying, wiggling, sashaying. The traffic is barely moving, so I won't cause an accident.

I don't know what it is about Megan Thee Stallion, but the rhythm of her voice is pure magic. The pain in my back and hips eases a few notches, and I don't feel so inclined to scream in frustration due to the discomfort and delay.

That quickly changes ten minutes later, when I realize the traffic is being rerouted, and the detour will add an additional hour to my drive to Maple Ridge.

By the time I finally arrive at P&T, my body, especially my neck, shoulders, and hips are screaming in pain. Megan Thee Stallion can only do so much if you're rerouted and your body hates the idea of that. Megan Thee Stallion can only do so much if you have to pay attention to the road without moving your body to her beat.

My back throbs. Pain slices through my shoulders. Fire blazes along my arms. I park in my employee spot near the building and rest my forehead on the steering wheel. I close my eyes against the pain, tears welling up.

Get moving. Things always feel a little better once you're moving, once the stiffness lessens.

I inhale slowly through my nose, attempting to chase away the pain. It doesn't work, but it does help strengthen my resolve to get my ass in gear.

I tentatively climb out of the driver's seat and slowly zombie-walk to the building's back entrance. The fewer people who see me in this state, the fewer questions I'll have to deflect.

It takes a lifetime and a half before I arrive at my destination. I lift my keys, my shoulders screaming, unlock the door, and step inside. The busy sounds—the chatter and the laughter—from the main part of the café greet me.

That sound is the reason I love what I do. This place, my life's work, helps bring joy to people. Even if it's just the simple joy that comes from eating one of our desserts or a tasty meal.

I walk to the staff room and remove the bottle of ibuprofen from my desk drawer. I take two tablets with the remaining water in the glass on my desk. I'd left it there when I rushed out to drive to my appointment.

I lock my purse in the bottom drawer, grab the pair of jeans and a T-shirt I have stashed in my locker, and walk across the hallway to the washroom. I click the lock on the door in place and change out of my clothes.

The stiffness in my joints makes it more challenging to get in and out of my pants. I have to lean against the door to maintain my balance. I mutter a few colorful curses in my head.

Once the jeans are on, I pause for an elongated moment, catching my breath, my head resting on the door. *I've got this.*

I plaster on a smile that hopefully isn't as fragile as it feels. Joesph's words from the night we broke up slither into my head, coil around my resolve.

"The woman claims she has chronic pain...the rest of us have to pick up her slack."

No one knows—other than Garrett—I'm dealing with this. No one suspects I might have rheumatoid arthritis, and I want to keep it that way. For as long as possible.

I don't want people to think I'm not capable of doing my job, to feel like they need to pick up my "slack." And I don't want anyone to know how much I'm struggling.

This, whatever it is, won't define me.

What I'm doing with P&T, what I'm doing for the community, what I'm doing to help support the women-owned small businesses in the area, those are what define me.

I zombie-walk down the hallway toward the counter at the front of the café. Too bad it isn't Halloween. Then I could pretend my awkward gait is part of my costume.

I might be able to plaster a smile on my face and fool everyone, but how can I make it look like I'm walking normally?

And how the hell am I supposed to work on the expansion today when my body doesn't want to cooperate? But if I don't work on it, Troy's crew will have to do it, and that will put everyone behind schedule and add to my expenses. That's why I had opted to do some of it myself.

Anastasia and Clara are busy serving customers at the counter. I wave and smile at the three regulars crowding the countertop to place their orders. They return the smile and wave, like members of the family they've become. The P&T family.

My smile widens at how important every member of this family is to me. They are what gets me out of bed in the morning when my body is temporarily uncooperative. Their smiles brighten my days, even when I'm not feeling anywhere close to a hundred percent.

Dr. Edwards and Dr. Holmes told me I need to rest whenever my body demands it. I was technically resting on the drive to Maple Ridge, and that didn't seem to help my hips or back or knees in the slightest. They're still grouchy. Still pissed at being forced to endure the ride.

Anastasia turns and meets my gaze. "Hey, you're back."

"I just got here. And now I'm going next door to work on the expansion. Do you two need anything?"

"No, we should be good for now. Have fun."

I chuckle. She makes it sound like I'm spending my afternoon at Disneyland. "Will do."

I head for the kitchen and check how things are going with Jess and Keshia.

"We're good, other than we're getting low on the pumpkin curry," Keshia tells me. "It's been extremely popular today."

"Wow, that's great. Guess word got out I added it to the rotating menu last week. I'll make more before I go next door." I grab the ingredients and start chopping the vegetables and preparing the food. My body quickly gets into the flow, my motor memory kicking in.

My hips sway to Keshia's show-tune playlist. My movements become less jerky, less robotic as one song merges into the next.

The pain and stiffness don't entirely diminish, but they do eventually become less crippling. It doesn't hurt that I'm doing something I love. Cooking is my source of comfort, the thing that relaxes me—whether I'm at home or at Picnic & Treats.

With the curry simmering on the stove, I go next door.

I pick up the sledgehammer—my earbuds secure in my ears, my helmet and goggles on—and I swing at what remains of the counter. The sisters who bought the business took the glass shelves, so I just need to remove what's left.

My body falls into the satisfying rhythm of swinging the sledgehammer in time to Aalia singing "Do It to Me."

As she sings of golden kisses, my thoughts drift to Garrett and the kiss from ten days ago. The way his lips moved against mine...and mine shamelessly, soundlessly begged for more. The way my body was left humming for the rest of the night, so close to getting what it wanted. So far from getting what it needed.

No, no, no. Stop thinking about the kiss.

Thinking about it won't get me anywhere. It won't conjure Garrett out of the blue. It won't make him finally see what's in front of him.

It won't help me move on from my stupid, stupid, *stupid* unrequited feelings for my best friend.

27

GARRETT

I recline on the wingback chair, my brain in a temporary fog after pushing out a hefty word count so far today.

I've returned to my old routine over the past week. The only major difference is I now spend lunch with Peony and Athena. And I no longer pick up food from P&T.

Which means I haven't seen Zara since I kissed her ten days ago, other than the time she came to see Peony. But Mom was here, and it would have been too awkward to talk about the kiss then. And then there was the time I bumped into Zara at the grocery store...but she was with Emily. And I also couldn't talk to her about the kiss when I saw her on Main Street while I was shooting some videos to post on social media. She was with Jess and Troy.

If not for this stupid deadline, I'd be able to go to her apartment and make sure things aren't awkward between us. I mean, it shouldn't be. It was barely a kiss. Nothing to get awkward over.

Yeah, you just keep telling yourself that.

A happy squeal outside my window tugs my attention to Peony and Athena in the backyard.

Also, if not for this stupid deadline, I'd have more time to get to know my daughter. Other than the one time almost two weeks ago, when she let me carry her home from the playground, we haven't made that much progress with her accepting me as her father.

It's not like I've been able to go to the playground with Athena and Peony either.

My deadline has stolen that possibility from me.

I pick up my phone and type out a text to Zara—at least that hasn't changed since the second kiss. Our brief phone calls and texts have seemed normal, as if we had never kissed. Clearly the kisses haven't had the same effect on Zara that they've had on me.

Me: Hey, how are things going?

I hit Send.

It's Friday afternoon. Usually, I would be joining my brothers and our friends for our weekly game night, but that won't be possible this time. I'll be away this weekend with a large group of retired soldiers, who are participating in the Wilderness Warriors canoe trip. To make up for lost time, I need to stay home tonight and work on *Untold Mercy*.

Which means I can take a short break now and spend it with my daughter.

I put my laptop on the desk and go outside to join Peony and Athena. Athena is running in slow motion while Peony chases after her. They don't notice me watching them, smiling at how much fun they're having.

Fun I'm missing out on.

Peony taps Athena on the leg, a wide goofy grin on her face.

Athena feigns surprise, her eyes round. "Oh, no! You caught me."

I step onto the grass. "Can I play too?"

"Of course," she singsongs. "We're playing tag." Athena

swiftly stretches toward me and taps my arm. "And you're *it*. Run, Peony!"

Peony squeals again and runs in the opposite direction. With my long legs and her much shorter ones, it will only take three strides to catch her.

I crouch like a frog and leap forward. "*Ribbitt. Ribbitt.*"

"Oh, no. Someone turned your daddy into a frog." Athena snickers. "You think he's like the frog on *The Princess and the Frog*? If his true love kisses him, will he turn into a prince?"

The mention of kisses has my brain reeling again, and the memory of my lips on Zara's plagues me for the millionth time in the past ten days.

That's not the only memory that replays in my head. The sight of her erect nipples pressed against the thin fabric of her T-shirt has appeared in more than one dream.

Stop. Thinking. About. The kiss.

I leap several more times, my thighs burning, no doubt thanks to my hard run with Kellan a few hours ago. "*Ribbitt. Ribbitt.*"

Peony giggles uncontrollably and flops sideways onto the grass.

Leap. "*Ribbitt.*" Leap. "*Ribbitt.*" Chuckling, I collapse next to her and roll onto my back. Wispy clouds dot the blue sky above us.

Peony pushes to her feet. I expect her to go to Athena like she normally does, but she clambers onto my stomach, surprising the air out of my lungs with an "*Oof.*"

She giggles once more and wiggles farther onto my abs, her knee poking into my side.

Other than the low laugh, I stay motionless. Two weeks ago, I couldn't have imagined a moment like this, where she trusted me enough to voluntarily get this close.

And now I can't wipe the grin off my face if I tried.

Peony wiggles and squirms until she's sitting on my stomach. It's not exactly comfortable for me, but hell if I'm pointing that out.

"*Ribbitt. Ribbitt.*" The movement in my abs from making the noise shifts Peony up and down.

"*Wi-witt. Wi-witt,*" she says, trying to imitate me.

Athena kneels next to us. "What an adorable little froggie." She pats Peony on the head.

A mark I haven't noticed before peeks from beneath the scooped neckline of Athena's T-shirt. It's not a tattoo. More like a raised scar, the color faded to pink. There's almost a pattern to it, but it's hard to tell for sure. Her top hides most of it.

"What happened?" I point to the scar.

Athena looks where I'm pointing and readjusts her neckline to cover it. "Oh, it's nothing. It's the mark of a fairy. Some might say it's the magical kiss of one." The last part is said in a god-awful imitation of an English or Irish accent.

Translation: she doesn't want to talk about it. Fair enough. I have scars on my body I don't want to discuss either. Even Zara, my brothers, and my parents don't know how some of them came to be.

Athena straightens to her feet. "Are you two ready for dinner?"

Peony shifts to lie on her stomach again and wiggles off me.

"Yes, please. Thank you." In one smooth move, I rock to my feet and stand.

Peony lifts her hands above her head. "Up."

Her arms aren't raised in front of Athena like they usually would be. Peony is holding her arms up to me, an expectant look in her eyes, my favorite toothy smile on her face.

And my heart responds with a booming, *Hell, yes.*

I don't make her ask twice. Wearing a shit-eating grin, I hoist her in my arms.

My phone pings in my pocket. It's probably Zara. I want to

check my phone to make sure she's okay, but I also don't want to end this moment with Peony and put her down just yet.

I fly her around the backyard, doing whatever it takes to make her laugh and squeal with joy. But after several minutes of dipping and twirling her in the air, my arms and shoulders and upper-back muscles start to burn.

"Coming in for a landing." I lower her onto the grass and pull out my phone.

> Zara: I'm doing good. Miss seeing you.

I type my reply.

> Me: Me too. So…about that kiss.

My finger hovers over the send button.

Do you think about it too? Do you want to do it again, even though we shouldn't? It's not that way between us. We're just friends. Good friends. The best of friends.

I delete the last part of the text, leaving only the first two words, and hit Send.

> Me: Kick everyone's asses tonight.
> For me.

Unless I was called away on a search and rescue mission for several days, I usually got to see Zara daily. And for plenty of those times, it was just the two of us hanging out together.

Not seeing her as much as before feels unnatural. Like part of me has been hacked off.

28

GARRETT

Two hours after I disappear into my office following dinner to write and post on social media, I reemerge and head to the kitchen to grab a glass of water.

Peony's and Athena's voices are coming from the living room, and I take a detour to see what they're up to.

They're at the coffee table, working on a bright, colorful jigsaw puzzle with jungle animals on it.

Or rather, Athena is putting the puzzle together. Peony is taking it apart.

Athena doesn't seem to care that Peony is destroying it as quickly as Athena is putting it together, if her smile is any indication.

I sit on the couch and watch Athena slot the tiger's face into place. "Hey, what are you two doing?"

"We're putting together this jigsaw puzzle, aren't we, Peony?" Athena's smiling eyes meet mine.

Peony waves at me and ducks down. Only the top of her head and the two buns perched on either side are visible above the coffee table. She pops back up, holding a book, and toddles to where I'm sitting.

She puts the book beside me and toddles to the sectional cushion where Poppy is flopped on her side. She grabs her by the leg, returns to where I'm sitting, and puts her next to the book.

The board book Kenda used to read to Peony.

Her favorite book.

Peony leans her chest onto the cushion, the surface of it dipping under her slight weight, and she awkwardly brings her leg up. Then in an impressive combination-wiggle-roll move that would impress even the Olympic gymnastics judges, she pulls herself onto the couch.

She crawls onto my lap, sits upright, and reaches for her panda, which is too far away for her to grab. "Poppy." The sweet strawberry scent of her kiddy bubble bath lingers on her skin.

I hand her the panda.

Athena beams at us. "I think she wants you to read her the book."

I show it to Peony. "You want me to read this to you?"

She taps the cover several times like it's a drum.

"I can do that," I tell her. Inwardly, I high-five myself.

I open the book and read the story, making funny voices for each of the animals. Peony giggles at each one, so hard, at one point she almost rolls off my legs and onto the couch.

I loosely wrap my arm across her stomach like a seat belt, keeping her in place, and finish reading the story.

Reading her this book...the one that she loves because it reminds her of her mother...it's like...witnessing the Northern Lights, a solar eclipse. There's no other feeling like it.

I just hope this, the way Peony is currently responding to me, isn't temporary. I hope I won't wake up tomorrow and find out we've retreated five steps overnight.

"Do you want Daddy to put you to bed?"

My breath catches at Athena's question, and I brace for Peony's reaction.

She peers up at me shyly. There's no indication, no warning sign she's about to have an epic meltdown, like I've witnessed more times than I care to admit. This time, she seems almost... eager. "Bed."

"Wanna fly there like a bird?" I ask. That gets me a rapid nod.

I lift her above my head and carry her to her room. Peony is flying backward, giggling, with Poppy dangling from one of her hands. She calls out, "Whee!" like she did at the playground almost two weeks ago, when we were there with Zara.

Shit. I'll miss her this weekend while I'm away with the army veterans.

Between that and my deadline and the increase in social media I'll have to do for my upcoming release, I worry my progress with Peony might stop moving forward—and might even take several steps back.

And I have no idea how to prevent that from happening.

"Birdie and Poppy coming in for a landing." I make a *brrrr* engine noise as I swoop Peony toward her bed.

I lay her on the mattress and pull the bedding to her chin. "Good night, little flower." I boop her on the nose. This makes her giggle some more. "I'm leaving tomorrow morning, probably before you're up. But I'll see you Sunday night." I boop her once more on the nose and give her panda a pat on the head.

FRIGHTENED SOBS RIP ME AWAY FROM THE SCENE I'VE BEEN writing nonstop for three hours and tear at my heart.

I put the laptop on my desk and rush from the room. The sound is coming from Peony's bedroom. Her door is open and the soft glow of her nightlight barely illuminates past the threshold onto the wood flooring.

A softly spoken voice stretches from the doorway, Athena's words too quiet to make out. Whatever she's saying seems to do the trick. Peony's sobs aren't as loud now, but that doesn't stop my feet from moving to the bedroom.

Usually, I don't do anything when Peony wakes from a bad dream. I let Athena go to her and do what she can to make things better. But I'd be a fool, now that Peony is slowly accepting me, to not try to chase away her fears and comfort her.

Peony is sitting on Athena's lap, safe in her arms, and sobbing against her chest.

"What happened?" I gentle my tone, strengthen my resolve not to let her tears send me running this time.

Peony turns her head at the sound of my voice, spots me in the doorway, and releases a soul-crushing scream, pitched almost high enough to shatter windows.

A scream that seems to go on forever.

"Turn the light on," Athena hurriedly says, concern and panic hovering beneath the surface. "She doesn't know it's you."

I flick on the overhead light. The bright glow floods the room, chases away the shadows.

"Look, Peony. It's your daddy." Athena keeps rocking Peony in her arms. "He's not going to hurt you."

Her words aren't enough to calm Peony. I'm not even sure she can hear them over her strained screams.

"*Shhh*, baby girl." Athena hums a song I don't recognize, but it appears to have a calming effect on Peony. Her screams fade by slow, sobbing increments. "It's just your daddy. He won't hurt you."

"You're safe here, little flower." I walk farther into the room. Her face is still buried in Athena's chest. She doesn't turn to look at me.

I crouch at the end of the bed. "I won't let anyone hurt you. You're safe."

When I was little, the possibility that monsters lived under my bed was very real. My father would come in my room each night and shine a flashlight under the bed and in the closet and chase them away. Something tells me it won't be as simple as that with Peony.

"I promise you're safe." Careful not to further scare her but also needing to reassure her, I place my hand on her back. Her little body stiffens briefly under my touch.

Her eyes meet mine, and her tear-soaked features morph into relief.

"I have a security alarm to keep out the scary people and monsters." As well as stalkers who become fixated on me—the reason I got the system after the one time.

I don't know how much of what I'm telling her Peony understands, but I keep talking, voice low, tone soothing. Maybe just hearing me will be enough to reassure her she's safe from whatever haunts her dreams.

I pat Poppy's head with my finger. She's squished between Peony and Athena. Only the top of the panda's head is visible. "You and Poppy are safe. I won't let anything bad happen to you."

Athena continues rocking Peony on her lap, and within a few minutes, Peony's eyes drift shut.

Athena shifts her onto the bed. Peony whimpers, but her eyes remain closed.

"Don't worry, baby girl. I'm right here." Athena points to the overhead light, indicating for me to turn it off. "Can you grab my pillow and comforter from my room? I'll stay with her for a while."

"Sure." I turn off the light, fetch her bedding and phone, and hand them to her. "I'll be in my office."

I would volunteer to camp out in the room, but after Peony's reaction to me before I turned on the light, I don't think my sleeping on her floor would be a good idea. It might only make things worse if she woke up from another nightmare and didn't realize it was me.

I return to my laptop, but now that the flow of words has been interrupted, I can't get back into the story.

I close my eyes and try to visualize in my head the scene playing out. But instead of the image of William Lockheart and Safina Berry, it's Zara and me. And instead of the argument they were embattled with, I'm kissing Zara in the forest where the scene was taking place.

The only thing the visualization exercise accomplishes is it makes me want to kiss Zara again. For real.

But she hasn't brought up our last kiss. It could be it did nothing for her—and unlike for me, she doesn't need to get the thought of kissing me out of her system. It was never there to begin with.

Pride is a swift kick in the ass at that realization.

I need to get out of here. To get some air. My brain is still spinning from what happened with Peony a short time ago, and I need to settle it if I want the words to flow once more. That might be all I need to regain my focus. I still have another few hours of writing to push through tonight, and I won't be able to do that if I can't stop thinking about Peony or the kiss with Zara.

I text Athena.

> Me: Going out for a bit. Call me if you need anything.

> Me: Or if Peony wakes up from another nightmare.

I drive toward Windermere Lake, intending to walk along the beach and watch the moon's reflection ripple on the water's surface. But as I approach the turn-off that will take me to Zara's apartment, I change my mind about what I really need.

I need to see Zara. To talk to her. To hang out with her for a few minutes. I'm dealing with withdrawal from not seeing my best friend for so long. That's why I can't stop thinking about the kiss. Just seeing her again, without anyone else around, should stop the withdrawal symptoms.

It's late enough Zara should be home from our weekly Game Night, but it's not too late yet that she's probably asleep.

In case she is, I park in Visitor Parking and send her a text.

> Me: I'm downstairs. Can I come up?

Three little dots appear, and I hold my breath, waiting for her reply.

> Zara: Sure. Give me a sec to buzz you in.

> Me: I'm in my SUV. Will text when I get to the entrance door.

I jog to the entrance and text her. She buzzes me in.

> Zara: The apartment door is open.

The elevator is on the main floor, so I take it instead of wasting time with the stairs.

The door opens on her floor, and I rush to her apartment, my long stride quickly eating up the distance. I open the apartment door and enter her foyer.

At the sight of Zara, standing in her living room, my heart clambers into my throat, making it difficult to swallow. She's wearing loose-fitting velvet lounge pants and a silky black camisole, and *fuck*, my best friend looks goddamn irresistible. Sexy. Mouthwatering.

Her last boyfriend—what's-his-name—was an idiot to give her up. To throw her away for his ex-wife.

I'm vaguely aware of Beyoncé singing in the background as I kick off my shoes.

I walk toward Zara, unable to stop staring at her. It's not like this is the first time I'm seeing her in this outfit. But something about seeing her now, like this, is...is having a whole new effect on me.

"I—"

"I think we should kiss again." Zara's words are a fast-moving train, flattening what I was going to say.

It takes a brief moment for her words to register in my head. I stare at her for a rapid heartbeat, stunned. There's not enough space in my head to get my thoughts together, and I clumsily blurt out, "You do, do you?"

"I do." She sucks her plump bottom lip into her mouth. "But only if you do."

I'm too busy staring at her mouth, imagining what it would be like to suck her lip between my teeth, that I almost miss her second sentence.

My gaze flicks up to meet hers. How could she possibly think I wouldn't want to kiss her again?

"I do." My voice is a featherlight murmur. All I seem capable of is getting lost in her beautiful, chocolate-brown eyes.

The subtle jasmine scent I associate with Zara wraps me with a need I never knew was possible. Just thinking about her lips on mine...I can barely draw air into my lungs.

She tilts her head up, her eyes telling me all I need to know. I lower my mouth to hers, giving her time to change her mind.

Christ, I hope she doesn't change her mind.

My mouth doesn't meet hers. It just hovers there as I breathe in her scent, her breath fanning my lips. Shit, I want to taste her so badly...

Her mouth meets mine before I can finish the thought. Like last time, the kiss is the gentle brushing of lips. But unlike then, the light press of my lips against hers, the tiny taste, the small sip of perfection, isn't enough. I want to drown in her kiss, to become intoxicated with it. To savor it.

Zara parts her lips on a gasp, so quiet I barely hear it. And without a twinge of regret or self-doubt or a second thought, I plunge my tongue into her mouth, unable to hold back any longer.

Fuck. Fuck, she tastes...she tastes like chocolate and the finest scotch and heaven all rolled into one.

She grabs a fistful of my shirt and pulls me to her. Our bodies crash together, erasing the space between us. Zara makes a tiny sound, and it's the tinder tossed onto a campfire. Heat and desire flare in me, consume me, devour me in the best possible way.

I slide my fingers into her hair and cradle the back of her head. Tilting her head more, I deepen the kiss.

The kiss becomes a hungry exploration of her mouth, a slow dance of tongues, the drawing out of the moment. Zara moans, and I greedily absorb the sweet sound. The vibration reaches every cell, every nerve, drives every electrical current in my body.

And for the first time in a while, I feel alive. Like I can face all the problems heavily weighing on me. The book deadline. The stress of being a single father. The unknowns when it comes to Peony. As long as I'm kissing Zara, everything will be fine.

The kiss, the taste of her, the warmth of her in my arms—it all feels so good.

So addictive.

Christ, I was an idiot thinking I could easily walk away after one more kiss.

There's no way I can't *not* kiss Zara again. But how on earth do I navigate this new terrain between best friend and something more without risking a train wreck?

29

ZARA

The last thing I expected after I left Simone and Lucas's house was that Garrett would show up at my apartment, and I would declare we should kiss again.

The words had slipped out without thought. And once they were freed, I didn't want to snatch them back—especially not after he'd agreed we *should* kiss.

But we weren't talking about the brushing of lips, like the accidental one more than two weeks ago. That kiss left my body tingling, and I couldn't stop thinking about Garrett's lips on mine.

And we weren't talking about the second kiss, which had been not much more than the brief touch of our lips.

This one is...it is...there are no words to describe it.

Of all the kisses I've experienced over the years, none of them compared to that third kiss with Garrett.

It's the type that ruins a girl for all the ones that follow. Other men's kisses. Kisses that don't belong to my best friend, the man I'm in love with.

We keep going, as if afraid to stop. Once our mouths separate, there likely won't be another kiss between us. Another chance for more of whatever this is to flourish.

For the first time in weeks, with Garrett's lips on mine, I feel like for now I'm on solid ground. I'm not walking across a frozen lake, unsure when and if the ice will crack under my weight. Leaving me stranded, unable to get to shore.

I hook my arms around Garrett's neck, the pain in my shoulders giving me a moment of peace. I don't let my brain analyze what the kiss means. I just enjoy it for as long as I can.

But eventually, I loosen my hold on him and step away, ending the kiss, fighting to regain my senses. Because. *Well...I... wow. Um. Wow.*

Garrett looks at me like I'm a math problem he's trying to solve, except math was never his strong suit.

It was mine—and even I can't figure out what just happened and what it all means.

"I needed that." Garrett's voice is an awed whisper. His warm brown eyes remain locked on mine.

"Me too." My voice is not much louder, my pulse thundering in my ears, waiting for his next words, his next decision. Waiting to see if he plans to slice me across the heart, to leave me to bleed out.

"So," he drawls, as if he's as lost as I am. I want to kiss him again, to feel his lips on mine, to prove to myself I didn't dream what just happened. But that wouldn't be a good idea.

Not until we have talked.

"So," I say, echoing Garrett's unspoken question.

He returns to pacing, telling me without words he needs to think.

I make myself comfy on the couch, legs curled to the side, and I watch him figure things out for himself. I'm clearly not the only one whose thoughts are a tangled mess over what just happened. But I also get the sense the kiss isn't all that has him conflicted.

"How's Peony doing?" I ask after a long, agonizing beat.

That question is all it takes to get him to stop pacing, and he drops down next to me. The exhaustion in his eyes vanishes, replaced with a spark of excitement. "She let me read her favorite book to her before bedtime." The grin that curves across his face is so bright, it would have brought me to my knees if I weren't already sitting.

"That's great. So things are getting better between you two?"

His grin and the spark in his eyes falter, clinging to a fraction of their previous brightness. "Because of my deadline, it's been hard to spend as much time with her as I should. But we're slowly getting there." He turns his gaze to the ceiling, his neck resting on the back of my couch. "And I'm currently looking for a therapist for her. She gets nightmares." Heartbreak for his daughter furrows his brow, pulls down on the corners of his mouth. "She had one before I came here."

His reason for being in my apartment now makes sense. He's so stressed out at whatever his daughter is going through, he needed a distraction. No matter how small it might be.

A dopamine rush. That's what the kiss was about. Nothing more.

"A what?" Garrett asks, eyebrows lifting, his gaze back on me.

Oh, shit. Please tell me I didn't say that out loud. "Huh?" I reply, playing innocent.

"You said something. What was it?" He gives me the look that warns me he won't let it go until I tell him.

I could lie, but he and I don't lie to each other—other than the part about how I'm in love with him.

"Our...our kisses. They're a dopamine rush. A stress reliever."

He huffs a sound that says he's never thought of it that way until now. "I could sure use the stress relief with everything going on."

That makes two of us.

"So maybe...um...maybe that's what you need. To kiss. More often." I mentally kick myself at the suggestion. *Way to go on telling him to kiss other women.*

He slowly nods, as if contemplating my idiotic comment. "Except I'm not interested in dating anyone. I have a daughter to think about now. The last thing I need is to get messed up in a relationship." A raw emotion crosses his expression, but it's gone before I can further dissect it.

"I know what you mean. I've got enough going on without worrying about a relationship too." Especially after what happened with Joseph. And the last thing I want is to end up with another jerk like him, who thinks chronic pain is all in the head.

Sure, I could quiz the men prior to dating them about their opinion on chronic pain, but if I haven't told my friends and family about it yet, why would I tell a stranger?

"So maybe this shouldn't be a one-time thing." Garrett sits up straighter. A hopeful smile curves his mouth, gleams in his eyes.

"What do you mean?"

"You and I"—he points between us—"we kiss whenever we need it. Purely for stress release. For the dopamine rush."

Part of me wants to laugh out loud at the ridiculousness of what he's suggesting. But the other part is nodding, one-hundred-percent on board. "That's not a bad idea. And anytime one of us needs a hit of dopamine, they go to wherever the other person is and we kiss." It might work.

My heart groans that it's a stupid idea. I ignore it. What does it know? In college, it thought it would be a brilliant idea for me to fall in love with Garrett, and look where that's gotten me.

"Right. But we should probably keep this quiet," Garrett says. "Just between us. We don't tell anyone, including your brothers and my brothers, or Simone, Jess, Emily, and Avery."

"Good idea." Simone and Em would think it was a bad idea or would get things all wrong. They know my feelings for Garrett go deeper than they probably should. And my brothers...they just wouldn't understand. "The only people who have to know about our deal is you and me." I hold out my hand to shake on it.

Garrett has different plans. His mouth christens mine with a stamp of approval, and I sink into the kiss, wondering why we didn't think of doing this sooner. We really should have done this sooner.

My brain doesn't allow me to lose myself in the kiss for long. It screams, *We need to set ground rules, boundaries, if this will work.*

I want to bat it away, tell it to get lost.

But it does make a valid point, even if I would prefer it made that point *after* we finished kissing.

I pull away ever so slightly, my breathing and heart rate already runaway trains, and rest my forehead on his. "We need ground rules." My voice flows out husky and low.

"What kind of ground rules?"

Willing my heart to get control of itself, I shift away from him on the couch. I need distance between us if I'm going to get this out. "This is just about us kissing. No sex." I'm not sure our friendship would survive if we took it that far. Not with how I feel about him. This proposition is risky enough as it is.

A flicker of something crosses his face. "Okay. Kissing only."

"And if one of us should find someone else"—if he should change his mind about Athena being more than Peony's nanny—"our kissing experiment ends."

"Right." His lips squish in the way that tells me something else is on his mind, but he doesn't plan to tell me what it is. "Anything else?"

Lord, this is crazy. But crazy or not, it might just work. I snicker. "If I were a lawyer, I'm sure I'd come up with something. But I'm not my brother, soooo..."

Garrett coughs out a laugh. "I can only imagine the long list Jerome would come up with."

I lean in and kiss Garrett again, not wanting to give him a chance to list some of those things. It's a deep, knee-wobbling kiss that is all tongue, my hands threaded through his hair. I could get addicted to Garrett's kisses, which is probably not a good thing.

Well, more addicted to them than I already am.

Temporarily sated, I reluctantly pull away, an inch separating our mouths.

A long shaky breath fans over my lips—his breath—and his eyes slowly open, as if he needed the extra moment to regain his senses.

"I should get going." Garrett pushes to his feet. "I've got a few more hours to write before calling it a night. And I want to make sure Peony is okay."

I begrudgingly unfold to a stand. My muscles ache at the effort, but the intensity is nowhere near as bad as it was this morning. I keep the wince off my face, though I can tell from Garrett's frown I didn't do a good job.

"I'm just getting old." The lie floats out on a chuckle. When his frown doesn't smooth away, I add, needing to distract him from the truth, "I really am fine, Garrett. Just tired." That isn't a lie.

I walk him to the door. "Well, have fun this weekend with the warriors." I kiss him, deeply again...to further distract him from the reason behind the wince.

And because I can.

30

ZARA

I put the hammer in the toolbox on the workbench and stretch my torso from side to side. I'm not hungry, but it's already afternoon, and after all the work I've been doing on the expansion this morning, I should eat something. Plus, I need to make a bunch of calls regarding the grand reopening celebration for Picnic & Treats.

It's a sunny day, with a few wispy strands of cotton-like clouds in the sky. Might as well make those calls at the park while I enjoy the warm weather, before I drive to Simone's house to meet her two foster girls. Simone, Emily, Jess, Avery, and I will also be discussing ideas on how P&T can support women-owned businesses in the area. Small businesses like Simone and Emily run.

I retrieve my bag from my desk and head out. It's Saturday, and the only reason I'm here is because of the expansion. Otherwise, I would have bailed a few hours ago, after I made the lunchtime specials on today's menu.

I walk along Main Street, the pain in my body manageable compared to this morning. The stiffness in my muscles is also less noticeable.

A steady flow of vehicles slowly drives past, obeying the speed limit. It's the typical weekend traffic at this time of year, with outsiders coming to spend a day sightseeing, hiking, climbing, or canoeing in the mountains.

The sidewalk is busy with tourists and locals checking out the various stores. Several yards ahead of me, Athena is crouched next to Peony's stroller.

"Krista!" someone calls out farther down the sidewalk. The voice is loud enough to startle a few people, including Athena, who jerks her head in the direction of the voice.

She stands, her shoulders stiff with tension, but she hasn't yet noticed me.

Athena might not have seen me, but the same can't be said for Garrett's daughter. A wide grin breaks out on her face, and she zealously waves at me with both hands. "Za-wa."

That gets Athena's attention. She turns her head my way, but not as fast as she did when someone called out a few seconds ago.

"Hey, Peony. Athena." I approach them and lower to a crouch, holding the side of the stroller to keep my balance. "And good afternoon to you, Poppy. Where are the three of you off to?"

I flash Athena my friendliest smile. I've seen her a handful of times since she arrived in Maple Ridge, but we haven't had a chance to get to know each other.

From what I can tell, she could use some friends. She barely leaves Garrett's house during her off hours. Of course, it doesn't help he's on a deadline and she's been working a lot of overtime.

"We were just going for a walk," she explains. "To the library."

My knees and hips scream for me to straighten, and I do as they demand. "You walked all the way here?" That's a five-mile hike from Garrett's. Athena doesn't drive. According to Garrett, she's waiting for all the documents she lost in the fire to be reissued.

Athena shrugs. "It's a nice day. And Joanne is picking us up soon and will drop us off at home."

"I bet she's excited to spend time with her granddaughter." Garrett told me she's beyond thrilled to finally have a grandchild.

Athena's eyes search my face, and the thin wall she has erected between us seems a little chillier than normal. "She is."

Her hand goes to the pendant around her neck, and her fingers trace over the flowers etched in the silver. And just like that, the chill in her eyes thaws a tiny amount, and an ounce of tension drains from her shoulders.

"That's a pretty locket. Does it have special meaning for you?" I haven't seen her without it on, but that doesn't mean anything. It's not like I see her all the time.

She doesn't respond, so I pull the tiny silver, oak-tree charm from under the neckline of my T-shirt. "My grandmother gave me this. The oak tree symbolizes strength and wisdom and reminds us we're connected to nature." It was my birthday present from Mimi when I turned six, but I started wearing it again after she died late last year. "It makes me feel closer to her," I explain.

"It's pretty." Athena fingers her locket once more. "The love of my life gave this to me." A sad smile bends the corners of her mouth.

"He did? Does he live near Maple Ridge?" Or do they have a long-distance relationship going on between them?

Her smile doesn't go anywhere; it just seems sadder now. "Heaven."

Oh. "I'm so sorry for your loss. My grandmother's dead too." I shift on my feet, the discomfort in my hips, lower back, and knees growing more intense now that I'm standing still. "So, you have the afternoon off? Once Joanne picks up Peony?"

"I do." The sadness in Athena's voice is palpable. It could be because she misses her love. Or her friends. Or because of any number of things. I doubt it's because she has the afternoon free.

"Have you been to Barside Brewery? It's a bar the sister of one of my friends owns. She and her girlfriend own and run it. Maybe you and I could go there for a drink. Say in an hour?" I have time to do that and make my calls before I meet my friends at Simone's house.

"I...I don't know."

"I bet Emily would love to join us. Have you met Em yet?"

Athena shakes her head.

"Oh, you'll love her. And Jess. She might be able to join us too. Plus Avery." Then we could all head over to Simone's together.

"Maybe...maybe another time. We...Peony and I should get going." She crouches next to Peony's stroller, her body clearly not struggling with chronic pain and muscle stiffness.

She smiles at Garrett's daughter, her face lighting up like that of an ethereal creature. "You ready to go on another adventure?" she asks Peony. "Maybe to the stars?"

Two guys in their late twenties walk past us. One glances in Athena's direction, and he elbows his friend. "Damn, that's one hot piece of ass."

Athena's smile vanishes. The tight expression that takes its place is scorching enough to melt plastic. She shoots upright, standing a few feet in front of them.

"I'm not a farm animal, nor am I any part of one." Her voice is low with warning, sharpened to eviscerate despite the Texan drawl that isn't usually there. And I blink, watching the usually docile, ethereal creature transform into something mind-blowingly fierce—and a little frightening. "If you think I am, then your mama obviously dropped you on your head when you were a scraggly newborn." The Texan accent has vanished from Athena's voice as if it was never really there.

Why try to hide it?

Her fierceness reminds me so much of Kenda, and my heart aches once again at how much I miss my friend.

She also...she also reminds me of *me*, especially when I was a kid and stood up to bullies who targeted my friends. Back when I'd thought I was invincible.

An irritated frown crosses the man's face. His friend snickers, looking ready to give the guy grief for Athena's reaction.

Athena's smile returns, demure in a way I've never seen from her until now. And it's fully directed at Peony, as if she hadn't just spoken to the man that way. As if her mask had slipped, allowing the real Athena to peek out, and now it's back in position.

Or perhaps it's the other way around.

I have no idea which is the real Athena and which is fake.

Part of me wants to step in, to keep things from getting uglier—which I will do if the men don't get the hint and leave. Another part is ready to stand back and watch where things go. I sense if Peony wasn't here, Athena would have really let loose her feelings about the man's sexist comment.

He opens his mouth to say something—or catch flies—but his friend shoves his arm. "Let's get out of here before she takes a chunk out of *your* ass." Laughter tints the friend's tone. "Jesus, my sister would love her." He chuckles as the two of them walk away.

I don't hear what else they have to say. I'm too busy staring at Athena as she fusses over Peony like none of that just happened.

"Damn. That was beautiful." Lauren walks up to us, her sleek black hair swinging down her back in a long ponytail. She's a few years younger than me and is wearing a long-sleeved floral dress and cowgirl boots. "It's about time someone put Chris in his place." She grins at Athena. "Hi, I'm Lauren."

"Athena." Athena's mouth bends into an uncertain smile.

"Nice to meet you, Athena." Lauren levels her grin at me. "Hey, Zara. I can't wait to see what you're doing to Picnic & Treats."

"Thanks. I was going to call you this afternoon. I'm planning a grand reopening celebration, and I'd love it if you could perform a few sets." I then tell Athena, "Lauren is an incredible singer and musician."

I fill Lauren in on the date and time.

"I would love to perform. And it should work for my schedule, but I'll get back to you later this afternoon to let you know for sure. I have to run now. I have a lesson with a student in ten minutes. It was nice meeting you, Athena. And your cute little girl." Lauren waves at Peony and hurries off before I can correct her about Garrett's daughter.

"Peony and I should get going too." Athena offers me a soft smile. "It was nice seeing you again, Zara."

"You too, Athena." *Ask her.* "Are you originally from Texas?" At the sudden coldness in her eyes, I add, "I noticed your accent when you got mad at that guy."

"No idea what you're talking about. I'm from North Carolina." Athena starts pushing the stroller, clearly done with our conversation.

I blink, taken aback by her sudden change in mood. I quickly recover and wave to Garrett's daughter. "Bye, Peony."

Peony returns my wave as Athena pushes the stroller past me.

Strange. Why would she suddenly have a Texan accent? Was she an actress in her past life who played a Texan at some point? But why deny it?

I shake the thought from my head, not wanting to fall down a rabbit hole. I continue walking to the park, letting my thoughts shift from what I just witnessed and my brief conversation with Lauren to the new twist in Garrett's and my friendship.

What would Athena think if she knew of Garrett's and my new dopamine-fix, kissing arrangement? Maybe she wouldn't care what the two of us did. We are consenting adults, after all. And I could be wrong, and she could view him as nothing more than her employer.

Or maybe the wall she seems to have erected between you and her has everything to do with your friendship with Garrett...

Maybe she's hoping Garrett will help her get over her previous love. Sure. Maybe. But the woman clearly isn't over the man she was with. She's wearing his locket.

Thank the Lord I read romance and not thrillers—other than Garrett's books. Otherwise, I might believe she was the nanny out to destroy the single father's love interest, because the woman is in the way of the nanny getting what she wants.

The father.

31

ZARA

"This is Kylie." Simone points to the six-year-old standing in front of me on the grass. Big blue eyes stare at me, heartbreak glistening in them.

Simone then points to the younger girl. "And this is Zoe." The blue eyes of the blond two-year-old are no different than her sister's, prompting me to want to hug the two girls.

A bright-pink scar cuts across Kylie's forehead, near her hairline, the ends dipping like an upside-down smile. It's the only visible scar I can see on her, a symbol of the accident that claimed their parents' lives. It's the invisible scars, though, that will mark them forever.

Kylie tugs nervously on one of her long dark-blond braids. Her other arm is protectively around her sister's shoulders, as if she's afraid if she lets go of Zoe, she'll lose her like they lost their parents.

I kneel to their level, my body bitching at how bad an idea that is. I ignore it. It's a little grumpy from the renovations I was doing this morning. "It's nice to meet you two."

Zoe looks away, Snowball snaring her attention. The white

240

cat is crouching in the grass, getting ready to pounce on something. Most likely a cricket.

Kylie nods at me but doesn't say anything. She doesn't need to. Her eyes say it all. I can't imagine what they're going through. Like Peony, they lost their parents not that long ago. A car accident. But unlike Peony, they had no family to take care of them. No nanny who was familiar to them.

Snowball is too much of a draw for Zoe, and the little girl slips out from under her sister's arm and wanders over to the cat. Kylie follows after her.

I awkwardly try to stand, the pain in my knees and hips flaring from the movement.

Simone's hand hooks under my arm, and she helps me to my feet. "You okay?"

I roll my eyes like a sassy teen, even though my body feels like it belongs to someone six times that age. "I just slept funny. And I was working on the renovations earlier. My body isn't used to all that exercise." I chuckle, my laugh genuine. "I'm not like your husband and Garrett, Kellan, and Troy with their brutal runs."

She flashes me a look that says she gets what I mean, but at the same time she doesn't buy my excuse. She knows there's more to it than I'm letting on.

The creak of the side gate leading to the backyard saves me from having to spill my secrets.

Emily, Jessica, and Avery walk through the archway, carrying dishes to add to the ones already on the patio table. The guys are away for the weekend and Avery's boyfriend, Noah, is working the afternoon shift at the police station.

Zoe's attention shifts from Snowball to Bailey, who is wearing her *Service Dog in Training* vest, and she runs over to Jess's dog. Kylie trails after her like a watchful parent, her guarded expression dropping as soon as she spots Jess's golden retriever.

Simone introduces Emily, Jess, and Avery to the girls, though I'm not sure Kylie heard any of the names. She's watching Bailey with rapt interest. Jess explains to the girls that Bailey is currently on duty and what that means.

"So Jasper can't play with her?" Kylie's gaze goes to the house where Jasper, Simone's golden Labradoodle, is currently standing by the patio door, eagerly waiting to join us.

"No," Simone explains, "but we can let Jasper out to play with *you* if you'd like."

Kylie enthusiastically nods, the heartbreak in her eyes softening a smidgen.

We watch as the two girls play catch with Jasper. Kylie throws the ball, and Jasper chases after it. His antics have the girls laughing, and a relieved smile eases onto Simone's face.

"Jasper has been a lifesaver," she explains. "Kylie talks to him more than she talks to Lucas and me. She's been through so much. But at least she can vocalize her needs. Most of the time. Zoe can't, but she seems to be adjusting to the situation better than her sister."

Jess pours a glass of lemonade from the pitcher and hands it to Emily. "Are they seeing a therapist to help them cope?" She grabs another glass and fills it.

"The child welfare agency gave us a list of resources for helping the girls, but I'm looking into private counseling for them. It's helped Lucas and me cope with the loss of Lily. And I thought we could also try family therapy."

"Family therapy?" I ask, surprised. I'm positive this isn't something foster parents normally would do for a child.

"We want to give the girls the best possible chance at this new life they didn't ask for. And I thought family therapy would help us navigate any speed bumps before it's too late."

"Those girls won the foster-parent lottery when they were assigned to you and Lucas." I hug her, then I get my friends up to speed on how things are going between Garrett and Peony.

"I'm looking forward to introducing the girls to Peony," Simone tells me. "It might help all of them, in one way or another."

"I think that would be good for her. She sees other kids at the playground, but Garrett told me she keeps her distance. It's like she doesn't know how to interact with them." I have no idea if that's normal for someone her age.

"She's nineteen months old. At that age, toddlers play alongside each other. Parallel play. But they don't interact and play together until between the ages of two and three years."

I sip my lemonade and put the glass on the table. "I should probably read up on toddlers and their developmental milestones. So I can help Garrett and have a better idea what I'm doing."

A sly smile slips onto Simone's face. "So, you and Garrett, huh?"

I huff a laugh that sounds slightly stilted to my ears. The other four women at the table don't seem to notice. "You know it's nothing like that." Thank the Lord they don't know of the kissing arrangement between Garrett and me; otherwise, Emily would be planning his and my wedding before I could blink. "Our friendship is the same as it's always been. And he's not looking for a relationship right now. Not when his focus is on his book deadline and Peony."

"He told you that?" Avery asks, the only person at the table who doesn't know I've been in love with Garrett for almost a lifetime. She and Jess didn't grow up in Maple Ridge. Both of them moved here last year.

"He did. But that's nothing new. I don't remember the last time he was interested in being in a romantic relationship." I really don't—even though that's not the Garrett I grew up with. He'd had several girlfriends in high school and college prior to him and Kenda becoming a couple.

But after that? After he retired from the Marines?

Nothing—other than the occasional one-night-stand hookup and the time with Kenda that resulted in Peony.

Simone pushes to her feet and picks up the kid-sized travel mugs from the table. "Wonder why that is? It's not like there's a shortage of women in Maple Ridge and the surrounding area who are interested in him." She walks to where she's set up the blanket for Kylie and Zoe and hands them their lemonades. "And once it gets out that he's a single dad, his"—she glances down at the two girls and shrugs—"his *you-know-what* appeal will dial up even more."

I snort-laugh. "Really? I mean, sure, I can see the appeal. Especially when Peony finally let him carry her last week. It was...appealing."

"Ovary-exploding appealing?" Avery dances her eyebrows up her forehead.

A dreamy sigh escapes Emily. Like me, she's currently single, but I can tell from her expression it's not Garrett she's sighing over. It's the other Carson brother—the one not married or in a committed relationship—she's thinking about.

"My ovaries didn't explode." They totally combusted. "But I'm sure if other women see him carry her, their ovaries will detonate."

"Maybe he'll change his mind about being in a relationship," Simone says, a little too optimistically for someone who is deeply in love with her husband. "Maybe one day he'll decide Peony needs a mother and be more open to the idea of finding someone to fall in love with."

My heart tightens at that prospect. A prospect that won't be me—even if we have the kissing arrangement between us. It's temporary. A dopamine rush. A form of stress release. Nothing more. "Maybe."

My phone rings in my jeans pocket, and I pull it out without looking at the screen. It's Abby's bell tone.

"Sorry, I've got to get this," I tell my friends and answer the call.

"Hey, Zara." Panic laces Abby's normally calm tone, and my hackles instantly rise. "We've got an emergency at the café."

"What kind of emergency?"

"It's raining. Inside."

Oh. Shit.

32

ZARA

I wake up Monday morning to not only the usual aches that hijack my body, but to a pain in my left eye, like something is jabbing at it. Tears flow down my face and my vision is slightly blurry.

I groan, wishing I didn't have to get up yet, but I have a meeting with Troy and Mr. Cartwright in an hour, to discuss the damage to Picnic & Treats. A burst pipe in the ceiling caused Saturday's unexpected rainstorm.

I stumble out of bed, exhaustion a rusty iron armor covering me from head to toe.

I repeat in my head several times what has become my daily morning mantra: *Just get moving. The stiffness will be gone in no time.*

I zombie-walk to my closet and flick on the light. A sudden pain stabs my eye with a red-hot needle, and I groan again, louder this time, my hand flying to my face.

Shit.

I loosely cover my eye with my hand. The pain decreases a little but still holds on tight.

I grab my clothes and slowly walk to the bedroom door,

246

where I pick up a pair of stylish sunglasses from my dresser. Garrett once joked they make me look like a sexy librarian spy. I'll happily take boring old nerdy professor if they stop the pain.

I slip them on and head for the bathroom.

Bracing for the intense pain, I flick on the light and slide the sunglasses down my nose. Contrary to how it feels, I don't have a knife sticking out of my eye, but it is red and watery. *Great. Conjunctivitis.*

Keshia had pink eye last year while on vacation, and it went away on its own. I'll just have to wear the sunglasses in the meantime.

I take my painkiller, have a shower—careful not to further irritate my eye—and head out to Picnic & Treats.

Because I don't know what kind of damage we're dealing with and if it's okay to have the café open until it's fixed, Picnic & Treats is temporarily closed. That means I'm the only person here when I enter through the alley door. Usually, Keshia and someone else would be in the kitchen, chopping onions, carrots, and whatever else I need for the day.

Lord, please tell me P&T won't be closed for long.

My business insurance covers any losses the unexpected damage might incur, but it won't make up for lost profits. And I need to pay my employees who were scheduled to work the missed shifts. It's not their fault we might have to be closed for several days.

I turn on the coffee maker and brew myself a latte. Then, with my travel mug in hand, I shuffle through the café, assessing the damage once more. The ceiling is stained from the water, but I still have a ceiling. It didn't collapse.

I could really go for one of Garrett's stress-reducing kisses right now. But between him catching up with his writing, because he was away this past weekend, and my current pink-eye status, kissing him is out of the question. For now.

The bell above the door jingles, alerting me Troy is here. He walks through the doorway with Mr. Cartwright following behind.

"Thanks for coming," I tell them and brace for the wise-ass joke about why I'm wearing my sunglasses inside. To my relief, neither man comments on them. I don't feel like discussing my pink eye with anyone, much less Garrett's brother.

We spend the next hour with Troy inspecting the café and discussing what needs to be done, since the water damage could lead to mold. He's then on his phone, contacting the company that will perform its magic to dry out the ceiling.

Troy tells me it's going to take a week to clean this up, which means the café will be closed for way too long.

By the time we're finished, my head is spinning with details, the early-morning fog crowding my brain again.

I see the men out, refill my travel mug, and visit the only person I want to talk to right now.

Mama.

I'm not the only person who has descended on her. Samuel's Lexus is in the driveway. I park next to it and walk up the path to the house.

I open the door, without bothering to knock first. "Hey, Mama. Samuel?" I call out in case I'm interrupting a private conversation.

"We're in the kitchen," Mama replies.

I kick off my sneakers but keep my sunglasses on and walk down the hallway to join them. Mama and Samuel are sitting at the kitchen table, coffee mugs in front of them. Sunlight reflects off the white walls and granite counters. These are the same white counters where I spent many hours during my teens, cooking with Mama by my side.

"Didn't expect to see you today, honey. Thought you'd be at work." Mama's warm smile is the one that always made things seem better when I was a kid. Even now, it helps a little.

"Picnic & Treats is closed for the next few days while the mess from the leak is dealt with." I'd told them about it yesterday during our weekly family dinner. "So I'm just spending the day working on plans for the grand reopening. And I'm contacting some women-owned small businesses in the area about possible partnerships with P&T."

"What's with the sunglasses?" Samuel pushes imaginary glasses up his nose.

I shrug and head for my chair at the table. "It's nothing. Just a case of pink eye."

"Have you seen Alyssa 'bout it?" The corners of his mouth twitch. "I mean, Dr. Cole?"

I shake my head and pull out my chair next to his. "Figured it would go away on its own." I lower my ass onto the chair, my body groaning at the effort.

"If it's viral, sure. But not if it's bacterial. Then you'll need antibiotic drops." He turns toward me and makes a come-here gesture with his finger. "Lemme have a look."

A smug smile tugs on my lips. "Thought you weren't supposed to diagnose and treat family."

"I'm just gonna take a look. And then you're gonna call Dr. Cole to have her diagnose and possibly treat it." He gives me the big-brother look that warns me he won't drop this until I do as he tells me.

I snort out a short laugh. "And if I don't? Are you gonna hold me upside down by my feet like when we were kids?"

He raises his eyebrow, a rumble of a chuckle rolling from him. "If that's what it takes."

Mama laughs, amusement dancing in her eyes. "You two never change. You're just lucky, Zara, Jerome isn't home to gang up on you with Samuel."

"Nah. You'd save me like you always did when I was a kid. Because I'm your favorite." I flash Samuel another smug look, and he chuckles again, a little louder this time.

"I have no favorites," Mom diplomatically points out.

"You're just saying that so you don't hurt my poor brother's feelings." I would wink at him, but that would involve taking off these sunglasses, and I'm not willing to risk the pain from the bright sunlight just yet.

"Nice attempt at deflecting," Samuel says, unfolding from his chair. "But I would feel better if you'd just let me see your eye." The humor has vacated his expression. I won't get my way on this.

I lower the sunglasses and wince at the sunlight streaming through the kitchen window. Tears well in my left eye and stream down my face, which only seems to make the other eye well up too, not wanting to miss out on the fun.

Samuel lifts my chin and inspects the eye. "That's not pink eye." The declaration is followed by a series of questions. How have I been feeling lately? Then he questions me about my stress levels. And if any other part of me hurts?

He doesn't tell me what he's fishing for, but I can tell from his concerned frown whatever he suspects is going on isn't good. He removes his phone from his jeans and taps away at the screen. "Hey, Michelle. It's Samuel Thompson." He chuckles at whatever the other person said, not having bothered with speakerphone. "I do remember that..."

His expression becomes serious once more. "Is there a chance you can slip my sister in to see you later today?" He lists the symptoms related to my eye, followed by my answers to his questions. "That's what I'm thinking too. Let me check with her..."

He lowers the phone. "Has Dr. Cole done any blood work, X-rays, or anything else to figure out what's causing the pain?"

"I haven't seen her recently about it. But her locum, Dr. William Edwards, set up a referral for me to talk to a rheumatologist in Eugene. The results were inconclusive. Dr. Holmes said it might be early stages of rheumatoid arthritis, and he would revisit things in six months."

Mama sends me a look that says, *Why am I only hearing about this now?*

I hope my answering glance is something along the lines of, *Whoops. Sorry. Didn't want to worry you.*

Samuel relays the info to the person on the other end of the line. They talk for another moment or two and then end the call.

"Dr. Michelle Isaacs can see you at two thirty. She's an ophthalmologist in Portland." He turns to Mama. "Can you drive Zar? I'm on shift this afternoon."

"I can. What's going on?" She splits her worried gaze between us.

"It's possible she has uveitis."

Mama's frown deepens, echoing my sentiments. "What is that?"

"It's the inflammation of the eye that is usually linked to several other medical conditions. If it's what I think it is, it can't be ignored. It will need to be treated with corticosteroid eye drops and eye-dilating drops for about a week." He ignores my groan. I hate anything that involves putting things in my eyes. "And because uveitis is a warning symptom for more serious issues in the body, Dr. Cole will want to investigate what else is going on with your chronic pain."

"What else is going on?" I parrot, my mind spinning with everything he's telling me. "So it might not be rheumatoid arthritis?"

"It could be. Both are immunological disorders. Uveitis is also a symptom of other conditions, like psoriatic arthritis, ankylosing spondylitis, as well as systemic lupus, herpes, syphilis, Crohn's disease, tuberculosis."

Lord Almighty, I'm sorry I asked. "Well, I definitely don't have herpes or syphilis. And the rheumatologist said I don't have the ankylosis one."

"That narrows things down a little bit. Book an appointment with Dr. Cole. Let her know you possibly have uveitis and you're seeing...never mind, lemme do it." He taps on his phone again.

"Hey, you can't book an appointment for me." I grab for his mobile, only for him to turn away from me. "I haven't given the clinic permission for you to do that."

He ignores me. I would roll my eyes if I could, but that would hurt.

"Hey, Alyssa." His voice goes soft, like he's seducing her, and I barely keep from rolling my eyes.

I would give him a hard time about it when he gets off the phone, but I'm suddenly not in the mood to tease him.

He tells her everything that's going on and asks if she can fit me into her schedule in the next day or two. He then ends the call. "You have an appointment Wednesday morning at eleven a.m."

BY THE TIME MAMA DROPS ME OFF AT HOME WITH MY prescription for two different eye drops, my mind is churning over everything that has happened since I woke up this morning. The news that P&T will be closed for the week while the water leak is dealt with. The diagnosis of uveitis.

The possibility the eye inflammation is linked to the chronic pain.

The possibility it has nothing to do with that, and something else is attacking my body.

And on top of all that, the eye drops have to be applied hourly.

Lord, I really hate life right now.

I grab a glass of water and swallow down two ibuprofen tablets. My body is screaming from the drive home from Portland, and I don't have the energy to do much. And that includes applying the eyedrops. But I don't have a choice in that department if I want my eye to get better.

So, I suck it up and head for the bathroom. A stream of colorful cusses spill from my mouth as I attempt to apply the hateful medications—drop-by-missed-drop—to my eyes. I try to remind myself they'll make things better, but my inner cheerleader has called it a day.

After the torturous session is thankfully finished, I heat up the leftover jambalaya in the fridge and curl up in front of the TV. I keep on my sunglasses and search for something I'm in the mood to watch.

What I want is to get back to the romance I was reading, but that isn't an option right now. Not until my eye feels better.

I pull up *Game of Thrones*, which I'm currently rewatching, and try to eat my dinner even though I'm not all that hungry.

I've been half paying attention to the show for the past hour, squirming to get comfy, my food half-finished, when my phone pings on the coffee table with a text.

> Garrett: I'm downstairs. Is now a good
> time?

33

ZARA

I stare at my phone. Maybe the reason Garrett is outside my apartment building is because he's here for a stress-relieving kiss. If there's ever a time I could use one, now would be it.

My body and mind have been tied into one gigantic messy knot, and I don't know how to untangle it.

Under normal circumstances, one of Garrett's kisses would be enough to pick away at bits of the unruly knot. But I'm not exactly kissable with how utterly delightful my eye looks.

On the other hand, after the day I've had, I really want to see my best friend.

> Me: Yes. I'll buzz you up. Apartment door unlocked.

I unlock the door and carry my half-eaten dinner to the kitchen.

I cover the food and return it to the fridge. I'll eat it tomorrow. My appetite should be back to normal by then. It's been off for a few days, but that's not surprising with everything going on.

The apartment door clicks open, and Garrett is standing in front of me in the kitchen before I can tell him I'm in here. The corner of his mouth lifts in an ovary-exploding smirk. "Sexy librarian spy. I need to add one to my book."

It takes me a second to figure out what he's getting at. Oh, right. The sunglasses. "Sexy librarian spies are always a win for any book. I highly recommend them."

He shortens the distance between us and cradles my hips in his hands. His long, strong fingers curve along the swell of my ass, leaving my skin under the lounge pants humming from the near contact. "Are you gonna remove your sunglasses so I can kiss you?" An adorable divot creases between his eyes. "Why are you wearing sunglasses inside?"

"I was watching TV and my eyes are sensitive to the light."

The divot deepens. "Since when?"

"This morning. I saw an ophthalmologist this afternoon, and I have uveitis. Inflammation of the eye. I'm taking drops for it. It'll be better in a few days." I smile at him as if this is the only thing I've had to worry about today. As if my body hasn't declared World War III on me. "I should probably have told you that before you rushed up here. You might not want to kiss me."

He leans in and ghosts his lips along my jaw. "Can I kiss you here?" His voice is a rough rumble coasting the shell of my ear, sparking shivers that skip across my skin.

"Uh-huh," I manage to get out on a shaky breath.

"What about here?" His lips trace my neck in a teasing caress, and an answering wetness pools between my legs.

"Oh. Yes. Definitely there." The words carry out on a delirious moan.

He slowly drags the opening of my silk top to the side, revealing my shoulder, and skims his lips over the exposed skin. "How are your shoulders doing?"

"Better." It's not a lie. They aren't as achy today compared to my hips and back.

"Anywhere else that hurts?" He glides his hands down my arms.

Everywhere.

"My neck is a little stiff. And my"—I swallow, my mouth suddenly dry—"my hips."

"You want me to massage you? Would that help?" His voice comes out in a low, seductive purr, and my entire body deliciously tingles.

"It might," I whisper, unable to make my words any louder.

He threads his fingers with mine and leads me into the bedroom. Releasing my hand, he walks to the curtains and slides them shut. The faint glow peeking through the fabric is the only light in the nearly dark room. "Does that help with the light sensitivity?"

I cautiously slide my sunglasses down my nose, testing my inflamed eye's reaction to the dim light. The pain I've been experiencing all day, whenever the eye is exposed to light, doesn't assault me. "That's good."

"Alright. Do you want to change into something else? To make it easier for me to massage you."

"I can put on my sleep shorts and tank top."

"That should work." He turns so his back faces me, and I take a brief second to appreciate the view before his words sink in.

"You want me to change here?" *With you standing there?* The words come out husky—not at all how I had planned. I can blame the view of his tight ass and broad shoulders for that. I swallow.

"I promise I won't look. Or I can leave if you want?"

"No, that's fine." It's not like we haven't changed in the same room. He's never sneaked a peek at me.

Even if I secretly willed him to.

I remove a pair of sleep shorts and matching tank top from the dresser drawer and deposit my sunglasses on my nightstand. I change into my sleepwear, my movements awkward and stiff from the long drive to and from Portland. "Okay. You can turn around."

In the dim light of the room, I feel his gaze travel down my body like the caress of silk on my skin. It's dark enough he can't see my nipples through the top from where he's standing. Can't see I'm braless.

He pats my mattress. "On your stomach. Where's your lotion?"

"In the bathroom."

"Right." He disappears out the door and returns with the jasmine-scented lotion.

I swallow again at my body's reaction to him, at the nakedly raw gut feeling I have that he's seeing into places I've kept hidden from the world. I climb onto the bed, crawl to his side, and lie on my stomach, my head on the pillow, arms folded under it.

I close my eyes. Deep secrets exposed or not, I'm not missing out on this massage when it might ease some of the pain.

The mattress dips under Garrett's weight. He straddles my hips and brushes my coils to the side. His large warm hands spread across my shoulders, and with gentle but firm pressure, he starts to unknot the kinks in my neck, kneading them with his calloused thumbs. Unwittingly forcing me to bite back a moan.

He continues to meticulously chase away the discomfort that has been plaguing me all day. Once he's finished with my neck muscles, his hands travel the length of me, spending time on those parts of my body that have been especially bitchy lately.

My groans of delight and hisses of pain guide him, no

doubt encouraging him to keep going. "I might need to start calling you Golden Hands."

His fingers glide to my butt muscles, and my breath hitches. The muscles clench, and then relax, not wanting to give him a reason to skip them. The gap between my legs silently pleads for his fingers to drift off course, to call on my pussy.

Nope. Not happening. We agreed we're not going there. Kissing only.

"How's that?" he asks once the massage is finished and I'm a content limp noodle on my bed. A *very* content limp noodle.

"Much better. Thank you." I make a move to roll onto my back, but the fabric of my tank top doesn't get the message that I'm moving. It accidentally shifts to the side, and I inadvertently flash a naked tit.

The world goes momentarily still, all the air in the room sucked out. Neither of us moves. Or breathes. Or speaks.

Then mortification kicks me in the ass, and I jerk the fabric back to where it should be. It's not enough, though, to hide my nipples, taut from having Garrett's hands on my body. They press perkily through the cotton.

Garrett rears up as if a venomous snake is coiled next to me, keeping him in his place. "That's good. I...I should get going. I have a few more hours left of writing to do tonight."

"Right." I push to a sit, my legs dangling over the side of the bed, and I cover my chest with my arm, blocking his view of my eager nipples. "Good luck with that." I fashion my voice so it sounds relaxed, upbeat. Perhaps a little too upbeat. But if Garrett notices, his expression gives nothing away.

"Thanks. And good luck...good luck with your eye problem." The last part is rushed out so fast, I almost laugh at how adorably awkward he sounds. And maybe I would have if that hidden part of me wasn't shaken to the core.

The apartment door clicks shut, and hollow silence packs the space Garrett recently filled.

34

GARRETT

Thursday morning, my words flow onto the page—a mountain stream fed by the early spring melt-off. That might have something to do with Safina—the Zara-inspired character—being in the scene.

It's a steamy scene—as steamy as it can get when I'm the one writing it.

I hadn't intended for it to unfold as it had. But I couldn't get the picture of Zara's naked breast from three days ago out of my head. The perfect fullness of it. And the hard, rose-brown nipple that has since fueled my lust-filled dreams.

And the next thing I knew, while writing this morning, the argument between Safina and William had shifted directions, and clothes started flying. Their clothes.

For some reason, the scene felt right. Correction. The scene felt like it fit, but I have no idea if I used the right words or if it came out sounding cheesy.

Maybe Zara could check it out and give me feedback.

I rub my hand down my face, imagining her reading the scene, only for her to burst out laughing. But better her than a reviewer or a reader. They won't be laughing...unless it's so bad, it's funny.

A text pings on my phone.

> Tyson: Deploying next week for twelve months. Hoping to bring family to visit you once I'm stateside again.

> Me: Looking forward to it. Can't wait to challenge your ass on the local trails.

I'm sure he'll whip *my* ass on them—not that I'll admit that to him.

I return to working on my novel.

A giggle outside the window a few minutes later yanks my attention from the laptop screen to my daughter. Athena is blowing bubbles while Peony tries to catch them. But the breeze keeps playing games, pushing them away, preventing Peony from touching them.

I could use a brief break from writing, so I put my laptop on the desk and join them in the backyard.

"Hey, you two. What are you doing?" It's a rhetorical question.

Peony points to the bubbles floating up. One bumps into a branch and bursts. "Pop!" Peony's toothy smile grows wider.

I chuckle. "You know what? If you fly, you can catch the bubbles."

Peony watches a few more bubbles bump into branches, then holds up her arms. "Fly!" She bounces up and down, her feet not leaving the grass, her knees doing all the work. "Fly! Fly!"

Her trust in me has grown considerably in the past two weeks, and a bubble-light warmth fills me. I hoist her up, laughter rolling through me.

It might be time to introduce her to my father and Kellan

again. To introduce her to Lucas and Troy. To see if she'll give them a chance now she has accepted me.

"Okay, Athena. More bubbles." I nod at her.

She pulls the long hoop from the solution and blows a stream of bubbles.

"Ready to pop them?" I lift Peony toward the closest bubble.

She pokes it with her finger, and it bursts. Peony and Athena cheer.

I move her to another bubble. She claps it between her small hands. We chase a few more, Peony popping each one.

My phone rings in my pocket. I consider ignoring it. I'd rather not interrupt the precious time I have with my daughter before I have to get back to work. But it's the tune I programmed for Emily, and she would only call me at this time of day if it was important.

I lower Peony onto my hip, her little legs straddling me, and answer the phone with my other hand. "Hey, Em. What's up?"

"Hi. I'm sorry to interrupt you while you're working, but Zara has her rheumatologist appointment this afternoon. I can't drive her anymore because I'm now dealing with a work crisis. I know you're super busy with your deadline, but can you take her?"

I frown—and not because Emily barely took a breath in all that. "What rheumatologist appointment?"

Emily mutters something that sounds suspiciously like, "Oh, shit."

"What rheumatologist appointment?" I repeat, my tone harsher this time.

Peony squirms in my arm. I crouch, lowering her to the ground. She toddles off after a small butterfly flying around the flower beds.

A thickening silence stretches on the other end of the line. I walk along the stepping stones leading to the garden beyond the hedge. "Don't make me ask a third time, Em."

"She has an appointment this afternoon in Portland," Emily says, defeat carrying the words on a sigh. "I said I would drive her, and Kellan was fine with that. But he got called away on an emergency and I need to stay here...and no one else is available to drive Zara to Portland."

My frown deepens. "Why does she need to see a rheumatologist?"

A bird somewhere above my head squawks as if in reply, and Peony's faint giggles reach me from the other side of the tall hedge.

"Samuel and her family physician suspect Zara's eye inflammation and her chronic pain might be linked." None of what she's telling me is news—other than the rheumatologist appointment.

Why didn't Zara ask me to drive her when she found out about the appointment? Why didn't she tell me what Samuel and her physician suspected?

I get the location and time deets from Em and text Zara.

Me: I'll pick you up at 1 p.m.

That will give us enough time to get there.

Zara: Pick me up for what?

Me: Your rheumatologist appt

That you never told me about.

Zara: You don't need to come. Em's driving me.

Me: Change of plan. Emergency came up.

Zara: You can't drive me. You have a deadline!!!

Me: And you have an appt. Your appt
trumps all.

Granted, my publisher and the movie studio might not see it that way, but that's not my concern right now. Zara is.

Zara: Really, Garrett, you don't need to
drive me. I can drive myself.

I snort a humorless laugh and speed dial her number. She picks up on the second ring.

"If you could drive yourself," I say before she can respond, "you wouldn't have asked Emily to take you. A few hours won't kill the book. Besides, I need your feedback on a scene I'm working on." Specifically, the steamy one.

"What kind of scene?" Suspicion swings in her tone, and I picture her dubiously eyeing her phone.

"One that involves the kind of books you, Em, and Simone like to read."

"Romance? You're talking about romance novels?" A silent chuckle wraps through her vowels, dangles from her consonants.

"Yup, I'm talking about romance. We can discuss it when I pick you up in two hours."

Her low, throaty laugh pours through the phone line, teasing me. "Can't wait."

We end the call, and I return to where Peony and Athena are playing.

Peony toddles to me, her little legs moving quickly. She stops and lifts her arms. "Fly! Fly!"

Her wide toothy grin is too irresistible to say no to, even if I should return to work. I scoop her up under her arms.

Holding her high, I do a lap of the small area of grass. Peony makes a funny spluttering-engine noise that sends Athena doubling over with laughter and has me chuckling.

We finish the lap, ending up at the patio. I press a light kiss on Peony's forehead. It's just a small kiss, the kind a parent gives their child. The kind I've witnessed Athena do plenty of times.

It's a test. To see just how far we've come. To see if Peony is ready to accept me as her father. To accept *me*, the man who this amazing little girl has wrapped around her fingers.

Peony stiffens in my arms, and it feels like we're back to where we started, when she showed up in my life.

A portion of my heart crumples at her hands. Falls to the ground like a dying leaf, ready to be crushed under foot.

But then the tension seems to fizzle from her body. She rests her head on my chest, where my heart is thumping loudly for her, and all the air in my lungs whooshes out in relief.

I tighten my arms in a small hug, letting her know she's safe. I don't want to put her down, to let go of her now I've built this level of trust between us. A thinly woven trust, easily broken if not treated with the utmost care.

Her trust is one of the most precious things in this world.

She is the most precious thing.

But as much as I don't want to let go of my daughter, I don't have a choice. I can't let Zara down either. And I have to get in more words before picking her up for her appointment.

Is this what parenting is? Juggling so many plates and trying not to drop any. Hoping if one cracks, the outcome won't be devastating.

I don't know how my parents managed. Mom worked part time as a nurse, but she also had three boys—four once Kellan became part of the family. She helped us with our schoolwork, took care of us, drove us to hockey practices and games. Yet, she was still there for her friends and neighbors if they needed a helping hand.

I always suspected Mom was a superhero. Now I'm a single father, trying not to let any plates fall, I'm more than ever convinced of it.

"As much as I want to stay and play with you two," I tell Peony, "I have to work a little longer and then drive Zara to Portland. But I'll be back in time for your bedtime."

I look up in time to catch Athena's frown. The grooves in her forehead swiftly smooth away, leaving me to wonder if I imagined the annoyed expression. Or maybe it was worry. Or jealousy.

None of the emotions make sense, so I brush her reaction aside. It was nothing more than my imagination, the side effect of being a fiction author. She's not a character in any of my books, past or present. The last thing I need to do is interpret her reactions as if she is.

I really know nothing about Athena—about her past, her family, her life goals—so I can't possibly know what she's thinking. And I shouldn't mentally accuse her of thoughts that aren't truly there.

Once *Untold Mercy* is with my editor, I'll make more of an effort to get to know Athena. Make more of an effort to get her to open up to me. As employer and employee. As friends.

I put Peony down on the grass. Another butterfly flutters by the hydrangeas, and Peony toddles over to check it out.

"Don't worry about making lunch for me," I tell Athena. "I'll grab something quick before I leave."

I return to my office, post an update on social media about the shitload of Advance Reader Copies the publisher is giving away of my upcoming release, and then semi-disappear into my work in progress. But it's hard to focus on the words; my thoughts keep drifting to how Zara needs to see a rheumatologist. The cause of her pain is beyond her family physician's level of expertise.

And that's making me antsy.

My word count has spluttered to nearly a standstill by the time I get ready to pick up Zara.

Even though I told Athena not to worry about making me

lunch, a sandwich sits at my place on the kitchen table. Athena is on the couch, reading to Peony from one of the picture books.

I sit at the table, watching them as I eat, wishing I could join them. But I have no intention of making Zara miss her appointment. I have no intention of not being there for her.

Zara is waiting for me outside as I pull up in front of her building.

Her brow creased, she climbs onto the passenger seat of the Explorer. I can't read Athena's expressions, but I know Zara's as well as I know my own.

"You're not a burden, so get that thought out of your head. I'm happy to help you out." I'd do anything for Zara. She's got to know that by now. "I'm more than just your kissing buddy." The corner of my mouth quirks up, and my gaze drops to her lips. The full lips I can't wait to kiss again.

Zara's thigh bounces on the car seat. Damn, she's nervous as hell. Usually, the leg bouncing is reserved for when she's super stressed. If we weren't sitting in the Explorer, needing to get going, I'd kiss her.

I reach over and thread her fingers with mine. "You don't have to do this alone, Zara. I'll be there for you. If you want." I squeeze her hand and pull away from the curb.

"I know. I just hate going all that way for nothing. I saw a rheumatologist in Eugene a few weeks ago, and he thought I *might* have early rheumatoid arthritis. What makes this rheumatologist any different?"

"Maybe this one will have more definitive answers. Your physician referred you to them for a reason." One person can't be an expert in everything. If my FBI contacts can't answer one of my book-related questions, they get the answer from someone who *is* an expert on the topic—as long as the information isn't classified.

"Hopefully you're right."

I release her hand and steer right onto the busy residential street. We drive past single-story homes and the scattering of cars parked in front of them.

"How are the renovations going?" I feel out of the loop compared to normal because of my deadline.

"Not bad. I'm also in the process of planning a grand reopening. Lauren McNair has agreed to perform during the afternoon."

"That's great." Her eclectic mix of country, pop, and '70s-style pop-rock music has gained her quite a following in the area.

"I'm also planning a sampler menu for the day, so people can try out the different foods that usually rotate on the menu."

I briefly shift my eyes from the road in time to catch a wry smile curving her mouth. "So, you want to tell me why you need my romance novel 'expertise'?" She air quotes the word.

I'm more interested in finding out why she never told me about the previous rheumatology appointment and how she might have rheumatoid arthritis, but I let her take the lead in the conversation. I explain the scene I'm working on, and that I'm upping the level of romance in the story compared to in my previous books.

She laughs my favorite throaty chuckle. The sound of it slightly eases my own concerns about what's going on with her body. Concerns I don't want to give voice to...in case that's all it takes to make them come true.

"I can definitely help with that." Her lips twitch, as if trying to hold back more laughter. "Just how steamy are you looking to write? I'm assuming not super spicy, since that's not what your books are known for."

I have no idea what that entails, but I can guess. And she's right. That's not what my readers expect from me. "Maybe midlevel steam."

"I can loan you the romances with scenes appropriate for

your book. And I'll mark the pages—with the kissing and the spicy times—so you don't have to read the entire novel."

"That'll be great. Thanks."

"And I'd be happy to read your scenes and give you feedback, so you don't get any WTF reviews." The sexy laughter returns to her tone, hitting me square in the groin, causing my cock to perk up.

I swallow a groan. *What the fuck?*

This is Zara. My best friend. The woman I shouldn't want. The woman who has been sneaking into my dreams lately. Dreams I had in college and she starred in more times than I want to confess to.

Dreams that would put those spicy scenes she's referring to...to shame.

35

GARRETT

Zara and I arrive at the medical building with ten minutes to spare. She's been squirming in her seat for the past thirty minutes. Discomfort or nervousness creases her brow, her teeth pressed into her pinkish-brown, plump lower lip.

I find an empty parking spot not far from the entrance. Zara climbs out of the Explorer but doesn't move beyond where we're parked, her eyes on the building. Uncertainty wars on her face.

I walk to her side of the SUV and cup her cheek. Her jasmine-scented skin is soft beneath my fingertips. "Hey, you okay?"

Her beautiful brown eyes meet mine, the emotion in them unchanged. "Can I have a kiss?"

"You can definitely have a kiss. Anytime you want." I capture her mouth with mine, and her lips part, giving me access to the sweet heat of her mouth.

Christ, I've missed her. Missed this.

My tongue strokes hers, and I'm eager to distract her for even a few seconds from whatever awaits her upstairs. The warm spring breeze brushes against us, as if wanting to get in on the action. Small birds from a nearby tree chirp their approval. I deepen the kiss.

It's been six days since I last kissed her. Six days since we made the deal to kiss whenever we need a dopamine hit.

While it might be six days since my mouth tasted hers, it's been only three since I had my mouth on the smooth skin of her neck. Three days since I first wanted to suck on her perfect nipple.

Just the thought of that makes me hard.

Zara's hands rest on the outside of my thighs, and her thumbs stroke a teasing caress over my denim-covered skin. Her touch is intoxicating, and it isn't helping my situation. But that doesn't stop me from taking one more swipe of her mouth with my tongue, memorizing her taste.

I pull away, not wanting to, but we're going to be late if we don't get going. "You ready to go upstairs?"

She nods and winces.

"Your neck?"

"Yes. And everywhere else. My body isn't a fan of long car rides these days. I'll be fine once I move around." She takes a couple of steps toward the front entrance, but her movements are stiff, robotic. It's like each step takes tremendous effort, but her expression barely reveals anything, a mask pulled into place.

Shit, I've never seen her like this. The caveman part of me wants to hoist her up and carry her to the rheumatologist's office. But she won't appreciate it. She's stubborn. Independent.

She'll pinch the skin on my arm if I try.

I speak from experience.

I hold out my arm for her to take, and we slowly walk to the main entrance. "I forgot to tell you," I say, as if we're out for a casual stroll. "I found a child-play psychologist for Peony." I'd meant to tell Zara during the ride to Portland, when she asked me how Peony was doing, but then we started talking about something else, and the thought slipped my mind until now.

"That's great. What does Athena think about the person?"

"I haven't told her anything about it yet. Simone gave a list of names the other day, and I contacted a few of them." I talked to one of them on the phone and felt instantly at ease with her.

Hopefully, Peony feels the same way with the therapist. And if not? I'll try someone else on the list. "We have an appointment with the therapist in two weeks. 'Cause Peony can't talk yet and tell the therapist what's wrong, it could end up taking a lot longer for the benefits of therapy to be seen."

"I can imagine it is more challenging. And frustrating for you and Peony." Zara flashes me a smile. "But see? I knew you'd be an amazing father."

"I'm not sure about that yet. But I am trying. We'll see how *that* goes when I take her to my parents' next week for dinner, so she can finally meet my brothers." And to see if Peony is more accepting of my father now that she's more comfortable with me.

"That's all you can do. Try." Zara smiles at me again. This time something stirs inside me, an emotion I can't name, and an intense craving to kiss her once more broadsides me.

But there's no time for that.

Not if we want to make it to the rheumatologist appointment on time.

I'M SITTING IN THE WAITING ROOM, FLIPPING THROUGH MY SOCIAL media account, responding to comments left on my recent posts. Someone calls out my name, and I jerk my head up to see who it was.

The woman in scrubs who took Zara to the exam room stands by the front desk and looks to where I'm sitting.

I stand. The murmuring in the room intensifies, like a swarm of locusts descending on a field.

"The author," a woman to my right whispers. "He's a *New York Times* bestselling thriller author."

I don't look to see who said it. The nurse approaches me and is the only person here who has my attention. I've had people approach me at restaurants because they recognize my face from my books. Normally, I'm happy to talk to fans, to let them know I appreciate them. I wouldn't be where I am today without them.

But this is one of those rare times when I don't want to be recognized, when I don't want to be approached.

The only thing I care about is what's going on with my best friend.

The nurse nods at me. "You can come back now."

She walks me down the corridor and points to a closed door. "You can go in. The doctor will be here in a minute, to talk to you and your girlfriend."

I don't bother correcting her on the girlfriend status and open the door. Zara is sitting fully clothed on one of the seats across from the exam table. Above the table is a close-up painting of a bear inspecting a butterfly on a daisy.

"The nurse brought me here," I say, taking the seat next to Zara. "But I can leave if you want."

"No, stay." Zara reaches for my hand.

Mine engulfs hers. "How did it go?"

"Pretty much the same as the appointment with the last rheumatologist. Lots of prodding and questions."

The door opens, and a tall woman of Asian descent enters the room. She looks to be in her late forties, a few laugh lines creasing at the corners of her eyes. Her dark hair is pulled up in a low bun.

She smiles at me. "Hi, I'm Dr. Winfrey."

"Garrett Carson."

Her eyes widen a tiny amount. "As in the thriller author?"

I chuckle, less reluctant to admit to it here than in the waiting room. "That would be me."

"My husband's a huge fan of your books."

My hand finds Zara's again. I never know how to respond to comments like this, when it's someone the person knows who's the fan. "Thank you."

Dr. Winfrey sits on the rolling stool. "So, Zara. I've reviewed your lab results, X-rays, and have a better picture of what we're looking at. Do you know anything about axial spondyloarthritis?"

Zara shakes her head. "Is that like ankylose...um. I can't remember what Dr. Holmes called it."

"Ankylosing spondylitis?"

"Yes, that's it. Dr. Holmes ruled it out because the pain was first felt in my shoulders. And my HL-something-or-other was negative. And he said something about the X-rays. Something about no signs of—" She waves her hand at Dr. Winfrey in a whatever-you-just-called-it gesture.

Dr. Winfrey gives her a patient, knowing smile. "Dr. Holmes's specialty doesn't include spondyloarthritis. HLA-B27 is a marker for the condition, but it's predominantly found in Caucasian patients. Having the marker doesn't mean you will go on to have axial spondyloarthritis, but the lack of it often leads to misdiagnosis."

My brain is spinning with all these foreign medical terms. I squeeze Zara's hand. The bear in the painting above the exam table symbolizes protection, the butterfly healing. I can't protect Zara from the condition, but whatever she needs, I'm here for her.

"He's also old-school," Dr. Winfrey adds. "You don't present with the SpA symptoms most commonly seen in men. Men usually experience pain in the base of their spine first. Women present the disorder differently, often with pain in the shoulders and the neck before anywhere else. That's why it usually takes longer for women to receive the proper diagnosis compared to men."

She turns her laptop to show an X-ray. "Your X-rays are negative for spine fusion. Which is a good thing. You have what is referred to as Non-radiographic Axial Spondyloarthritis. The other subtype of axial spondyloarthritis is ankylosing spondylitis, which is what Dr. Holmes was talking about."

She explains for a few minutes on what the condition means in the long term and about the complications Zara might experience. "Spondyloarthritis is different from other forms of arthritis. In the other forms, patients do better with lots of rest. In SpA, that tends to exacerbate the stiffness and pain. Which is why you experience more stiffness and pain when you get out of bed and why you've had trouble sleeping. The condition is also linked to loss of appetite, which you mentioned you've experienced over the past few weeks."

The last part is news to me. Hell, a lot of what Dr. Winfrey just said is news to me.

Apparently, Zara's been keeping things from me, not letting me know the full extent of what she's been dealing with.

Dr. Winfrey hands Zara a pamphlet. "This contains more information on SpA and tips for managing the pain, including different types of recommended exercise. Such as yoga. Going for walks. We have other pain med options we can try, but I would like to see if we can manage the condition with lifestyle changes first."

"Okay." Zara appears relieved compared to when we arrived at the clinic, the small crease between her eyes smoothing out.

"It's possible you'll experience flare-ups from time to time that exacerbate the pain. This is often the case during periods when you're dealing with high levels of stress. If that's the case, you might need to go on one of the other drugs for the short term or longer. The goal is to give you the highest quality of life possible, while using the holistic treatment approach as outlined in the pamphlet."

High levels of stress. That would make sense. Zara has been under increased stress lately with the expansion and the issue with the broken pipe at Picnic & Treats. Those could be what triggered the eye inflammation and why lately she looks so exhausted—more so than she usually does when she's stressed.

I take the pamphlet from Zara and flip through it. "Are there any restrictions with exercise?"

Zara laughs, the soft sound a low rumble in her chest. "I'm pretty sure that daily killer run you and Kellan go on would fall under the category of *don't even attempt.*" The corners of her mouth quirk into a quick grin.

"I recommend starting slow and listening to your body, Zara," Dr. Winfrey says. "Pushing yourself too hard might only make things worse. If your body tells you to slow down, slow down. If it tells you to get moving, get up and move. Go for a walk. Do some gentle stretches."

Her mouth curves into a reassuring smile that she splits between Zara and me. "I know it's a lot to take in. Read the pamphlet. It's by the Spondylitis Association of America. Their resources on the website should answer a lot of your questions too. I'm here to answer any others you might have, and I can provide additional guidance if you should need it."

Zara and I nod. My mind whirls with all the ways I can help her manage the condition that is conducting warfare on her beautiful body.

"If you have any questions referring to your specific case," Dr. Winfrey adds, "you can contact my office. I would like to see you in three months, to keep on top of things with your condition. But if you experience flare-ups that make the lifestyle changes—such as exercise—too difficult to do, let me know so we can alter your medication, if necessary."

Zara visibly relaxes with the last hit of information. She now has answers, a direction to take. And now we know what she's dealing with, I can help her. Because hell if I'm letting her face this alone.

She's my best friend.

The woman who has stuck by my side since the day she told my elementary-school bully where to go.

Zara and I walk to my Explorer in the parking lot. Her movements are stiff again, no doubt from sitting so long on the drive here and during the appointment. And now we have a long drive home.

"Do you need to get back to Maple Ridge right away?" I ask, my hand on the SUV passenger door handle.

Biting her bottom lip, she eyes the Explorer like it's a mouse scurrying her way. "I'm not expected anywhere anytime soon. But don't you need to get back to work?"

"I have a bit of time before I need to get back." I don't, but screw rushing to go home just yet. I don't want to make things worse for her by hitting the road so soon. "There's something I want to buy. And I thought we could go for a walk, in a nearby park, before we head home."

Zara's eyes brighten and turn skyward as if in a silent prayer of thanks. She knows why I suggested the walk. "What do you wanna buy?"

"You'll see."

I drive to a store that sells outdoors sports equipment, and we walk to the kids section.

"A child backpack carrier?" Zara's gaze roams over the metal frame with the canvas seat and zippered bag at the base of it.

"I've been wanting to take Peony on hikes on the local trails. This will let me do that. And I thought maybe you and I can go for daily walks around the lake or on Warrior property. This way Peony can also join us. If that's okay with you." Of course, all this would be a lot easier without the ticking deadline.

Excitement sparkles in Zara's eyes, its shine a backdrop to the skeptical bend of her mouth. "I would love it if Peony joins us. It won't be like those killer runs you go on with Kellan, though, will it?"

"Definitely not. It's about me spending time with Peony and helping you manage the spondyloarthritis."

It's about helping my best friend and being the father Peony deserves.

Being the father Cooper and Clarke don't get to be, because I failed them.

I couldn't save them after we accidentally triggered the explosion that stole them from their families. I failed to predict the building would be booby-trapped.

The ever-present guilt roaring under my skin has intensified since discovering I have a daughter. Peony is a constant reminder of how Cooper and Clarke are missing out on seeing their kids grow up.

"We'll take things as fast or as slow as you need." The last hike she went on with my brothers and our friends was more than a year ago.

Her lips slide into a grin that says she's going to hold me to that. "Sure. I'll do anything if it helps with the pain. But are you sure? What about your deadline?"

"It will be fine." I turn back to the child carrier, hiding the truth in my eyes that proclaims it will be anything but fine.

Just two months and twenty-three days to go till the book is due.

36

GARRETT

The following Thursday, I buckle Peony into her car seat and hand her Poppy. Athena climbs into the front passenger seat of the Explorer.

"Are you sure you'd rather not stay here?" I sense Athena would rather avoid going to my parents for dinner.

"No, I need to be there for Peony." She clicks her seat belt in place.

"My mom will be there, and Peony likes her." And trusts her. "Plus, Lucas and Simone's foster daughters." Maybe being around other young kids will make things easier for Peony.

I don't have time for dinner with the family, but I also don't want to delay introducing Peony again to my father and Kellan. And introducing her to Troy and Lucas, who haven't seen her yet.

After what happened at the playground with my father, I decided to wait until she was more comfortable with me before introducing her to the rest of the family. The goal is to help her feel like she's part of it. To feel safe and loved with all and any of us.

My brothers' vehicles are on the street in front of our

278

parents' house when we arrive. Athena removes Peony from her car seat while I grab Peony's bag from the trunk.

I join them at the back passenger door. Athena is staring at the house, chewing on her bottom lip. "You ready to see Granny? And Grandpa? And meet your uncles and Auntie Simone?" I tickle Peony under the chin and am rewarded with a giggle. "And you get to meet Butterscotch. You'll love Uncle Troy's little dog."

After much deliberation and consultation with my brothers, we decided Butterscotch, Jasper, and Bailey should also join us for dinner like they normally would have pre-kids.

Jasper is here for Kylie's and Zoe's benefit, and Bailey is here for Jess. After everything Jess has been through, she needs her psychiatric support dog by her side, even if Bailey is still undergoing her training. And while Jess might not be Troy's wife—not yet, anyway—she is very much part of our family.

Like Zara is, yet you didn't invite her to join us.

Not having Zara here feels wrong. Like part of me is missing. But she's coming over to my house later, so I'll see her then, for our evening walk.

A yawn powers its way to the surface, reminding me of what the book deadline and the daily walks and having a daughter cost me in terms of sleep last night. I barely cover my mouth in time to stifle the yawn.

Just two months and sixteen days, and then I can finally catch up on missed sleep.

"Tired?" Sympathy softens the anxiety creasing Athena's pale features.

"I'll be fine. What about you? Is Peony keeping you up with her nightmares?" The dark circles under Athena's eyes give it away.

Once therapy helps Peony deal with her demons, Athena will start getting more sleep too. I still have to tell her about it, but something's been stopping me—this niggling fear that

Athena won't approve even though I know play therapy is a good idea.

"No more than the moon is made of blue cheese," Athena says with a straight face, and my mouth quirks into a half smile.

"What does that even mean?" It's another of her most random, off-the-wall comments, which I'm getting used to.

She shrugs, confirming what I suspected she'd do. End of topic. Let's move on to something else.

"Have you heard anything 'bout your replacement ID and Social Security Number yet?" It's been more than a month now, and I'd prefer to start wiring her the money instead of handing over large amounts of cash, like I had to do the other day.

"No. Not yet. But you know how slow the government can be. A snail flattened by a tire moves faster." She kisses Peony on the temple. "Are you excited to meet the dogs?"

Peony tightens her hold on Poppy, squishing the panda against her body. "Yes!"

A symphony of little girl giggles reaches us as I open the wooden gate to the lush backyard I designed, planted, and nurtured.

Leafy plants make a soothing backdrop to the colorful spring flower beds framing the lawn. The large grassy area surrounds an odd-shaped pond with a waterfall, the gentle rush of the water usually calming. But now that we're here, facing so much uncertainty, the water thunders in my ears.

It's the newest additions to the backyard that put me at ease. Bringing Peony here wasn't a mistake. She'll be fine. Happy, even. Mom went all out here when it comes to her granddaughter, Kylie, and Zoe. A turtle-shaped sandbox, small slide, and water table now occupy one side of the lawn, each plastic toy cheery in color.

I shouldn't be surprised at the extent Mom has gone to for the three girls. I would've been more surprised if she hadn't turned the backyard into a mini wonderland.

"And how's my little princess doing?" Mom gushes, smiling warmly at Peony from next to the picnic table. Peony grins and waves at her from Athena's arms.

A small bark shifts Peony's attention from her grandmother to the golden Cavapoo sitting next to Troy.

"Doggy." Peony points to Butterscotch and squirms in Athena's arms.

I ask, "Do you want me to introduce you to Butterscotch?" And by default, my brother.

She nods, her gaze on the small fluffy dog.

I hold out my arms for Athena to pass me my daughter. A contemptuous frown narrows her eyes, and for a fleeting second, she looks like she plans to bail, taking Peony with her.

And maybe she would have if Peony hadn't stretched her arms out to me.

I don't know what Athena's problem is. It's like she's refusing to trust my family—which doesn't make sense. Mom has been nothing but supportive of Peony and Athena.

I take Peony from Athena and walk toward Butterscotch and Troy. My hand is secure on Peony's back, letting her know she's safe, nothing bad will happen to her. No villains will drop from the trees. No monsters will leap from the bushes.

No one will hurt her while she's in the protection of five retired Marines.

"Athena, why don't we go get some drinks?" Mom tells her. "Figure you and I can talk. Get to know each other a little better."

"I'm not sure I should leave Peony alone."

"She won't be alone." Mom smiles indulgently at Athena. "She's with Garrett. She'll be fine."

The slight downturn of Athena's mouth wordlessly says she disagrees, but she gives a small reluctant nod. "Okay." She and Mom head inside the house, and the back door clicks shut behind them.

As Peony and I draw closer to Butterscotch, everything shifts. Peony's body trembles under my touch and fear widens her eyes. The countdown in my head doesn't have time to commence. A high-pitched wail explodes from her little lungs, the noise so loud, so terrified, anyone on the street could hear it.

My heart clambers into my heart, the fast *dumb-dumb-dumb* echoing in my ears. Athena was right; bringing Peony here was a mistake.

Mistake or not, I need to fix this. I stop walking and pivot so we are no longer facing Troy and Butterscotch. But that doesn't seem to make a difference. Kellan and Lucas and my father are now in front of us by the pond. There's no missing them.

She makes eye contact with them and the intensity of her wails picks up, an air-raid siren signaling an incoming threat.

Shit. Now what?

Distract her. That's what I need to do.

I carry her to the blue hydrangeas and gently rock from side to side. "Do you see the pretty flowers?" I point to them. "Do you know what color they are?"

Peony continues wailing, the sound not quite as loud as before, but just as shrill.

"They're blue. Do you think they're pretty? Okay, not as pretty as the flower you're named after. Your mommy loved peonies. See that plant?" I point to a cluster of dark leaves. "It will produce beautiful peonies in a few months. Beautiful." I kiss the crown of her head. Her soft coils tickle my lips. "Just." Another kiss. "Like. You."

Peony's sobs start to slow to a hiccup. Still rocking from one foot to the other, I point to the different plants and tell her their names.

"What has you so scared, little flower?" I eventually ask her, my tone soft and inquiring. "You're safe here. My brothers— your uncles—and your grandfather will do everything in their power to protect you. That's what we do. We protect the people we love. And I know if you give them a chance, you'll love them. And they'll love you like I love you."

I pat her panda on the head. "Do you think Poppy would like to go down the slide Granny bought you? She can go *wheeeee* all the way down." I bend my knees in a quick dip.

Peony holds Poppy up. "Wheee!" Her sweet voice is thick with tears, tinged with a touch of joy.

I chuckle. "That's right. Wheee!" I brush my thumb over her wet cheeks. "Can I introduce you to your uncles now? We'll take it slow."

Part of me wonders if I should wait until after her first play therapy session next week. But a larger part—a part that might be an idiot when it comes to this parenting thing—tells me to try again but take smaller steps this time.

"We're just gonna meet Butterscotch. You can stroke him. He'd like that. You don't have to talk to Uncle Troy. Is that okay with you? You want to see the doggy?"

"Doggy," she whispers, her voice hoarse from crying.

I drag in a slow breath. *You've got this, soldier.*

With the level of care taken when dealing with an IED, I walk toward Butterscotch and stop three yards from him. I nod at Troy, who lowers himself to the ground, so he's sitting behind his dog.

"It will be okay," I tell Peony. "My brother won't hurt you. He's a really nice guy, just like his dog." I sit on the grass, positioning myself so Butterscotch is between us and Troy. Butterscotch flashes Peony a doggy grin and lowers to his stomach.

Peony clings to my side, her gaze torn between the dog she wants to stroke and the man who is a stranger to her. Her lower lip trembles, and I brace for the wailing to recommence. I'm ready to intervene if it does.

I stroke Butterscotch. Pride warms me at how Peony feared

me just four weeks ago. Now, she's holding on to me, like I'm a life preserver in fast-moving flood waters.

"Butterscotch is a very special dog," I explain, still stroking him. "He has magical powers, so when people stroke him, they don't feel so nervous. He volunteers with Uncle Troy at the Veterans Center, making people feel better." I doubt she understands any of what I'm telling her, but her grip loosens on my shirt, and she slowly inches toward Butterscotch.

Troy remains silent, watching Butterscotch perform his magic. The dog wielded the same magic on Jess when she first moved to town and was struggling with complex PTSD and anxiety.

Peony crouches in front of Butterscotch and follows my lead, gently stroking him with one hand. The other arm crushes Poppy against her body.

Kylie and Zoe giggle and squeal as they play with Jasper in my periphery. Peony continues stroking Butterscotch, her attention fully on him.

"Peony, that's Uncle Troy." I point to my brother, who's sitting cross-legged on the grass.

She tears her attention from Butterscotch and stares at Troy, trepidation narrowing her eyes.

He waves at her and offers her a small smile. "It's nice to meet you."

Her gaze moves from Troy and surveys the rest of the backyard, to where Kylie and Zoe are throwing Jasper's ball to him while Lucas supervises.

Peony points at Jasper. "Doggy." She then points to Simone, Jess, and Bailey. The three of them are watching the girls play. Bailey is lying next to Jess's feet and has on her *Service Dog in Training* vest. "Doggy," Peony repeats, referring to Jess's golden retriever.

"That's Bailey. She's a working dog. She helps Jess feel safe. Like Poppy makes *you* feel safe." I pat her panda on the head and gesture with a wave of my hand to Lucas and Simone's golden Labradoodle. "That's Jasper. Do you want to visit him?"

Or is meeting Troy enough for now?

She buries her face into my side, turning her head slightly to peek at the dogs—or their owners. I can't tell which.

I stroke my thumb across her shoulder blades. "That's okay. You can meet him when you're ready." I'm talking about Lucas, but my comment could refer to any of the males in the backyard—canine or human.

I nod my thanks to Troy. He returns the nod in a silent reply and pushes to his feet.

He and Butterscotch walk to where Jess, Bailey, and Simone are standing. He wraps his arms protectively around Jess's waist, and she leans into him.

A flash of longing hits me like the crack of lightning during an electrical storm. And a sudden, unexpected need to have Zara by my side swells in me. We wouldn't be able to kiss, since we're keeping this new twist to our friendship to ourselves. But still...I miss her.

I wish she were here.

Mom and Athena walk out of the house, carrying plastic glasses and a pitcher of lemonade. They place the stuff on the table, and Athena rushes over to join Peony and me. I have a feeling she witnessed through the kitchen window what happened, but Mom kept her from racing out to be there for Peony.

Athena kneels next to us and puts her hand on Peony's back, just below mine, our fingers touching. "Hi, sweet kebab. How are you doing?"

Peony turns to Athena. "Nina." She scrambles onto Athena's lap and is instantly engulfed in her arms.

"I'm sorry," Athena coos. "I knew you weren't ready yet." She doesn't look at me when she says it, but I don't miss the tiny bite to her tone that's clearly meant for me. "But you did good, little one."

"She's meeting with a play therapist next week," I casually inform Athena. "I'm hoping the therapist will have suggestions on how to make her comfortable with my father and brothers." Since today didn't go as I had hoped.

Athena frowns, and the flare of anger in her eyes from earlier returns. Peony doesn't notice it. Her attention is on the dogs again. "What do you mean she's meeting with a play therapist?"

I shrug. I should have probably given her a heads-up sooner, but Athena is Peony's nanny. She's not her mother. It isn't something I needed to discuss with her.

My family—Lucas and Simone—were the ones I turned to for help. They are the ones who gave me the list of names. They were instrumental in me getting Peony the help she desperately needs.

"She's too young to see a regular therapist," I explain. "She doesn't have the communication skills yet for that. But I thought with everything she's dealing with, what with the loss of her mother and the nightmares, she might benefit from play therapy."

The anger in Athena's eyes twists and reshapes into hurt. "You could have mentioned it before booking it." Hurt might glare coldly at me, but that's not the emotion laying fire to her tone. It scorches with frustration and worry and the irate stomp of her foot.

I stare at her for a beat, a frown creasing my brow. "Didn't realize I needed your approval. She is my daughter after all." I raise an eyebrow in emphasis.

"I didn't say you needed my approval. But a heads-up would have been nice."

"A heads-up? A heads-up for what, exactly?"

She tightens her hold on Peony as if afraid I'm going to rip my daughter from her arms. As if protecting Peony from me… and my plans.

Peony squirms, her attention on the two girls and Jasper.

"Sorry," Athena murmurs and loosens her grip. "I…I just want to know…that's all." Accusation burns in her tone, but all the steam behind it has fizzled.

My own anger at the situation snaps and crackles under my skin, but for Peony's sake, I let Athena's comments and attitude slide. I don't bother to remind her that I did let her know about the play therapy…a few moments ago. I could have waited until after Peony and I returned home from the appointment.

"So when exactly is it?"

"A week today. The therapist is in Portland, so I'll be taking the afternoon off for it."

"Is…is Zara going with you?"

The emotion in her tone, prickly with thorns, sets me on edge. "No, she's busy with the café expansion." Not to mention the drive would be hard on her. I keep my voice even, void of any emotion that indicates my irritation.

The jaggedness smooths from Athena's expression, and a smile curves on her mouth. "That's good. That you're taking Peony to see someone. Can…can I go with you? In case I have questions for the therapist?"

I frown at her sudden shift in attitude, unsure why it makes me feel more unsettled than it should, but I still nod in reply. Why the sudden pivot when she found out Zara wouldn't be coming with Peony and me?

I brush the question aside. The abrupt change doesn't matter. What matters is Peony, and how therapy could make a big difference in her healing after the loss of her mother.

37

ZARA

I open the front door to Garrett's house. Peony's delighted giggles greet me, the sound coming from the living room. I slip off my shoes and walk toward the back of the house, carrying my yoga mat with me.

Garrett is sitting on the couch with Peony on his lap, a board book open in his hand. "'Where is my shoe?' Lucy Mouse squeaks." Garrett says the dialogue in an adorable, high-pitched voice that has Peony giggling again.

Damn. The two of them together are too cute for words.

I lean the yoga mat against the couch and sit next to Garrett, close enough that our shoulders almost touch. Garrett tosses me a quick smile without missing a beat and continues reading the story.

This is the life I once dreamed of. A life with Garrett as my husband, reading to our children. But then I discovered he and Kenda were secretly hooking up and had inadvertently fallen in love, and the dream ruptured, its spiraling death long and painful.

And now here I am, the dream almost reality.

Except Kenda is Peony's mother, and Garrett will never love me the way he loved her.

But Kenda is dead, and you're the one he's kissing.

Yes, for the dopamine rush and stress release. With everything going on—the spondyloarthritis diagnosis, the expansion, the delays because of the burst water pipe, planning the grand reopening, talking to local women-owned small businesses about possible partnerships—anything that reduces my stress level is greatly appreciated.

Especially when stress is the trigger that causes my SpA symptoms to worsen.

And worsening symptoms will screw up my ability to function.

Further adding to my stress...

It's a never-ending cycle. One I'm trying not to get caught up in—a tornado that never dies. Always spinning, spinning, spinning.

Athena walks into the living room. Her gaze falls on me and a small frown wrinkles her forehead. I can't tell if she's jealous I'm sitting next to Garrett, or if she's frustrated with me for some other reason.

"Hi, Athena," I say a little too brightly.

She nods like she's been doing since we first met. Resigned. No doubt wishful I would just flutter away like a bug caught in a stiff breeze, even though I've given her no reason to feel that way. A small smile tilts on her mouth, but I can't tell if it's genuine or if it took effort to plaster it onto her face.

Garrett is busy reading the book to Peony and doesn't notice Athena's reaction to me.

There's nothing I can do about the situation. She's Peony's nanny, and Garrett needs her if he plans to finish his book on time. It's not like she's done anything wrong. So, hell if I'm rocking the boat. Not at the risk of capsizing it. She adores

Peony and Peony adores her back, and that's the most important thing.

I dunno. Does she have a thing for Garrett? Does she see me as competition?

I almost snort a laugh at that. The last thing I am is competition. Sure, Garrett and I are kissing, but we're not a couple. We're just friends—and that's all he sees me as. His friend.

Garrett finishes the story and closes the book. "Bedtime, little flower. Say good night to Zara."

Peony waves at me. "Night-night, Za-wa!"

"Good night, sweetheart." I wave at her, and while Garrett and Athena put her to bed, I check my social medias.

Garrett, Peony, and I usually go for a walk in the evenings, but I went for a walk on my own earlier, since they were at his parents' place for dinner.

He returns to the living room alone. "It's nice out. I thought we could go in the backyard."

Guilt and shame thicken in my throat, making it difficult to swallow. I'm not the only one stretched well beyond their limit. Yet here he is, taking time from his busy writing schedule to help me because my body is at war with itself. "You sure you have time for this?"

"I'm sure. Besides, it benefits me too, after spending the day with my ass in the chair. It wouldn't hurt to learn a few yoga poses."

Garrett grabs a bath towel to use as a yoga mat, and we head outside.

We walk down the stone path to the section of the garden that's out of view of the house. The grassy spot is peaceful, with a wooden bench to one side, currently in shadow from the nearby trees. Flower beds skirt the rest of the area, other than where the tall hedge separates this part of the garden from the one closest to the house.

Quiet and secluded, it's the perfect spot for practicing yoga.

I slowly inhale a lungful of crisp mountain air, clearing out some of the cobwebs that have made themselves at home in my body with the spondyloarthritis.

I'm releasing the air when Garrett turns to me. His mouth is on mine before I can register what's going on.

My lips part, welcoming him in. I'm vaguely aware of dropping my yoga mat onto the grass, of my arms looping around his neck, of my body pressing into his, hungry for his heat, his touch.

Hungry for his everything.

Our kiss deepens, and our tongues wrestle and stroke, taste and devour. Every part of me tingles with need. Want. Desire. I moan softly into his mouth, never wanting the kiss to end. Desperate to stay in this bubble forever.

This kiss and the other ones from him are exactly like I had dreamed about all those years ago, when the yearning for my best friend became as real as the sunset, as real as the mountains gazing down at us.

The kiss starts out frantic, an unquenchable thirst. But after a few moments, it settles into slow sips of an intoxicating beverage that can be felt all the way to my toes.

We eventually come up for air, our breathing ragged, foreheads kissing.

"I needed that." Garrett's growled words breeze over my lips. He straightens, our body's shifting but still touching.

I loosen my hold but don't let go of him. "Bad dinner at your parents?"

"Peony started crying when I tried to introduce her to Troy. And things didn't improve when she saw Dad, Lucas, and Kellan."

My heart breaks for Garrett. He was so hoping Peony would accept the men in his family now that she has accepted him as her father.

"Things did eventually get better after I distracted her, but she wanted nothing to do with them." His lips press in a defeated line. "If not for the dogs, my mom, Simone, and Jess, we would have left. She wasn't scared of them. She was only scared of my father and my brothers."

Like she was at first—after arriving in Maple Ridge—afraid of Garrett.

The question is why? Why is she so scared of them when they have done nothing to warrant that level of fear?

"I'm so sorry, Garrett. I know you were hoping things would go differently. I thought maybe they would too." I lower my arms from around his neck. "I wonder why she's having a hard time trusting your father and brothers. Did the shooting really mess her up that much? Or has she always had trouble trusting men?" From the sounds of it, she hasn't had any interactions with men since arriving in Maple Ridge, other than Garrett's family.

"I know. It's not like her mother was leery—unless someone did something to give her a reason to be that way."

"You're right. Kenda was a social butterfly, always happy to interact with everyone, no matter the gender they associated with." It was why she was such a great journalist. She had a way of getting people to open up to her. "So what would cause Peony to not trust men when Kenda wasn't like that? Do you think it's the shooting? Have you asked Athena?"

"I haven't." He scoffs out a humorless half laugh. "I'm not sure she would even give me a straight answer if I did. She's super private. About everything. But it makes sense that Peony doesn't trust men because of the shooting."

"Maybe Peony's therapist will figure it out. Eventually."

"I hope so." Garrett bends to retrieve the towel he dropped on the grass. "Ready to show me some yoga poses?"

I unroll my mat next to Garrett's towel on the grass, and I show him a few of the moves I learned from a video I found online. The chirping of birds, the scampering of a squirrel in a tree, and the occasional rustle of leaves are the only sounds entering our peaceful cocoon.

"So, I found a video on the Spondyloarthritis website yesterday," Garrett says as we're coming out of the final pose. The way he stresses "So" snags my attention, like a big fat highlighter squiggle on a page. "The presenter on the video mentioned that orgasms increase the pain threshold by a hundred percent."

I splutter out a laugh and sit on my mat. *This should be interesting.* "They did?"

Garrett drops his ass next to me on my yoga mat. "She did. Whatever that means."

I hold out my hand so it's level, my science background geeking into high gear. "Okay, say this is the pain threshold." I wiggle my hand. "If the pain stimulus from the injury or disease is below this threshold, the person doesn't experience pain. But once the amount of stimulus is enough to reach this threshold"—I wiggle my hand again—"then you feel pain. The more neurons activated, the greater the pain." That's the simple explanation. The only explanation he needs to know for the sake of this discussion.

"So if the video is right and orgasms increase the pain threshold"—I move my hand up—"the amount of pain I'll feel will be less...or nonexistent." Sounds good to me.

"That's not a bad deal. Plus, who doesn't love a good orgasm?" Garrett's rough, rumbled chuckle hits my girl parts in all the right ways. Or maybe that was due to how the word *orgasm* rolled from his mouth, like melted chocolate.

I grin. "Right? But unlike painkillers, orgasms are side-effect free. You can't go wrong with them." Side-effect free, other than they can be highly addictive. But I don't bother mentioning that.

"True. The only downside is the benefit supposedly only lasts twenty-four hours."

I snicker like a fourteen-year-old boy in sex-ed class. "Well, that's disappointing."

Another low, sexy laugh rumbles through Garrett, and heat flickers in my belly.

"Isn't it? But that's no different than with painkillers." He lifts his shoulders in a slight shrug. "I'm guessing from your initial reaction, orgasms don't give you any sort of pain relief? So maybe the info in the video was theoretical."

I lie back down onto my side, my elbow propping up my head. "Maybe it is theoretical and maybe there's truth to it. I wouldn't know. I haven't been given an orgasm in..." One. Two. Three years? That can't be right. "...in a very long time."

Garrett's eyebrows shoot up, the surprise on his face down-played by the one-sided twitch of his lips. "Are you telling me that what's-his-name never gave you an orgasm?"

"You mean Joseph?" I almost snort the last part out.

"Yeah, him."

"He...um...well...we never had sex. He wasn't in a rush to take our relationship to the next level." Probably because he was in love with his ex-wife.

Garrett mutters something that could have been, "Christ, he really was an idiot." He shakes his head as if unable to compre-hend my ex's reaction to sex. "So you haven't had orgasm-inducing sex in a while."

"More like no *sex* in a while. Period."

"What about orgasms from your own hand. Or have you never touched yourself?"

I snicker again. I can't believe we're having this conversa-tion. "I have. Both my hand and vibrator have given me orgasms, but the orgasms weren't strong enough to impact the pain. Or maybe what you saw in the video is fake news." A chal-lenge, unexpected and seductive, sits in my tone. At the thought of Garrett touching me, of him giving me an orgasm so earth-shattering the impact is felt throughout my body...I swallow.

My pussy tightens in a wave of need, and wetness rushes to between my legs. Lord, if this is how my body responds to the mere thought of Garrett touching me, what would it be like if he actually did?

The air in my lungs whooshes out on a shaky breath.

My gaze searches his, probing the depths of his warm brown eyes, the silent questions humming in my brain.

His breath softly hitches. "Zara." The low, rough rumble of his voice hits me in all the right places, cranks up my need for sweet relief. A different relief than what my painkillers bring me. "Do you want me to give you an orgasm? So we can see if the video has any truth behind it?"

"Like a scientific experiment?"

The kissing we've been doing is one thing; what he's suggesting is in another stratosphere. I love our friendship, the way we're always there for each other. The way he knows how to make my day brighter when it feels like I'm stuck in a never-ending storm.

He is my heart.

My soul...even if he doesn't realize it.

But what he's proposing isn't the typical friends-with-benefits arrangement. He's talking about a side-effect-free, adjunct painkiller. How can I argue against that?

"Exactly like a scientific experiment," Garrett says, looking genuinely earnest.

"Okay." The word is drawn out as all kinds of questions and scenarios spin in my head, snagging on the possibilities. Stumbling on how it could all go wrong, on what it could do to our friendship. "Just so we're on the same wavelength, what are you proposing?"

38

ZARA

Garrett leans in, his warm breath brushing the shell of my ear. "I want to touch you." His voice is a low growl. "Make your panties wet. Make you come with my name on your lips. I want to finger fuck you, Golden Girl."

Oh. My.

"Wh-when?"

"Now." His voice is lace with smoldering, dirty thoughts, and I'm close to fanning my flaming face with my hand.

My panties are ready to incinerate, and he hasn't even touched me yet. "Okay." It comes out this time more of a squeak than an actual spoken word. I clear my throat. "Okay."

His fingers glide over my hip and sloooowly travel along the outside of my thigh. The teasing touch is enough to ignite every nerve ending in my body, like the opening colorful blooms in a grand fireworks display.

Guess we're really doing this.

I shift position, lying on my back, and widen the space between my legs.

Garrett's fingers caress languid circles on my inner thigh, inching their way up, up, up. I'm surprised I don't wiggle down to get them that much sooner to the part of me that aches for his touch. Although if he goes any slower, I might do just that.

Garrett lowers his head to mine, pauses for a beat, and captures my mouth with a heart-shattering kiss.

My lips instantly part, and my tongue rejoices at dancing with his again. We explore each other's mouths, the kiss deepening more with each passing second. I've always suspected he would be a good kisser, but this...the way he consumes me, worships me...it's everything and so much more. I'm close to orgasming from his kiss alone.

He brushes his fingers along my seam. "Fuck, you're already hot for me." The hungry growl in his voice has me whimpering. "Are you wet for me too?" His lips brush mine once more, and his fingers press against my clit, the touch teasing, full of promise.

A starving need has me widening my legs. I want him, this, more than I want oxygen.

He draws tight circles around my clit, bringing me closer to the edge. I don't remember the last time it felt this way, and he's not even touching me skin on skin.

A needy groan escapes me. Garrett swallows it, his mouth on mine. The glide of his tongue...the stroke of his fingers... perfectly synchronized. He's playing me like an instrument. I'm the violin to his bow. Each move of his hand, each flick of his tongue, elicits a whisper, a whimper, a moan.

His hand moves away from my core, sliding up to the waistband of my yoga pants. Yoga pants, which until last week, I never used as they were intended. And now they're experiencing an entirely new type of lesson in flexibility.

Garrett's fingers slip under the waistband and continue south, reclaiming that which he had teased only moments ago. "Fuck, you're so wet," he murmurs as his fingers slide along my lips, slick from the way he's got my body panting for him.

He continues to work me up, my body tightening with each pass of his thumb over my super-swollen clit.

I brush my fingers along his hard length, visible through the cotton of his running shorts. A strangled groan falls from him, and I have to bite back a satisfied grin.

Garrett shakes his head. "Not this time. This is about you, and only you."

I cling to the *Not this time* as his finger presses inside of me, curving to find that magical spot. Another thick finger joins it, taking me closer to the edge. *Not much further.*

My body bucks and writhes, searching for sweet relief. *So close. Ever so close.*

"Come for me, Golden Girl." The growled words vibrate against my neck, the final push I need to collapse over the ledge.

White-hot liquid heat pours through every inch of me, and I cry out from the intensity. Then I'm floating skyward in a body that feels unrestrained, the tether holding me to my body disintegrating.

My ragged breaths fan my lips as I come back to myself. I should probably care I cried out and possibly alerted Garrett's neighbors to what we are doing.

I probably should care, but right now, I can't find it in myself to give a damn.

A smile lazily curves my lips as I take in the gorgeously deep shades of orange, red, and mauve stretching across the sky. "Wow. It's been a while, but I don't remember it ever being that good." I turn my head to Garrett.

He's sitting upright next to me, watching me expectantly. His smile is pure smug satisfaction, and I barely keep from rolling my eyes. "Glad you enjoyed it."

I snort a laugh and push up to sit, my body still feeling like it's floating somewhere in the heavens. "Don't let that go to your head."

But he's a man—of course his ability to give me an orgasm will go to his head.

"So? Did it work?"

Work? It takes a beat to figure out what he means, and I catalog how my body feels. Maybe it's just a placebo effect, but the earth-shattering orgasm seems to have helped with the pain. "There's...there's definitely something to that video. I mean, my body still aches, but...but it's like the volume has been turned down a bit. Like...like background noise that isn't quite as loud as before. If that makes any sense."

Now, if only I didn't need to have orgasms once a day to keep up this benefit. It's not as simple as popping a pill, given that Garrett and I don't live together.

And we're not a couple.

The other downside of this holistic approach to pain management is I've stumbled, as feared, across a new addiction. A Garrett-induced orgasm addiction. Since when were orgasms this mind-blowing? This *wow*?

If only my vibrator were as capable as Garrett's hand.

If only *my* hand were as capable as Garrett's fingers.

A rustle of leaves has me turning to the sound. The noise wasn't caused by the wind. More like an animal. A large animal.

"Um, you haven't had any bears or cougars wandering through your backyard lately, have you?" I whisper, straining in the dimming light to make out what could have caused the leaves to rustle like that.

"No, why?"

"I thought I heard something. Over there." I point to the hedge that separates this part of the garden from the garden closer to the house.

Movement catches my eye near where I'm pointing. Then whatever caused it races in a flash of floral toward the house.

I groan, covering my heated face with my hands. "I think Athena witnessed our experiment." I drop my hands from my face and lean back on them, my cheeks still burning. "She was standing by the hedge, but I don't know how much she saw."

Garrett shrugs, not at all flustered. *Of course.* "What difference does it make?"

I huff a near laugh. "Such a guy response."

"It wasn't like we were naked." His mouth tilts into a smirk and amusement dances in his eyes.

"Having someone watch me while I come isn't on my bucket list." Not even close.

Garrett chokes out a laugh. "I was watching you. Does that make me a peeper?"

"Well, no."

"Am I supposed to not watch you next time?" He closes the distance between us, until his breath brushes the shell of my ear. "Because that would be a shame," he murmurs. "You're sexy as fuck when I give you an orgasm."

Oh, damn. Garrett's dirty talk has my pussy clenching and the air in my lungs coming out in raspy little pants.

I don't remember him ever referring to me as sexy. "Er, thank you. I think," I say, hastily pulling myself together in my mind. "But that's beside the point."

The adorable divots he gets between his eyes when he's confused spring to life. "What point?"

"I think Athena has a thing for you."

His expression shifts, his eyebrows lifting, and he stares at me as if I'm losing my mind. "What are you talking about? She's Peony's nanny. My employee."

"Doesn't mean she can't have a thing for you." Lord knows I've had one long enough. And I'm positive I'm not the only one who has felt the same way, crazy stalker women notwithstanding. "It's just this feeling I get around her. It's hard to explain."

Hard to explain to a man who's been clueless all these years that I'm in love with him.

And now that I have a chronic illness, the closest I'll come to being in a relationship is what Garrett and I now have between us. A secret arrangement. Kisses for hits of dopamine. Orgasms for medicinal reasons.

At the end of the day, I don't want to be a burden to him or anyone else—which I will be if the disease progresses and flare-ups become a constant battle.

"I'll talk to her." He pushes to a stand.

I scramble to my feet. "You can't. What if I'm wrong? It'll be all kinds of awkward." For Athena. For Garrett. For me.

And if she does have feelings for him like I suspect, that will be all kinds of awkward too. For all of us.

39

GARRETT

Maybe it was the way Zara fell apart in my hands last night or the way she called out my name... whatever the reason, the moment I sat at my laptop this morning, the words flew onto the page.

I even skipped my lunchtime run with Kellan. I didn't want to risk the flow of words hitting a wall while I was gone.

By dinner, the words finally petered out.

I cut into the chicken breast on my plate. "If it's all right with you," I tell Athena, "I'm going out tonight. Unless you have plans." I don't want to assume she's available to stay here with Peony just because she hasn't discussed them with me.

But then, I can't think of a time when she has had plans. Even when Mom comes over to spend time with her granddaughter, Athena hangs around the house.

"Where are you going?" The soft smile on her face is directed at Peony, the suspicion in her tone only for me.

"Zara's apartment. My brothers will be there for Game Night, and we need to discuss last-minute details about this weekend's excursion." Plus, I thought I'd give Zara another orgasm, since their benefits only last approximately twenty-four hours and I'll be away for two days.

Guilt digs deep holes in my gut, knowing I should stay home with Peony in case she wakes up from a nightmare. I hate relying on Athena to do that, even if she's been there for Peony from day one, whenever she's had a nightmare.

You'll only be gone a few hours. You'll be there if Peony wakes later on.

"So, you and Zara…" The rest of her words are left hanging, the wince in her tone filling the gap.

"Are friends. As you know." I don't bother to get her to clarify what she's really asking. What Zara and I are is not up for discussion. With anyone.

Athena pushes a bite-sized piece of chicken around her plate. "Are you sure about that?" Her attention remains glued on her food.

Peony picks up a chunk of cooked carrot from her unicorn plate and shoves it in her mouth. The toothy grin she flashes at me wraps my heart in a sweet hug. I miss her, and I haven't left for the trip yet.

"Yes, I'm sure." I pull out my phone and snap a photo of Peony. She grins at me again, and I snap another photo.

"You're not posting that on social media, are you?" The frosty snap to Athena's tone startles Peony and me. Peony stares at her with tearful, round eyes.

I frown, the creases in my brow solely for Athena. "I haven't posted on social media that I have a daughter, and I have no intention of posting photos of her." I keep my voice calm so as not to further upset Peony, and I flash her a reassuring smile.

She returns to playing with her food, babbling something I don't understand.

"Plenty of influencers and authors post family photos on social media to build a connection between themselves and their fans," I tell Athena. "But I don't plan to do that. My life is private. Not that it's your choice if I post about her."

As far as I know, it's not public knowledge in town that I have a daughter. Some people might have seen me with Peony, but the news hasn't made it yet to the Maple Ridge grapevine.

Athena huffs a small, irritated sound. "You've posted photos of yourself on the Wilderness Warriors social media accounts," she counters.

Technically, Avery, who works for us, posts those photos. "Yes, but that's different. All the people in those photos are adults, and they agreed to be in the pictures. And those photos are on social media for reasons that have nothing to do with my author career." Such as showing what some of the military veterans have accomplished, despite the challenges they face due to a life-altering injury they got while deployed.

"I am doing everything I can to protect my daughter," I remind her. I have no idea how the conversation veered so far to the left. But at least we're no longer on the off-the-wall tangent of Zara and me.

The doorbell rings, saving me from continuing this wayward conversation.

I walk to the front door, at this point happy to see whoever is on the other side of it...even a canvasser.

I swing open the door to find a man standing on the stoop. George and his family live five houses down from me. This is the first time, that I know of, he's dropped by my house. He's a contract lawyer and a fan of my books, but whenever we talk, it's usually in front of his property or mine.

"Sorry to interrupt you," he says rather cheerfully. "The postal service dropped off a letter for you in my mailbox." He hands me the envelope. My name and address are typed on it, but there's nothing to hint who it's from.

I give him a chin nod and smile. "Thank you. I appreciate you dropping it off."

"Thought it might be important." He turns to leave. He's not the kind of man who likes to pry into people's lives. He's not here to fish for intel to feed the vultures, though I'm sure by now there are questions circulating as to why Peony and Athena are living with me.

I shut the door and open the envelope. Inside is a single folded sheet of paper with a typed message.

Garrett,

I just wanted to let you know how excited I am to read your next book. I can't tell you how many times I dream about you. How many times I touch myself while reading your words.

I don't read beyond that. I don't need to. This is similar to how the stalker began her letters. What concerns me is that whoever sent this knows my address. Usually, letters are sent via my agent. And the ones forwarded to me are vetted first by her assistant.

I'm tempted to crunch the paper up and toss it into the recycle bin. But in case I'm dealing with a new stalker, I'll give the letter to Noah, so he can keep it on file at the police station, should things progress beyond this one.

I WALK WITH KELLAN AND EMILY TO THE ELEVATOR AFTER GAME Night ends. Lucas, Simone, Troy, and Jess left the apartment not that long ago. Emily needed to talk to Zara about an upcoming wedding Em is coordinating for a client. Zara is catering the event.

"I can't believe you two lost," Em says, almost a little too gleefully. "I've never seen you and Zara so off your game. Pun intended."

"We were letting you and Kellan win for once." I wink at her, and Kellan scoffs. Those two are a force of their own when we're playing partner games. But then, usually so are Zara and I.

I pat my pockets as the elevator door opens. "Shit. I forgot my phone. Go ahead without me." It's on the coffee table... where I purposely left it.

"See you tomorrow. And don't be late." Kellan might be saying the words to me, but I'm not the one he's referring to. Troy and Lucas have a habit of being late on Saturday mornings, because they're fucking their girlfriend or wife right before they head out to the Warriors property.

"Okay." My mouth slides into a smirk, acknowledging that of course I won't be late; I'm not Lucas or Troy.

I walk to Zara's apartment in record time and knock on her door. It opens, revealing the woman who's been on my mind all evening. I step into the apartment, closing the door behind me with a soft click.

And then my mouth is on Zara's.

It was torture sitting next to her during Game Night, unable to touch her. But now, with everyone else gone, I no longer have to restrain myself.

I deepen the kiss, but it's not enough. I grab the back of her thighs and hoist her up. Her legs wrap around my hips, and I push her against the wall. I rock into her, my cock getting the wrong idea. It hardens in my jeans.

Zara lets out a shuddering moan. "My bedroom," she murmurs on my lips.

I don't bother to reply, my thoughts focused on how much I want to taste her. On how much I want to hear her cry out my name.

I walk toward her room, our mouths busy making up for lost time. Making up for the long stretch tonight when I just wanted to touch her, kiss her, but couldn't because my brothers and our friends were here.

I lower her onto the bed. Her skin softly glows in the light spilling into the room from the hallway. Christ, she's fucking gorgeous. A goddess. A siren. Luring me willingly to my demise. Her subtle jasmine scent is the last nail in my coffin, the one I'll happily hammer in myself for the chance to taste her.

I brush my thumb across her nipple, hidden under her T-shirt and bra. She shudders beneath my touch, her inhale a whispered gasp.

"Can I?" I lift the hem of her T-shirt enough to reveal a thin strip of her golden-brown stomach, enough so she knows what I'm really asking.

She nods, her lips parted, her eyes dark with want, and I tug the fabric up the rest of the way.

I help her remove the top. Then I peel off the rest of her clothes, waiting for her permission with each one until she's sitting on her bed in only her violet lace bra and panties.

I stand motionless for a beat, barely able to draw oxygen into my lungs, my gaze worshiping every part of her.

She lifts an eyebrow and gestures to my body. "Are you forgetting something?" The corner of her mouth curls up. "I'm not the only one who is gonna be naked here. You said 'next time' I'd get to see you."

She pushes the button of my jeans through the hole. Her fingers brush the hard length pressing almost painfully into the denim, and I suck in a sharp breath. "Oh, and I bought a box of condoms this afternoon. They're in the drawer. If you're interested..." She points to the bedside table. "If you want to have sex with me." Her voice is low and smoky, a sweet dab of honey mixed into a cock-arousing elixir. "Because...because I want to have sex with you."

Fuuuuuuck.

"Are you sure?" Because, damn, while I crave to be wrapped in her, to be snug in her tight heat, I need to make sure it won't affect our friendship. Ensure she also definitely wants what she's offering.

"I'm sure. I know when we agreed to our kissing arrangement, I said no sex. But that was before..."

"Before you found out one of the benefits of orgasms?"

Her mouth curves into a huge-ass grin. "Exactly."

We quickly shed our clothes until we're standing in nothing but glorious nakedness. All I'm capable of is staring at my best friend, the ability to speak gone.

Zara's gaze is a mirror of mine, taking in my body the same way I'm perusing hers. Her eyes linger on my tattoos and the scars that war has left behind. Scars I've never told her about. That I've never told anyone about, other than those in the military with the necessary clearance.

I've always thought she was beautiful, but seeing her like this, like a bronzed goddess from one of the African myths she loved as a kid, is too much. I'm almost afraid to touch her in case she vanishes, like smoke on a breeze.

Afraid of somehow messing this all up.

I skim trembling fingers on the silky skin of her shoulder and down her arms to her breasts. Her sultry, rose-brown nipples beckon for my touch, and a groan slips out from deep in my chest.

Christ, I want to explore every part of her body, learn her through and through. Know what sounds she makes when she's close to coming with me inside her. What sounds she makes when she falls apart. I want to see what pushes her to the edge, what makes her whimper, gasp, call out my name. What makes her shatter in my arms.

I want to know everything.

I lean down and tease a taut nipple with the tip of my tongue, circle it, draw it into my mouth, suck on it hard.

"Oh. Yes. Garrett." Zara tangles her fingers in my hair, tugging on it. The sharp pull on my scalp makes my cock grow that much harder.

I continue tormenting her nipples, first one and then the other.

My hands trailing along her sides, I sink to my knees. "I've been waiting all day to taste you." All day. All week. All time.

Her breath hitches and her beautiful brown eyes widen with an array of emotions, lust shining the brightest.

I lift her feet, one at a time, onto the mattress, opening her up to me.

Modesty has her closing her knees, and I gently guide them apart. "Keep open. I want to see you." I take my time appreciating the sight, the buffet laid out, groaning at the delicacies awaiting me.

Her delectable scent has me desperate to taste her, to eat her out. To send her soaring to the stars as she chants my name.

Zara leans back on her arms, her eyelids heavy, and I take a mental picture to have something to remember her by this weekend. To keep me going during those moments when I miss her the most.

I separate her folds and feast on her with my tongue, drawing out her moans, her greedy gasps. I lick every sip of her divine taste, not wanting to miss a single drop. Her needy sounds encourage me to keep going, and I push my finger inside her, eager for her soft heat to wrap around it.

Zara's fingers tighten in my hair again, causing me another shot of pleasure and pain. Damn, even without me saying anything, she instinctively knows what I need, what I crave.

I slip another finger inside her.

I work her body with my fingers and my mouth, pushing

her to the edge of release, enjoying her sweet taste, her sweet whimpers, her sweet moans.

"I'm going to come." Zara's warning rides out on a groan. "Want you. Inside. Me. Now."

"Not yet. We're trying a new experiment."

Her eyebrows lift. Interest gleams in her eyes. "What experiment?"

"We're going to see if two orgasms are better than one. Maybe it will be enough to keep the pain threshold elevated for almost forty-eight hours instead of only twenty-four."

And if it doesn't...well, I still get to enjoy watching her fall apart, not once but twice.

Zara's lips curve to one side. "I knew there was a reason I loved science. And ex-ahhhhhhh," she cries out in response to my fingers thrusting inside her, my thumb circling her clit.

Her soft heat pulsates around my fingers, drawing them in, and I come close to groaning at the thought of it around my cock shortly. She flops on the bed, falling apart against my fingers, her knees squeezing together.

While she recovers from the first of the orgasms I plan to give her tonight, I open the nightstand drawer and remove the unopened box of condoms. "You bought a supersized box?"

She makes a small agreeing noise. "I believe in being prepared."

I frown at the box. We agreed to end our kissing arrangement if Zara wanted to start seeing someone else, but we haven't laid any ground rules for the pain-reducing orgasms. "Prepared? As in, having sex with other men...in addition to me?"

Zara snorts out an affronted laugh. "Exactly how much time do you think I have in a day with everything else going on in my life right now?"

Fair point. "Does that mean it's just me?" *Please, tell me it's just me.*

"It's just you." She nods at the box in my hand. "So, are you gonna put on a condom so we can return to our science experiment?"

She doesn't have to ask twice. Chuckling, I rip open the box like a starved bear who just found a wrapped steak, and I remove a foil square.

Zara yanks it from my fingers and rips open the package. Bottom lip caught between her teeth, she pumps her hand along my hard length several times.

My cock jerks in response, and a deep groan slips out of me. "I'm not going to last much longer if you keep doing that."

My favorite grin spreads across her perfectly lush, kiss-swollen lips. "You're very bossy, Garrett."

"And you're driving me crazy, Golden Girl."

"Happy to oblige." She rolls the condom down my length and gives my balls a light but firm squeeze, rapidly pushing me to the edge of the cliff. Her satisfied smile tells me she knows exactly what she's doing to me.

Sexy, breath-stealing tease.

I cup the back of her neck and take a second to kiss her senseless, tormenting us both with the delay in uniting our bodies. Our tongues dance and glide, the sound of our groans the accompaniment.

I pull away the barest of distance. My next words mist her lips with my command. "In the middle of the bed."

"Yes, sir." She salutes me and turns, gifting me with a great view of her ass.

I give it a light slap, eliciting a giggled yelp from her. "Are you trying to tease me?" I ask, grabbing her hips between my hands and preventing her escape.

She wiggles her backside and laughs at my resulting groan. "Maybe. But you're so much fun to tease."

"Next time," I tell her. "Next time I'm taking you just like this." I run my thumb along her swollen seam, and I'm rewarded with her whimpered moan. Just how I like it.

I release my hold on her hips and follow her onto the center of the bed.

She lies back, and I guide the head of my cock along the slick length of her pussy. Teasing her. Torturing myself. *Christ*, I want her so badly.

I position the blunt head of my cock against her entrance and lock eyes with her. I slowly push inside her, relishing her hot wetness coating my length. I keep going until I'm buried balls deep. Zara's legs wrap around my hips, holding me close.

She feels so perfect.

Us, like this, feels so perfect.

I begin thrusting, worshiping, learning my best friend's body inside and out...and appreciating every second of it. Sweat forms on my skin.

"Oh, God. Garrett." My name rides out on a heavenly moan past her parted lips, and never has my name sounded so good.

My mouth tugs up to one side, my gaze remaining on hers. "Enjoying this, Golden Girl?"

"Most definitely." Her voice is low and husky, the words pulled out like saltwater taffy.

Just hearing it has my balls tightening and heat building low in my belly.

I keep thrusting inside her, taking us higher and higher and higher. Never wanting to end this but knowing I'm not going to last much longer.

Zara's tight heat squeezes my cock in a wave of desire, and I groan out my appreciation.

"Garrett, I'm gonna come." She gasps out the words.

"Come. And I'll catch you." My words are growled, my thread of control rapidly fraying.

Zara screams out as her soft heat convulses around me and sends me tumbling over the edge.

An edge I'm happy to fall off.

"Christ, Golden Girl." I grunt out my seemingly never-ending release.

Satisfied beyond belief, my body now boneless, I collapse next to her on the bed. *Damn.* I don't remember the last time sex felt that mind-blowing. That...*wow.*

40

GARRETT

I stir awake to the warmth of the early morning sunlight shining on my face and a subtle jasmine scent teasing the air. My eyes are still closed, and I have morning wood to rival all others, no thanks to the dream I just woke from.

I open my eyes and blink the room into focus. When the room doesn't morph into the one I usually wake up in, I snap my eyes shut, hoping the simple act is enough to reboot my brain, and when I reopen my eyes, my familiar beige walls and blue bedding will be back.

I wait a beat before trying again. But the view doesn't change when I reopen my eyes. The large canvas painting on the wall facing me is still there. The painting of several Black women in brightly colored traditional outfits, performing a celebration dance against a neutral backdrop.

Memories of last night flicker into focus. Of collapsing on the bed, exhausted, the used condom tossed into the bathroom trash can. Of lying down next to a drowsy Zara after she'd come hard around me. Of thinking of how I should head home, but I just needed a moment to recover. Of thinking how right Zara felt—warm and naked and spent—in my arms.

314

My eyes widen. *Oh. Fuck.*

I sit up abruptly. According to the alarm clock on Zara's nightstand, it's 8:30 a.m. Not only have I overslept, I'm not at home.

Where all my things are.

Where my daughter is.

Double fuck.

I scramble out of bed, the erection I was sporting dying a rapid death.

Zara groans, but it doesn't sound like the sexy noises from last night when I made her come. Twice. This is a groan that comes from pain.

I pause instead of grabbing my clothes scattered around the room. I walk to her side of the bed, kneel in front of her, and stroke the side of her face. "Hey, what's wrong?"

She blinks at me like I'm a mirage, then slowly pushes herself to sit. "I'm fine." She winces, unable to fasten on quick enough the mask everyone usually sees.

"You're in pain?"

"No more than normal." She gives me a smile I assume is meant to be reassuring. "I'll be fine in a few minutes. Once I've taken my ibuprofen. And walked around for a bit. And done a few yoga poses." Her smile fades to a frown. "How come you're still here? I thought you were leaving last night. And getting in more words before bed."

"I fell asleep."

"Me too." She touches her hair, as if just realizing she forgot to wear her bonnet, then shifts her legs from under the covers. Her movements are slow and hesitant.

I wish kissing every inch of her body was all it took to make her feel better, to chase away her pain completely.

I grab my boxer briefs from the floor and yank them on.

"Shit," Zara exclaims. "You're late."

I locate my jeans and tug them up my legs. "I know. Kellan's gonna kill me."

"Only if he knows you're late because we had sex last night and you fell asleep here. But he doesn't know, right?" She lifts her eyebrow; I shake my head. "So he'll just think you're late because of Peony."

She has a point. I'm not about to admit to Kellan, or any of my brothers, the real reason I'm running behind. Zara and I agreed, what the two of us are doing is no one else's business. It's our secret. And I'm not breaking that vow 'cause I fell asleep in her bed.

I lean down and give her a swift kiss. A barely-there touch of lips. Anything more, and I'll have a hard time leaving. "Have a good weekend. I'll see you when I get back."

Pulling on my T-shirt, I head to the living room, snatch up my phone from the coffee table, and bail as if the hounds of hell are trying to take a chunk out of my ass.

If Kellan has any say in it once he reads my text, the hounds could be doing exactly that.

I don't bother with the elevator and sprint to the entrance of the stairwell. I practically hurl my body down the staircase, taking the corners tight. Luckily, no one else is in here. No one is at risk of me accidentally plowing into them.

As I pull out of the visitor parking, I send Kellan a brief voice text.

Me: Running late. Will be there shortly.

It's a lie. I still have to shower, eat, and grab my gear for the weekend. Most of it is already packed. I just have to throw in a few last-minute items.

Kellan doesn't reply to my text. If fate is shining on me, Troy and Lucas also fucked up and are running behind, because they squeezed in a quick fuck before leaving Jess and Simone.

Lucky guys.

There wasn't enough time for me to give Zara another orgasm.

I park on my driveway, sprint to the front door. A screaming toddler tantrum welcomes me when I open it, the high-pitch wails coming from the kitchen. *Shit.* I don't have time for this. Kellan will be kicking my ass into the next solar system as it is.

But knowing that doesn't stop me from heading to the source of the noise.

I walk into the room as Peony releases another high-pitched scream from her very healthy set of lungs. She's sitting in her highchair, her tear-stained face red, the room looking like a casualty of war. Except instead of land mines, food has exploded all over the place.

And standing in the middle of it all is Athena, her mouth gaping as she stares dumbfoundedly at my daughter.

"Hey, little flower." I walk to her chair, my tone the gentle touch of a bomb disposal technician.

Wide, wet eyes meet mine. She stops screaming, but her sobbing is now in full force. She lifts her arms, making it clear she's ready to escape the confines of her chair.

I unbuckle her and gently bounce her in my arms. "Hey, little flower, what's all the fuss about?"

Peony rests her cheek on my shoulder and heaves out a tiny sigh.

Rocking from side to side, I wipe my thumb over her other cheek, slick from her tears, and glance at Athena to see if she has any clue what's set Peony off.

Athena doesn't respond to my silent question. If anything, she seems irritated. Her eyes are narrowed, and if she were a cartoon character, she'd have steam coming out of her ears.

Having no idea what bee bit her in the ass, I walk to the sink, grab Peony's washcloth, and wipe the smeared food from her top.

"Rough morning?" I wipe her hands. Her glistening eyes

almost bring me to my knees. The way her bottom lip is pushed out in a pout doesn't help my case either.

I check the microwave clock and inwardly groan. "How about we get you changed? Then I'll read you your favorite book."

I grab Poppy from the table and hand her to Peony. Surprisingly, the panda avoided being a casualty of the food war.

Athena follows us into Peony's bedroom. "Where were you?" Accusation drips from her words, the edge of her tone razor sharp.

"That's none of your business." I attempt to take the sting out of my words, but my frustration at the situation—my falling asleep at Zara's, being late, coming home to find my daughter throwing a fit—hampers my success at altering my tone.

I'm wearing last night's clothes, so I can't bullshit my way out of this and pretend I'm just returning from a run. Plus, she knows I'm behind schedule. I would have usually left by now for the cabins.

"She woke up wanting you," Athena's tone doesn't soften. "And you. Weren't. Here."

Joy pokes up unharmed through the thorns of guilt, and I have to fight back a smile. Peony is upset because I wasn't there for her. She wanted *me*, her father. A month ago, I wouldn't have believed that would even be possible.

Athena huffs and shakes her head, her eyes narrowed.

"I don't need your permission to come home late. I'm not a teenager, and you're not my mother." Okay, not my finest retort. She's not accusing me of being a teen who ignored his curfew. But I am a father, and my falling asleep at Zara's was inexcusable.

Peony's bottom lip trembles, a warning she's about to scream again.

I flash her an unsteady smile. "I'm sorry." The words are meant for Peony, but maybe I should say them to Athena too. "I shouldn't have come home so late. I shouldn't have taken for granted that you're here. You're Peony's nanny. You're not her mother."

Athena draws in a sharp, wounded breath—which doesn't make any sense. I didn't say anything that isn't true.

I walk into Peony's closet. "My staying out was unacceptable, and it won't happen again." I remove Peony's green top, with small ladybugs all over it, from the hanger. "Do you want to wear this one?"

Peony's arm stretches toward it. I hand it to her with a full-out grin and head for her dresser.

"Why were you so late?" The accusation in Athena's tone is now nothing more than a frayed thread, the rest of her tone either disappointment or hurt.

"I think Athena has a thing for you."

Is that what this is about? Athena is reacting like this because she *possibly* has a thing for me?

I open the top drawer. "I guess all my late nights working on the book finally caught up with me." I remove a clean pair of jeans from the drawer.

That explains why I fell asleep after my earth-shattering orgasm with Zara. I usually don't stay at a woman's house after having sex with her. I leave after an appropriate amount of time.

Kenda had been the exception...until now.

I carry everything to the changing table, sit Peony on it, and hand her the toy maracas. I remove her dirty clothes and proceed to put the ladybug top and jeans on her.

As I dress her, she shakes the maracas and giggles when I pretend to dance to the off-beat rhythm. I don't care I look like an idiot. Anything to bring a smile to her face.

I toss the dirty clothes into the hamper, grab Peony's favorite book from the nightstand, and carry her to the living room.

I sit on the couch, with her on my lap, and read her the story. This, of course, takes longer than it should. Peony likes to discuss—in her toddler language—the different pictures. And I'm not rushing her just so I can get out of here. My top priority is to make sure she feels seen and loved.

"I need to have a quick shower," I tell her after it seems like she has finished discussing the story with me. "Then I'm heading out to meet your uncles and the men we're taking camping and canoeing." I kiss Peony's head, between the two little buns perched on either side of it. "But I'll be home tomorrow night. Be good for Athena."

Peony wiggles off my lap, apparently finished with our conversation.

I help her onto the floor. "Granny will be coming over later to play with you and take you to the playground," I add as she toddles to her toy box.

After a quick shower and equally quick breakfast, I head out. My brothers have finished loading the supply van by the time I arrive at the main cabin on the Wilderness Warriors property.

"It's about time you showed up," Kellan grumbles. "Your excuse had better be good."

"Peony was upset. So I stayed to help defuse the situation." That's close enough to the truth. Hell if I'm telling him the rest of it.

41

—————

GARRETT

The campfire crackles and pops in front of us as we devour the tasty dinner Troy and Lucas prepared after a day of canoeing and hiking.

Now, the group of fourteen men—including my brothers and myself—are relaxing at the secluded campsite and enjoying the camaraderie that comes with these trips.

"Do any of you have kids?" Jake asks my brothers and me, after the rest of the group has shown off photos of their children.

"My wife and I are fostering two young girls," Lucas tells the other men, a wistful smile on his face. He misses Kylie and Zoe. I can tell.

I feel the same way about Peony. It's the strong tugging in my heart, the empty void twisting in my chest. A jigsaw puzzle missing an important piece.

I honestly don't know how Dad so easily walked away every time he was deployed for months at a time—leaving behind his wife and three young boys. But maybe that's the point. Maybe that's the reason he retired from the Marines earlier than he had planned—it hadn't been easy for him either.

321

Two days. That's all I'll be gone for. Surely I can handle that.

Lucas taps on his phone and passes it to Jake.

"Cute kids." The phone is passed around the circle and eventually stops at me. The two girls and Simone are grinning at the camera. Jasper is sitting with them, a grin also on his face.

I pass the phone to Kellan, who's sitting next to me on the downed tree trunk. He glances at it, and one of his rare smiles crosses his face. A smile usually reserved for kids who mean a lot to him—like the kids on the hockey team he coaches.

"What 'bout you three?" Jake's gaze shifts from Troy, to me, and then Kellan.

"Happily single and kid free," Kellan replies, his mouth not bothering with a smile this time.

"I'm happily taken but no kids. Yet." Troy doesn't show the group a photo of Jess. After what she went through last year, when the media tracked her down, he's even more protective of his girlfriend's privacy than he would have been with anyone else's.

The men's attention moves to me.

"I have a daughter." I figure it's safe enough to tell them that. It's not something I can keep quiet for much longer. So far, not many people have seen us together. But that will change once I've sent the book to my editor. Then I'll be able to spend a lot more time with Peony, which means people will see us together as we frequently venture out in public.

"You have any pictures of her?"

"Of course." I remove my phone from my pants pocket and scroll to the photo I took last week of her playing with her peas.

Jake studies the picture. "Damn, she's quite the cutie. Any photos of your wife or girlfriend?" Respectful of my privacy, he doesn't flip through the photos to check for himself.

"Nope. Her mother died a few months ago."

"Sorry for your loss." He passes the phone to Paul as the rest of the group echo his condolences.

"Thanks. It's not public info—about me being a father—so if you could keep it to yourselves, I'd appreciate it."

The men all nod.

Paul looks at the photo, and a fleeting look of recognition crosses his face. I brush it off as nothing more than my imagination. It's hardly likely he's seen her before. He's confusing her for someone else. He's from Baton Rouge, Louisiana, and not from North Carolina.

"Who's looking after your daughter while you're here?" He passes the phone to the next person.

"Her nanny and my parents."

Technically, for now, it's just Athena and Mom. But once Peony is no longer scared of my father, he'll be happy to jump in and spend time with her. To take her places. To show her how to fish. To be the grandfather I know he's eager to be— even if he hasn't been as vocal about it as Mom.

The phone makes its way back to me, and I sneak a quick glance at Peony's grinning face. Then I go to the folder with one of my favorite photos of Zara.

It's not the photo of her in a black bikini, with gold paint smeared on her body, but this photo is equally hot.

She's standing in the lake, her purple and gold one-piece showing off her curves.

I'm not a great photographer, not even close to one, but somehow I captured *this* photo, with the sun hitting her from behind, the angle just right. Her skin glows like that of a bejeweled goddess. Like a water nymph sparkling in the rays of the setting sun.

It's the photo no one knows about.

"Is that Zara?" The surprised, murmured voice comes from next to me. Kellan.

I shove my phone into my pocket, putting a halt to that

conversation. I can't let my brother know I have...I have what for her? Sexy feelings? Deep, caring feelings beyond our friendship?

I shake my head. All I know is I can't wait to see her again.

THE FOLLOWING THURSDAY, I PLACE THE ADVANCED READER Copy of *Unfallen* on my desk. I add a map of New York City and a leather journal to the setup and shoot a couple of photos for social media. The midmorning sunlight through the window gives the pictures the perfect, mysterious vibe.

Next, I record a video, but this time I'm holding the book open and I smile for the camera. "The Advanced Reader Copies of *Unfallen* are now in reviewers' hands. Just three more months and four days till the book is out in the world. Can't wait for you to read this gripping thriller. What are you looking forward to seeing in the book? Comment below..." I point down and tap on the Stop button.

I create several posts, upload them to my socials, and head to the kitchen for a glass of water. Peony and Athena are playing with the wooden blocks on the coffee table in the living room. Poppy is sitting next to the small tower.

I wave at Peony. She waves back and flashes me a toothy grin, then chats animatedly to Poppy.

Athena pushes to her feet and walks to the kitchen, her expression solemn. "Peony's sick. Maybe you should cancel her therapy appointment."

I walk over to the coffee table and crouch next to Peony. "Hey, little flower. Athena said you might be sick."

Her grin returning, Peony straightens and throws herself at me. Her arms go around my waist, and I return her hug. I might be new to parenting, but she seems fine to me. She doesn't even have a hint of a cold.

I place the back of my hand on her forehead. She doesn't feel hot. "She seems fine. And I have no intention of canceling the appointment." It would be different if Peony really was ill—ill beyond a mild cold. "Jada Biles is highly recognized for her work with young kids who've experienced trauma."

Displeasure presses Athena's lips into a flat line, but she doesn't say anything more on the topic. Her glare says it all.

"We'll leave around one thirty," I remind her. "I'm assuming you're still coming." From the way she's trying to get me to change my mind, though, maybe it would be better if Athena stays home.

Why the hell is she so against Peony seeing a therapist?

"I'm still coming." Athena heaves out a disgruntled breath and picks up a block from the floor.

"You sure? You don't seem all that excited about going."

"I doubt playing with toys will make a difference." She huffs. "She already does that here." Athena waves to the blocks on the coffee table. "Play therapy sounds like a waste of time, if you ask me."

I ignore the comment and blow a raspberry on Peony's cheek. Peony giggles. "Daddy has to work a little longer. Then after lunch, we'll drive to Portland to visit a special lady." Who can hopefully get to the root of why Peony becomes scared around men. And hopefully Jada will have some suggestions as to how I can help my daughter with that and the nightmares.

The little princess is fast asleep when we arrive at the professional building. I pull into an empty spot on the street in front of an older single-story house. The lawn is slightly sloped, the grass recently mowed.

Athena jumps out of the passenger seat as I kill the engine. She races to Peony's side of the SUV and opens the door. "Hey, baby girl, we're here."

Her reaction is odd given her opinion about Peony seeing a therapist. I doubt she's in that much of a rush to get to Jada's office.

In the elevator, Athena gently bounces Peony in her arms as if to soothe her. But Peony doesn't seem nervous. If anything, she looks curious as she glances around the elevator, her eyes sweetly rounded. The only person who is clearly nervous is Athena.

"She'll be fine," I tell her, barely resisting the urge to take Peony from Athena, in case Peony starts to think there is a reason to be nervous.

We easily find the clinic and walk into the brightly lit waiting room. The comfy chairs scattered in the space are neutral colored, topped with aquamarine cushions. Light-green trees add a painted splash of color to the beige walls.

No one else is in the room. On the desk is a sign that reads, "Please take a seat. Jada Biles will be with you shortly."

Peony points at the large aquarium along one wall and squirms in Athena's arms. Tropical fish swim through the water and dart between the aquatic plants.

Athena lowers her to the floor and looks around the room. Annoyance squints her eyes, flattens her lips. Even her body is tense. Tension rolls off her and tries to get under my skin.

Peony toddles to the aquarium, but she's too short to see inside it. She turns to me and lifts her arms. "Up."

I hoist her onto my hip. While we wait for Jada, I point out the different fish, including a clown fish that swims past. "Look, there's Nemo."

"Are you Garrett and Peony Carson?" a woman asks behind us.

I turn to find the person whose photo is on the clinic's website. Jada Biles is a tall, curvy woman with smooth mahogany skin and platinum-blond hair trimmed close to her scalp. Her black pants and light-pink T-shirt loosely skim her body.

"Yes, that would be us," I reply. "And this is Athena. Peony's nanny."

I've already explained on the phone how Peony came to live with me and that I only recently found out that I had a daughter. I also told her Athena has known Peony since birth.

"I'm glad you could both come." Jada's eyes shimmer with kindness directed at my daughter. "It's so nice to finally meet you, Peony. I'm looking forward to playing some games with you. Do you like sand?"

Peony tilts her head to the side but doesn't respond. She aims a shy smile at Jada and rests her head on my chest.

"You love playing in the sandbox at Granny's and Grandpa's house, don't you?" I say to Peony.

She lifts Poppy for me to see, as if that answers Jada's question. And the curve of her lips widens into a grabs-me-by-the-heart grin.

"Why don't we go into the playroom and get to know each other a little better?" Jada suggests.

I nod. Athena makes a soft noise that sounds like a grunt. I barely refrain from frowning at her, wordlessly telling her to get over whatever her issue is with Jada. For Peony's sake, she needs to give Jada a chance before she dismisses this as a waste of time.

We follow Jada into another room, which is decorated much like the waiting room.

"I thought while your daddy and Athena tell me about your days, we can play with the sandbox." Jada leads us to the square sandbox on the floor. A bunch of plastic toys lie scattered on the sand, including a dog, a dinosaur, a policeman, a man, and a car. Some of them look realistic—like the dog and the dinosaur. The others are bright colors and cartoonish.

"Today is just about me getting to know Peony and vice

versa," Jada explains to Athena and me. She had told me this on the phone when I spoke with her a few weeks ago. It's to help Peony to learn to trust Jada.

Peony picks up the dog and plays with it on the sand. While Peony plays, Jada asks us about Peony's daily routines. Jada's attention remains on Peony. Some of her questions are also directed at my daughter.

Peony doesn't reply to any of them. She picks up the car and pushes it through the sand.

"Did she have nightmares before she lost her mother?" Jada asks Athena.

"No," Athena responds after a long beat. "They started soon after her mother died."

Peony grabs the plastic man and dumps him on the sand face up. Her lips press into what looks like concentration, and she picks up the toy shovel. She scoops sand onto the man and keeps going until he is buried deep under it. Her face scrunches, and she pounds the wide mound with the shovel.

The toy policeman meets the same fate, buried under another pile of sand.

Icy prickles crawl up my spine, and I look at Jada, hoping she knows what Peony's actions mean. Jada's watchful expression doesn't give away what she's thinking, but she leans forward like she's mentally taking notes.

And I can't help but wonder if Peony is just afraid of the man...or if it's also his uniform she fears. Or does she fear something deeper, something darker?

42

ZARA

Monday afternoon, I'm working the front counter of Picnic & Treats when Garrett enters with Peony in his arms. Athena is with them. Today was Peony's third weekly session with the play therapist, and they always come here to get her a treat after the drive from Eugene.

Peony grins at me, and I can't believe how big she's getting. It's only been a few days since I last saw her, but damn, what are they feeding her?

Athena is also smiling, which I suspect has nothing to do with me...and everything to do with the desserts in the display case. Turns out, Athena has a weakness for my lemon raspberry cupcakes, as I discovered two weeks ago.

"Za-wa." Peony waves hi to me.

"Hey, you three." I swear my ovaries do their usual happy dance at seeing Garrett with his little princess in his arms. His little princess in an adorable light-green dress with appliqué daisies all over the tulle. Two white bows decorate her hair.

After raising four boys, his mother loves having a little girl in the family to dote on. She was the one who bought Peony the dress.

I'm not the only one who thinks Garrett and Peony are adorable together, as the dreamy sigh from one of the nearby customers can attest. The woman is no more immune to them than I am.

My ovaries aren't the only things reacting to the sight of Garrett. My clit aches for his touch, like a dog in one of Pavlov's experiments.

It's been three and a half weeks since Garrett and I conducted our experiment. Three and a half weeks since I discovered firsthand the pain-control magic of orgasms.

But it's been sixty-six hours since my last one.

Sixty-six excruciatingly long, lust-filled hours.

I'm barely keeping myself from climbing over the counter and dry humping him. And it has nothing to do with pain-relief management.

"Do you want the usual?" I do my best not to rub my legs together, to ease the growing ache and give away my body's reaction to him. "I can bring it to your table."

"Yes, a lemon-and-raspberry cupcake for me," Athena confirms with a small smile. While I still suspect that she would prefer I'm not in their lives, she has warmed up to me a smidgen. I can thank the baked goods for that.

"You want a unicorn cupcake or a chocolate chip cookie?" she asks Peony.

Peony points to the collection of cute, kid-sized cupcakes in the display. Her favorite.

Garrett passes her to Athena. "Why don't you two grab the table in the corner by the window, and I'll bring the drinks?"

Athena walks off with Peony.

Muffled hammering filters through the wall separating this part of the café from next door, where Troy's crew is working on the expansion. Another week and it will finally be finished after several unexpected setbacks.

And starting tomorrow, Picnic & Treats will be temporarily closed, while they work on joining the two areas into one.

But that doesn't mean I get to take a vacation. *Au contraire.* I'll be working on the last-minute details for the grand reopening.

"How's the pain? From one to ten?" Garrett drops the volume of his voice. The deep cadence of it washes through me in a warm, delicious shudder.

My staff knows about the spondyloarthritis, but they're the only ones, so I appreciate his caution. Even so, it doesn't keep me from rolling my eyes. "You don't have to ask me every time you see me."

"Yes. I do. We're in this together. I'm part of your treatment plan."

I snort out a laugh. But he does have a point. He's a very important part of the plan—and not only because of the orgasms.

We're still walking together in the evenings. But I don't know how much longer that will last as his deadline draws closer. His book is due to his editor in just under two months.

"Okay, Mr. Treatment Plan. It's a six." This is a big improvement over what it used to be, before my diagnosis and lifestyle changes, which has included making sure I eat healthier, cutting out highly processed foods, and following the Mediterranean diet.

"What was it yesterday? Since you ignored my text last night."

"The same. And I didn't ignore your text. I just didn't see it."

The truth is, I did see it. I didn't respond because I knew he needed to get back to his novel, after his weekend excursion in the mountains. Coming to my apartment to give me an orgasm wouldn't help him with the deadline.

I fetch the drinks for him and put them on a tray. "How did play therapy go?"

"Not bad. It would help if Peony could tell her therapist what's going on in her head. Today, she played with the sandbox again, and like with the first appointment, she buried all the plastic characters who were men."

"Does the therapist have any idea why she did that?"

Garrett shakes his head, the movement slow, too many unknowns rusting the movement. "Not specifically. She has trust issues with men, but Jada doesn't know why. It could be related to Kenda's death. Or it might have a deeper root."

"What did Athena say about that?"

"She didn't say much. She agrees it could be because Peony witnessed her mother being shot." Garrett puts his hand on the countertop.

I give it a squeeze, telling him without words that I'm here for him and Peony. "Why don't you take the drinks, and I'll bring the treats."

I grab the two cupcakes and walk with him to where Peony and Athena are sitting next to the window. I don't get to spend enough time with Peony, so I'll steal whatever precious seconds I can, even if it's just delivering her food.

"Daddy!" Peony says from her highchair, her toothy grin directed at him.

"Oh, that's so sweet. She called you Daddy." I swear I'm smiling at him as much as she is. My eyes mist, and I blink the tears away.

Pride beams on his face, and the warmth of it pours into my heart like a ray of sunshine. "She started calling me that this morning."

"I'm so happy for you. You two have come a long way." I put her plate on the table in front of her. "Here you go, Princess Peony."

Excitement rounds her eyes as she takes in the adorable cupcake, with its closed-smiley eyes and a sugar-cone horn in the fringe of rainbow curls.

She reaches toward the cupcake. "Uni-corn."

"So, this is your little girl," a male voice says from behind me, a Southern drawl to his tone.

I turn to see who it is but don't recognize the tall man with dark, military-shaved-short hair.

I might not recognize him, but he seems to know Garrett. The man smiles at him like they're old friends.

"Hey, Joffrey." The amusement in Garrett's tone is equally friendly. "Yes, this is Peony." His gaze shifts to Athena, and then to me. "Joffrey was one of the Army veterans who joined us on the climbing trip this weekend."

"One of the best climbs I've done in a while." The man turns his smile on me. "You have a beautiful daughter, ma'am."

On instinct, I glance at Athena. Her complexion has paled to almost the same shade as the white-washed table, but she's also scowling at the man.

"She's not my daughter," I hurriedly point out.

Athena ducks her head and begins peeling the paper from Peony's cupcake. But her reaction isn't what has me worried.

It's Peony's.

She frantically squirms in the highchair, leaning away from the man, looking as if she plans to throw herself out of the chair—like someone in a burning building whose only chance of escape is to jump from a third-story window. Then she releases a wail so loud, so panicked, it startles the nearby patrons.

Garrett and I both make a move to her, but it's Athena who shoots to her feet first and hastily lifts Peony out of the chair.

"Is it okay if I take her to the staff room?" she asks me, cradling Peony against her chest, blocking her view of us. Peony's little body trembles in her arms.

"Go ahead."

She levels Garrett a look so poisonous, I reverse a step from the force of it. *What the hell?*

From the confusion creasing Garrett's brow, it looks like he's wondering the same. He didn't do anything wrong, so why is she mad at him?

Carrying Peony, Athena rushes to the hallway, like a mouse spotted by a circling hawk.

"I'm sorry." Joffrey's gaze follows Peony and Athena as they hurry away. "Didn't mean to scare her."

"I know." Regret roughens Garrett's tone. "She witnessed a man shoot her mother a few months ago."

"Shit, man. I'm so sorry. Both for what just happened and for your loss."

Garrett excuses himself to check on Peony, taking the two uneaten cupcakes with him.

Joffrey returns to a table where two other men are sitting, looking a little stunned, like everyone else, at what just happened. Or maybe something else has them surprised.

I walk to the front counter, stopping on my way at a table where two women are talking, their plates empty except for some crumbs.

"The ALS is draining me," the blond woman says to her friend, without giving me a second glance as I pick up her plate. "I rarely have time for myself. I constantly have to do everything for him. For better and for worse..." She huffs, the sound harsh. "Whoever came up with the line has never looked after someone with a chronic illness."

I don't stick around to see what her friend has to say. I hurry to the kitchen, trying to keep the comment from tangling with the ghost of Joseph's words. Trying to keep it from spreading through me like poisonous fungus.

I put the plates in the dishwasher and head to the staff room.

"He thought she was her mother," Athena scoffs, her voice barely audible through the closed door, and I freeze, my hand pausing midway to the doorknob.

"She's not the one who plays with her." Bitterness reshapes Athena's voice into something barbed and cutting. "Or is there for her when she has a nightmare. She's nothing like Kenda. How can anyone think she could be Peony's mom?"

I wait for Garrett to defend me, to explain spondyloarthritis makes it more difficult for me to get down on the floor and play with Peony.

I wait for him to remind her I must take care of my body, which takes more time than I'd like, so the spondyloarthritis doesn't impact my quality of life as much.

I wait for him to remind her I have a business to run, but that doesn't mean I don't want to spend time with his little girl.

I wait for him to say all these things, but he doesn't. He remains silent.

The time I spend with Peony is usually just during our evening walks with Garrett. I wish I could spend more time with her. To be cool Auntie Zara, who gets to hang out with her and do all the fun things Peony wants to do.

But while the spondyloarthritis does slow me down and my work takes time from my schedule, it doesn't mean I don't love Peony. It doesn't mean I don't secretly wish she was my daughter, that I haven't been waking up from dreams about Garrett, Peony, and me as a family.

The washroom door opens, revealing the man who I've been waiting to defend me. Peony is in his arms, and there's a damp spot on her dress.

I blink owlishly. "Hi? I didn't realize you were in there." So who the hell was Athena ranting to in the staff room?

Whomever it was, her tirade seems to have stopped for now. The staff room is quiet.

"She got icing on her dress, so we were just cleaning it off." Garrett smiles at his daughter.

"I was going to get something from the staff room, but

Athena's on her phone and I don't want to interrupt." Especially considering what she's saying about me.

"You sure? Athena doesn't have her phone with her. She forgot it at home when we left for Portland."

So who the heck is she talking to?

The door opens, and Athena steps out. I peek past her. She's the only person in the staff room.

"We're heading out now," Garrett tells me. "Are you coming over later?"

"I probably shouldn't. I have a meeting with some of the small-business women whose products I'll be stocking here soon." A meeting that wasn't stopping me from seeing Garrett tonight...until I heard Athena's cutting rant.

She was talking to herself. That's who she was ranting to.

"You've also got to keep up with the treatment plan," Garrett continues, oblivious to my inner turmoil. "Otherwise, your symptoms will worsen."

His words are a slap to the face, though that's not what he intended. They're just one more reminder Athena is right. I could never be Peony's mother, not in the way Kenda was for her daughter. Not in the way Athena is now, in Kenda's place.

"I will. Don't worry. I'll be fine." I curve my mouth into a smile for Peony's benefit. "Bye, Princess Peony." I wave at her.

Don't let him see how much Athena's words hurt.

As soon as I turn away from them, I give in to the heavy pull of gravity on the corners of my mouth.

And my heart sinks with it.

43

———

ZARA

The July 4th sunlight streams through the partially closed bedroom curtains, telling me it's time to get up. I have a busy day ahead of me, finalizing plans for the grand reopening next week.

But afterward, once all those big events have passed, I can take things easier and respect the limitations spondyloarthritis has placed on my body. I can take the metaphorical bull by the horns and craft it into something we can both live with, in relative harmony.

I flip over to check my alarm clock. At the sudden, unwelcome movement, my body wails at me, like a toddler throwing a tantrum.

I feel like crap. But it has nothing to do with the SpA—and everything to do with the symptoms that hit me yesterday. I'd played ostrich when I woke up yesterday morning, shoving my head in a hole and pretending I didn't have a sore throat. Pretending I wasn't getting sick.

Ignoring the symptoms didn't make them go away.

And now they're too drastic to pretend they don't exist. The aching body. The chills. The headache. The exhaustion. The brain fog that swept in overnight with no plans to dissipate in the morning sun.

Of all the days for me to get sick, it had to be July 4th—one of the busiest days of the year for Picnic & Treats.

Get out of bed and move around. You'll feel better in no time.

I half-heartedly shove the bedding aside and cautiously swing my legs over the edge of the mattress as I sit upright. Being hit with a sledgehammer would hurt far less than this. *Shit.*

I lower my feet to the floor and slowly stand, testing my balance, testing what my body thinks of my plans.

My legs wobble under my weight, and I grab the corner of the nightstand, steadying myself.

Once I'm positive my equilibrium won't fail me, I take a tentative step.

My muscles scream, *What the hell do you think you're doing?* and I drop my ass back onto the edge of the bed.

I gauge the distance between me and the bedroom door. I don't exactly want to stay in bed all day. My body will hate me if I even try. But I'm not sure I can make it to the living room either.

I pick up my phone and speed dial Keshia's number.

"Good morning, Z," she cheerfully chirps.

"I'm not gonna make it in," I grumble, the words sandpapering the lining of my throat. *Ouch. Goddammit. Ouch.*

"You sound terrible." The sweet sympathy in her tone is a soothing balm to my soul. Too bad it doesn't do anything for the symptoms. "Do you need me to cover your shift?"

"Could you? I know you have plans to spend today with Tyler. And I hate to ask." She wasn't scheduled to work because it's a holiday.

"He texted last night. He and the guys are in Portland. So no plans."

"Portland? What happened to you two spending the day

together?" Lord, why am I so surprised? This is Tyler we're talking about. The king of letdowns when it comes to his girlfriend.

A fluttering sigh comes from Keshia's end of the phone line. "Oh, well. What's a girl to do?"

Dump his sorry ass. That would be my first suggestion. She can do so much better than him. And hopefully she realizes that before she wastes too much more time on a man who's only capable of loving himself.

"I'll make it up to you," I promise her.

"Don't worry about me and P&T. We're good. You just make sure you get lots of rest. Is there anything you need? I can drop it off on my way."

"No, I'll be fine." Maybe I can crawl to the bedroom door since my legs aren't in the mood to walk there.

We end the call, and with a groan, I lie down on the bed.

The bright side of brain fog is it dulls the memory of what Athena said during her rant that I overheard last week, when she was in the staff room. I haven't been able to stop replaying it in my head. The downside?

I glance longingly at the spicy romance novel on the bedside table. I don't have energy to read it.

There are always audiobooks.

I lift my phone and stare at the screen. I just don't have the brain capacity right now to download an audiobook app, create an account, and find something worth listening to.

Maybe if I go back to sleep, I'll wake up feeling better.

"Hey, Golden Girl." The familiar, low husky voice intrudes on my restless dream, and a warm hand touches my aching head.

I'm vaguely aware of a soft moan, a moan possibly falling from between my dry lips. I slowly blink my eyes open. It takes a moment before the man sitting on the edge of my bed comes into focus.

He's wearing his faded blue T-shirt that hugs his body just right and his jeans.

"What are you doing here?" My voice is scratchier than it was when I spoke to Keshia on the phone. Flames creep along the tender lining of my throat. On top of that, my nose feels like cotton balls have been stuffed up it, warping the sound of my voice even more.

"I took Peony to P&T to visit you, but Keshia told me you were home, sick. I dropped Peony off at home then came here. Is it the spondyloarthritis? You're having a relapse?"

I shake my head, the movement minute. "No. An annoying summer cold." Usually, summer colds don't hit me like this, but with everything going on with my body, maybe the SpA made the illness feel worse than normal.

I try to shift on the bed, but the pain is a twelve. I can hardly move. I'm only capable of groaning.

"Did you have your meds today?"

"No. I haven't been able to get as far as the bathroom." The press of my bladder confirms it. If I don't get up soon, I'm going to humiliate myself.

I can tell from Garrett's expression the second the same thought crosses his mind. The part about me needing to go to the bathroom. Maybe not so much the part about humiliating myself.

"I'll be right back." He disappears out the bedroom door. A moment later, the rush of running water taunts me.

Not helping me here.

Praying my bladder doesn't fail me, I squeeze my legs together. The action only worsens the muscle pain. It does nothing to ease the need to pee.

Garrett returns and scoops me up in his arms.

My arms go around his shoulders, and I try not to notice the press of his hard chest and abs against my side. Try not to notice how delicious he feels. "You shouldn't come near me. You'll get the plague too." *Little late for that warning.* "And Peony will get sick." I don't need to give Athena yet another reason not to like me.

Plus, it won't help him with his deadline.

He gives my body a light squeeze-hug. "I'll take my chances."

Of course he will.

He carries me to the bathroom. "Why have you been avoiding me for the past week?"

"I haven't been avoiding you." I've totally been avoiding him —ever since I overheard Athena's tirade in the staff room. Every time I replayed her sharp words, they shredded me on the inside a little more. "I've been busy. With all the planning I've been doing for the grand reopening." It's the truth though.

He lowers me onto the closed toilet seat. "I'll give you privacy while you do your thing." He points to the toilet. "And I'll help you into the bathtub once you're done." A slightly panicked expression crosses his face, lifting his eyebrows. "Unless you need help with..." He waves at me and the toilet.

"No, I'm good," I say a little too quickly. If I wasn't feeling like hell had stomped on me and if I wasn't mortified at the thought of him helping me with the toilet, I'd burst out laughing at his equally mortified reaction.

Garrett leaves, shutting the door behind him. With the help of the counter, I stand on shaky legs, lower my sleep shorts and panties, and do my business.

Once I'm finished, I flush and wash my hands and brush my teeth. My eyes go to the mirror, and I die a little more on the inside. I don't look like crap. I look a hundred times worse than crap.

I don't have the energy to fix my less than substellar appearance. All I can do is remove my sleep bonnet and fluff my hair. It will have to do. It's not like Garrett and I are dating and I don't want him to see the real me.

He has seen the real me plenty of times—including when I have a cold.

Knocking comes from the other side of the door. "You ready?"

"Yep. Ready."

The door cautiously opens, and Garrett steps into the small space, his body almost bumping into mine.

He turns on the tap for the bathtub and picks up the bottle of bath salts from the counter. He unscrews the lid and sniffs the contents. "It smells like you."

"It's jasmine."

He pours some into the water. The light, floral scent is barely noticeable through the congestion in my head.

He returns the bottle to the counter and strips out of his T-shirt.

I don't say anything or question what he's doing. I lean against the bathroom door and appreciate the delectable view of his muscled abs and chest. A girl's gotta make the most of moments like this whenever she can...even when she feels like crap.

Especially when she feels like crap.

His shorts, socks, and boxer briefs come off next. I wasn't expecting him to join me in the bathtub, but he won't see me complaining or protesting. I just watch the way his muscles stretch and contract, commit the view to memory for a rainy day. Damn, he's fine. More than fine.

He turns off the water and helps me remove my T-shirt, a light blush spreading across his sun-kissed cheeks.

"You've seen me naked several times. How can you be embarrassed now?" I would giggle at how adorably-bashful the usually unflappable Marine is, but that would only hurt. Everywhere.

"'Cause those times I was planning to give you orgasms and be buried inside you. This seems…"

"Different? Intimate?" Just saying the second word feels like a caress to my soul.

He lifts his shoulders. "Yeah, something like that."

He helps me shimmy out of the rest of my clothes, placing them next to his on the counter. I can tell he's doing his best not to check me out, but I keep catching the accidental glances, like featherlight brushes to my skin.

He steps into the bathtub and offers his hand. I take it and join him in the water.

We sit, sloshing the water in gentle waves, my butt settling between his powerful thighs. I lean against him. Heat laps my aching muscles, and I moan in satisfaction.

I rest my head on his shoulder and close my eyes. "Thank you. This is my idea of heaven—minus the pain and sore throat and congestion."

"You're welcome." His arms go around me, and he tenderly rubs his thumb along my arm. "You wanna tell me why you've been avoiding me for the past week?"

Dammit. I walked right into that trap. He knows I won't be able to escape him, escape the question—not while we are like this, in the bathtub. Not while my body isn't in the mood to comply with my wishes.

What am I supposed to tell him?

I've known Garrett most of my life, and we've been close friends for the better part of it. It's not in my nature to keep things from him—other than how I'm in love with him.

But admitting what I overheard the other day, when Athena was ranting about me to herself…it's too much.

Garrett kisses my wet shoulder. "You can tell me anything, you know that, right?"

I open my eyes and nod.

He kisses my neck, sending a shower of sparks through me in spite of my cold. "So tell me."

I ease out a slow breath. It does nothing to relax me. "It's just something I overheard Athena saying last Monday in P&T's staff room, after Peony freaked out."

"What did she say?" There's an edge to Garrett's voice I can't unravel through the brain fog.

I roll my bottom lip between my teeth, figuring out the best way to address his question.

"What did she say?" he presses when I don't respond, still in thought.

The words cling to the back of my throat, pleading for me to lie. To come up with something less hurtful. Maybe I could even convince myself the lie is true. That she never said what I overheard. "She was complaining how…it really doesn't matter what she was saying. She loves your daughter, and that's what's important."

"I don't doubt she loves Peony." He continues caressing my arm, his touch lulling my brain into doing whatever he asks of me. "But what I want to know is what she said that had you avoiding me."

I swallow, and it feels like I've tossed gasoline onto the flames in my throat, their heat lashing the tender lining. "She couldn't believe how anyone could confuse me as Peony's mother. After Joffrey thought I was her mom. She said I'm nothing like Kenda." Something I already know and don't need the reminder of.

I'd realized it in college, when Garrett fell in love with her and didn't see me as someone he could love that way.

"She also said I'm not the one who plays with Peony, nor am I there for her when she has a nightmare. And she's right. I'm not. Athena is more capable of being Peony's mother than I am." The reality of those words still cuts deep. "Not that I'm trying to be her mother," I rush out. "No one could ever take Kenda's place."

What Garrett and I currently have between us—the kissing and sex—isn't about us being a couple. It isn't about us falling in love and making a family.

"It's just...her words reminded me how much the spondyloarthritis impacts my ability to be a mother."

"In what way?"

"I always have to worry about triggers that might cause the symptoms to worsen. And while things have improved due to the lifestyle changes I've made to keep the flare-ups under control..." I draw in a breath, too quiet for Garrett to hear. What I'm about to say will forever put me in the friend zone. To have him see me as nothing more than Peony's doting "aunt." "Things have improved, but I'm not a hundred percent. You've seen me with yoga. It's a struggle for me—the getting up and down."

"And you think those things will keep you from being a mother?" Confusion twists its way through his tone, ties it up with a pretty bow.

"They make it more challenging. I can't play with Peony as easily as Athena can."

"But you can do so much more than that."

I smirk—not that he can see my mouth with my back pressed against his front. "You mean make adorable unicorn cupcakes?"

He chuckles, the low rumble vibrating through me where our bodies touch. "Being able to make those certainly doesn't hurt." He kisses my shoulder once more, and a different kind of fire than the one in my throat sparks to life low in my belly. "I take it you want kids?"

It's an honest question. We've never really talked about whether I want to have kids one day or not. Just like we've never discussed whether they were in his future either.

"I do. One day." Not that I've found someone I want to have them with, if you exclude the man I'm currently reclining on.

But even if I do find a man one day who wants to have kids, things might not be so simple. For some women, pregnancy can trigger spondyloathritis symptoms to worsen. They spend most of their pregnancy in more pain than normal. There's no way to predict how things will play out.

"Well, for all it's worth, I think you'll be a great mom."

My mouth eases into a small smile, but the reality of the truth—I'll never be the mother to *his* kids—prevents it from growing wider. "Thanks."

Garrett plants a soft kiss in the crook of my neck. "Is the bath helping any?"

"Yes." I only wish it could last for a few more hours.

But he cannot stay here, with me, for much longer. Even if he didn't have the book deadline rushing toward him at full speed, it's a holiday and he should be spending it with his daughter.

His fingers move between my legs, sending a wave of need through me. "Do you want me to give you an orgasm?" His low, gravelly voice against my ear is almost enough to have me coming right here. And now.

"Yes, please." My breathy tone floats out on a light moan.

GARRETT SITS NEXT TO ME ON THE COUCH AND PICKS UP THE romance novel from the coffee table. "Ready for story time? I thought I would read to you."

He flashes me a playful grin, then shifts on the couch, piling pillows at the end of it. Seeming satisfied with the result, he pats between his legs. "Sit here."

I move my ass to where he's indicating and lean back on him, like I did in the bath.

"Comfy?" His warm breath fans over my cheek.

How could I not be? With Garrett? Like this? "Definitely." After the orgasm he gave me, the pain in my body has eased off slightly. The cold in my head and chest is another matter.

He puts on his reading glasses, and *damn*, he looks as fine as ever in them. I don't know what it is with those dark-framed glasses, but they drive up his sex appeal—and leave me practically drooling.

Garrett's arms go around me, and he opens the book to the last page I was on.

I close my eyes and listen to his deep melodic voice. If this is what male narrators sound like, I might need to start listening to audiobooks after all.

Or convince Garrett to read to me more often.

"I can't believe she didn't just kick him out of the vehicle," Garrett says after he's been reading for a while. "Why is she giving him a second chance?"

"Because she loves him. Because she knows deep down, he isn't as messed up as he thinks he is."

"*Hmm.* He sounds pretty messed up to me."

"Most people are, one way or another. As you know, Mr. Thriller Author." The corners of my mouth twitch. "But that's the beauty of romance. It's a chance for the hero and heroine to untangle what they think are the messiest parts of themselves." I absentmindedly draw circles on the inside of his wrist with my index finger. "But it's the other person who helps them eventually see that part of themselves clearer. And they realize they aren't as broken as they had originally believed. And it's only then they can progress to the happily ever after. Together."

"Guess I've never thought of it that way."

"That's because you don't read romance." I playfully poke him in the side with my elbow. "Speaking of which...how's the romance in *your* novel going?" I haven't gotten over how he's actually adding spicy scenes to the story.

"Not bad."

I shift forward and glance over my shoulder at him. "You're not planning to kill off the woman, are you?" I can't believe he did that in one of his novels and dared to call the subplot a "romance."

His fingers trail along my cheekbone and tuck a wayward coil behind my ear. "After the grief you gave me last time?" He chuckles. "Definitely not."

"What's she like? The woman your character falls in love with."

Garrett doesn't answer right away, his eyes probing mine. "Smart. Generous. Kind. Loyal. There's nothing she wouldn't do for her friends and loved ones. She's the kind of person who makes someone feel seen, worthy." His gaze drops to my lips. "She's the kind of person who welcomes people into her circle and makes them feel like family."

"She sounds amazing."

His eyes flick up to mine again, and a smile plays on his mouth. "She is."

44

——

GARRETT

I spend the next few hours reading to Zara and watching a sappy movie with her. I ignored her initial protests, telling me I needed to leave so I can spend time with Peony or work on my book. Eventually, she gave up trying to figuratively push me out the door.

She's right though. I do need to work on my book. It's a holiday, and in theory, I get to take the day off to spend it with family. To spend it with Peony. But the reality is, I don't have that luxury right now. Not until the book is finished.

Zara is more than ready for a nap by the time I stand to leave. I cover her with a throw and kiss her forehead. "Text if you need anything."

She nods on her pillow, her eyelids half-closed. "Okay. And thank you, Garrett. For everything." Her congested, honeyed voice comes out drowsy.

"Anytime."

Zara might be napping, but Peony certainly isn't when I walk into my living room after returning home. Peony is giggling and bouncing on the couch cushions Athena has laid out on the floor.

"Hey, little flower."

"Daddy!" She practically hurls herself at me.

I catch her and swing her above my head, which elicits another round of giggles.

"You ready to go to Granny and Grandpa's house?" I blow a raspberry on her cheek. She giggles some more and throws her arms around my neck, her exuberance almost strangling me.

Usually, I would hang out at the Fourth of July celebrations that Maple Ridge throws each year, but I'm skipping it this time. Peony's play therapist recommended not taking Peony to it, 'cause of the trauma she's working through. It might be too overwhelming for her.

Athena picks up a couch cushion and returns it where it belongs. She's quiet, her thoughts clearly somewhere else. And she appears so...fragile. That's the best way to describe her right now.

Her hand goes to her necklace, and she fiddles with the pendant.

This isn't the first time I've seen her like this, but she seemed fine this morning. Her mood shifted when I left Peony with her so I could check on Zara.

If Athena was anyone else, I would assume she was annoyed I ruined her day off by expecting her to look after Peony while I was at Zara's. But Athena was the one who insisted she didn't want the day off. That she was happy to look after Peony so everyone else could enjoy the celebrations in town.

I'm guessing the reason she's acting off is because I went to see Zara. "Zara means a lot to me," I tell Athena, using the same caution one would use for a wounded animal. "And I'd like it if you two could become friends."

Athena's head whips to me, surprise or uncertainty rounding her eyes. As if I had slapped her.

"She's going to be a major part of Peony's life," I remind her. "So—"

"You're...you're marrying her?"

I choke out a laugh. "No. Definitely not." An image flickers in my head of Zara standing in front of me in a wedding gown last summer, when we were pretending to be bride and groom so Jess could practice taking wedding photos. Just seeing Zara dressed in white, the long slit of her floor-length gown revealing golden flashes of her leg, had my cock threatening to harden in my pants.

I had recited in my head the names of all my favorite hockey players—in reverse alphabetical order—to keep everyone from seeing the effect she had on my body.

"But...but you're dating her?"

I shake my head, sorry for stepping on this land mine. For suggesting Athena becomes friends with Zara. The last thing Zara and I want is for this new twist in our friendship to go public, for Athena to out us. "We're not dating."

Her eyebrows scrunch together. "So you're just using her for..." She glances at Peony in my arms. "S.E.X?"

"I'm not using her for S.E.X." Why would she think that I am?

Because she doesn't know the benefits orgasms have on pain control.

And I'm not about to discuss them with her.

Her frown deepens. "You're not dating her, and you're not using her for S.E.X? Then why have you been kissing her?"

"It's complicated."

Athena snorts and picks up another cushion from the floor.

"I'd appreciate it if you didn't mention to anyone you saw Zara and me kiss." I assume she hasn't already. She doesn't seem to know anyone in town, other than my mother. And I would have heard if someone had blabbed to Mom about Zara and me kissing.

"So you're ashamed that you've kissed her?"

"Of course not." Never.

"Do you want to date her?" There's no accusation in her tone this time. Only curiosity.

"I don't date," I say truthfully, though it's none of her business.

Understanding lightens her eyes, and she tilts her head to the side, as if to get a better read on me. "So, you just have S.E.X with women." Her eyes narrow. "Do you pay for it?" The words are spoken with a hard huff to her tone. "Or just hook up with women you meet?"

I'm sitting under a microscope, and she's studying me like I'm some sort of biology experiment.

Peony squirms in my arms, ready to be put down. I lower her to the floor. "I've never paid for S.E.X." Have no interest in paying for it either. Not that I've ever needed to. Finding a woman who wants to screw has never been a problem. "Anyway, we're getting off topic. I can't order you to be friends with Zara. But you'll find she's a good friend to have. And she wants to be your friend."

Athena stares at me and then blinks. "She...she wants to be friends?"

"Why wouldn't she?"

"Because I'm your employee."

"That doesn't mean you can't be friends. I'm not talking about you two becoming besties. But wouldn't it be nice to have someone in town who you can talk to? About women stuff?" Or whatever it is women talk about.

The corner of her mouth quirks up. "Okay."

"Good. We should get going. My parents are expecting us." The only reason I'm taking Athena along is because it might be easier on Peony if there's another person she knows and trusts at my parents' place.

Zara had planned to join us, but she obviously can't make it now.

Lucas, Simone, Kylie, and Zoe are already in my parents' backyard when we walk through the side gate. So are Kellan and Troy. Emily and Jess are volunteering with the hayrides in town, so they won't be here until later.

"Okay," I say to Peony as I carry her, the midafternoon sun kissing the back of my neck. "Should we try this again with your uncles? Remember, I'm here, and no one will hurt you. They just want to get to know you."

Peony's expression doesn't give any hint that she understands me. Her gaze is on Simone and Lucas's two girls playing with the water table.

Athena and I walk across the recently mowed lawn to the girls.

Zoe spots Peony in my arms and points at her. "Baby!"

Peony grins at the two-year-old. Mom has taken Peony to visit Simone and the girls a few times, so Peony knows Zoe. It's just Lucas who Peony hasn't gotten to know yet or spend time with.

"Hey, girls." I kneel beside the table and lower Peony to the ground. She immediately plays with the table, scooping water onto the grass.

I laugh. "I don't think that's what you're supposed to do with the water."

Lucas walks over to us, his steps hesitant as if he's gauging Peony's reaction to him. He crouches between Kylie and Zoe on the other side of the table. Peony eyes him leeringly, the yellow scoop still in her hand.

I put my hand on her back, reassuring her I'm here. Nothing bad will happen.

My oldest brother picks up the red cup, fills it with water, and pours the contents into the small tray elevated above the table. Water rains from it onto the table below. And onto the rubber duck floating on the water.

A delighted smile breaks out on Peony's face, though I suspect this isn't the first time she's seen the table make rain. She splashes her hands in the water, creating waves that send the duck bobbing toward Lucas through the shower.

He pours more water into the tray. Peony grins at him.

But the smile only lasts a fraction of a beat. It falls away, and her expression turns uncertain, her little brow wrinkling.

A screw in my chest tightens, a reminder of how much I'd hoped things would move in a positive direction today between Peony and her uncles. That this would be the start of the family Kenda envisioned when she wrote her final letter to me.

Lucas appears undaunted by her sudden change in demeanor, and he returns his attention to Zoe. It's clear from the way Zoe and Kylie interact with him, any nervousness they'd once felt around him has gone.

Anyone who sees the way the three of them respond to each other would think they're a family. A father with his two daughters.

Seconds later, Peony's brow smooths out. She splashes the water again. Has Lucas done it—melted her distrust? I hold my breath, hoping it's true.

As the afternoon moves on, Peony's walls crumble. A large part of that is surely due to the way Kylie and Zoe respond to my father and brothers. The way the girls talk to them, play with them, laugh with them.

And I also credit the change due to the hockey game, with the toy sticks and the rubber ball, that broke out on the lawn a short time ago.

Peony taps the ball between the two small pylons that make up the goal. It slips past Troy, the goalie.

Kylie and Zoe cheer, and Kellan flashes Peony a quick, rare

smile. She grins at him, as if realizing just how special the smile he's gifted her is.

The game continues, with Mom declaring at the end that both sides are the victors. "Who wants their reward—strawberry ice cream?"

"Me! Me! Me!" both Kylie and Zoe excitedly respond, jumping up and down, waving their arms.

Peony mirrors their reaction, her legs pumping up and down, her feet never leaving the ground. But she doesn't care. She's giggling all the same, her sweet face glowing. The three girls rush over to the table with Mom.

"Any particular reason you were smelling like flowers when you first got here?" Lucas asks, eyebrow raised.

I frown, having no idea what he's talking about.

Oh, shit. Zara's bath salts. I didn't consider that when I climbed into the water with her. I only noticed *she* smelled incredible, like she always does, while I was reading to her.

My chuckle is forced, but it sounds somewhat genuine to my ears. Good enough to fool my brothers.

Lucas, Troy, and Kellan watch me, seemingly waiting for my reply.

"I didn't smell like flowers." I glance at Athena. She has moved near the back door, far enough away to not overhear us, and isn't looking my way. She's standing there like an outsider, a statue, worry carved into her expression.

Troy shoves his hands into his shorts pockets. "You did. You smelled like Zara."

I huff out a laugh. "You're imagining things. I went to see her because she's sick, and I hugged her. Maybe her smell rubbed off on me, then."

Sounds like a reasonable explanation. One that doesn't involve me joining a naked Zara in her bathtub.

I turn my head again to check on Athena, to see if she's still worried when there's no reason to be. Peony is having a good time.

Athena is no longer standing where she was a second ago. No one is. And the side gate is now partially open.

Where the heck did she go?

GARRETT

The following Wednesday, I turn on the news, intending to watch it for only a few minutes. For a thriller author, it's often a good source of inspiration for stories or scenes in a book.

Peony is in the kitchen, pretending to help Athena make dinner. Neither of them are paying attention to the TV, the volume turned low.

Athena hasn't seemed quite as "off" over the past couple of days as she did at my parents' house last Thursday. But even after I found her pacing on my parents' driveway, working out a stitch in her side, she's been twitchy.

A picture of a man in Marine dress uniform appears on the TV screen, and the single beat of my heart thuds so hard, my chest wall reels at the impact. I know that man.

Tyson had gotten the stomach flu during my final deployment. Instead of going on the mission he had been assigned to be part of, he'd stayed behind while he recovered. And I'd taken his spot. It was the mission that cost Cooper and Clarke their lives. Cost each of their families a son, a husband, a father.

The mission where I failed to protect them.

The woman newscaster on the TV is explaining that First Lieutenant Philip Tyson died during a militia attack in Syria. His funeral is scheduled for next week in Alabama.

Heart heavy, I turn off the TV and pull on my everything-is-fine mask. For my daughter's sake.

Athena removes a casserole dish from the oven and places it on the granite counter. Peony removes a plate from her toy oven and puts it on the toy counter.

I crouch next to her. "Mmm. Dinner smells delicious." I point to the empty toy plate. "Did Zara teach you how to make that?"

Pride beams in Peony's smiling face. "Zawa."

"That's right," Athena says. "Just like she taught me how to make Southern baked mac and cheese yesterday, when Peony and I went to her apartment."

Cooking seems to be the only common ground between Athena and Zara. The cooking lesson—Athena's suggestion, not mine—was a tiny step toward them possibly becoming friends. Eventually.

I straighten to my feet. "Mmm. It smells good."

I help to set the table and buckle Peony into her booster seat. "How are things going with getting your replacement ID and Social Security Number?" I ask Athena. It's been almost two months. "Any word on them yet?"

Athena places the casserole dish in the center of the table. "Nothing yet. You know how bureaucrats are always getting tangled up in red tape? Guess this time they used duct tape. And that stuff's impossible to untangle." She slides me an amused smirk and returns to the stove. "I'm sure they'll get around to them soon enough."

THE EARLY EVENING SUNLIGHT KISSES A WARM GLOW ON ZARA'S face, highlighting her beauty. After hearing that Tyson is dead, more than ever, I crave to get lost in one of her kisses.

But Peony is sitting in her car seat, waiting to be removed, and I don't need her to witness me kissing Zara. It might not mean anything to her now, but there probably will come a point when she'll wonder about why Zara and I kiss.

Maybe not now.

Maybe not next month.

But it will eventually happen. And the reason I'm kissing Zara is a discussion I'd rather not have with my daughter. At any age.

"I don't think I'll ever get tired of walking here." Zara closes her eyes and tilts her face to the sun. "It's so peaceful."

"It is." The quiet that's only experienced when surrounded by nature—the rustle of leaves in the gentle breeze, the drone of a flying insect near my head—fills me with the same peace. It's the tranquility only felt in the mountains or by the lake or on Wilderness Warriors property.

I unclip Peony's harness and remove her from the car seat. Her attention is on a bird of prey circling over the meadow.

She points at it. "Bird."

"That's right. The bird is looking for dinner." Likely a poor unsuspecting field mouse hiding in the wild grass. But I'm not planning to explain that circle-of-life lesson right now to my daughter. Let her learn it from *The Lion King*.

I set her up in the carrier and hoist it onto my back. I adjust the shoulder straps and snap the chest strap into position. Peony rocks in the seat, hinting for me to get going.

Zara and I begin our hike on the dirt path that cuts through the meadow. The path is wide enough, in most places, for us to walk alongside each other.

I brush my knuckles across Zara's hand, needing her soft skin to ground me against the memories that haunt me when I least expect them. Peony happily chats away, oblivious to the physical connection between Zara and me.

"Is that so?" I say, pretending we're having a conversation. Her chatter is an endless babble of incoherent words, along with clearly spoken words and ones I can easily decipher.

But as much as I try to remain present, to listen to my daughter, to remind myself I'm on U.S. soil, not enemy soil, my thoughts return to the smoke-and-dust-filled Afghan house, when I watched the light in Clarke's eyes extinguish. I had begged him to hold on, told him help was on the way...

Warm, soft fingers squeeze my hand. "Are you okay?" Zara's smooth, honeyed voice eases into my thoughts. Her voice doesn't banish the memories grinding in my head, but it does quiet them for a beat.

I nod, my gaze on the path.

She squeezes my hand again. "I'm here if you want to talk."

The memory tightens around my chest like a band of fire. Its smoke pours into my lungs, fills the empty spaces. Suffocates me. I stop walking, close my eyes, and draw in a lungful of pine-scented air, grounding myself for the first time since learning Tyson is dead.

I take another long breath, relieved the ground doesn't drop away from under my feet, and reopen my eyes. "I found out today one of my Marine brothers, a close friend, recently died. During a bomb attack in Syria."

"I'm so sorry, Garrett." Compassion, not pity, shines back at me from her beautiful chocolate-brown eyes, further grounding me.

"The funeral is next Tuesday. In Fort McClellan. Alabama," I ramble on, unsure how to respond. Too many people I know have been dying lately. People whose lives have been prematurely cut short.

"Are you going?"

"I am." I owe it to Tyson. He saved my life more times than I care to remember.

"Then I'll come with you." Zara says, with the same fierce certainty she had when she stood up to my elementary-school bully without a second thought.

"You don't have to do that. You're busy with the renovation and the grand reopening."

She strokes my hand. "You're right. I don't. But I want to." Her eyes brim with understanding, as well as another emotion I don't bother to examine too closely. Possibly...love? No, it can't be that.

Going to Tyson's funeral will be tough for many reasons. Cooper, Clarke, Tyson, and I were a tight-knit group, but I couldn't even go to Cooper's and Clarke's funerals—something I'll forever regret. I had been in the hospital at the time, recovering from the explosion that stole them from me.

"Thank you," I whisper to Zara. "I would like it if you came to his funeral with me."

For the briefest of seconds, denial lets me have a taste of another set of words—words about how I really feel about my best friend. *Shit, I think I'm falling for you, Zara.*

The words are quickly locked away, the box tossed into the deepest lake. And once they're gone, the only taste left in my mouth is the sour mix of fear and grief, regret and relief.

Fear I'll fail her like I failed Cooper and Clarke. Like I fear at some point I'll fail my daughter.

Relief Zara isn't falling for me—because it would only be messy and complicated if she did.

And more complications are the last thing either of us needs.

46

———

ZARA

My phone rings from the kitchen counter. I snatch up the phone in time to see it's my cousin, Serena, calling. "Hey. How's New Orleans doing?" I grab the duster from under the sink.

"It misses your fine ass. How's Maple Ridge?"

"It misses *your* fine ass." I kneel in front of the middle shelving unit in the living room and stare at the empty spot next to the wooden elephant. The spot where a framed photo of Garrett and Kenda and me—taken during college—usually stands.

The photo also isn't on any of the other lower shelves.

"And how's Garrett doing?"

I can't see Serena, but I can tell she's grinning at the phone. She has known about my secret, not-so-secret crush on my best friend longer than Emily and Simone have. "He's doing good. How's the guy you recently started seeing?"

I drop to my stomach and look underneath the shelving unit as Serena animatedly talks about him. Dust bunnies have formed a committee under the shelves, but there's no sign of my photo.

362

Peony was here yesterday. Maybe she picked it up and moved it somewhere else.

I check under the couch and the armchairs and the coffee table, but the photo isn't under any of them. Where the heck did it go?

THREE DAYS AFTER I SPOKE TO MY COUSIN ON THE PHONE, I'M standing in the newly expanded Picnic & Treats, doing a mental happy dance. It's Saturday—and the grand reopening of the café. Lauren McNair's powerful voice fills the space as she sings one of her popular songs. A song about girl power and how supporting each other will make the world a better place.

Six little kids, including Peony, are dancing to the music in front of the small stage set up for Lauren. Athena is standing to the side, dancing with Peony. Both look carefree, big silly grins on their faces.

I record a short video to share with Garrett once he gets back from his Wilderness Warriors weekend excursion. I wish he was here to celebrate with me, but at least Peony and Athena showed up.

"The turnout for the event is crazy." The equivalent of a huge smile is in Abby's tone.

"I know." My tone matches hers. "I didn't anticipate it being this big."

It's been like this since the celebration began three hours ago.

A teenage girl and her two friends walk through the entrance. She laughs at something one of them says. I blink at the memory of the last time I saw her two and a half months ago. The day Joseph dumped me. The day her drunk father came into P&T and smashed the chair.

She looks nothing like she did that day. Now she appears happy, relaxed.

Abby returns to the counter, and I walk over to the three teens. "Hi. Sarah, right? How are you doing? I was here that day your father..." I leave the rest of the sentence flapping in the wind, unsure of the best way to end it.

Her eyebrows lift. "Went apeshit?"

That's one way to put it.

"Things are better. My aunt found out what happened and moved to Maple Ridge and is staying with me. Dad called her after he landed in jail." Her voice falters on the last part.

One of Sarah's friends puts her arm around Sarah's shoulders in support.

"My mom died unexpectedly from an aneurysm just before last Christmas. Dad didn't handle it well and started drinking. A lot. And all the time."

Oh, Lord. I can't imagine what she's going through. "I'm so sorry for your loss."

"Thank you. My aunt pushed for Dad to go into rehab, which is where he is now. She also got me into grief counseling, and he's doing it too."

"I'm glad to hear that. Please let me know if there's anything I can do to help."

She nods like she's heard that so many times and is going through the motions, even though she's not sure how sincere the person is.

"I mean it."

She smiles, the tilt of her mouth genuine. "Thank you."

We talk for a few more minutes, then I leave the three friends and make the rounds, checking how everyone is doing.

A man approaches me, carrying a big bouquet of flowers. Carl, a veteran who Garrett is friends with. "Hey, Zara. I've got a special delivery for you." He holds out the flowers for me. His wife owns the floral shop in town. "And congratulations on the expansion. It looks great."

"Thank you. And thank you for the flowers. Any idea who they're from?" The beautiful array of colorful blossoms includes my favorite, jasmine.

"You'll have to open the card to find out." He winks at me and leaves.

I carry the bouquet to the front counter, remove the plastic wrapping, and open the card.

> Golden Girl,
> Sorry I couldn't be there for your big day. I'm so proud of you. We'll celebrate when I get home Sunday night.
> Garrett

My silly heart swoons at the sweet gesture. *Don't read too much into the flowers.* Sure, Garrett has never given me any before, but that doesn't mean he's in love with me. It just means he knows how much the celebration and reopening means to me. Right?

My family, including both brothers, walks into Picnic & Treats. My parents are holding hands, smiling with the same pride in me on their faces that I witnessed growing up. They're the same two individuals who were there for each other, through the highs and the lows, during the season Dad battled testicular cancer thirty years ago. Dad swore Mama's love and devotion were what helped him get through it.

Helped the family get through the ordeal and be stronger.

A brazen picture of a much older Garrett and me saunters into my head. Of him giving me flowers just because. Reading to me like he did when I was sick. Kissing me as if I'm the sun, bathing him in adoration and warmth.

A dreamy, wistful sigh escapes me.

Mama pulls me in for a big hug. "I'm so proud of you, sweetheart." With the grand sweep of her hand, she gestures to the busy café. "This is incredible. What you've accomplished is incredible."

The softhearted expression on her face tells me she didn't doubt for a second I'd be able to pull it off—spondyloarthritis be damned.

I hug my father and my two brothers, Samuel and Jerome. Kim steps forward, carrying Sidney in her arms, and I squeal. My niece is not only the daughter of one of my closest friends from childhood, she's just a few months younger than Peony.

I hug Kim, the award-winning photographer responsible for Garrett's *Golden Girl* nickname, then I kiss my niece on the cheek. "I've missed both of you."

After we catch up for the next few minutes, they leave to take Sidney to a table that has just opened up by the windows.

A few tables over, a young couple is walking away from where Emily is sitting. I recognize the bride-to-be glow on the woman's face. The couple is newly engaged.

"How's it going?" I ask Emily and sit in the empty seat across from her. She isn't a full-time wedding coordinator, but her business has been growing steadily for the past two years. She's also busy as Kellan's full-time office assistant. The assistant he cannot survive without. She occasionally meets with potential clients here.

"It's going really well." Emily's glow is brighter than the one the bride-to-be who just left had. "I've just signed another new client. Their wedding is planned for during the holiday season."

"That's great. I'm so excited for you." I'm practically buzzing with excitement for her.

"Thanks, but what's that saying? Always a bridesmaid,

never the bride?" She lets out a self-deprecating laugh and rolls her eyes. "I'm always the wedding coordinator, never the bride."

She picks up one of her photo albums and shoves it into her oversized bag. "Maybe I should just ask Kellan to help me find a boyfriend...since he doesn't see me as anything other than a friend and office assistant."

My gaze flickers briefly to the counter and the large bouquet from Garrett. "Or you could just tell him how you feel about him?"

She lifts her eyebrow in a silent question. She's clearly asking me when am I planning on telling Garrett I'm in love with him.

"You never know," I say, sidestepping the deep crevice of the question. "Kellan might get jealous of all the men he's helping to set you up with, and he'll finally realize he's madly in love with you."

"Or you could do the same with Garrett. And before you know it, I'll be arranging *your* wedding." She rubs her hands together, as if she's eagerly anticipating that fictitious day.

I pick up one of the glossy pamphlets from the table without really seeing what's on it. "You mean with another man or with Garrett?"

"Definitely Garrett." She taps the pamphlet in my hand.

More specifically, she taps the photo on the front page. The photo Jess took last year of me in a white gown, my hair in an elegant upsweep. My hand cups Garrett's face and our noses are kissing. It's a gorgeous photo, capturing the joy of our make-believe wedding day, our fairy-tale love.

Capturing the happiness we felt in that moment, even if the love in Garrett's expression was faked.

Too bad the same can't be said for me.

"You really should tell Garrett how you feel about him," Em insists. "Before it's too late."

47

GARRETT

Zara and I sit in the pew near the middle of the church and wait for the funeral service to begin. I'm vaguely aware I'm tightening my hold on her hand. She's the lifeline keeping me tethered to the spot. So much loss. So many families missing those they loved. Not just Kenda's daughter and Tyson's family. But all the families who have lost a loved one to gun violence or while protecting the most vulnerable.

Shit, I miss Tyson. And I miss Clarke and Cooper. They were my friends, my family.

A movement in my periphery has me turning my head. An officer in Marine dress uniform walks down the aisle. I can only see the back of him, but it's as if all the air in my lungs has been sucked out.

Clarke.

But that's impossible. Joshua Clarke is dead and buried. I might not have been at his funeral, but I do know that much.

Driven by the haunting failure of my past, I release Zara's hand and stand. Only one thing has my attention, and it isn't the man in the coffin waiting to be laid to rest.

368

I stalk down the aisle, following after Clarke, ignoring the puzzled glances sent my way.

He walks to the main doorway and pulls open the door. The bright sunlight spills in, creating an ethereal glow that outlines the man. Like he's a spirit sent from heaven.

I trail after him, stepping into the stifling hot air. Stifling, but free of the stench of death and despair. I keep following him, scrambling to find purchase on all the things I want to tell him. The same old apology hovers on my lips.

It's only once he gets to the path leading to the sidewalk that he stops and turns, giving me a clear view of his face.

A face that doesn't belong to Clarke.

Of course it doesn't. He's not visiting from heaven. He's not here to blame you for failing to protect him from the explosion. For failing to save his life.

I release a long breath, trying to calm my heart. I can't go back inside to watch the service. Not yet. I need to regroup first, find my footing. I walk to the nearby bench in the shade of a flowering magnolia and sit.

My forearms resting on my thighs, I stare at a discarded cigarette butt on the ground and disappear into my memory of the day everything went to hell.

As I sit on the bench alone, ignoring the occasional person walking on the sidewalk, I attempt more than once to will myself to stand. To return to where I left Zara in the church. To go watch the service. But the sweltering heat of the day has me glued to the bench. Sweat trickles down my back, under the white dress shirt and black suit jacket.

I'm vaguely aware of the steady hum of vehicles driving past the church, but that's the only noise that filters in.

I have no idea how long I've been sitting on the bench when the church door opens, and people file out.

Shit. I couldn't even get my ass off the bench and go inside and sit through the service. I left Zara to mourn a man who was a near stranger to her. I left Zara to do what I couldn't.

I keep staring at the ground, unable to look at the faces walking past me.

She sits beside me on the bench. Her familiar jasmine scent gently embraces me, and for the first time since stepping inside the church, I breathe a little easier.

Zara rubs soothing circles on my back. She doesn't say anything but continues to ground me with her touch.

I finally look up at her, and tear-glistened eyes meet mine. "Sorry for leaving like that." Shame is a heavy winter coat draped over my shoulders in the summer heat.

"You wanna talk about it?"

I shake my head. She's got enough going on without me dumping my problems on her. I take her hand and straighten to my feet.

I don't release her hand as we walk to the parking lot. And when we stop at the passenger side of the rental car, I still don't let go.

I cup her face with my free hand and kiss her. Kiss her like she's the life preserver keeping me afloat. My tongue glides over hers, and I get lost in the kiss for a little longer, paying attention to how her soft body feels against me, how she tastes, how her sweet moans escape with each flick of my tongue.

I capture each of her sounds and rest my forehead on hers. I can't tell her why I'm unable to open my heart to someone, why I don't deserve love in return, but there is one thing I can do that will benefit us both.

"I could use an orgasm right now." The words come out broken, splintered. Pained.

She squeezes my hand, her breath fanning my kiss-swollen lips, and whispers, "I know."

Two days after Tyson's funeral, I'm sitting on my patio with Kellan. The turkey club sandwiches Athena made us while Kellan and I were running sit on a plate in the middle of the table. I bite into my sandwich. The low whirl of the vacuum inside reaches us through the open windows.

Peony is preoccupied, following a bug hopping through the sunny patch of grass.

"Who else knows what happened?" Kellan asks, grabbing another sandwich from the plate. I've just finished telling him about how Cooper and Clarke died.

I won't tell Zara about it, to let her into the horrors I experienced there. But I can tell Kellan, the one person who knows what it was like in Afghanistan, who experienced the same nightmare.

"You mean other than the military? And now you?"

He nods, his face free of what he's thinking after I dumped that all on him.

I wouldn't have told him if he hadn't called me out on it during our run. He knew something was off the moment we started up the trail, but it wasn't until we were cooling down after our final sprint that he brought it up.

"No one. And I want it to stay that way." I give him a meaningful look over my sandwich.

"You know it wasn't your fault, right?"

I huff out a humorless laugh as Peony walks toward us, poking at whatever is in her hand. "I might not have put the bomb in the building, but I should have listened to my gut when it told me something was off."

Peony stops in front of Kellan, cutting off whatever rebuttal he might have said. "Hi!" She grins at him and shows him the purple petal on her palm.

"What do you have?" He leans down and picks up the flower.

"You!"

"Is this for me?" He points to himself.

She rapidly nods, then toddles to me and stretches her arms across my sprawled legs. "Daddy. Up."

I hoist her onto my lap, happy for the distraction, and bounce her on my thighs.

This, I can handle.

Talking about how I'm skilled at failing the people I love, like I failed Kenda and Cooper and Clarke, is something I'd rather not do with Kellan. Or anyone.

Peony giggles and chats with Kellan as if they're life-long friends. He replies, though neither of us knows what she's saying. But that doesn't matter.

What matters is she's cheerfully talking to us and is smiling.

The fear she initially felt toward us has vanished. In its place is a trust I will fight for, to make sure it never dies.

Kellan's phone rings on the table. He checks the screen and accepts the call. "What's up?"

He doesn't have his phone on speaker, but his gruff tone softens, giving away the caller is Emily. I don't think he realizes his voice does that whenever she calls him.

"Okay....Okay...." Anger flickers in his expression, but his tone is neutral, the anger obviously not directed at Emily. "I'll be right there." He ends the call and stands.

"Work emergency?"

He grunts—and just like that, he's back to his shut-down self. The result of his fucked-up biological mother who abandoned him as a young child and a father he never knew.

"Bye, Peony." He waves at her, but the smile he usually flashes for her benefit is now nothing more than a fizzled light bulb.

I tickle Peony's tummy as he heads for the side gate. "How 'bout you and I search for fairies?" While Athena finishes whatever she's doing inside. Then she can look after Peony while I work.

"Fai-wies."

We walk through the backyard, checking the trees with the tiny doors and windows on the trunks. Zara and Jess were busy last weekend, setting up the fairy homes while I was away as a surprise.

Athena is standing on the patio, flipping through a stack of envelopes in her hand, by the time we return.

"Any sign of your replacement ID and Social Security Number?"

"Not yet." She continues flipping through the stack, her expression not revealing her thoughts about the delay. If it were me, at this point, I'd be checking into what was taking so long. "They will come when they come." She hands me the mail with a shrug.

I just don't get how she can be so nonchalant about the long wait. It's like she's not interested in having a bank account.

"You do realize I will be telling the IRS that I'm paying you for childcare?" For all I know, she wasn't planning to file her taxes for this year, which is why she isn't in a rush to get a bank account. But I have no intention of being dragged into her mess if that's her plan.

"I know." She walks to the large toy truck on the grass and picks it up. "I'm sure everything will arrive in plenty of time for that."

Let's hope so—otherwise the government really needs to get its act together when it comes to these delays.

I kneel next to Peony. "Daddy's going back to work now. Can I have a hug first?"

She tries to scramble onto my bent leg in an attempt to hug

me. I scoop her up, balance her on my thigh, and embrace her. She returns my hug, her little body crushed against me. I kiss her cheek and lower her to the ground.

I straighten, wave bye to her, and walk to the house as I check through the stack of mail. Nothing exciting. And no letters from Annie Wilkes 3.0.

Two others have also shown up at my house following the first one a month and a half ago. I handed each letter over to the police.

I flip to the last envelope. My name and address are handwritten on the front. I don't recognize the return address. The only thing I do recognize is the town it came from.

Cooper's hometown.

The one his family moved to following his death.

The handwriting doesn't look familiar. It might have been a while since I last saw his wife's writing, but this isn't it. Her handwriting is unmistakably feminine, the letters smaller and neater.

I carry the mail into my office, toss the rest of the stack onto my desk, and open the last envelope. I put on my reading glasses and remove the single sheet of lined paper.

Garrett,
You sit there in your fancy house, making more money than you could ever need because of those shit books you write.

Okay, not a fan of my stuff. I should toss the letter into the recycle bin, but something compels me to keep reading. Stupidity, perhaps?

It's obvious you don't give a crap about the people you've hurt. The people who cared about you when they shouldn't have bothered. It should have been you who died that day in Afghanistan. My brother should have been the one who came home.

You don't even care what you did to his family. Cassie struggles every day with the loss of the man she loved and still loves. Their kids still struggle every day, waiting for their mother to be the next one who disappears from their lives. All because of you.

You know what pisses me off most? That you never did time for your gross negligence. There was no punishment for your crime against my brother, against the woman he loved.

I hope you burn in hell when it's your time to leave this world.

Cooper's brother didn't bother to sign it, but I can picture in my mind the man who wrote the letter. Austin. Cooper's younger brother.

Shit, how did he even know what went down when his brother died? He's right, there was no trial. I didn't do anything wrong—other than not listen to my gut. Ultimately, it was the enemy who ended Clarke's and Cooper's lives with the booby trap that Cooper accidentally triggered. *But you were there. And now, you're here—and they're dead.*

My gut churns. The familiar sickening feeling of guilt resurfaces, and too much saliva coats my mouth. *Why did it have to end that way?*

I swallow back the pain and pull open my desk drawer. I shove the letter inside, remove my glasses, and rub my weary eyes.

Fuck. How do I make up for what I've cost their families? I reached out to their wives after I returned stateside, but at the time neither wanted to talk to me, caught up in their own grief. Instead of trying again later on, I clung to my guilt, letting it fester deep beneath the surface.

Guilt that flared up once more after Peony showed up, motherless, on my front stoop.

48

———

ZARA

Garret: Have to cancel tonight. Sorry.

Sitting on the staff-room couch, I reread the text he sent me this morning.

Then I reread the five other identical texts he had sent me, starting the day after we returned to Maple Ridge from Alabama.

He was so devastated at the loss of his friend, he couldn't even sit through the service. And the way he fucked me afterward—hard, desperate, a quiet anger hovering at the edge—further confirmed his devastation.

On top of that, he's drowning in stress from his rapidly approaching deadline. A deadline that might be more manageable if not for Wilderness Warriors, Peony, and Garrett's unofficial role in my treatment plan.

It's no wonder he's been canceling.

My chronic medical condition and I are a burden to the man I love. Just as I feared we would be.

Another text pings on my phone.

Emily: I'm here!

I grab the bag of samosas from the coffee table and walk down the hallway to the main sitting area of the café.

Even with the expansion, there aren't any empty seats. Picnic & Treats is one of the hottest spots in town, even more so with the new programs I now offer...including a monthly book club meeting for spicy romances.

Despite my crushing realization about Garrett, I can't keep the grin from my face at seeing what I've accomplished. Picnic & Treats and the work I'm starting to do with the small-business association...those are my crowning glories.

Too bad my crowning glories can't give me orgasms.

Or kiss me the way Garrett can.

No man can kiss me the way he can.

"Text me if you need anything," I tell Anastasia, who's working behind the front counter.

Then I join Emily standing near the main entrance. She's wearing a yellow sundress covered with daisies and is carrying a picnic basket. A bright smile shines on her face.

Emily is a perpetually sunny day, happy to share her warmth with everyone. After receiving Garrett's latest text, I'm more than delighted to absorb that warmth. To bask in its glow.

We stroll along the sidewalk to the local park and find an empty bench overlooking the pond to sit on. The sweet scent of freshly mowed grass and the lazy last days of July ease my lingering stress.

Emily's phone rings, and she checks the screen. "Sorry, I have to get this. It will only take a second."

I nod and flash her a reassuring, I'm-good-with-that smile. I inhale deeply and repeat several times in my head my daily mantra: *I choose to remain positive so my body can heal.*

Chronic pain is often linked to depression, and pain and depression can become a vicious circle. The more intense the pain, the worse the symptoms of depression. The worse the symptoms of depression, the more intense the pain...

It's a cycle I've been working hard at not getting caught up in, which isn't always easy to do.

I open the photo app on my phone and visit the positivity vision board I created last weekend. The uplifting photos and quotes make me smile and remind me that I've got this.

Sure, the vision board won't cure my chronic pain, but there is something to having a positive mindset. The creation of vision boards is just one more thing in my arsenal to help manage the pain. The added bonus is that it is side-effect free.

I slip my phone in my purse as Emily ends her call. "Did Melody and Hunter figure out what they want for their rehearsal dinner?"

"They did. They sent it to me just as I was walking out the door. I'll forward it to you once I get back to the office."

"Thanks." I open the bag of samosas sitting next to me and offer one to Emily. "I don't know how you do it all. Working for Kellan and running your own business." Especially at this time of year, when she's dealing with more weddings than normal.

"Ha. As if you aren't super busy with everything you've piled on your plate."

I shrug half-heartedly. "*Touché*. But I am doing a better job with balancing everything, now that I know about the spondyloarthritis and how to manage it better. Lord knows what might have happened if I hadn't been properly diagnosed." The uveitis was bad enough. I'd rather avoid the condition worsening and have other painful and annoying symptoms dumped on me.

We talk for a few minutes about the upcoming small weddings I'm catering and she's coordinating.

"Have you seen Kylie and Zoe lately?" Emily asks once we've finished the business talk.

"I did. The other day. They're doing well, all things considered." I eye her suspiciously. Emily is vibrating with excitement. More excitement than expected, even for Em. "What's going on? Why are you so happy?"

"I'm always happy."

"Uh-huh. But right now, you're like supersized happy. So, what gives?"

"I'm just happy for Simone and Lucas. Especially now that they're starting a family."

"You mean...because they became foster parents?" I pop what's left of my samosa into my mouth.

Emily chews on her lip. It's her deliberation expression. Her weighing-the-pros-and-cons face. Whatever she's dying to tell me, it's big. "No. Because they're planning to adopt Kylie and Zoe."

I gape at her for a heartbeat, her words turning into bubbles of excitement and happiness for one of my closest female friends. *Adopting.* Simone and Lucas are going to be parents. The parents they would have been a decade ago if not for the drunk driver.

Emily presses her finger to her lips. "You can't mention it to anyone—Simone plans to tell everyone soon—but they've fallen in love with the girls and don't want to see them bounced around the system."

"Wow, that's great. And it doesn't surprise me. Simone and Lucas have so much love to share."

"They do. It's a slow process, and they're not asking the girls yet, given they've only recently lost their parents." She tilts her head to the side. "What about you? Would you like to be part of Garrett and Peony's family? As more than just a friend?"

I startle at her question, though I shouldn't be too surprised she asked it. It's also clear from her expression that she knows the answer. "You love Peony like she's your own daughter, don't you?"

"How could I not?"

"You just have to tell Garrett you're in love with him and *poof*." Em waves her hand like she's Cinderella's fairy godmother.

I grab another samosa from the bag and pull a chunk of fried dough from it. Filling falls to my lap. "But he doesn't feel the same way about me, so why bother?" I doubt even Cinderella's fairy godmother could help me there.

"You're wrong. I've seen how he looks at you, Zara." Emily's words float out on a dreamy, wishful sigh.

The corners of my mouth twitch, and I barely restrain a snorted laugh. "Looks at me? How does he look at me?"

She doesn't get the chance to answer. A good-looking man in his early forties, pushing a woman in a wheelchair, approaches our bench. "Is it okay if I sit there?" He points to the empty spot next to me.

I shuffle my ass closer to Emily, giving him more space to sit. "Absolutely!"

Okay, I might have said that with a lot more enthusiasm than probably either he or the woman were expecting. *Anything to get me out of that conversation with Em.*

The woman chuckles. She's extremely pretty. Her golden hair is tied up in a messy bun and she's wearing a shell-pink dress. But what is especially breathtaking about her is the long, delicate vine and butterfly tattoo traveling up her arm.

Her husband, if their wedding rings are anything to go by, leans down and kisses her.

And I swear Em releases another long, dreamy sigh.

Or maybe that was me.

"Are you visiting Maple Ridge?" she asks the couple.

"Yes," the woman replies as her husband sits on the bench. "We're from Portland. I love the mountains and keep hearing how pretty this town is. So, we thought we'd celebrate our wedding anniversary here."

"Happy anniversary," both Em and I exclaim at the same time. "How long have you been married?" I add.

"Fourteen years. Fourteen crazy years with lots of ups and downs." She grins at her husband. "Not to mention more medical appointments than I care to think about." She rolls her eyes, her smile waning only a tiny amount. "But Nick has stood by my side when I'm sure there were things he would rather be doing."

He takes her hand and kisses the back of it, making my insides swoon a little. Okay. A lot.

"You're my best friend. The woman I love. There is nowhere I'd rather be than with you."

It's a sign. That's what Emily's smug look is trying to say. *The universe is sending you a sign. You and Garrett belong together.*

What am I supposed to do about that? Tell Garrett the truth about my feelings for him?

Or maybe the Universe could help me out and be the one to tell him.

49

ZARA

Two days after Emily and I talked to the married couple in the park, I show up at Garrett's house, buoyed by words of the husband's undying love and support for his chronically ill wife.

I don't know if it's right or not, if their love is a sign I need to tell Garrett how I genuinely feel about him. But sign or not, it's time I tell him the truth. I owe myself that much.

Garrett didn't send any texts today to cancel on me, so I ring his doorbell. I don't even bother to try to see if the door is unlocked. Athena prefers it locked for security reasons, and Garrett has gone along with that request. Even if he knows I'm coming over.

It seems like forever since I last saw him, and I miss him. I miss the mind-numbing sensation of his lips on mine, and I miss his achingly sweet kisses that flutter deep in my soul. Kisses that leave me feeling like I'm the most precious thing to him, other than his daughter.

The front door opens, and Garrett steps onto the stoop. "Hey." For a millisecond, he stares at me, like I'm some sort of white-clad angel sent from heaven.

Then his lips are on mine, and he kisses me as if I'm the oxygen he's thirsty for.

He's not the only one who's thirsty. I greedily gulp him down, my fingers knotting in his hair. All lingering fears about his true feelings for me are temporarily shoved aside.

I keep kissing him, embracing the dopamine rush, embracing Garrett until he eventually releases me. And even then, I don't want to let him go. But I have to for now.

He presses his lips to my brow. "Thanks. I needed that." His low voice comes out rough, scraping deliciously against my kiss-flushed skin.

"Me too," I whisper, searching for the confidence to tell him I am in love with him. The confidence I had after talking to the couple the other day, but which seems to have momentarily fled.

He opens the door before I can pull together a reasonable string of words to convey my feelings.

I make small talk with Athena in the kitchen while Garrett rounds up the stuff we need for hiking.

Things are a little easier now between Athena and me, but the ghost of her wall remains. Solid, uncrumbling.

Baby steps. Things will get better in time, as long as she isn't crushing on her boss and believes I'm somehow keeping him from her.

A few times, I've come close to asking if her feelings for him have ventured into the unprofessional arena. But the last thing I want is to piss her off with my questions and make things rocky between us again.

Peony comes rushing around the corner and practically hurls herself into my leg. "Zawa."

"Hey, Princess Peony." I crouch and hug her.

As I straighten to my feet with Peony in my arms, I catch the tail end of Athena's scowl. Guess nothing has changed between us—at least not when it comes to Peony. It's as if Athena is jealous of my relationship with Garrett's daughter, but why would she be? That doesn't make sense.

More than likely, I'm reading way too much into her expression.

I'M SWEATY AND MY MUSCLES ACHE MORE THAN NORMAL BY THE time Garrett, Peony, and I finish hiking my favorite trail on the Warriors property. Not once did I find the right moment to tell him just how much I care about him. But the confession is not the kind of thing you do when the other person has a toddler strapped on their back.

"Are you still coming over after you get Peony to bed?" I ask as he carefully removes his sleeping daughter from the carrier. The warm evening and the rocking motion of the carrier have lulled her to sleep.

"Do you want me to?"

"Yes, please." No matter what I think about or do while I pleasure myself, my body refuses to come apart at my touch the way it does for him. No one else's touch will suffice but Garrett's.

But I'm not about to admit that to Garrett. No need to have his orgasm-inducing powers going to his head. I'd never hear the end of it.

"Alright. I'll be there as soon as she's settled in bed." He straps the sleeping Peony into her car seat.

By the time Garrett shows up at my apartment, I've showered, practiced yoga, and answered a bunch of emails. Em's advice from two days ago buzzes in my brain. *"Tell him you love him."*

Garrett walks to where I'm standing in the brightly lit

kitchen. In a heartbeat, his mouth is on mine, and my thoughts are all scrambled in my brain.

His lips not straying from mine, he lifts me onto the counter. He widens the space between my legs and pushes up the hem of my skirt, revealing my underwear. His eyes darken.

Satisfaction at his response sings through my body. He wants me as much as I want him. No words need to be exchanged. We just know. The way we quickly learned how to read each other's body, to read the signs of what we need. It's all instinctual when it comes to us.

He runs his tongue along his bottom lip as his thumb trails along my pussy. I drag in a sharp breath, every part of me singing for joy, for him. Every part of me humming with an ache so different than what usually wrecks my body.

I suck my lip between my teeth, and his eyes go even darker with lust, igniting a power in me, a confidence I've never had with another man. I'm doing this. Making him react this way.

His thumb draws tight circles around my clit, teasing the throbbing bundle of nerves hidden under my panties. "Fuck, you're so wet, Zara." He pushes the panties aside, baring me for his naked perusal, and that only makes me wetter.

He separates my lips and takes a long lick of my pussy. "Christ, you taste so good."

My head flops back, lengthening my neck, and a moan vibrates low in my chest.

A thick finger presses inside me and curves into the magical spot that will have me coming apart too soon. He pumps his finger while his thumb continues to create its own magic on my clit, each stroke taking me higher and higher and higher.

Another finger joins the first. "Not much further," he says, his hoarse, deep voice finding new, tantalizing ways to push me closer to the edge. His hot breath brushes my mound.

His tongue flicks my aching clit again, and a tsunami-sized

wave of euphoria crashes through me, heat flooding my lower belly with mind-numbing relief.

"Ooooh God, Garrett." The words fall out on an endless groan.

He kisses my brow after a beat as the euphoria lulls to gentle waves lapping the shoreline. His gesture is so sweet, so tender, it melts me further into my newfound bliss.

He lowers his forehead to mine.

"I love you." The hushed, unvetted sentence falls past my lips and mist over his with a kiss.

I freeze, the words echoing in my head, my eyes saucer wide. I can barely breathe, almost hoping he didn't hear them. Almost hoping he did. This wasn't how I had planned to tell him.

Had I ever planned to really tell him?

But that doesn't matter now. It's too late to yank the words back. To hide them away.

I'm not the only one who's unmoving. It's as if Garrett has been turned into the stone statue that stands in the middle of his parents' pond. And I'm sure if I put my hand on his chest, I'd find his heart equally motionless.

But even knowing that, I cannot hold back the feelings I've held in check for so long. "I've been in love with you since college. I've never stopped loving you."

I halt the spill of words to gauge his reaction, but what I see on his face is enough to lacerate my heart with a thousand tiny cuts.

His eyes are squeezed closed as if I'm causing him pain, as if I'm the one destroying *his* heart. Behind him, the hum of the refrigerator reminds me I'm sitting on the kitchen counter, too stunned at myself, at his reaction, to jump down. To adjust my clothes. To hide my shame.

Garrett shakes his head, and a long breath hisses from him. It's only then he opens his eyes.

"I can't do this, Zara." His voice doesn't come out apologetic. Or warm. It's cold and unyielding. It's laced with anger...anger that, somehow, I've betrayed him.

A sledgehammer slams into my heart, pulverizing it into something unrecognizable, something barely beating. I inhale slowly, gathering the remaining pieces. Taping them together so he can't see my pain.

Garrett steps away, his face a mirror of the horror spilling inside me. But his doesn't hold the regret, the grief, the longing twisting through me. Regret I can't snatch back my words. Regret I can't tell him I didn't mean them. Can't beg him to forget what I said.

I can't lie to him like I've been doing for more than a decade when it comes to my love for him.

So I do the only thing I can to preserve what little dignity I have left. I hop down from the kitchen counter and adjust my clothes.

My movement snaps Garrett out of his stupor. The anger has smoothed off his face, replaced with some other emotion. Annoyance? Agony? Regret?

"I can't do whatever this thing is between us anymore. I need to focus on Peony and keeping her safe. And happy." He rubs his side below his ribs where one of his scars is located. "I failed two of my closest friends in the Marines, and they lost their lives. Their kids lost their fathers. Their wives were left widowed."

He steps back, the canyon between us growing wider, deeper. "I don't deserve love, but I still want to be friends with you. Like before."

Like before.

I want to touch his arm, to let him know he does deserve love. But another thought keeps me from reaching out. A toxic thought I can't shake.

I'm a burden.

I have a chronic illness with symptoms that strike when I least expect them. Symptoms triggered by stress. Symptoms that can make being a mother to Peony challenging.

The husband from the park the other day is strong enough to stand by his wife's side as they deal with her life-long chronic illness. But not every man is like that.

Not every man is like my mother, who stood by my father's side through the worst season of his life.

And maybe that's part of the reason Garrett can't love me. Maybe it's not just that he thinks he doesn't deserve love. Perhaps he doesn't possess the same strength as the husband and my mother.

That's the easy explanation, the one I want to cling to, to rationalize his reaction. But the truth is, Garrett has never loved me the way I want to be loved. The way I deserve to be loved.

Kenda has always been his one true love, and I can't compete with that.

I slowly nod and find the voice that has shattered alongside my heart. "I understand." I clear my throat of the tears clogging it and will them not to fall while he's still here.

Please go. Please go before you see how much you've eviscerated me. Before you see how steep the walls are that I have to climb to finally move on once and for all.

Garrett walks to the apartment door as if he hasn't just torn my heart from my chest and driven over it. "I'll see you Monday," he calls over his shoulder. "For our evening walk."

Except I have no intention of walking with him. Not for the next while. I need some distance while I put my heart back together.

I swipe at the falling tears and wait for the door to close.

It's only once the resounding click echoes through the hallway that I can gather my thoughts, use them to tape the pieces of my heart together, and pad it against future pain.

Maybe even pad it against taking another foolish chance like that again.

I walk to the coffee table and pick up my phone. I deliberate my options for a heartbeat, then send Emily a text.

> Me: Never tell a man you're in love with that you love him when you're not sure if he feels the same way.

> Me: It never ends well.

Em responds less than a minute later.

> Emily: Ben, Jerry, and I will be right over.

50

GARRETT

Eyeing the pink frosting smeared on Peony's cheek as she plays with her blocks, I pick up the mail Athena left on the dining table.

The amount of frosting on Peony's cheek is tiny, but it's enough to tell me she and Athena were at Picnic & Treats this afternoon.

I'm almost tempted to ask Athena if she saw Zara, who's canceled our hikes every day this week, but the handwriting on the top envelope immediately steers my thoughts away from that. Suspecting the letter isn't an apology from Cooper's brother for the last one he sent me, I head for the dimly lit cave of my office.

I toss the rest of the mail onto my desk and deliberate whether to bother with the letter or just toss it into the recycling unopened. Do I have the energy to deal with his theatrics or is this letter part of my punishment?

Fuck. I put on my glasses and rip open the envelope by the window where the afternoon sunlight still hits.

Garrett,

Do you regret how many lives you've hurt? How many others you've destroyed?

My brother was always there for me. He was there when I needed a guiding hand. You stole that. You took away the one person who I could trust for advice.

You don't care what your actions did that day. You don't care about anyone but yourself. You stole everything that was important to me. You destroyed his wife and his family.

That's the thing—I do care.

I glance at the calendar, though I don't need to see how many days remain until my deadline. I have the daily countdown in my head.

I could wait the fourteen days and then fly out once the manuscript is secure in Thomas's inbox.

I could...but I won't be able to focus on it until I talk to Austin. Until I see for myself how Cassie and her kids are doing.

Plus, I could use that time while I'm in Tucson to lock myself away in a hotel room for a few days and write without interruptions. Because if not for the frequent interruptions that come in the pint-sized form of my daughter, I'd already be finished with the manuscript.

And then I'll talk to Zara. We need to have a conversation that's long overdue.

I spend the next several minutes arranging my flight and hotel room, as well as checking that my brothers can handle this weekend's Warriors excursion without me.

A week away should give me plenty of time to finish the book, other than the final read through. And I'll FaceTime with Peony while I'm gone so she doesn't think I've abandoned her.

I drop the letter next to the government grant application

form for Wilderness Warriors. I need to give it to Kellan to sign before I leave for Tucson. It's due next week.

THE FOLLOWING AFTERNOON, I SIT IN THE RENTAL CAR OUTSIDE what was once Cooper's house, while I wait for Cassie to come home. The small two-story building is on a residential street with other older cookie-cutter homes.

Like me, Cassie has always been into gardening, and that doesn't seem to have changed since Cooper's death. Colorful flowers fill the yard and wooden planters on the porch. It's not exactly the long-forgotten garden I half expected based on Austin's letters.

I open the photo app and scroll to my favorite picture of Peony.

I captured the moment while Zara and Peony were building a sandcastle on the beach by the lake. Zara was wearing shorts and a crop top, her skin glowing in the late afternoon sun, her coils loose about her head.

Peony was wearing an orange-and-pink swimsuit and a huge-ass grin directed at my best friend.

The woman I love but don't deserve.

"I don't deserve love, but I still want to be friends with you. Like before."

Like before? How the fuck do I expect things to return to what they were before I knew how she tasted? Before I knew how right she felt tight around my cock? Before I knew how incredible she felt in my arms, her subtle jasmine scent teasing me?

Shit, I miss my daughter. And I miss Zara.

I lean my head on the headrest and close my eyes. I hadn't meant to keep my distance from Zara since her bombshell. I've just been so busy with the damn book, with trying to be a good father, with the increase in my social media presence as I gear up for the release of *Unfallen* next month.

Each time I thought I could slip away to see Zara, something popped up and killed that plan.

Okay, maybe I was also stalling. Yes, we had great intentions when we started kissing and having sex—for stress release and pain reduction. But I never expected to fall in love with Zara. Both in college and then again years later.

Or maybe I never stopped loving her for all those years in between. I just buried it deep down, kept myself in denial, afraid to ruin the good thing with Zara.

I open my eyes and send Kellan a text—so I can distract myself from thoughts of Zara for a moment.

Me: Did you find the form?

I'd been in a rush to get to the airport and forgot to drop the grant application off at his house. He had texted while I was on my flight, asking where I'd put the form.

I look up and my thoughts about the form come to a sudden standstill. Cassie is walking on the sidewalk, her long blond hair cascading over her shoulders in loose waves. She hasn't changed much in the years since I last saw her—back when her husband was alive.

While she might not have changed, the two kids with her have. The youngest is now eight and is a mini version of her mother. The boy is ten and looks so much like his father, it feels like a ballpoint pen is stabbing my heart.

Cooper's daughter skips along, appearing carefree. His son and Cassie are laughing at something one of them said. They're not what I was expecting after reading Austin's letter.

That's not to say they aren't hurting from Cooper's death, but they seem to have done a better job moving forward than Austin let on. Better than he is doing.

I climb out of the rental car and approach the trio. Cassie doesn't pay much attention to me at first. She's listening to what her son is saying. Then her eyes meet mine, and surprise and recognition widen them. "Garrett?"

A hesitant smile forms on my face. "Hey, Cassie."

Her smile is *not* hesitant. It grows wide and welcoming, and she hugs me like we did all those years ago. She's the same woman I frequently chatted with when her husband and I were deployed and Skyping with our families. I would jokingly interrupt his conversations with his wife, and he would do the same when I was talking to Zara.

She takes a step back and playfully looks me over. "I see being a bestselling author hasn't changed you at all."

"I'm sure my drill sergeant would disagree. He'd probably claim I've gone soft."

She snorts a laugh and invites me into the house. I remove my shoes and follow her down the hallway to the kitchen. Framed photos cover the walls. Photos of the kids as they have gotten older. Photos of Cassie and Cooper together. Photos of a happy family, with an expectant mother, and a father, and their toddler son. Some of the photos I've seen before. Many are new.

Cassie suggests the kids go play a game, and they run off into the living room.

The kitchen looks pretty much like I remember, although the walls are now pale yellow. The pine furniture is the same, maybe a little more scratched with use.

"So, what's new with you lately, Garrett? Any other women in your life? Or have you finally realized Zara is your soulmate?" She walks to the fridge, pulls out a beer, and hands it to me.

I take it from her. "Thanks."

We sit at the table, and I tell her about Peony, show her the photo of Kenda's and my daughter. The combined noise of a computer game and the kids' laughter from the other room creates a background soundtrack to Cassie's and my conversation.

"Oh, she's adorable! Who's looking after her while you're here? Zara?"

The doorbell rings as I'm about to answer. Cassie pushes to her feet. "I'll be right back."

While she's gone, the competitive, teasing banter between her two kids keeps me company, and I drink some beer.

A man's voice reaches the kitchen, the words indistinguishable. Cassie laughs, the sound of it growing closer.

The moment he steps into the room, I recognize who he is.

The asshole who's been mailing the letters.

His gaze lands on me as I stand from the chair, and a ferocious storm blows into his expression. Without warning, he charges across the room and swings a fist at my face.

51

ZARA

Peony yawns for the second time in the past several minutes and picks up a wooden block from Simone's living room floor.

She walks to the lopsided tower Zoe and Kylie have been working on and puts her block on top. The tower sways a fraction of an inch, readjusting to its new center of gravity. But physics isn't on her side, and the tower crumples.

Kylie and I reach for it on instinct, but we're too late. The entire structure collapses, clattering loudly on the wood floor.

Jasper jumps to his feet from his dog bed, his nap now over, and barks. At the same time Peony lets out a disgruntled shriek, her gaze on the ruined tower.

The shriek quickly settles into full body sobs. Every inch of her trembles, the rattling aftershocks of an earthquake.

Jasper barks again, eager to play with the girls.

Simone strokes him, and the attention calms the golden Labradoodle.

Kneeling next to Peony, I gather her in my arms and gently rub her back, wanting so much to absorb her frustration, to turn it into a harmless puff of smoke. "Hey, it's okay, Princess Peony. It's not a big deal. But I do think it's someone's naptime."

She looks forlornly at me, her bottom lip pushed out. Tears drench her face, and her mouth opens, the subtle warning that another round of high-pitched, ear-shattering wails are about to commence.

"It really is okay, sweetheart." I pick Poppy up from the floor and hand her to Peony.

Still sobbing, she buries her face in the panda's fur.

"Let's get you home now." I kiss the crown of Peony's head and stagger to my feet with the aid of the coffee table for support. I rock her from side to side. "Say bye-bye to Auntie Simone, Kylie, and Zoe."

Peony's tearful face peers up from Poppy's side, and she waves at them, her bottom lip still pushed out in a pout. "Bye-bye"

By the time we arrive at Garrett's house, her eyes are shut, the rise and fall of her chest slow and even. She looks so adorably peaceful like this, I hate having to move her and risk waking her.

I park my car in the shadow of the trees on one side of the driveway, leaving space for Joanne's car once she gets here, and kill the engine. Peony doesn't stir.

I climb out and open her door. "We're home, sweetie," I say softly, so as not to startle her. "I'll just put you down for a nap in your bed, and by the time you wake up, Granny will be here."

Peony doesn't so much as blink open an eye at my voice.

I was at Picnic & Treats earlier when Joanne phoned and asked for my help. Athena has the afternoon off, and Joanne was looking after Peony, because Garrett has gone out of town for a week, which was news to me.

But then a medical-appointment spot opened up. She phoned to see if I could look after Peony for an hour or two.

And I was more than happy to help out. I haven't seen

Peony since last Thursday. Instead, I've come up with excuse after excuse as to why I can't go for my usual walk with Garrett.

I'm not ready to see him just yet.

A litany of questions still burns on my tongue. Questions about how Garrett is doing. If he's almost finished with his novel. I also wonder what he was talking about when he claimed the death of his two friends was his fault.

I never mentioned the last part to Emily when she came over with Ben & Jerry's. And I didn't mention it to Troy and Kellan on Friday night, during our weekly Game Night. A Game Night that only consisted of Troy, Jess, Kellan, Emily, and me, because Garrett, Lucas, and Simone were home with their kids.

I unbuckle Peony's car seat harness and remove her and Poppy from the car. She stirs in my arms, her head on my shoulder, but otherwise remains comatose.

I carry her to the house, leaving my purse and her bag in the car. I unlock the front door, step inside the house, and key in the password to the security system, disengaging it.

A hollow silence stretches endlessly around me like a tomb. So different to what it usually feels like in Garrett's home—especially now that Peony lives here.

I can't tell if Athena is somewhere in the house, out of earshot. Or she might be in the backyard, enjoying the warm summer day.

I put my keys on the hall table, next to the vase filled with flowers from the garden, toe off my sandals, and walk deeper into the house. A few months ago, this place resembled a man cave. A nicely decorated one, but a man cave no less. Now, flower-filled vases decorate the hallway, living room, and kitchen. In the living room, floral cushions crowd the couch. Cushions that weren't here several months ago.

The light sage throw that complements the cushions is another addition that had nothing to do with me. It's like

Athena is weaving herself into the family, becoming an important thread integrated into the delicate pattern. But at the same time, I can't tell if she longs for Garrett the way I do, if she sees herself as one day being his girlfriend or his wife.

Before I stupidly, idiotically confessed I was in love with him, Garrett told me she hadn't made any moves that suggest she sees herself fitting into his life that way. Maybe helping to decorate your employer's home is part of the nanny job description.

I walk down the hallway to Peony's bedroom. Her curtains are open, allowing the late afternoon sunlight to stream across the hardwood floor. I peek through the window into the backyard, but it doesn't look as though Athena is out there.

I have no idea what Athena does during her spare time. I don't think Garrett knows either. She's private about what she does when she's not working...like she's private about a lot of things.

Peony blinks herself awake and slowly straightens in my arms.

I smile softly at her. "I take it you've finished your nap?"

She looks at the floor. "Daisy."

"You want your elephant?" I'm grasping for bent straws here. Her panda is named after a flower, so it makes sense her elephant would be named after one too.

She nods, eyes puppy-dog wide.

Her floppy stuffed elephant isn't on the floor or the bed or the bookshelf. Nor is it on the rocking armchair.

I lower Peony to the floor and walk over to the toddler bed. I get down on my stomach, peer under the bed, and pull out a board book, a red ball, and a yellow plastic donut-sized ring.

But no Daisy.

I search through Peony's toy box, but it's not here either. "Let's look in the living room. She's probably there."

We head back to the living room. When a cursory glance

around the room doesn't result in Daisy, we look under the coffee table and behind the couch and on the bookshelves. But still no sign of the elephant.

"Any idea where you last saw her?" I ask Peony.

She takes one last quick scan of the room and takes off running down the hallway. I follow her.

She stops outside of Athena's bedroom door, which has been left slightly ajar. Not giving any thought to Athena's privacy, Peony pushes the door open and enters the room.

I stand motionless in the doorway, watching her wander around the room like she's on a mission. "I don't think we should go in there, Princess Peony. That's Athena's room. It's private."

"Nina." Peony points at the bed and drops to her knees next to it.

Like the rest of the house, Athena's bedroom is immaculately tidy. The only messy thing about her room is her bed. Her bedding is askew, haphazardly dangling over the side, forming a small puddle of sheets on the floor.

"You think Daisy's under there?" I gesture to the queen-sized bed.

Peony attempts to push the bedding aside, like branches of a weeping willow hiding a cave entrance.

I kneel next to her and lift the curtain of bedding. "Do you see it?"

Peony lies on her stomach and peers under the bed. Giggling, she stretches toward what I'm guessing is Daisy.

But it seems to be too far out of her reach, unless she's planning to crawl under the bed to retrieve it.

"I'll get it," I tell her and flatten onto my stomach.

Blindly groping, I move my hand along the floor, searching for the stuffed elephant. The familiar ache in my shoulders and back protests the awkward movement.

As I breathe through the pain, wishing orgasms were in my near future, my fingers brush against a book.

Peony's bright eyes shine at me, and she giggles. "Daisy!"

Oh, Daisy isn't a toy. It's a character in one of Peony's picture books.

I slide the book from under the bed. But it's not a board book like I was expecting. It's a sketch pad with a flat metal box sitting on top. A metal box containing colored pencils. The quality kind artists use.

Peony shifts to a sitting position and pats the book, as if that will magically open it.

Athena must be okay with Peony seeing whatever's inside it. Otherwise, Peony wouldn't know about the book. I ignore the voice telling me it still doesn't give me the right to be in Athena's room, and I open the book to the first page.

A breathtaking drawing of a young woman's face stares at me. Her straight black hair frames delicate features, and long dark eyelashes accentuate sad eyes. But the most heartbreaking part is that the girl has no mouth. She has a nose and those expressive blue eyes, but it's as if Athena never got around to drawing the mouth.

Or she had another reason for leaving it out.

I flip through the next couple of pages. They contain more sketches of girls who could be in their late teens or early twenties. There's something disturbing yet beautiful about each one.

I trace my finger over the green-eyed girl, as if that's all it will take to erase her pain. These pictures and Athena's talent don't come as a complete surprise. I remember the image she drew several months ago, when she came to Picnic & Treats and drew the sketch of a girl using only a crayon.

I turn the page. This time I'm not met by the exquisite eyes of a young woman. It's a sad bunny that stares at me. It's cute, like the kind of picture you would find in a children's book.

Peony points at the bunny. "Daisy."

Ahh. So this is the mysterious Daisy.

I keep flipping the pages, pausing on each one to appreciate what I'm looking at, only to eventually realize the pictures of the various woodland critters, in their natural habitat, represent some kind of story.

Peony points to the wolf, and her adorable face pinches into a scowl, like she just ate something bitter. "Bad."

"Is he the villain?"

She doesn't reply, but instead helps me turn to the next page, where more of the story plays out.

I flip past a few more pages to one with a bear on it.

Peony points at the drawing and scowls again. "Bad."

Ah, the story has two villains. "Has your daddy seen this? It's really good. You think maybe Athena should consider a career in illustrating children's books?" Possibly also writing them.

The last page of the sketchbook doesn't contain a drawing of the bunny or any of the woodland critters. A sketch of Kenda smiles at me. A sketch accompanied by the familiar photo that at one point also included Garrett and me. Our existence has since been cut away. Disposed of.

How very metaphorical.

I flip the photo. My handwriting is on the back.

True friendship stays strong, no matter the distance.

What the hell? I wrote those words on only one copy of the photo. The copy that was in my apartment. The copy that recently went missing.

Why would Athena steal the photo and cut it up? It's not even Garrett's picture she kept...not unless that part is under her pillow.

A muffled sound, so quiet I almost don't hear it, comes from somewhere in the direction of the front door.

Shit. Athena.

The last thing I want is to be caught in her room, going through her things, even if I apparently had the right to, given she stole the photo from my apartment.

I return the photo to where I found it, close the sketchbook, and quickly shove the book and the box of pencils under the bed.

I make sure the bedding looks close to how we found it and usher Peony toward the door, hoping to get out of Athena's room before she finds us here.

A thick wall of a man steps into the doorway, blocking our exit. A surprised shriek catapults from my lungs, the sound barely louder than my now racing heart. I stumble back a step.

I'm not the only one who screams. But Peony's scream isn't one of surprise.

It's a scream of terror. The kind of terror that turns you cold from the inside out.

52

ZARA

"Who-who are you?" I ask the hulking man standing in the doorway to Athena's bedroom. Gray peppers his short dark hair, and a scar cuts across the outside corner of his eyebrow. He's wearing jeans and a plain blue hoodie and is holding something in his hand, but I can't make out what it is.

Joanne didn't mention anyone coming over to do work on Garrett's house. She must have expected to return from her appointment before the man arrived.

Peony's arms wind tightly around my leg from behind me. Her screams morph into uncontrollable wails. She presses her face into the back of my leg, muffling her cries, but her arms remain in place.

With a little patience and gentle coaxing, I untangle myself from her hold and lower to a crouch. "Hey, Princess Peony. It's okay." But as I say the words, the sharp claws of an unsettling feeling dig into my stomach. The man didn't bother ringing the doorbell. He just entered the house like he belongs here.

Maybe Garrett is fine with that, but something about the situation doesn't sit right.

I kiss Peony's cheek, trying to comfort her, her small body trembling in my arms. She's still leery with men she doesn't know. And given the size of this man and his muscles, it doesn't matter how sweet he might be, he's intimidating as hell.

"Where's Nina?" The man's low, harsh tone comes close to that of a wolf baring its fangs, dispelling any belief there might be a sweet bone in him.

I push to my feet with Peony in my arms, the growing ache in my joints reminding me I'm due for ibuprofen soon. "You have the wrong house. You better leave or I'll call the cops." I infuse my voice with indignation and an unspoken promise that I will carry through with my threat.

He doesn't need to know, though, I left my phone in my purse.

Which is in my car.

The whisper of a voice pokes at me. *Is it possible Peony hasn't been mispronouncing Athena's name? It really is Nina?*

But that can't be right. I saw the letter Kenda wrote for Garrett. She referred to Athena by that name. And not once has Athena let on her name is something else.

"I'm not going anywhere until you tell me where Nina is." The man's voice doesn't soften. If anything, it grows scarier. Somehow, deadlier.

"I have no idea where she is. I only know she's not here." Now get out of Garrett's house.

The man reaches behind the waistband of his jeans and pulls out a gun, which he points at Peony and me, sending my heartbeat skittering to a standstill, blood pooling to my feet. "Not a good enough answer."

"I-I really don't know where she is."

He steps back from the doorway and gestures with a wave of the gun to the hallway. "Move!"

I do as I'm told, my mind spinning a thousand miles an hour. Garrett taught me self-defense, but none of the lessons will be of any use in this particular scenario, with Peony in my arms. Plus, the risk of her getting hurt is too high.

"We're going for a ride." The man points toward the front door.

Fuck. Now what? We won't stand a chance once we get into his vehicle.

His dark expression warns me to get moving. I slowly walk to the door, my mind still spinning. His heavy footsteps follow me. I don't have to look over my shoulder to know the gun is aimed at my back.

Peony hiccups a sob, her body still trembling. Her crying isn't as loud now, but her fear pumps through my veins with the rapid beat of my heart.

"Let me put her in her room first." As long as Peony is safe, I can breathe a little easier. Joanne should be here soon, so Peony won't be left alone for long.

"No. She's coming with us." He attempts to smile at Peony, but the curve of his mouth only makes him look that much more menacing. The increased trembling of her body confirms it.

I turn from him, using my body as a shield between him and Peony, who's perched on my hip. "Why? She's just a toddler. She hasn't done anything wrong." And neither have I. Whatever his issue is with Athena, it's exactly that—between him and her.

It has nothing to do with Peony and me.

"She's coming with us," he repeats, his tone not leaving room for negotiation. But that doesn't mean I won't try. For Peony's sake.

"Where are we going?" I'm stalling for time while I think of a way to get him to leave without us.

His irritated frown makes it clear he has no intention of answering my question, and he gestures again with the gun for me to get moving.

If Peony was older, I could put her down and fight the man while she hid. But she's too young to understand what I'm saying if I tell her to run and hide.

And she won't be able to get away from him fast enough should he quickly overpower me.

He opens the front door and waits for me to step outside.

I make a move to put on my sandals.

"No shoes." He shoves me hard in the back, sending me stumbling toward the doorjamb. I regain my balance in time to keep from slamming into the wood.

The sinking sensation in my stomach grows heavier. But even then, I pray for a miracle. Any miracle. No matter how small. Anything to help us get away.

I step onto the stoop. Any hope of escape dies a rapid death. He didn't come here alone. A tall, white muscle-bound man in a black T-shirt and black jeans is leaning against the passenger door of the black SUV now parked on the driveway. It's behind my car, preventing my escape should I be able to outsmart the men.

His tattooed, tanned arms are folded over his thick chest, but the gun casually held in his hand doesn't skip my notice.

Fuck. Fuck. Fuckfuckfuckfuck.

What the hell did Athena do to bring these two men searching for her?

The dense garden of trees and shrubbery provides privacy between Garrett's property, his neighbors, and the street. Usually, I appreciate that privacy, that sense of seclusion.

Now, it's a prison wall, preventing everyone from seeing the danger Peony and I are in.

And now, that same thick garden, beyond the driveway and flower beds, mocks me with the possibility of escape.

A very slim possibility.

Odds are great Peony and I won't make it to the cover of dense leaves in time. We'll be shot first.

The late afternoon sunlight shines through the leaves, painting dappled patterns on the driveway. Even the shadows don't have a solution for getting out of this predicament alive.

"She's not here," the man behind me tells his...his friend. "But I got the child." His voice sounds different this time, like he's talking through a mask.

I glance back at him, and a new wave of fear engulfs me. A tsunami-sized wave. The thing he was holding earlier that I couldn't identify? It was a mask, like the rubber kind worn at Halloween.

A wolf mask.

Peony referred to the picture she saw in Athena's sketch pad as *bad.*

This man...the wolf in the sketch pad...is it a coincidence or was Athena drawing this man in wolf form? The wolf that represents my new nightmare.

The man-wolf shoves me toward the SUV, and I stumble once more, the rough surface of the driveway digging into my bare soles.

"It's illegal for babies and young children to ride in a car and not be in a child seat," I remind them. Neither man looks the sort to care about child safety, but maybe they'll surprise me.

"Hey, Zara."

At Emily's cheery voice, a jolt of hope shoots through me, and my muscles turn rubbery. The relief is short-lived, fear and panic overriding it. And a wave of dizziness hits me, steals my ability to speak, to scream, to cry out in warning.

I turn my head to where she's walking up the driveway.

"Kellan sent me to pick up some..." Her gaze shifts from the two men who caught her attention and back to me. Her face is pale, eyes owlish. "What-what's..." Her hand moves slightly, inching to her dress pocket.

Movement in my periphery is the only warning I—

BANG.

My heart stops beating for a fraction of a second, the world around me suddenly quiet, other than the ringing in my ears. A sharp, acrid smell taunts me.

Then the flapping of wings and panicked squawks fill the air as birds in the trees take flight. The sudden movement and noise send my heart rate into overdrive.

Ice-cold horror immobilizes me, and I watch Emily collapse onto the driveway. Fear and confusion and anguish root me to the spot.

"Em!" Her name scrambles out on a broken scream. I can't tell if she sees or hears me. Her hair covers her face.

Blood seeps from her torso and spreads across the ground. And that's all it takes to shake me from my shock. To tell me this isn't a bad dream I'll wake up from and everything will be fine. I need to save her. Now.

My focus narrows on Emily, and everything else, other than the screaming toddler I'm clinging tightly to, fades into the background.

In my mind, I'm racing over to Emily.

In my mind, I'm frantically stopping the flow of blood.

In my mind, I'm checking her pulse and performing emergency first aid.

But in reality, Peony is snatched from my arms. In reality, I'm being handcuffed, kicking and screaming, and shoved into the back of the SUV.

In reality, heavy metal music is turned on, the pounding beat cranked up, and I'm told if I step out of line, Peony will pay the price.

Please be okay, Em. Please be okay. Please be okay.

I'm vaguely aware of moving my lips to my new mantra as I rock on the seat, my heart racing, my body a block of ice. Tears soak my cheeks and drip onto my lap. The wetness is not enough to smother the scream-ignited fire in my throat.

She's gotta be okay. A neighbor must have heard the gunshot. They have to be calling the police.

Please hold on, Em. Please hold on. Please hold on. Help is on the way.

The SUV screeches out of the driveway and speeds down Garrett's street.

Leaving Emily all alone.

I don't try to soothe Peony, who's screaming next to me in the child seat. I frantically look out the passenger window for someone who can help us, but the street is empty. No one is out taking a stroll or walking their dog or biking along the road.

And even if there was anyone, the way the handcuffs are threaded through the seat belt and my position in the middle of the back seat prevent me from banging on the window. The music drowns out the desperately distressed noises Peony and I are making. The loud pounding of the song matches each rapid beat of my heart.

We're in plain view, but no one knows we need help.

No one knows we're in trouble.

We're alone—and I suddenly understand Peony's fear of men a whole lot more.

53

GARRETT

Cooper's brother takes a swing at my face, his complexion redder than a stoplight. Unlike Cooper, Austin never served in the military. He doesn't know the first thing about fighting. That much is clear.

I step back, grabbing his wrist, and push his hand to the side.

My phone rings. I let it go to voicemail.

"What the hell is wrong with you?" My tone is the lash of a deadly whip. "Isn't it bad enough you've been harassing me? You don't come into Cassie's house and throw punches at her guests."

"You're no guest." His face contorts—nostrils flaring, eyes narrowing. "You're the man responsible for her husband's death. My brother's death."

"Austin!" Cassie's voice tug-of-wars between horror and dismay. "How can you say that?"

"He was the one who issued the order that resulted in the explosion." He jabs an angry, misguided finger in my direction. I have no idea what orders he's talking about. Likely ones he

412

pulled out of his ass. The mission was classified. Everything about it was classified.

"The explosion the Taliban was responsible for," she volleys back, her tone firm, unwavering, like a general warning a soldier not to be hotheaded. "The Taliban killed my husband and your brother, Austin. Not Garrett. Garrett loved Eli like you and I did."

My phone rings a second time. I let that too go to voicemail.

Austin scoffs, but even then, the anger in his eyes softens. His *eyes* soften. For her.

Oh, shit.

He's in love with her. When the hell did that happen? Is that why he's been sending me those letters?

"He messed everything up." He gestures at me with his finger again, but his attention is solely on Cassie. "Things would've been so different if my brother hadn't died. We would've had a chance."

Cassie closes her eyes, the pain from his words etched on her face, her shoulders rolling forward under the new weight of this truth.

Shaking her head, she reopens her eyes. "Austin, not again. Not now. Don't you see? We wouldn't have had a chance. We made a mistake. A night of weakness. One night. That's all."

My phone rings for a third time as I fight to process everything they're saying. Cassie cheated on Cooper. *Double shit.*

"How can you say that?" Austin bites out, apparently forgetting I'm here. Or maybe he doesn't care I'm hearing this monumental confession. About how he betrayed his brother, my friend.

Christ. To think I flew here when I have a book due in thirteen days, all because Austin is in love with Cassie. That must be why he's been writing to me—he somehow blames me for his lack of romantic relationship with his brother's wife.

At least the trip isn't a total loss. I can do some marathon writing in my hotel room over the next few days.

Maybe send the book to my editor a day or two early, and then I can finally talk to Zara, fix what I broke between us, and be the father my daughter needs.

I check my phone to see who's calling. Noah.

"I love you, Cassie." Austin's lovesick tone is back. "I've always loved you. Even before the two of you fell in love and decided to marry."

The call goes to voicemail.

I check who called the other two times. Also Noah. From his work number.

Maybe he's calling about Annie Wilkes 3.0. Whatever his reason for calling, it must be important given how many times he's rung in the last few minutes.

I take a step toward the doorway. "I should go." My words are for no one in the kitchen in particular.

"No, don't go." Cassie's voice is somewhere between resolute and exasperated. "What did you mean when you said Austin's been harassing you?"

My phone rings for the fourth time. Again, it's Noah.

"I've gotta get this," I tell her, inching toward the door. "It shouldn't take long though. And then we can talk." I accept the call and lift the phone to my ear. "Hey, Noah. What's up?"

A long beat of silence answers my question. For a second, I wonder if I accidentally sent him to voicemail.

"Garrett." His voice sounds oddly broken, and it's enough to freeze me to the spot. "Are you driving?"

My gut tightens at his question, and unease warns me this call isn't just to tell me the police know who's been sending the newest round of "love" letters. A cloud outside moves over the sun, casting the kitchen in shadow. "No. I'm not. What's going on? Is Peony okay?" The words spill out in an unstoppable rush.

"I'm sorry to call to tell you..." His breath comes through the line shaky, and ice-cold dread pumps through my body, paralyzing me.

"What's going on?" I'm vaguely aware of the room turning pin-drop silent as all eyes turn to me, the concern and anguish in my tone making it clear this isn't a social call. "Is something wrong with Peony? My family? Zara?" The volume of my heartbeat intensifies, echoes off the walls, at just saying the names.

"We don't know where Peony and Zara are. One of your neighbors reported hearing a gunshot." Noah's tone has shifted to work mode, like he's relaying the facts in court. "When I arrived on the scene...Emily had been shot."

My stomach free-falls to the kitchen floor, taking my heart with it. "Shot? Is she all right?" She has to be all right. This is Em we're talking about. If anyone can bounce back from being shot, it would be her.

A long, heavy sigh comes through the phone line. I know what he's going to say before he utters the words, but I still hope I'm wrong. *Christ, please be wrong.*

Why was Em even at my house?

"I'm sorry, Garrett. Emily didn't make it. She died at the scene."

At those final words, it's as if the weight of the universe crashes onto my shoulders, knocking the air from my lungs. My legs buckle, and I have to grab hold of the chipped kitchen counter just to keep upright.

Fuck. Fuck. Fuck. FUCK.

"My mother." I can barely get the words out, the sound of my voice splintered and strained. "Peony is with my mother." She's not with Zara. My daughter's okay. Mom probably took her to visit Dad, or they went to the lake or one of the other places they like to explore.

And maybe Zara is with them. I clutch tightly to that thin thread of hope with slippery hands.

"Your mother had a medical appointment. Zara was looking after Peony. The two of them were last seen at Lucas and Simone's house. Simone said that Zara took Peony home for a nap. No one saw them at your house, but a witness heard a woman and child screaming after the gunshot. And then Zara's car, as well as a black SUV, were seen racing from the scene. We're currently searching for both vehicles. Do you have any idea who the owner of the SUV could be?"

"Fuck. Black SUVs aren't exactly uncommon. Kellan and I both have one." Mine's at the airport parking lot in Eugene, so my Explorer isn't the vehicle witnesses saw.

Flames of fear lick inside me, stoking an anger deep in my gut. I scrub my hand over my face, hardly able to draw air into my lungs. I won't be able to pull in full lungfuls again until Peony and Zara are safe in my arms.

Noah asks me more questions, but none of my answers bring us any closer to figuring out who killed one of my closest friends, and where Zara and my daughter went. "I'll be on the next available flight," I tell him as I walk to the front door. "I'll text you once I have the flight info." I end the call.

"Wait, Garrett." Cassie's voice lassos me to the spot. I might not have told her what's going on, but she would have heard enough from my end of the conversation to get a pretty good idea. "You're in no state to drive to the airport. Let me drive you. Austin can bring me home after I drop you and the rental car off."

My eyes dart to the man who's been sending me harassing letters. I'm too exhausted to deal with his drama, to fight out whatever issue he has with me. It's nothing more than a pebble in the hell that is my life right now.

Wincing, he raises his hands. "Cassie and I obviously need to talk things through, but I won't cause you any more problems. I'm sorry." He doesn't elaborate on why he's sorry, but I doubt it's an apology for the letters.

It's just as well. I'm too emotionally and physically drained from Noah's news to deal with Austin; otherwise, I might just knock the crap out of him. If not for the letters, I wouldn't have flown here to deal with the issue. I would have been at home. Emily would be alive.

And my daughter and the woman I love wouldn't be missing.

But as much as I would like to blame him for everything that happened, the way I've been blaming myself for what happened to Cooper and Clarke, it's like Cassie said. The Taliban killed her husband. I didn't. The shooter killed Emily. Austin had nothing to do with that.

I wasn't the one who set up the explosive.

He wasn't the one who pulled the trigger.

MY PHONE RINGS. I'M SITTING AT MY GATE IN THE AIRPORT, MY computer open on my lap, waiting for the boarding announcement.

It's not Noah this time. Nor is it my mother or Lucas or Troy calling again.

It's one of my FBI contacts I use when researching my books.

I accept the call, relieved to have a brief moment where I can focus on something other than the new hell I'm in. A hell that closely parallels the book I'm supposed to be working on. "Roger."

I don't have it in me to make my voice pleasant. It comes out gruff. Strangled. Destroyed.

I rub my hand over the crack in the vinyl seat, wishing that was all it would take to reverse time, to prevent me from getting on the plane to Tucson.

"Garrett. First, I'm sorry about everything that's happening. This probably isn't a good time to call, since I'm not sure if you give a damn right now about the question you asked me the other day..." He lets the rest of whatever he was going to say trail off.

According to Lucas, the news media has already released information on the alleged kidnapping of my daughter. They've also mentioned Zara's disappearance, because it's linked to Peony's case. Emily's name hasn't been released yet, but details of her death have been.

If people in the airport have heard the news and recognize me, I wouldn't know. Until Roger's call, I'd been staring at my blank laptop screen, blocking out the world around me. I don't even have the strength to watch the news reports, to see what kind of narrative the stations are spinning.

I'm on a thin edge, barely keeping my crap together.

Barely keeping my fears and my grief off my face.

"No, it's fine," I tell Roger, my voice still rough. "Did you get an answer?"

He gives me the information I need for the book. An answer that has nothing to do with the storyline involving the kidnapping of a child, because right now, that's one of the last things I can handle. It's also an answer that won't require me rethinking part of the story, sending it in another trajectory. A trajectory I don't have time for...or the energy to think about.

A young woman with strawberry-blond hair like Athena's walks past. She doesn't look like Athena, but that doesn't keep my next thought from shaping itself into words. "I have a question that has nothing to do with the book. At least not this one. And it has nothing to do with my daughter's disappearance."

"Sure. Fire away."

I tell him about how Athena hasn't received her replacement ID yet. "She requested it over three months ago."

"It might have gotten lost in the mail."

"I've thought of that too. But both the ID and her Social Security Number? I was wondering if there might be another reason for the delays. Like the government offices are backlogged, and the ID and number are coming soon. I'd rather wire her the salary than keep paying her in cash."

The reality of what I'm saying hits with the force of a torpedo. I have a nanny, but the child she's supposed to care for is missing. A nanny who will also be frantic about Peony's disappearance.

My stomach cramps just thinking about how my little girl is gone and the police don't know where she is. She must be terrified, and I'm not with her to protect her, to comfort her, to make her feel safe. I want to tear down the fucking world and find her.

"Understandable....If she doesn't have a bank account, where's she keeping the money?" Roger asks.

"I haven't asked, 'cause it's none of my business where she's hiding the money. For all I know, it's in her sock drawer."

"Any chance she's spending it as soon as she gets it?" The question is straightforward, but I can tell his thought process is spinning through numerous possibilities. Possibilities I would be considering if this were a book I were plotting.

"If she is, she's not buying anything I've seen. She's bought clothes for herself and toys for Peony, but nothing that costs anything close to what I'm paying her." I've mentioned a few times to Athena that she could be earning interest on the money, but she just brushes my suggestion off, claiming the interest she's missing out on isn't much while she waits for the government to replace her ID.

"Is it possible she has a gambling addiction? She could be using the money to buy a credit gift card and using that to gamble online."

I close my laptop and wearily unfold to my feet. "Anything's possible." I begin pacing in the small corner area I've secluded myself in, away from most people. "But she doesn't demonstrate the usual signs of a gambling addict."

Signs I know about from research I'd done on the topic for one of my earlier novels.

"What's her full name, date of birth, and a general description? I'll see if I can find out what's holding up the replacement ID."

"Athena Williams." I give him the rest of the information he needs, other than her date of birth. I can only give him a rough estimate on her age. It's not like the topic of her age and date of birth have come up in conversation.

Roger promises to call me back as soon as he can.

I turn to the window and watch planes cross the tarmac. Why was the shooter at my house? What were they after? Why shoot Emily?

I stop my thoughts from spiraling down the route of *Untold Mercy*. That kidnapping was politically motivated. It has nothing to do with Zara and Peony.

My mind keeps steering to the same place. Annie Wilkes 3.0.

Just how far would a crazed fan go? The thought is enough to make me want to quit writing, if it means keeping the people I love safe.

Roger calls several minutes later. "Are you sure that's her name?"

His question short wires my heart, and it stutters a beat. "That's the name she told me. Athena is also the name my ex-girlfriend wrote in the letter Athena gave me, in the event something should happen." At the time, I had no reason to believe Athena Williams wasn't her real name.

"Are you certain she wrote the letter?"

"Pretty certain. I'm no handwriting expert, but it looked like Kenda's writing. But she only wrote the name Athena. Maybe that name is correct, and I got the last name wrong. But I'm ninety percent positive that's the name Athena gave me."

Roger seems to mull things over for a second. "Is she American born?"

"She hasn't given me a reason to believe she isn't, but she hasn't exactly been forthcoming about her life prior to Maple Ridge." My chest tightens. Every single muscle in my body tightens. *Fuck.* If Athena isn't who she says she is... "Are you telling me the woman caring for my daughter possibly isn't who she claims to be?"

"That's what I'm saying."

I rub the back of my neck, scrambling for any scenario that could explain why Athena lied to me. The same woman Kenda asked me to keep on as Peony's nanny.

The adrenaline-infused pounding in my chest is making it difficult to concentrate. My heart was already beating fast, but knowing Athena has been lying all this time...that she was looking after my daughter...has my heart rate picking up speed. If it beats any faster, it might jackhammer its way through my ribs.

My hand moves to my chest, and I rub the spot above my heart.

Just how well did Kenda know the woman she trusted our daughter with? The Kenda I knew in college would have requested a security check before trusting her child to a stranger. Or maybe she did request one and Athena passed it. But why not tell me Athena's real name if she knew it?

"Could she be in witness protection?" I ask.

"There's a *slim* possibility she is."

"Slim?"

"I don't have the necessary clearance to find out if she's in witness protection, but the delay in replacing her lost ID and Social Security Number is a red flag. That wouldn't be the case if she was in witness protection. Do you have a photo of her? I can see what I can find based on that."

"No. I don't have any." I didn't think I'd need to take photos of her. All the photos I've taken of Peony are of her on her own, with Zara, or with my family. There are bits of Athena in some photos, but nothing usable to identify her with.

And now that I think about it, Athena was careful to avoid being in any photos.

I think back to when she thought I might be posting pictures of Peony on my author social media accounts and she freaked out. It's possible she was just being cautious for Peony's sake—or maybe there was another reason she didn't want my daughter's face on social media.

Crap. I should have let Kellan dig deeper into her past. Perhaps she has nothing to do with what's happening, but that doesn't explain why she's been lying to me all this time.

"You need to contact the local authorities and let them know your nanny isn't who she's claiming to be," Roger tells me. "I'm sure they've already questioned her on your daughter's disappearance, and they might be looking into her claims about her lost ID, but it wouldn't hurt to keep them informed with what you know."

"Thanks. I'll do that."

"Let me know if there's anything else I can do to help."

I do as Roger suggested. I phone Noah and fill him in on the conversation.

"We've questioned her," Noah tells me as my flight's boarding announcement is made. "Her name is Krista Danes. She has an alibi and is clearly distraught that Peony is missing. We fingerprinted her, but she has no criminal record or red flags indicating she's linked to what happened."

"So why the name change?"

"She claimed she wanted nothing to do with her old name. Her father was abusive and she wanted to cut all links to him."

"And that included her name." My muttered words are for my ears alone. It makes sense now—the reason Kenda hired Athena. Kenda was the type of person who would hire and protect someone who needed saving from an abusive father.

Fuck. Fuck. Fuck. We're still no closer to figuring out what's going on.

The Maple Ridge police are no closer to finding my daughter and the woman I love.

I rub the spot over my heart again. The ache in my chest isn't a heart attack. It's something more serious. More painful. It's the gnawing fear, the sharp edge of grief, that if they aren't found soon, it will be too late.

And my reasons for breathing will be gone.

54

GARRETT

It's shortly after ten thirty in the evening by the time I walk into Eugene airport baggage claim. Lucas and Troy are waiting to one side of the carousel. The usual life in their eyes has been sapped; their mouths are a deflated line.

Something paralyzing shoots through my body, stalling my breath, my heart, my will to keep moving. I wasn't expecting my brothers to be here.

Shrieks of joy and well-wishes and laughter surround us from other passengers and their loved ones. A reminder that while my brothers and I are stuck in a well of grief, life goes on.

"Any word yet?" The question stumbles out of my suddenly dry mouth.

They shake their heads, and a tiny bit more air eases into my lungs. At least they're not handing me bad news. But even knowing that, hope fails to flare to life inside me. The emotion is little more than an ember, not ready to burn out just yet. It needs a lot more tinder before it can flourish.

Before I can fully breathe again.

I one-arm hug my brothers, the action saying more than

424

words can right now. We're there for each other, pillars of strength against the growing storm.

Even so, their wan faces warn they're clearly emotionally exhausted.

I'm exhausted. Drained-beyond-belief exhausted.

But I won't be getting any sleep tonight. Or tomorrow night.

Sleep won't be possible until Peony and Zara are safe and home again. Until they're in my arms once more.

"What are you two doing here?" They knew I drove to the airport. My Explorer is in the airport parking lot.

"We figured it would be better if you didn't drive." Lucas adopts his big-brother tone. His take-charge tone. "Noah is at your house and will update you on everything once we get there."

"Does he have any idea where they are?" That's the only update I need. That, and to find out who killed one of my closest friends and has the two most important people in my life.

Whoever did it...I want to see them destroyed. Burned to the ground.

"No. Not yet."

Troy and Lucas aren't the only ones waiting for me in baggage claim. Airport security has corralled a gaggle of reporters to one side. Questions are shouted, the raised voices little more than annoying static.

We walk past, my focus tunnel-visioned on the terminal exit. I've gotta get out of here before I lose it. Before reporters witness, firsthand, just how well I'm surviving.

"Any idea why Emily was at my house?" I ask Lucas once he and I are on the highway to Maple Ridge. Fields pass in a dark blur as I stare out the passenger window.

"Kellan sent her to pick up the grant application form."

Fuck. If I hadn't forgotten to drop the form off at Kellan's house, Emily would still be alive. *Christ, I can't even begin to...*

I close my eyes for a beat, pressure building in my chest. *Why did I have to forget to drop it off?* "How's Kellan doing?" The question squeezes past the lump in my throat, my voice rough and splintered.

"Did you know he and Em were dating?"

I barely keep from getting whiplash at how fast I turn my head. "Since when?"

It's been obvious for a while Emily was in love with Kellan. Obvious to everyone but Kellan, that is. But I got the impression he was happy to keep things as they were between them. As friends.

"Few weeks, maybe. They were keeping things quiet for now, since they weren't ready for everyone to get in their business. But I suspect his feelings for Em run deeper than any of us realized."

I don't know what to say. I can imagine the guilt Kellan's dealing with, having been well acquainted with the emotion myself. I wouldn't be surprised if he blames himself for sending Emily to pick up the contract from my house, instead of getting it himself.

But it isn't his fault. He couldn't have known. There was no reason to suspect someone armed would show up at my house. No reason to suspect someone would shoot her.

"What about you?" Lucas asks.

"What about me?"

"Something tells me Kellan and Emily weren't the only ones who were involved behind everyone's backs." The *busted* tone of his voice rings clearly in the SUV.

I inwardly groan. Not because he's figured it out, but because I fucked everything up. I thought I didn't deserve Zara. And then when I finally pulled my head out of my ass, cast my demons aside, realized Zara's it for me, she disappeared. Has possibly been kidnapped.

She put her brave heart on the line, and now she's out there somewhere and has no idea how much I love her.

Has no idea she's the oxygen to my flame.

The air I need to breathe. The blood in my veins.

The woman I want to wake up to every morning, to fall asleep with in my arms every night.

Instead of being reassured I love her, that's she's my heart and soul, she's probably scared and in great pain.

Lucas pulls into my driveway an hour later. Police cruisers are parked on the street, a warning to reporters I'm not interested in talking to them.

It doesn't mean I won't be. Noah told me there will be a press conference, a time when I will plead for my daughter's and Zara's safe return. But until then, I need space to process everything.

I walk toward the front door. The dense wall of trees and bushes in my yard shelters me from prying eyes beyond the driveway.

My brain commands my legs to sprint to the door and see if Noah has any new information since the last time my brothers talked to him. But my body doesn't have the energy to push past the weight of my grief.

Blood, visible in the light spilling from the stoop, stains the driveway. And something sharp reaches inside me, yanks my heart into my throat.

The contents of my stomach heave and churn, but even if I do hurl, I haven't eaten in over twelve hours. There's nothing much to splash on the driveway. To mark the spot where the nightmare became more real.

White tape outlines where Emily took her last breath. Where all her hopes and dreams and ambitions died. Bile rises in my throat, and my hands shake.

I bend forward, palms braced on my knees. I attempt to suck in air. If whoever took Peony and Zara killed someone like

Emily, what will keep them from doing the same to my daughter and Zara?

Inhale....Exhale. One breath at a time.

I release a shaky exhale, straighten, take one last glance at where Emily lost her life. "I'm so sorry, Em." Grief cracks my voice. "I'm so sorry I wasn't here to protect you."

Noah and Officer Hunt are in the foyer with a red-eyed Athena when Lucas and I walk through the front door. Athena is clutching Poppy to her chest, her pale cheeks wet with fresh tears. One look at me, and a loud sob escapes her.

But that's not what I focus on. It's the panda in her hand that has my heart squeezing painfully.

Shit. Shit. Shit. Peony doesn't even have Poppy with her. She never goes anywhere without her panda. She can't even sleep without it.

It's a ridiculous thought. There are bigger problems than Peony not having Poppy with her. But ridiculous or not, I can't let it go. Poppy means everything to her.

"Any word yet?" The question is directed at Noah. My voice sounds like sandpaper has scraped over it, the grain roughened and scratched.

"Nothing yet." Noah doesn't have on his cop face. He has on his sympathetic-friend face. "I'm sorry for your loss, Garrett." He's referring to Emily. That much I can tell. His expression shifts into that of a police officer. Professional. Focused. Attentive. "We're doing everything we can to find them. We have the camera footage from your front door"—he nods at Lucas, who would have given it to him—"but all we can tell is that a man entered the house shortly after Zara and Peony did."

"Was he with them?"

"No. And we have no idea if she knew him. He put on some sort of wolf mask before stepping in front of the camera and entering the house—"

Athena's face flushes; her fists clench. "Because Zara didn't reengage the security system." Venom lances the word *didn't*.

I don't bother to respond. Irritation scorches in me that she obviously blames Zara for Peony's disappearance. I point toward the living room. "Maybe we should sit down."

"Sit down?" she screeches, the pitch almost high enough to rupture our eardrums. "Peony has been kidnapped and you want to sit down?"

"No, Krista—"

She flinches at the name. "I prefer Athena."

"No, Athena," I snap, the shell of my control slipping. "I want to tear the town apart, looking for my daughter and my best friend. But that won't get us anywhere if I go in the wrong direction."

"You're not doing anything, Garrett. You're letting the police and the FBI handle this." Noah's tone is a stern warning. Message clear. He'll arrest me if I get in the way of the investigation.

The five of us, including Officer Hunt, head to the living room, but none of us sit. I've sat long enough on the plane and on the drive back. I just want to pace.

I pick up Peony's favorite book from the coffee table, to have something of hers to hold. To help me feel closer to her.

I've read stories of people with the ability to sense someone who is missing, to know if they're still alive, to have an idea where they might be just by holding an object that belonged to them. I don't have that special ability.

Holding the book brings me no comfort, but I keep holding it, unwilling to let go.

"The man...the letters I've been getting. They sounded like they were from a woman." Did I get that wrong, and Annie Wilkes 3.0 is a man?

"We're not ruling out the possibility the cases might be linked. But we are expanding our investigation beyond the letters." Noah gets me up to speed on the latest updates—which contain nothing new since I last spoke with him. Zara and Peony aren't in any of the hospitals within the county and Zara's car hasn't been found. They've been trying to track her phone, but so far they have nothing.

I've texted Zara several times after news broke about the shooting, but she hasn't read any of them. I don't know if she has her phone with her or if the kidnapper tossed it.

Or maybe she and Peony escaped after Emily was shot and they're currently hiding. Unable to call for help.

Still clutching Poppy to her chest, Athena picks up a pillow from the couch. "She was supposed to be safe," she mutters, not looking at us. She vigorously fluffs the pillow, as if it has somehow wronged her. "Kenda said we'd be safe here."

I frown at Athena. "What do you mean you're supposed to be safe here?" My crisp voice startles her, her round eyes turning my way. "Safe from what?" Something about the way she said that...it doesn't sound like she's referring to Maple Ridge's low crime rate.

Athena's face crumples like a spring-time avalanche. She covers her eyes with her hands, her body shaking with the new round of tears.

I turn back to Noah. "Could this be someone hoping to profit? They falsely assumed, because I'm a *New York Times* bestselling author, my income is the same as Stephen King's, and they're planning to ransom my daughter?"

I'm afraid to voice my other fear. About Zara. If they do plan to ransom my daughter, will Zara be part of the deal? Or do they view her as disposable goods, and her life is as good as forfeit?

Muttering to herself, Athena resumes attacking the pillows under the guise of fluffing them.

Noah sends her a quick, puzzled frown. "It's a possibility. That's why the FBI is now helping with the case. They have resources that a police department like Maple Ridge's doesn't have."

Athena picks up the pillow closest to me. "He doesn't know I'm here. He can't know I'm here." Her voice is so soft, I just barely make out what she's saying.

"Who can't know you're here?" What the hell is she talking about?

Athena's fear-widened eyes meet mine. "Bernard."

55

GARRETT

"Bernard who?" I ask Athena, confused what he has to do with Peony's and Zara's disappearance.

Is Bernard her father? And what does he have to do with everything?

It's probably nothing. But her ramblings could end up taking the investigation in the wrong direction.

"According to him, it's German and French for 'brave as a bear.' But I don't know if it's his real name." Her accent slips into the Texan drawl I've heard from her one other time, and her gaze goes to the living room window overlooking the back-yard. "Like Josiah probably wasn't my boyfriend's real name either." Athena laughs a humorless, shaky breath. "Or rather, Josiah was my boyfriend before I was honest with myself."

"What does all of this have to do with Peony's and Zara's disappearance?" *Shit. Please tell me she isn't taking us down the wrong path.*

The twisting in my gut though, tells me to listen to what else she has to say. Like the iceberg that sank *Titanic*, there's more to her words than what's on the surface—as confusing as they might be.

432

Her eyes jerk to mine. "Josiah wasn't really my boyfriend. He just pretended to be one in the beginning. He pretended to care about me. Told me he loved me—unlike my parents. My father was an abusive asshole. To me, anyway."

She crosses her arms like a shield, Poppy pressed against her chest. "Josiah was never my boyfriend. Not like I had originally believed. He was..." She closes her eyes for a beat and releases another shaky breath. "Josiah was my pimp."

She watches Noah's and Officer Hunt's reactions, fear glossing her eyes. She's just admitted to doing something illegal. Something that could, in theory, get her arrested.

Arrested or not, she now has all of our attention.

"How long ago did you leave him?" My near-quiet voice echoes in the pin-drop silent room.

She walks to the bookshelves behind the couch and picks up a framed photo of Peony smiling at the camera. "You make it sound as easy as walking out the door and never looking back."

None of us say anything. We just wait to see if there's more to her story.

"I didn't clue in at the beginning what was going on. Josiah encouraged me to run away from home. He knew about my father. He pretended to be a concerned friend. Told me he loved me." Her Texan accent remains strong, and her mouth lifts into a one-sided smile, sadness drowning out any hint of humor. "I was so desperate for someone to love me, I fell for his lies. We didn't have much money. So he convinced me to have sex with a friend of his. Just this one time."

Hugging Peony's picture and Poppy, she returns to the windows overlooking the backyard. "I didn't want to. He told me I would do it if I loved him. So I did. The next week, it was a different friend he wanted me to have sex with. Again, if I loved him, I would do it...for us."

She traces her fingertip over the glass, as if drawing a small picture. "And then came the threats. If I didn't keep having sex with his friends"—she stops drawing to one-handedly finger quote "friends"—"he would tell the police I was selling my body for money, and I would go to jail. He then pressured me into doing other things that would get me in trouble if I was caught. Like stealing."

She leans her temple on the window. "I wanted to escape, but I didn't know how. I tried to leave him once. He beat the living shit out of me and told me the next time I tried that, he would kill me." Her voice grows steadily distant, like she's back with the man she once thought loved her. "He introduced me to another of his friends. Only this friend, he didn't want me to have sex with. He was Josiah's boss. And now The Bear—Bernard—was my boss. But I wasn't his only girl. He had a bunch of other girls he pimped out."

Christ. Once I get my daughter back, I'm never letting her out of my sight...until she's at least fifty.

I'll make sure she knows every day that she's loved, so she doesn't fall prey to assholes like the ones Athena is describing.

Even though what she's telling us has nothing to do with Peony and Zara, it's like watching a train wreck mid-collision. I can't turn away.

"I was stuck in this hell for years. Day in, day out, never knowing what to expect. Sometimes, I was beaten so badly by a john, I couldn't work for a week. Other guys weren't so bad. They were just there for the sex. One guy..." A soft smile lifts the corners of Athena's mouth, but she still doesn't look at us. She continues tracing on the window. "One guy was worried about me because of the bruises on my body. He asked me if I was okay. I thought maybe he would help me escape. He didn't. He walked out the door afterward and never looked back."

The movement of her finger against the glass slows, becomes more delicate. "And then one day I met Kenda. I was at a party, and she was there. I didn't know at the time she was doing research for an investigative piece she was working on.

She'd hoped this would be the big break she needed and was planning to expose the sex trafficking ring I was part of."

"Investigative piece?" I frown. "Why not tell the police what she suspected? Or had she planned to do that too?"

"She would have told the police, but she didn't know who to trust. Some of The Bear's best clients were cops." Athena draws a heart on the window.

"What is Bernard's last name?" Noah asks her.

Her shoulders twitch with a small shrug. "I don't know. I never heard anyone say it. Like I said, it's probably not even his real name." She fogs up the window with a long breath. "Kenda convinced The Bear he had nothing to worry about with her. He had no idea she was a reporter, which is why she was allowed to talk to the girls, even though she was hired as the housekeeper."

Athena erases the heart on the window with the heel of her hand. "I'd known for a couple of years by that point I was gay, but it took time at first for me to realize it. I thought my disinterest in men was due to my situation. I never said anything about it to The Bear. It wouldn't have made a difference. As long as I did as I was told, as long as I still brought in money, he didn't care what my sexual preference was.

"I fell in love with Kenda. And she..." Athena turns to me. "I don't know if she ever told you, but she was bisexual. In college, she had been crushing on Zara big-time, but she knew Zara was straight, so she went out with you instead."

Shit, I had no idea. It wouldn't have made a difference to me that she was bi, but I hadn't realized Zara was her first choice.

Like Zara had been mine. Only I stupidly hadn't voiced it at the time and had gone out with Kenda. "Was she ever in love with me?"

Not that it matters anymore. Kenda is my past. Zara is my future. But I am curious, given I had been in love with Kenda.

Just not as much as I had thought I was at the time. Not as much as I am now with Zara.

Athena's smile is apologetic. "She cared for you. A lot. But I don't think she loved you. Not in the same way you loved her. Not in the same way she and I fell in love."

Athena goes on to describe the sequence of events that resulted in Kenda going to New York right after she and Athena had fought. That was when Kenda and I bumped into each other and ended up having sex. Of how Kenda returned to the house where the girls were kept, needing more evidence for her story, needing to protect the girls. How she eventually realized she was pregnant. How The Bear found out about it and used the pregnancy to keep Kenda and Athena in line.

And later, he used Peony to keep them from escaping their hell.

Horror-induced rage surges through my body. The hot spike of adrenaline fists my hands. All this time...I didn't have a single fucking clue any of them had gone through that. I had no idea what Athena and Peony had survived. But so much now makes sense. "Is Peony terrified of men because of everything you've just told us?"

Athena nods, unable to look at me, her head down. "None of them ever touched her. Not in the way you might be thinking. But she saw enough not to trust men." Her hand goes to her pendant. "After much planning, we finally escaped. The three of us. Kenda and I had planned to begin a new chapter in our life together. Get married. Finally have our happily ever after." She swipes at her cheeks.

"She wanted to send her story to a major newspaper, like she had originally planned. But I begged her not to. I was afraid the cops would figure out I was one of the girls she mentioned, and I would be arrested for prostitution. And that was only the start of my petty crimes." Athena shoots another nervous glance at Noah and Officer Hunt.

"You finally had a chance to be happy, only for your stuff to be lost in the apartment fire and then Kenda was shot because you were in the wrong place at the wrong time." I shake my head at the senselessness of it all. If it hadn't been for the shooting though, I might never have known about my daughter.

"There was no apartment fire. I just told you that 'cause I didn't want to tell you what really happened to my ID. The Bear had it. He figured I couldn't go far without it. And we weren't in the wrong place at the wrong time. The men were The Bear's hired hands. They tracked us to the mall and didn't realize an on-duty cop was there. The cop shot them. Kenda had told me if anything ever happened to her, I was to come here." She looks directly at me. "You would protect Peony and me."

"Do you think whatever happened to Zara and Peony has anything to do with your past?" Or have we just been wasting time listening to a story—as heartbreaking as it is—that has sidetracked us from more pressing issues for the moment?

"I don't know. The mask...the one you said the man was wearing." She looks at Noah. "One of The Bear's men would wear a wolf mask. Like the kind you can easily find online or at Halloween. But no one knew I was here. I've made sure of that. Except..." Her gaze shifts briefly to the window. "One of the johns was in Maple Ridge a few weeks ago, but he wouldn't know me. I only recognized him because he beat up one of the girls and his face stuck in my mind after that." She shudders, her reaction to his memory saying it all.

"Do you know his name?" Noah asks.

"No." She turns her eyes to me. "But you do. He was one of the guests for Wilderness Warriors. He came into Picnic & Treats a few weeks ago, and Peony got upset."

"I think I know who you're talking about." I then explain to Noah and Officer Hunt, "We take photos while we're on the trips, to post on social media. Not all the participants agree to being photographed, but I can show what we do have to Athena. Just to make sure I have the right man."

"This lead might have nothing to do with Emily's death and Peony's and Zara's disappearance," Noah warns. "But we'll let the Feds know. Their Homeland Security special agents who deal with sex trafficking and exploitation will want to pursue that lead. And they'll want to interview you."

Athena nods, her hands clutching both Poppy and her pendant, her skin paler than normal again.

"You thought you were safe in Maple Ridge," Office Hunt says. "If Bernard was no longer your pimp, why are you worried he might have tracked you down here? Why would he bother?"

Good point. Why spend time looking for her and why kidnap my daughter and Zara when Athena wasn't in the house? If that's what really happened.

"If The Bear thinks I have info on him that I could turn over to the Feds, he would put a bounty on my head and send his men looking for me."

"Do you have information on him? Evidence Homeland Security might be interested in?"

Athena shakes her head, her shoulders slumped, expression worn. "I wish I did."

"What about an address? Do you know where we can find Bernard?" Noah asks.

She shakes her head once more. "Somewhere in New Orleans. He had a big white house. That's all I know. I'm originally from Texas. That's where Josiah found me."

I frown. "New Orleans? I thought you and Kenda were living in North Carolina. And the only reason Peony had been born in New Orleans was because Kenda went into labor while you and her were visiting the city." That's the lie she had told me because Louisiana is listed on Peony's birth certificate.

"I wanted to distance myself from that city as much as possible after what happened. We had escaped to North

Carolina, but we were just temporarily hiding out there. We were living in New Orleans when Peony was born."

Noah looks thoughtful. "Did you go anywhere in New Orleans—like a hair salon—where people would remember you? Maybe somewhere close to where you were staying?"

"I don't remember the name of the place. But it wasn't close to the house. One of The Bear's men always drove us there and stayed with us. And I doubt the women working there would tell you anything. They were as scared of The Bear as I am. Plus, I wouldn't be surprised if the owner was paid well to keep silent about what she suspected."

I share a worried glance with Noah. We have a possible location as to where Zara and Peony *might* have been taken... but just how hard will it be to find them in the city?

Assuming that's where the kidnappers were headed.

Assuming Zara's and Peony's disappearance is linked to Athena's past life.

56

ZARA

I stand in the ultra-tacky, straight-out-of-*Criminal-Minds* motel room and rock Peony in my arms. She fell asleep a few minutes ago, clearly worn out from her endless tears. I don't dare put her down on the bed, afraid if I do, someone will pop out of nowhere and snatch her away.

We're alone in the room, but that doesn't ease the quivering fear in my belly.

"It's gonna be okay," I murmur against Peony's temple, hot tears clogging my throat. "We'll be okay."

My body is captured in its own hell, every joint feeling like someone's taken a sledgehammer to it. My feet are sore. The small cuts from walking outside barefoot are a constant reminder that I'm without shoes. And my brain...my brain is foggy, my thoughts rolling in slow and distorted.

There's no phone I can use to call the local police or my family. That much I can figure out through the fog.

I don't know where we are, other than somewhere in Colorado or Kansas or Oklahoma. The two men who abducted us took turns driving, after they pushed my car into a ravine.

We stopped a handful of times so they could grab food, get

440

gas, or go to the washroom. Those were the times when I could change Peony's diapers, the conditions to do that often less than ideal.

Each time we stopped, they popped baseball caps on Peony's and my heads and big sunglasses on our faces. And I was reminded what the cost would be if Peony and I tried to escape or drew attention to ourselves.

Somehow, I kept her from having meltdowns at the worst possible times. But maybe that didn't matter. Maybe a toddler having a meltdown would have caused people to look away, disgusted I couldn't control my child. Disgusted I walked around without shoes.

We'd finally pulled into a motel thirty minutes ago, after we'd been driving for over twenty hours or twenty years. The early afternoon sun is hiding behind clouds, a thin strip of light peeking between the curtains.

My eyes are blurry and exhaustion is dulling my senses. I'm surprised I'm still standing upright. I sway on my feet, rocking Peony, gritting my teeth against the hammering pain in my shoulders. "It's gonna be okay," I whisper. "Auntie Zara will figure out a way to escape from these mean men."

Memories of Emily lying unconscious on Garrett's driveway destroy the dam holding back my tears. Someone must have heard the gunshot and called the police. Maybe someone spotted us. Maybe we'll be rescued.

Maybe the police will link our disappearance to Athena.

What if she has no clue who these men are? Has no clue what they want? Doesn't know where they're taking us?

But she must know. That would explain why she prefers being a shadow, why she hasn't attempted to get to know anyone in Maple Ridge.

She didn't want to be noticed.

She didn't want to be found.

I move closer to the window and peer between the curtains.

The motel parking lot is empty, other than the cursed black SUV. No guests out there I can signal to for help. No one to call the cops. No sign of life other than the man who shot Emily.

Beyond that is a road and open fields of nothingness. No place to run to. No place to hide. Not a single vehicle drives past the run-down motel. We're at least five miles from the gas station. Five miles from Burger Barn, where one of the men picked up food.

With each passing second, hope of being rescued is dragged into the pit of despair, weighed down by my sinking stomach.

Anger flickers and burns inside me, fueled by the helplessness that trembles through my veins. I move away from the window, the intense ache in my arms and shoulders causing them to shake. I'll drop Peony if I don't put her down soon.

But once I do that, I can look for paper and a pen and hide a note in the bed. Maybe whoever cleans the room will find the message and pass it on to the police.

I lower Peony onto the mattress. She whimpers, and her eyes flutter open.

I climb onto the bed, the mattress dipping under my weight, and lie next to her. I hold her close, giving her the illusion she's safe. She doesn't have Poppy for comfort. She left her panda on the floor while we were searching for Daisy and forgot about her until after it was too late to get her.

"Go back to sleep, Princess Peony," I whisper. "I'll protect you from the scary dragons."

Now we just need someone to protect us from those men.

Peony snuggles even closer to me and falls asleep again. I try to inch away from her, but she releases a small, distressed noise. I'll have to wait until she's fully asleep before I can look for paper and leave a message.

I close my eyes and imagine Garrett saving us like one of the protagonists from his books, or how he used to rescue people when he was a Marine.

Garrett. The man who I wish was the hero in my story. The man who never loved me like he loved Kenda.

Though with Peony's life in danger, and mine too, I can't bring myself to care about his friends-only feelings for me. I have bigger things to worry about, to fear.

Tears leak past my closed eyes and dampen the pillow. I just need a second to rest.

I JERK AWAKE TO THE BRIGHT SUNLIGHT SUDDENLY STREAMING through the window, and my heart jolts into a frantic pace, banging hard against my chest wall.

Peony stirs in my arms. The fog clouding my brain hasn't faded since I closed my eyes. If anything, it's denser. Unrelenting.

"Get up. Now." The cruel voice pushes through the fog, reminding me I'm not in Garrett's arms like I was in my dream. I'm back in my own hell. A hell with two evil men and a toddler I must protect.

Peony lets out a tired wail.

"Shut her up or I will." The growl of his voice makes me think of an angry Rottweiler whose favorite chew toy has been stolen. His scowl is equally terrifying, the thick scar slicing through the corner of his eyebrow amping up the effect. He's alone.

I sluggishly push to a sitting position, my body wanting to scream at the pain swallowing me whole.

Don't fail Peony.

As much as I want to curl into a ball and die, I can't. Peony needs me.

I still have no idea where we're going, or why they

kidnapped Peony and me when it's Athena they were looking for. The few times I asked were met with icy silence.

The man tosses two candy bars onto the bed.

"Candy? Can't you get us anything more...nutritious?" I've been careful with my diet because of the spondyloarthritis diagnosis, but the two men don't give a damn about a healthy diet for us. Junk food is all they've given us so far.

"It's this or nothing. Your choice."

My choice is to be back in Maple Ridge, but I keep that to myself and pick up one of the Snickers.

I tear it open, break off a piece, and hand it to Peony.

She eyes it with reluctance but a beat later takes it from my hand.

I open the other Snickers and take a bite of it. I'm not hungry, the pain in my body overshadows my appetite. But Peony needs to eat or else she'll grow cranky and get on the men's nerves. Though I'm not sure a toddler hyped on sugar is much better than a cranky toddler.

She takes a nibble of her piece, then eats the rest. I break off another chunk and hand it to her.

"We're leaving. Get your stuff. You can eat in the SUV." He points to the closed door.

"Where are you taking us?" Maybe he'll be more chatty this time.

"You'll find out when we get there." Okay. So, not chatty.

That doesn't stop me from asking the other question he never answers. "You were looking for Athena, so why do you want us?"

I've come up with a bunch of possibilities, thanks to Garrett's books. But I'd rather hear the truth. Even with the brain fog, my imagination is scary.

"You're only here to watch after her while we're on the road." He points to Peony, his message clear. I'm expendable.

The trembling that's kept my body prisoner intensifies. Even Peony can't miss my body's reaction to the news.

"But why do you want Peony?" Is Athena part of a child trafficking ring? She steals children and sells them to people who want to adopt a baby or young child? And...and for some reason she developed a conscience with Peony and decided to return her to her father?

My brain fog grows denser, preventing me from figuring out what all this has to do with Athena disliking me. Preventing me from figuring out if I'm on the right track.

Stay focused. For. Peony's. Sake.

The man waits for me to quickly change Peony's diaper, then has me gather up her things, and carry her out of the motel room. She clings to me like a koala to a tree, her body trembling as much as mine.

Frustration leaks out on a long sigh. Instead of searching for paper and a pen and writing a message, I fell asleep. No one will find my nonexistent SOS tucked under the bedding.

No one will know we've been here.

No one will know where to find us.

57

GARRETT

Seventy-two hours. That's how long it's been since Simone last saw Peony and Zara.

And we still have no idea where they could be—other than they could be possibly headed to or are already in New Orleans.

I pace for the thousandth time in what little available space there is in my living room. The room and adjoining kitchen are crowded with everyone waiting for news. My parents. My brothers. Zara's parents and brothers. Kim and Jess.

Simone is at home with the girls, anxious like the rest of us.

I haven't told anyone—other than my brothers—about what Athena told me. The last thing Zara's parents and brothers need to hear is that Zara is possibly in the hands of sex traffickers.

The police and FBI have swept my house for evidence. Now all we can do is wait.

And it's killing me.

I write heroes who take charge and save the day. I'm a fucking Marine, and I can't do a fucking thing to save my

446

daughter and the woman I want to spend the rest of my life with.

If I had been home...if I hadn't run off like an idiot to confront Austin...if I had been here like I should have, working on my book, Emily would be alive, fine-tuning the last-minute details for next weekend's wedding she was coordinating.

And Peony and Zara would be safe.

There has to be something I'm missing. A clue to tell the FBI where Peony and Zara might be found.

Athena is sitting in an armchair, her face, her body, her posture that of an anguished stone statue. She hasn't spoken since combing through hundreds of Warrior photos taken during the past few months. She didn't recognize in any of them the man who Peony freaked out over. I'm pretty sure it was Joffrey Winters, but he was one of the men who didn't want to end up on social media, so we never took photos of him.

We have no idea if the man is linked to Emily's murder and Peony's and Zara's disappearance. We have no idea if we're chasing our own tail.

No one has made a ransom demand, so we still don't know if that's the motive for taking them. And there's been nothing to suggest the kidnappers want Athena in their custody too.

The occasional murmur of voices or the sniff of a broken heart crack through the heavy silence in the room. The silence thunders in my ears, matches the echoing *boom-boom-boom* of my pulse.

I need to get out of here.

I just need a moment. A moment where I'm not reminded of how many lives will be forever changed if they don't come home. I'm having a hard enough time keeping things together for myself. I can't be strong for everyone else.

Outside, I walk across the patio to the grass and inhale the fresh mountain air. It doesn't make a difference. It doesn't fix my anger or my pain or my fear. It doesn't bring my daughter and Zara home to me.

I pick up a small stone from the flower bed and hurl it against a maple tree. Anger rips through my throat in a yell. The stone bounces off the trunk and lands a few feet in front of a fairy door.

"Fuck. Fuck. Fuck." I pick up another stone and another, each one hurled with the same force as the first. The stones litter the ground around the fake fairy home, and my lungs burn from all the yelling. But none of it makes me feel better. None of it brings Peony and Zara back to me.

The door clicks open. I turn to tell whomever it is to leave me the fuck alone. Unless they have news about Peony and Zara.

It's Troy—and the curse dies on my lips.

Only he can understand what I'm going through, after what happened to Jess last year. Not exactly a great comfort. Jess was tortured. Christ, please tell me the same thing isn't happening to Zara and Peony.

"How're you doing?" His tone tells me he knows the answer.

I grunt, not having enough words to give a reasonable reply, and begin pacing on the grass.

"It's never easy for men like us to sit on the sidelines and rely on someone else to save someone we love." He turns a patio chair to face me and sits, elbows on his knees. His expression is the same tortured one I recognize from when Jess went missing. He knows things Jess never told the rest of us about her ordeal. "You have to trust the cops and FBI to find that person. You have to trust someone who doesn't have the same thing at stake as you do—your heart. And that's damn near impossible."

"I just want to be out there looking for them." My eyes lock with Troy's. "I love Zara. I love her as more than just a friend." A dull ache sits in my chest at everything I want to tell Zara. Of how much I love her. Of how I plan to make up for the time I wasted denying my feelings for her. I want a forever with her.

"I know. Glad you finally figured that out for yourself." He flashes me a tired smile, which then flattens into a twisted line. "As for looking for them...unlike in your novels, this is real life. And killing the bad guys isn't an option for a civilian. Not when it could result in us doing time instead of the ones who should be locked away. We have to rely on the justice system to do its job."

I snort a laugh, the sound void of humor. "What about justice for Kenda? What about Athena and the girls who were lured into sex trafficking? Are they going to experience justice?" I drop onto the grass, as if the only thing that kept me standing was the bravery I no longer feel. "Fuck, why does this have to be so hard? Why can't they figure out who took them and where they went?"

The back door opens, and Noah walks to where we're sitting. He's in his uniform, so this isn't a friendly visit. His expression warns me he doesn't have good news.

A winter freeze turns my body cold, the August breeze unable to defrost it.

I would stand, but my legs refuse to work.

I can only stare at him. Stare and hope that's all it takes to kill the bad news on his lips. To make whatever he has to tell me not be true.

"The state troopers found Zara's car. Her purse and phone were inside it."

His words flick on the small amount of hope in me, and I push to my feet. "Where?"

"Down an embankment. In Cascadia State Park."

"They got out?" Hope in my chest expands into something bigger, brighter. "I'll let the Search and Rescue know. Zara and Peony might've taken shelter in the forest."

Noah lifts his hand, a *stop* gesture. "Other than the purse and phone, there was no evidence that Zara and Peony were in the car when it went down the embankment."

Hope deflates into a wrinkled balloon, and I frown. "What are you saying? You think someone staged the accident?"

"That's what it looks like. Possibly to distract us into pooling our resources to look for Zara and Peony near the site of the accident. But in case we're wrong, Search and Rescue has been called to the area. However, the FBI is still focused on the possibility they're in New Orleans."

I start walking toward the house, calling over my shoulder, "Okay, I'll head to the accident site now." I need something to do other than sit here like a helpless idiot.

Noah grabs my arm, stopping me. "You're not going to help them. You're family." He releases my arm. "The rules are clear when it comes to family members."

Fuck the rules. "I can't just sit here waiting."

"You don't have to sit here waiting. But you do have to let us do our job and keep out of the way. I mean it, Garrett. Go for a run with Lucas or Kellan or Troy. Do whatever you need to, as long as it has nothing to do with Peony's and Zara's disappearance. Or finding the man who murdered Emily." Noah's nostrils flare at the last part, a slight crack in his cop mask.

No one knows where Kellan is, so I go for a run on my own. My head is no clearer by the time I return home than it was when I left.

Athena is curled up in the armchair, staring into space, like she was when I left. From the sounds of it, everyone else has moved into the backyard.

"Hey," I say, still digesting the news she told me two nights ago about her and Kenda. How if things had gone according to plan, Athena would be Peony's mother and not her nanny.

"Hi," she replies, her voice lifeless.

"You said you prefer the name Athena, not Krista."

"That's right."

"But Peony calls you Nina. Why not just stick with that name?" I've been wondering that since finding out her real name isn't Athena.

"Nina was the name The Bear gave me." She shudders, the movement violent enough to notice. "So no way did I want to keep using it after we escaped. Athena had been Kenda's idea." Athena continues fiddling with her pendant. "The goddess of wisdom, war, and the crafts had been thought of as courageous. Kenda said anyone who had survived what I had was definitely courageous."

Kenda was right about that. "The name's fitting for you." I sit in the middle of the couch. "Did Kenda give that to you? The pendant?" I point at it.

Athena blinks, her eyes red from crying. "It's a locket. She gave it to me the morning she was killed but didn't have a chance to put any photos in it. We were going to do that when we got to California." She lifts her feet onto the chair and hugs her legs, her shoulders slumped forward.

"Why don't we fix that?" I head for my office and return with two small, newly printed pictures of Peony and Kenda. I grab scissors from the kitchen drawer.

Athena hands me the pendant, her curiosity-widened eyes watching me.

I sit on the couch, open the locket, and remove one of the stock photos. I put it on Peony's photo, a template for cutting her picture.

Tiny handwritten numbers stare at me from the back of the generic photo.

Without my reading glasses on, they look blurry.

"What are the numbers for?" I show them to Athena.

She shakes her head, her pale eyebrows disappearing under her bangs. "I have no idea."

I grab my reading glasses from the office and return to the couch. This time, when the numbers aren't so blurry, they make more sense. "They look like longitude and latitude directions. And possibly a lock combination." And now that I have my glasses on, there's no denying they're written in Kenda's handwriting.

The part of me that loves solving mysteries in the books I read, who as a kid would talk through plots with Zara for the books we read together...that part of me sits up and takes notice. Gets excited at what the numbers could mean.

I log them into my phone to see where they take me. They are exactly what I was thinking. The first two sets are longitude and latitude directions.

Hope plunges straight to my heart and spreads through my body. And for the first time in three days, a tiny amount of ice inside me thaws.

I dial Noah's cell phone. "I think I might have something."

58

ZARA

"**Z**awa!" Peony's gut-wrenching wail breaks through the brain fog, and I slowly blink open my eyes. Sunlight pours onto the bed from the window, the thick prisonlike bars painting ominous shadows on my body. The steady beat of Taylor Swift's "I Can Do It with a Broken Heart" plays from what sounds like several rooms away. The title, my new mantra.

I groan at the intense pain holding my body hostage and push up to sit a little too fast. I wince at the pain and frantically scan the nondescript room with two twin beds. "Peony?" Her name tumbles past my lips in an anguished cry.

My gaze settles on the playpen next to the window. The top of Peony's tear-streaked face peers at me from above the rim.

"I'm here, Princess Peony." I shuffle over to her, my muscles stiff and uncooperative, and I pick her up. My body responds unkindly to the movement, screaming vicious, silent curses.

I cuddle her, trying to reassure her without words that everything will be okay. I'll protect her. I'll keep her safe.

Peony clutches to me. I'm Poppy's replacement, a role I take seriously.

"It'll be okay." I close my eyes against the lie and press a soft kiss to her tear-salted cheek. I rock her, and her crying slows to a light sob.

Blurry-eyed memories trickle in of arriving at a house, the New Orleans heat and humidity embracing me like a long-lost friend distraught at the turn of events. Memories of being escorted to this room, being told a list of rules I can't remember. Of a girl who couldn't be more than eighteen or nineteen years old bringing food for Peony and me. Of her telling me to rest up, she would be back later.

The bedroom door opens, and the girl from earlier walks into the room.

Tilly's long golden-blond hair is twisted up in a messy top knot. She's wearing extremely short shorts and a crop top that reveals more than it hides, and she has the same odd mark I've seen on Athena's body, just below her collarbone. The mark that resembles the letters T and B turned sideways.

Tilly smiles at Peony, whose sobs have lulled to gentle hiccupping. "Hi, Peony. Do you remember me? You've gotten so big since I last saw you." She tickles Peony's side, drawing a sweet, tear-dampened giggle from her.

I frown, unable to take my gaze from the mark under her collarbone. What are the chances it's just a coincidence they have the same scar?

Scar—or brand?

Because that's what it looks like. Like Tilly and Athena have been branded.

I tighten my hold on Peony. What kind of fucked-up place is this?

"I brought you clothes." Tilly lifts the small, folded stack of clothes in her hands and some diapers.

Track marks scar her arms. She doesn't seem high or strung out, but I could be wrong. I haven't had any experience with people addicted to heroin or whatever it is she shoots herself up with.

"What is this place?" My sleep-deprived voice comes out rough. An echo to how my body and my brain feel.

"Peony's home. Yours too." She sets the clothes on the bed I woke up on.

"I have a home. Thanks. In Oregon." I glance around the room again, searching for any clues as to what this messed-up building could be. There are no pictures on the walls, nor are there any religious symbols, like a cross, decorating the space. "Is this...is this a cult?"

I don't know much about cults—other than what Kenda told me. She wrote a paper on cult culture for one of her sociology classes.

Tilly shakes her head slowly but doesn't look too certain of her answer.

Kenda was smart. She wouldn't have fallen for the mind tricks cult leaders use to recruit new members. But I could see her becoming involved with a cult, with the goal of pitching an exposé to a newspaper or magazine. Or to do research for a book.

I roll my shoulders, working out the stiffness and pain from holding Peony. "Thanks, but I'm not interested in being part of a cult." Or whatever is going on in this house.

"You'll like it here," Tilly says sweetly, but the ghost of a plea ripples through her tone. "You'll get to have fake lashes and pretty nail extensions." She wiggles her fingers at me, showing off her long red nails with flowers painted on them. "And pretty clothes."

"I like the clothes I have at home, thanks." I kiss Peony's temple, branding her with the message that she's with me. "So that's where we're going. Home." I stumble-walk past Tilly, Peony held securely in my arms. Every muscle and every joint and every ounce of dignity protest the movement.

They can protest all they want. Peony and I are getting out of here, spondyloarthritis be damned.

I just need to find a phone and call my cousin Serena. She'll come get us. And I'll call the authorities and Garrett. And find out how Emily is doing.

My body trembles at the memory of her on the ground, bleeding. I switch the picture in my head to her sitting in her hospital bed, working on the final details for the upcoming weddings she's coordinating. Nothing will keep her down from doing what she loves.

Peony still on my hip, I walk along the stretched-out hallway, my heart beating in my throat. We pass a series of closed doors.

A white man with shaved-short dark hair, wearing a crisp white shirt and gray trousers, steps into the hallway from a room just ahead of me. My heart stops, and a gasp tumbles past my lips. Then my heart restarts, the pounding in my chest faster and louder than the rap beat playing nearby.

The man smiles. He's tall and bulky, maybe in his midfifties, his body a mix of muscle and overindulgence.

I take a step back, putting distance between us.

His smile is charming, but there's a hardness in the gleam of his eyes, the set of his jaw, that sends a galloping shiver through me. "How are you settling in? Zara, isn't it?" His thick Southern accent wraps around an unspoken threat in his tone.

I take another step back, shifting Peony onto my other hip, and angle my body to put distance between her and him. My gaze flicks to the stairs a few feet away and back to him.

"I hear we have a mutual acquaintance. A mutual friend."

I have a feeling *friend* isn't the word Athena would use to describe this man.

A barrage of questions circles through the fog in my brain. Questions I want answers to, but I don't know where to begin, or if I can trust anything he says. I just want to get out of here, with Peony. I just want something for the pain.

"The men who kidnapped us said you wanted Peony. Why? She's not your daughter." I'm making a huge leap here, assuming he's the one responsible for what happened.

"What makes you think she isn't my daughter? Rosaline and I had an...arrangement." His words are polished, a steel blade, his underlying meaning ready to draw, quarter, and eviscerate me.

I stare at him, muddling through what he's saying. Who the hell is Rosaline? Does he mean Kenda?

No, it can't be. Kenda wouldn't have had sex with him. Not willingly, anyway. "I don't care what kind of arrangement you had; she's not your daughter. And you can't hold us against our will."

The man chuckles, a serpent planning to hypnotize its victim into complacency. "I'm not holding you here against your will. You're free to leave. But you leave, and Peony dies. Your choice."

He's bluffing. Murder is as illegal in New Orleans as it is in Oregon. He won't risk jail time just to keep me here.

"You don't look like enough of an idiot to believe you'll get away with it." I take a step toward the stairs, angling my body so it's still between Peony and him, the wall a shadow to my back.

What do I do now? The fog in my brain mixed with terror is making it harder to figure out my next step.

Each thought takes tremendous effort.

Each thought is draining my dwindling energy.

Each thought is drowning in an ocean of hopelessness.

Stay strong. For Peony.

"Should we test your theory? See if I can get away with it?" The smile returns to his face, and a chill forms low in my stomach.

He shifts the recipient of his smile to Peony. She tightens

her fists on my T-shirt, her body trembling against mine. And a high-pitched wail, so frightened, so shattered, erupts from her.

I rock her, straining to keep the pain from my face, to prevent the truth of my body's betrayal from being broadcast. Especially to this man.

I press my lips to her temple and hum the opening melody of "Spirit" to try to soothe her. It doesn't do much. The only way she'll feel safe is if we're millions of miles from this place. And in her father's arms.

The man shoves his hands into his trouser pockets, the move deceptively casual. "So I guess you haven't figured it out yet? About Rosaline? About who killed her?"

I stare at him, my arms visibly shaking from the effort of holding Peony. There's no way I can hide that truth.

His mouth slants to one side, and I shudder once more at the cruelness reflected in the gesture. "A random mall shooting. Isn't that what they called it? Nothing random about it though."

Mall shooting? He really does mean Kenda?

"So pretty. You'll be a nice addition to my stable." He tenderly wipes calloused fingertips along my cheek.

I jerk my head away from his hand. An unreleased growl coils up deep in my throat.

He snatches my chin and roughly yanks it to face forward again, forcing me to look at him. "Take her to her room. We'll give her two days to recover from the trip, then she can join us for the next party. I have a few men in mind who'll appreciate her." His hand moves down to the V of my T-shirt, and he yanks the fabric aside.

I jerk away once more, but this time with my entire body. The startled movement is so violent, my back bangs into the wall.

Undeterred by my reaction, or maybe encouraged by it, he traces the skin below my collarbone on the same spot where Athena's and Tilly's matching scars are located. My skin crawls and prickles at his touch, but I'm too frozen with fear, with anger, with disgust, to move—my fight-or-flight instinct bailing on me. "Perfect. We'll also need to brand her."

"You sure about this one?" The high-pitched Texan drawl from behind me belongs to a female, and I turn to it. A tall, dark-haired woman approaches us from the top step of the staircase. "Wolf said she has trouble walking."

"As long as she can spread her legs—that's all I care 'bout."

Spread her legs.

The meaning of the words doesn't hit me like a cement truck failing to stop at a red light. It hits me with the force of the meteor that rendered dinosaurs extinct.

My already rapidly beating heart starts beating that much more, louder, harder—powerful aftershocks rattling my rib cage.

The woman is maybe two or three years younger than me. A curtain of silky hair swings against the lower curve of her spine. Her pencil skirt and sleeveless blouse aren't as revealing as Tilly's clothes, but they still show off acres of smooth tanned skin.

She flashes Peony a look of disgust, her frosty eyes two soulless dark orbs.

Peony presses her face into my chest, muffling her cries. Her tears soak through my T-shirt.

"What about Nina?" The woman's gaze takes me in from head to toe, but she keeps what she's thinking off her face. "Wasn't the goal supposed to be to bring her back here? It wasn't to get another girl."

"Let me worry about Nina. We've got something she wants. Nina will cooperate just to keep the little girl safe." The stiffness in his voice speaks of a man who requires complete respect from those addressing him.

She gives an answering nod and grabs my arm. Her fingers press painfully into my muscles.

Or it would be painful if every inch of my body wasn't already aching.

Peony's sobs grow louder, the sudden jerking of my arm possibly frightening her.

"Maybe give her something"—he nods at me—"to make her more compliant." He doesn't spell out what that is. He doesn't need to. The fog in my brain from spondyloarthritis is bad enough. I don't need to add drugs to my system too…even if they will temporarily help dull the pain.

"I'll do whatever you want." My tone isn't defeated. It's earnest. Hopefully earnest enough to convince them I'm telling the truth. Earnest enough to buy myself time, while I figure out how to get away from this hell.

The woman escorts me back to the bedroom, her spine stiff, hand still hooked on my arm. She glares at Tilly, who's sitting on her bed, painting her toenails. "Tell her the rules, then get downstairs. You're working tonight."

She huffs as if the two of us are an inconvenience and leaves.

"She's pleasant," I mutter and sit next to the stack of clothes Tilly had put on my bed.

I blow a raspberry on Peony's cheek, hoping it will distract her enough to get her to stop crying. Not that I blame her. I'd be crying too if I could get away with it. But crying won't get us out of this situation.

The smirk Tilly flashes me isn't so much a look of amusement—it's more of a shudder. "That's Lola. She's a bottom bitch. You don't want to get on her bad side. She's meaner than Satan on his worst day."

"Bottom bitch?"

"She's like The Bear's right hand. She used to be like the rest of us but worked her way up to where she is now."

I pick up the crop top from the pile of clothes. "Lovely. So much for feminism and protecting your fellow sisters."

Tilly's gaze darts nervously to the open door. "Never trust her, no matter what she says. She's not on your side—even when she pretends to be."

Tilly needn't worry. There's no way I'd trust that woman. The only person I can trust to get Peony and me out of this place...is me.

59

ZARA

The next day, I still have no idea how to escape this fortress before I'm forced to do what no little girl dreams of doing one day.

I stiffly move from one yoga pose to the next, silently cursing the lack of a yoga mat on the bedroom floor. Cursing I have to practice yoga without ibuprofen or clothes better suited for the activity. The boy shorts keep riding up my ass.

Yoga hasn't been enough to control the warfare battling in my body. It's just something to distract me. Distract me from curling up in a ball, from sobbing uncontrollably.

And maybe, just maybe, the increased blood flow to my brain will stimulate an idea for getting out of this place.

Peony is asleep in her playpen, worn out from playing with me and Tilly earlier this afternoon, worn out from her most recent bout of tears.

I shift into warrior pose, breathing through the stiffness and pain.

I am strong. I feel no pain. I am a warrior. I am Peony's warrior.

Breathe.

During the past twenty-four hours, I've learned that Rosaline really was Kenda, based on the description the other girls gave me of her. And I've discovered there are six girls in this house, ranging from eighteen to twenty-six years old. All were coerced, in one way or another, to be part of the sex trafficking ring.

Two of the girls believe they made the choice to be here. They haven't figured out yet the only person benefitting from the arrangement is the man who calls himself The Bear. The money he gives them doesn't come close to a fraction of minimum wage. The pretty clothes, the fake nails and lashes, the blowouts—none of it is worth what these girls are forced to endure.

Queen E limps into the bedroom, the bruises on her face still dark from when a john beat her two days ago. According to Tilly, it was on the menu. Like numerous other horrendous acts I'm sure none of the girls in this house are *willing* participants for.

She smiles at me, but there's only sadness in her eyes. "Your hair looks good."

I was taken to a salon this morning for my "makeover," and she had insisted on a blowout for me.

I couldn't even tell anyone there I needed help, to plead for them to call 9-1-1. My "boyfriend" was standing by my side the entire time. From the nervous glances the stylists kept giving him, I could tell they knew he wasn't really my boyfriend. I also sensed they wouldn't be willing to risk their safety to help me.

I've never felt so alone before.

Are Peony's and my photos on the news yet? Maybe. But even if they are, with the thousands of people reported missing, would we be nothing more than a blip on the radar?

Peony might be more than a blip because she's the daughter of a popular thriller author. That's bound to have led to national news coverage of her disappearance, right?

I cautiously move out of warrior pose, my body uncooperative. I wobble slightly, then regain my balance—a feat in itself with the fog occupying my brain.

Candi storms into the room I share with Tilly. Her face is red, her fake-lash-rimmed eyes narrowed, her ire aimed solely at Queen E. "Where the fuck is my brush, bitch? I know you have it."

Queen E scowls as much as she can with a bruised and swollen face. "I don't know where the fuck your brush is. I didn't use it."

There's no point in telling Candi to save her energy for the real enemy. She hasn't realized The Bear—and not the rest of the girls in the house—is the bad guy. She sees him as her savior after she ran away from her abusive father. In her mind, if not for The Bear, she would be living on the street instead of in this large house.

Candi's eyes narrow some more at Queen E, and she turns to me. "Lola and The Bear are waiting for you downstairs."

"Why are they waiting for me?" A shakiness that wasn't there a moment ago sneaks into my voice. The last time the bottom bitch was waiting for me, I ended up with a nasty bruise on my jaw and another warning of what would happen to Peony if I didn't cooperate.

All because my body is slowing down on me, and I didn't move as fast as Lola wanted.

"I think I heard something 'bout you being branded."

At Candi's final word, fear and panic slam the brakes on my heart, and my breath skids to a standstill. My heart restarts, beating faster, harder, louder than its new normal. The new normal it's been reset to ever since the man-wolf stepped into Garrett's house.

Candi shrugs like it's no big deal. Like I'm getting my teeth cleaned at the dentist. "And you're supposed to bring the baby with you." She waves half-heartedly toward Peony's playpen.

I bite back the urge to say, "Like hell I am." Candi doesn't care if I take Peony down or not. It's what will happen to Peony if I'm not here to watch over her that keeps me from voicing the thought out loud.

Not every girl in this house cares what happens to Peony. Not every girl in this house has mothering instincts like Athena and Tilly.

Taking her downstairs isn't my favorite option either. But I haven't been given a choice, so I lean over the side of the playpen, where Peony's still sleeping, and stroke her face. "Hey, Princess Peony. Time to wake up." *We have to visit the ugly troll and his she-witch.*

Peony sleepily blinks her eyes open, then scrambles up to her sleeper-covered feet. Her small fingers curl over the top of the playpen, steadying her. "Zawa."

She used to smile at me whenever she said my name. Now, her bottom lip just trembles. Any joy she might have once had has been sucked drier than the desert.

I promise you, you will get to see your daddy again. Someday soon.

If Kenda and Athena found a way to escape, so can I. The Bear doesn't want to risk a repeat of that with any of the girls here, so it might take longer than I'd hoped. He's recently imposed extra security at the house.

But I swear on Mimi's grave, Peony and I will escape.

She'll have the chance to live the life she deserves.

A life filled with happiness and love.

I will away the fresh round of tears clouding my vision, pick her up, and carry her downstairs. It feels like I'm carrying a school bus on my shoulders, and with each step, I sink farther into the carpet.

But if the plan is to brand me...well, that hardly makes me want to rush.

I shuffle-walk into the living room that permanently smells

like stale cigarette smoke and beer and something else I'd rather not identify. The large-screen TV on the wall, from the sounds of it during the past three days, is only for watching sports. And facing it, like we're in an upscale sports bar, are the leather couch and half a dozen leather armchairs. Each probably costs more than the income that any of the girls in this house make in a year.

It's late afternoon, but the curtains are closed. The only light in the room comes from the floor lamps positioned throughout the space.

I search from where I'm standing for something that could double as a weapon. Search for something that could aid in Peony's and my escape. A sharp-looking knife—a hunting knife, possibly—lies on the dining-room table, but The Bear is looming next to it. He'll be armed before I get close to the weapon.

The knife isn't the only thing on the table. A candle stands next to it, the flame dancing ominously.

"For God's sake," Lola grumbles. "You weren't told to be slow." Her gaze shifts to Peony, and her eyes frost with pure loathing. "Maybe we should punish the baby for your indolence."

I drop my gaze to the floor. Being submissive is against my nature, but it's better to be submissive than anger the she-witch. "Sorry, I moved as fast as I can."

"Why the hell did you have to be disabled?" she mutters. "No one has time to wait for you."

I don't argue the disabled comment. I'd rather she believes that's the reason I'm slow than to know the truth and shoot me up with whatever several of the girls are strung out on.

"Put her on the couch." Lola's tone is sharper than the knife on the table.

My chin lifted just a fraction, I walk to the couch, my arms quaking from the effort of carrying Peony downstairs.

Grab the knife and get out of here. Stab those assholes if you have to.

If only it were that easy.

I bend at the waist to put Peony down on the couch, my body still trembling. The trembling has less to do with the spondyloarthritis than it does about what's going to happen.

Peony clings to me, her eyes as round as saucers. "Noooooooooo."

"It's gonna be okay," I whisper on her temple, tears stinging my eyes at the lie I'm trying to convince us both of. "This will be over before either of us realizes it. I just need to put you on the couch for a few minutes. That's all. I promise."

Her hold on me loosens just enough for me to put her on the couch, but she's still screaming, tears streaming down her cheeks.

She's barely out of my arms before Lola snatches hold of my wrist and drags me to where The Bear is standing, heating the knife blade in the flame.

The reality of what they're planning to do sinks in, lighting a match to horror and terror. The emotions sizzle and burn like an out-of-control fire, destroying the last ray of hope I had clung to.

My eyes widen. "NoNoNoNoNo." I struggle and scream, yanking at Lola's harsh grasp, and try to push her away with my other hand. "Please don't."

The bulky man-wolf grabs my arm. I frantically slap at his face, his arms, his chest—anything and everything my palm can make contact with. But nothing seems to faze him.

Peony continues screaming, her high-pitched voice growing hoarse.

He shoves me onto the chair and catches hold of my arms. Using his body weight, he pins them to the armrests. Undeterred, I wiggle and squirm and kick out. I beg, I plead, I shout obscenities. I fight for my life, for the right to have a say in what happens to my body.

But his stone grip doesn't loosen.

"Sit still, or we'll brand the baby too." The cold hostility in Lola's voice flicks a switch inside me, and I stop moving, the fight ripped from me.

Please don't touch her.

I try to say the words out loud, but my voice fails me, the lining of my throat burning.

The lingering fog in the periphery slips in and clouds my brain, and I brace for what will no doubt be the worst pain of my life.

Music clicks on. Some sort of country song I vaguely recognize. One I hope to never hear again. The volume is cranked up, not to the point of deafening, but loud enough to mask any noise I might make from being heard outside.

I close my eyes, unable to look at Peony, unable to take the fear in *her* eyes. She's screaming and crying, but I don't have strength left in me to tell her I'm okay. The lie forms a knot in my throat, preventing the words from escaping.

A sharp, scalding pain cuts into my skin, again and again and again. The faint acrid smell of burning flesh taunts me.

Through the fog, I hear my never-ending screams, my throat burning more intensely with each one.

A loud knock echoes from the front door. It's nothing more than my imagination. A delusion. Brought on by the pain.

I keep screaming...wishing, praying, pleading to who-knows-what that the knocking isn't just in my head. That someone has finally found us. That after everything we've been through, we get to go home.

Yelling and a bang that seems to vibrate through the house follows the knocking. But the stinging cut of the knife and the burning has stopped. That's all I care about.

Dazed, I open my eyes. Three angry, two-inch lacerations

form a pattern above my right breast. Blood spills down my body, staining my thin, white tank top.

Men and women in FBI vests stream into the room, guns drawn. The music is turned off. Words are yelled, and heavy footsteps thunder up the stairs. Crying and screaming and cussing from the second floor follow a moment later.

The selling of sex is illegal in the U.S. These girls are all victims, coerced to sell their bodies, but the law doesn't see it that way. In the eyes of the law, it's not just the pimps who are criminals—these women are too.

Which means, if law enforcement believes I've traded sex for money, I'll also be branded a criminal. I could be facing time in prison.

None of that matters for now though.

Pushing past the numbness, I propel my aching, bleeding body to the couch. Peony is the only thing that's important.

I gather her in my arms. "It's gonna be okay. You're going home to your daddy."

She wails into the side of my chest not dripping blood. I kiss the top of her head. "You're going home to your daddy."

An FBI agent approaches us. And I keep whispering the words into Peony's hair, a new, denser fog spreading through my brain.

60

GARRETT

I remove the pan of mini blueberry muffins from the oven and put it on the counter. They don't look too bad. Actually, they smell and look exactly how they're supposed to, unburned and golden brown.

Athena is staring out at the dimming evening light through the living room window overlooking the driveway. The same place she's been standing for the last two hours.

"They're here!" The girlish pitch of her voice gushes out loud and excited, and my currently already faster-than-normal heart rate spikes.

Athena takes off running, sprinting past the coffee table and couch. I toss the oven mitts onto the kitchen counter and follow right behind her.

She unlocks the front door and flings it open without stopping to put on her shoes. She rushes toward the black SUV pulling up to the house. Her feet are bare, but she doesn't seem to care.

I shove my feet into my sneakers, tie them up, and jog over to join her.

She bounces on the spot next to the open passenger door and frantically waves at Peony.

The woman agent removes my daughter from the car seat. Peony's hugging a stuffed dog, shadows of exhaustion painted under her eyes. A physical exhaustion. As well as the emotional strain that could only come from the ordeal she has been through. Twice.

Hopefully with time and therapy and plenty of love, she will eventually heal.

And be the carefree little girl she's meant to be.

Athena reaches for Peony. The agent gives Athena a small, placating smile and shifts her body slightly, putting herself between them.

"Are you Garrett Carson?" she asks me.

Peony's sad eyes meet mine. Eyes with more knowledge of the world than someone so little should have.

Her face brightens, the reaction tugging deep in my chest and leaving me dizzy with relief. "Daddy!" She stretches her free hand toward me, answering the agent's question.

And that one word is all I need to hear.

My heart climbs into my throat, and my vision blurs for the first time since learning she and Zara were missing. I'd been able to hold back the tears all this time, but seeing my daughter, hearing her voice, getting to hold her warm body in my arms...those are the things that finally pull down the dam, rip loose the floodgates.

I gather her in my arms, my tears dampening her hair. She's alive. My beautiful, sweet little girl is alive. I hug her and kiss her cheek.

Her arms go around my neck, holding on tightly to me, and she rests her head on my shoulder. Little hiccupped sobs vibrate through her body, and wetness spreads through my T-shirt where her face is pressed against it.

"Christ, I've missed you." Tears clog my voice, relief and

happiness buff it to a shine. I hug her once more. I can't stop hugging her.

I sniff back the tears and release a steadying breath, inhale her sweet smell. "Who's your friend?" I pet the toy dog on its head.

"Doggy!"

Athena holds out her hands for me to give her Peony. But unless Peony wants to go to Athena, I'm not letting go of my daughter just yet.

Athena loves her, has been there for her during their darkest days, but that's not enough for me right now. She'll have to be content for a few more minutes knowing Peony is safe and those men won't kidnap my daughter again. They've been arrested and face countless charges. Athena will have to be content knowing *she* is safe; she can finally start her life over.

And I'll do whatever I can to help her. I owe her that much...and so much more.

I thank the agent for bringing my daughter home to me.

"You're welcome. She's a sweet little girl. And brave too." The agent looks down at Peony, and a gentle smile touches her mouth.

A small, shy smile bends on Peony's mouth, and she buries her face into the side of her stuffed dog.

"Is Zara okay?" I haven't heard anything about her since she and Peony were rescued. All I was told was Peony would be arriving home within the next few hours.

The agent's brow creases. "Zara?"

"My friend who was kidnapped with Peony."

"I was asked to escort Peony to Maple Ridge. No one mentioned anyone else."

Fuck. Fuck. Fuck. Why do I have a feeling I've been kept out of the loop? That something has happened to Zara?

I tell myself she's on another flight, but I have a hard time believing that. Peony trusts Zara. Why would FBI agents separate them?

The agent talks to me for several minutes, letting me know that victim support will be in contact, and then she and the police officer who drove her here leave.

Peony yawns.

"Do you want me to get you ready for bed?" Athena asks Peony, holding her hands out to Peony again.

Peony shakes her head, exhaustion slowing the movement. "Daddy."

Hurt flashes on Athena's face. The kind of hurt where her heart has been ripped out and stomped on. But she quickly hides it from Peony, from me, with a smile that ghosts her mouth.

"You can help me get her ready," I tell Athena, wanting to lessen the sting of rejection.

Once Peony is asleep, I return to my office and dial Zara's number. I'm sent to voicemail. I don't leave a message. What I want to say needs to be said to her face.

I phone Samuel. He answers right away, and I leap straight in with my most pressing question. "Do you know when Zara's coming back? The FBI agent who flew with Peony told me Zara wasn't with her."

"No one told you?"

Anxiety grabs my stomach in a vise and twists. "Told me what?"

"She's in the hospital in New Orleans. Her spondyloarthritis symptoms have worsened, and she wasn't in any condition to fly yet."

Christ. Between the kidnapping and witnessing Emily being murdered, I can't imagine how bad the symptoms got. Or how she would have been there for my daughter, even though Zara's body felt like it was a nuclear plant on meltdown. "When is she coming home?"

"Not for a few days. Maybe a week. My parents are making arrangements to fly out. And I'll be joining them."

I'm relieved Zara won't be alone, but at the same time, I want to be the one with her. The one sitting by her side. Holding her hand.

After we end the call, I open my inbox on my laptop. Because Peony was kidnapped, my publisher and the movie production company extended the deadline, which had originally been a week today. I send them an update on the situation and let them know I am on track with making the deadline—give or take another week or two. I CC my agent.

For now, that weight has been knocked off my shoulders.

The familiar cries of Peony having a nightmare come from her room, and I rocket to my feet. Both Athena and I reach Peony's room at the same time.

Now that I know the cause of her nightmares, I stare at the cracked-open door, momentarily at a loss for what to do.

Athena doesn't have the same qualms and hurries into the room. She turns on Peony's bedside lamp, casting the room in a soft glow and chasing away the deep shadows. Deciding it's safe to go in, I join her and kneel next to Peony's bed.

I stroke Peony's back and whisper soothing words.

Shit, what do I do? My daughter is here, in Maple Ridge, dealing with the trauma of what happened, both during the week she was kidnapped and for a good portion of her life. She has a play therapy appointment tomorrow. I never got around to canceling it after she went missing.

And Emily's funeral is in four days. A funeral Zara will miss.

I can't be in New Orleans, to be by Zara's side while she recovers from her ordeal. I need to be here for my daughter, and I need to attend the funeral.

Except...except I know Emily. I know the woman who was such a romantic she started a small wedding consulting business. She would be the first person to tell me to rush across the country and declare my love for Zara.

She would tell me if there was ever a way to honor her in death, making the grand gesture for the woman I love would be it.

But that still doesn't help me choose between the two most important females in my life.

Do I stay here with Peony? Or go to New Orleans to be by Zara's side?

61

ZARA

I open my eyes to find my cousin sitting in the chair next to my hospital bed. The same place she was sitting when I drifted to sleep. My parents were in the room earlier but must have stepped out while I was napping.

The smell of overly bleached sheets wafts in the air, the floral arrangements in the room softening the intensity. Floral arrangements from my parents. From my family. From my friends. The soothing clicking of Serena's knitting needles and the whir of the AC are the only sounds in the room. Reminding me that I'm safe. I no longer have to fear The Bear, or the men working for him, or Lola.

"So, Granny. When are you gonna make me a shawl?" I allow a small smile to flutter on my lips, my face and body aching less than they did two days ago. It's my soul, after learning Emily didn't survive, that is in worse shape, bouncing back and forth between grief and relief, happiness, guilt, and frustration.

Grief at losing my friend. Happiness Peony is with her father.

Relief that she and I are safe. Guilt I couldn't save Emily.

Frustration at how I'm stuck in NOLA for now, unable to be in Maple Ridge for her funeral. Unable to say goodbye to one of my closest friends.

And after everything I learned at the house where I was held prisoner and from the FBI, roiling beneath it all, like a smoldering pile of dry leaves in the depths of a forest, is anger. Anger that men like The Bear exist, preying on girls. Profiting off them. Mistreating and abusing them.

I tenderly nurture the anger, blow on the flames, keep them under control. Embrace them as a step forward in my healing from the tragic losses of Kenda and Emily.

Maybe one day I'll do something with that anger. Put it to good use.

But for now, my goal is to get better and return home. To see Peony.

Serena stands and puts her knitting project on her chair. "Do you want me to raise the head of the bed some more?"

"Yes, please." Breathing is easier when the head of the bed is upright.

It also helps that I'm not crying as much as I first did when the FBI told me about Em. I spent the first twenty-four hours sobbing, broken. But I know if I let myself fall too far down the well of grief, it will only make the spondyloarthritis symptoms worse, delaying my return home.

And Emily wouldn't want that. She would want me to embrace the day, to appreciate the small things, to smile.

To heal and live my life to its fullest. That's the very least I can do to honor the life, the friend, I lost.

Someone knocks on the door. "Come in," Serena says, answering for me.

Samuel enters the room, his clothes disheveled, like he slept on the plane after a long shift at Maple Ridge hospital and came straight here from the airport. "Hey, sis." He walks to the bed and gently hugs me, taking care not to get tangled in my IV tubing. "I just saw Mom and Dad downstairs. They'll be up in a few minutes. How are you doing?"

"Alive. Recovering. Desperate to go home." I flash him a pleading expression, as if that's all it will take to make it happen.

"Sorry, can't help you there. Wish I could." He walks to the other side of the bed and hugs Serena. "I'm not the only one who hauled their ass here," he tells me.

Jerome's here as well?

But it's not Jerome who walks in and sends my traitorous heart into a frenzied tailspin.

Garrett. He's here. And the lines of exhaustion creasing the corners of his eyes are even deeper for him than they are for my brother. But that's hardly surprising. His daughter was missing for four days. All things considered, he looks great.

Too great.

I can't tear my eyes away from him.

Wait. What *is* he doing here? The last I heard, Peony flew home to be reunited with him. Maybe I'm imagining he's standing in my hospital room, next to my bed. Smiling at me. Or maybe it's a side effect of the anti-inflammatory meds the rheumatologist put me on.

I move my hand under the blanket and pinch myself. I barely notice the pressure, but it's enough to prove to myself Garrett *is* here. The fact that I can smell the floral arrangements from friends and family and Garrett should also tell me I'm not imagining things or suffering from a delusion.

I keep staring at him, my body remembering how it felt when he touched me, how his talented fingers and tongue and other body parts made me fall apart in his arms. How he fell apart in mine. The great way he smells. The warmth of his breath when he laughs against my neck. How easy it is to talk to him. How I smile more when I'm with him than I do with anyone else. How I feel like the best version of myself when he's around.

Neither of us speaks. We just stare at each other, an odd tension vibrating the air molecules between us.

Someone clears their throat. Probably my brother.

I blink myself back to the hospital room. "Where's Peony?"

"She's at home with my mother." The deep rumble of Garrett's voice spreads over my body, slightly easing some of the pain. He really is here.

He nods at my cousin. "Hey, Serena."

"Garrett." Serena's teasing grin doesn't fool me, and I silently curse myself for telling her about the orgasm part of my previous treatment plan.

Garrett kisses my brow, and I almost swoon at his scent. "I was so scared when I found out you and Peony were missing." He cups the non-injured side of my face and strokes my cheek with his thumb.

His familiar calloused skin feels deliciously warm against my face. I lean into his palm, inhaling him once more, indulging in the Garrett addiction I can't seem to get away from.

"Maybe we should give the two lovebirds privacy," Serena tells my brother. I'm not looking at her, but the smooth laughter in her tone hints at a wide grin on her face. "And make sure your parents don't come in the room for say...um...ten or fifteen minutes."

The length of time for Garrett to give me an orgasm.

She laughs again, the sound just short of a snicker. "*Psst.*" She drops the volume of her voice to a conspiring whisper. "I think this is the part where he admits that he's been an idiot. And maybe gives her some of that treatment he's so gifted at."

"What treatment?" A scratching-the-head tone wraps around Samuel's question.

Serena pats my brother's arm like he's being silly and ushers him from the room.

"I was afraid I'd never get to tell you...I love you, Zara," Garrett says once the door shuts behind Samuel and Serena. Garrett's deep, rumbly voice should hit me in all the right places with the last part. Should, but the reality of what he's really saying sinks my heart, like a cinder block to water.

"I know." My voice catches on itself. "You love me as a friend." Always has and always will. Loves me as a friend but as nothing more than that.

He sits on the edge of my bed, next to my hip. "I don't just love you as a friend, Golden Girl. I'm in love with you." He's looking at me like I'm the Northern Lights painting the sky in vibrant colors. The way I've wanted him to look at me for the longest time.

And it just makes my next words even harder to say.

"I love you, Garrett. More than you can imagine...but I can't be with you. It wouldn't be fair to you and Peony." I swallow the building pain that has nothing to do with spondyloarthritis and everything to do with the chronic illness.

"What are you talking about? Peony loves you. And I love you." His thumb caresses my cheek again, and my stomach does a silly little flip. "I've been in love with you for the longest time. Since before Kenda and I ended up together."

I shake my head, trying to make sense of what he's saying. I misheard him. That's it. A potential side effect of the medications the hospital has me on. "No, you haven't. You've always seen me as just a friend." There's no accusation in my tone— just me telling it the way it is.

He drops his head like I'm causing him pain. "That's not true." His gaze meets mine. "I didn't think you felt that way about me. I should have been honest with you. I was just so afraid of losing you. But what I felt for Kenda is nothing like what I feel for you, Zara. You're the only one I've ever truly loved."

I cover his hand with mine and pull it away from my face.

He can't be touching me if I'm going to get out what I have to say unscathed. "Have you finished your book yet?"

"My publisher and the movie production company extended the deadline. Because Peony was kidnapped. But what does that have to do with me being in love with you?" A crinkle forms between the dark slash of his eyebrows. A confused crinkle, not a celebratory one.

"That's good. About the deadline." It would be heartless of them to still expect the manuscript on time when Garrett was more worried about his daughter than the book.

I adjust my position on the bed, wincing at the pain hammering my body. The emotional pain this conversation is costing me is not much better than the pain from the spondyloarthritis. "But you shouldn't be here. You should be in Maple Ridge with your daughter and attending Emily's funeral." Grief cracks my voice at her name, and I sniff. I close my eyes, fighting to regain my composure. It hangs from a thin wire when I reopen them. "But instead of being there, where you belong, where you're needed, you're here."

"I'm here because *you're* here. You're important to me, Zara."

"If it weren't for my chronic illness, I could've flown back with Peony." My tone is the calm of a teacher hammering home a point. *Please get what I'm saying. Please don't make me have to keep explaining.* My heart can't take it. "My injuries weren't bad enough for me to be hospitalized." I touch the spot under my collarbone where gauze covers thirty stitches. "But the spondyloarthritis is. That's why I'm here and not at home."

"I know. The physician explained all that when Samuel and I got here." Garrett threads his fingers with mine, and the reassuring strength of his hand grounds me.

But it's not enough to change my mind. "I don't want to be a burden, Garrett. To you or anyone else."

"Why would you think you're a burden?"

"Because I have a chronic illness that makes it difficult to do things. Especially when the symptoms flare up."

"So?"

"So I don't want to be a burden." What isn't he understanding?

"If our places were reversed, would you stop loving me because I had a chronic illness or because I survived an accident that left me disabled?"

I snort out a laugh at the ridiculousness of that question. "No. I love you no matter what."

"Exactly. You're not a burden." He leans down and brushes a kiss on my jaw. The tension in the air coils around us, drawing us closer. "You're my everything, Golden Girl."

I shift my head slightly to catch his gaze. The love I see reflected back at me has me sucking in a soft breath. *Is this real? Is he really in love with me?*

"You're a beautiful, strong, courageous woman. You protected my daughter under the worst possible conditions." His lips press ever so gently on mine. The touch lasts a fraction of a moment, but it still steals the air from my lungs. "And I would have flown halfway around the world to tell you I love you, regardless of the reason for you being there." His mouth hovers above mine, our stuttering breaths caressing. "I was going to apologize when I got back from Tucson for what I said and tell you I do love you. But everything happened before I had the chance."

The feel of him, his taste, his scent...my senses are thrown into overdrive. He kisses me again, this time lingering longer on my lips. "How 'bout for the next few days, we just focus on us. You and me. And on how I want to grow old with you. Because I love you."

His words are like aloe vera to the soul, easing my fears, my misgivings, my self-doubts. Words I never imagined I would hear from Garrett. Words I've longed to hear. And I believe him. He. Loves. Me.

And not just as a friend.

My heart pounds, my breath hitches, and a wave of tingles sweep over my body, our new reality winding around me in a loving embrace. "Okay." My reply brushes my lips in a whisper.

He slowly pulls away, his eyes searching mine. "Those men...did they touch you?" He traces over the bruised side of my face. "Other than here."

"No. Not in the way you're thinking." Thank the Lord for that. And thank the Lord Peony had never been touched that way either. Tilly confirmed that. She'd told me a lot of things while I was her roommate. Things I don't want to think about right now. I'd much rather think about this man in front of me —this wonderful, sweet, caring, sexy man...who finally, after all these years, is all mine.

A sexy glint lights his eyes. "So...so you're okay if I touch you?"

"Are you asking if you can give me much-needed orgasms... for pain relief?" A wide smile spreads across my face. "Because the answer is yes, please. But you might want to lock the door first."

"Good idea." He clicks the door lock and returns to the narrow bed. I scoot over to give him more room.

He lowers the head of the bed to make things a little more comfortable. Hospital beds weren't exactly designed with sex in mind. A nervous giggle escapes me at what we're about to do in a very public place. But heck if I'm changing my mind. I need him, this, so badly, I ache for it deep in my bones.

And not just because of what it means for my physical pain.

He's in love with me.

Garrett lies next to me and lovingly cups my breast with his hand over my gown, his thumb stroking the nipple. I give in to the sensation, my body celebrating his touch, and I arch into his palm.

Outside the room door, the regular hospital sounds click, squeak, announce, chatter, but inside the room...inside the room it's just us and our rapid breaths, my soft moans. Moans at his touch. Moans as I worship the feel of his mouth on mine. Worship the dizzying sensation of his mouth on my jaw, my neck, the shell of my ear.

"I've booked a hotel room." His breath blows hot across my skin. "Do you want to stay with me in my hotel while you recuperate, until it's safe for you to fly?"

"I would love to." The whispered words fall out on a quiet whimper as his fingers do delectable things to the ache between my legs. I widen the space between them, a wanton groan building deep in my throat.

Oh, Lord, I've missed this. Missed the way my best friend, the man who has my heart and my soul, knows how to play my body. Knows how to get me begging for more.

Garrett moves his mouth to my ear. "You ready to fuck my hand, Golden Girl?" The question rides on the low, throaty rumble of his voice, and I plunge closer to the edge of euphoria.

My "Oh, yes!" rolls out on a whimper, my body writhing and bucking against his hand.

Garrett's fingers sink inside me, claiming me. "And once you've been released from this hospital, it will be my mouth on this gorgeous pussy."

His words and his touch and his sexy voice are all it takes for the white-hot heat to consume me—in a giant wave of ecstasy and relief.

62

ZARA

Six days after Garrett told me he loves me, he and I enter his house through the garage door.

While I was recuperating in New Orleans, we spent a lot of the time cuddling in bed and talking. Talking and cuddling. He told me about Eli and Joshua—his two closest friends from the Marines—his reason for being in Tucson, and why he pulled away that day I told him I loved him.

Guilt is a shadow on his soul, because he wasn't there when the man broke into the house and kidnapped Peony and me. But he has agreed to talk to someone about the guilt, to make sure it doesn't linger and fester, shredding him up over time from the inside.

The FBI victim support team has also made sure Peony and I have the resources to help us fully heal from the ordeal. We plan to make the most of it, since Garrett and I want to ensure nothing gets in the way of making what we have between us solid. Forever.

But most of all, he and I agreed to talk whenever doubts about us sneak in. We won't let fear drive us apart.

He also told me Athena was never interested in him in the

way I'd thought she might be. I'll admit I never saw it coming that she's gay and Kenda was bisexual. My heart aches for Athena because of everything she lost: Kenda—the love of her life—and being a mother to the little girl who would be her daughter if not for the cruel events that had unfolded.

Events that ultimately resulted in Garrett finding out he has a daughter.

Peony's giggles come from the living room. My heart squeezes with a happy little *thu-dum*. I've missed her so much during the past week, even though we did frequently FaceTime.

Garrett and I walk into the living room. Athena, his mother, and Peony are on the floor, playing with her toys.

Peony looks up, and my favorite adorable grin bends on her mouth. "Daddy! Zawa!" She toddles to us and lifts her arms. "Up. Daddy. Up."

Garrett scoops her up and hugs her. She throws her arms around his neck and strangle-hugs him, her smile not going anywhere.

And my eyes prick with tears. Happy tears. Everything's-gonna-be-perfect tears.

Guilt tries to slither inside me, to coil in my stomach, to flatten my joy. But I don't let it, like I promised Garrett I wouldn't. I can't reverse time or take back what happened. And he convinced me that between Athena and his mother, Peony would be fine while he was with me in New Orleans.

"Oh, God, Zara. I'm so glad you're okay." Joanne hugs me tightly. "I was so worried about you." She looks at me with love in her eyes—the kind of love that says she's ecstatic I'm dating her son.

She turns her head to Garrett. "The statue you ordered arrived this morning. Lucas put it by the front door."

"Thanks."

"Statue? Did you get one of those big Greek goddesses for

your backyard?" A smile spreads across my face. I'm kidding about the statue. Well, mostly kidding.

"You'll see." The subtle nervous tension suddenly rising from him leaves me even more curious about the mysterious delivery.

I kiss Peony's cheek, inhaling her sweet toddler scent. "I've missed you."

She giggles and reaches toward Poppy and Doggy on the coffee table. I pick up the two stuffed toys and hand them to her. One of the FBI agents gave her the dog after we were rescued from the house. From what Garrett told me, she's been inseparable from it.

"Have you heard from Kellan?" Worry lifts Joanne's eyebrows and drops the curve of her mouth.

Garrett shakes his head, his expression a battle of emotions. Pain. Regret. Grief. "I texted him a few times, but he never got back to me."

Another thing I learned while Garrett and I were talking and cuddling was that Kellan and Emily had started dating. She'd failed to share that big news with me—much like I'd failed to share with her what Garrett and I were doing. She'd joked about asking Kellan to help her find a boyfriend, and maybe then he would finally see what was in front of him. Is that what happened?

"All your father and I were able to find out is he left town. But no one knows where he went or when he'll return. Troy got the impression it won't be for some time." Joanne sniffs, her eyes turning watery. "He finally let Emily in all the way, only to end up with a broken heart."

Emily touched so many people over the years. We'll be feeling the loss of her for some time. But the rest of us have each other to lean on, to help us get through the day without her bright light. Kellan has turned away from our support. Lord knows what that will do to him.

Athena looks toward the living room window, our conversation clearly making her uncomfortable. And sad.

Joanne sniffs again. "I'll let you three get reacquainted." She nods at Garrett, Peony, and me. "I'll call you tomorrow, Garrett."

"Thanks, Mom. For everything." Garrett walks her to the front door, taking Peony with him.

Once they're gone, I turn to Athena. "I'm so sorry for everything you went through. For what those men did to you." I don't have to elaborate on what I'm referring to. She knows.

"Thank you," she says, her Texan accent no longer hidden. "And I'm sorry you got caught up in it. I never suspected they were looking for me. I thought it would be safe coming here." Athena picks up Peony's squirrel pillow, her shoulders slumped. "Tilly and Queen E and the other girls? What will happen to them?"

"All charges and warrants against them have been dropped. The FBI is more interested in shutting down the sex trafficking rings than punishing the girls who were coerced to be part of them. But hopefully they will go hard on men like The Bear." I put my hand on her arm, letting her know I don't blame her for any of what happened. I hurt for what she's been through. For the situation she never asked for.

That none of the girls asked for. They all deserved a lot better than what life gave them. "They miss you. Tilly and Queen E. I told them you were happy. I hope that's true. Or at least that you're working toward being happy. Kenda would want that."

The small smile Athena gives me grips my heart. I want so much for her to have happiness. For her smiles to be big and wide and genuine—and not only for Peony.

"I know you've never actually liked me," I add, and a bright blush spreads up her neck and over her cheeks. "But I meant what I said before. I would like to be your friend, Athena."

"It wasn't that I didn't like you. I was jealous."

"Jealous?" That makes no sense at all.

"Because of Kenda."

That makes less sense. Garrett told me Kenda and Athena were romantically involved, but what does that have to do with me?

Athena laughs. The sound is less amused and more self-deprecating. "Garrett didn't tell you?"

"Er, tell me what exactly?"

We move to the couch, and I listen, stunned, as Athena tells me everything Garrett failed to mention while we were in New Orleans. Kenda's crush on me. How Athena had been jealous of me because I was Kenda's first love, and because I had photos of Kenda and she didn't.

I don't bring up the missing one I found under her bed, because I don't want to admit to going into her room without her permission, but I get now why she had the photo. And why she had removed Garrett and me from it. She wanted the photo of her love. She didn't need us in it—so she simply removed us.

The more Athena tells me, the more things fall into place from when Kenda and I had been close friends in college. I had been so clueless—much like Garrett had been clueless about how I'd felt toward him.

"Kenda and I had a lot in common," Athena explains. "We both came from abusive homes. Mine was more on the physical side. Her father was verbally abusive and very strict. That's why her father doesn't know about Peony. Kenda didn't want him to have anything to do with her."

Athena unfolds from the couch and walks to where a stray block lies forgotten in the corner of the room. "I could tell you and Garrett were close." She bends and picks up the block. "Kenda told me you guys have been like that since you were kids."

I stand, my body growing uncomfortable from sitting, and nod because it's true.

"I was afraid...I was afraid if you fell in love and got married, I would no longer be needed, and I would lose Peony. I was so scared." Her tone holds a fraying thread of jealousy her apologetic smile doesn't have. "That's why I put up a wall between us."

"You'll always be her family." Garrett's deep voice, thick with sincerity, startles us.

Athena and I look to where he's standing at the entrance of the living room.

"You might not be her stepmother like you wanted, but you're still her family. You'll still be family to her even when she no longer needs a nanny." He lowers Peony to the floor. She drops next to her toy xylophone and bangs haphazardly on it.

Garrett walks over to us and rests his hand on the lower curve of my spine. "Have you two finished talking?"

"We have." I share a relieved glance with Athena. Now that I know where she's coming from, we can reboot our relationship and send it in a new direction. "I hope this means we can finally be friends," I tell her.

Her face lights up like the Rockefeller Christmas tree. "I'd like that. Thank you. Both of you, thank you."

Garrett's hand shifts from my back, and he threads his fingers with mine. "There's something I want to show you," he tells me.

"Okay?"

We walk down the hallway to the front door. While I was talking to Athena, he moved my shoes here from the laundry room.

He pulls on his sneakers, and I slip on the ones he bought me in New Orleans. He doesn't tell me where we're going, and I don't ask.

Outside, he takes my hand and leads me to the spot on the driveway that causes me heartache. The spot where Emily died.

My stomach twists and my palms slicken and my pulse whooshes loudly in my ears.

There's no mark on the driveway where I last saw Emily—nothing to show this is the spot where my incredible friend took her last breath. A shipping box, three feet tall, stands in its place.

Garrett softly kisses me, and that's all it takes to ease the rush of adrenaline. To make it easier to breathe.

"I hope it's all right with you...I wanted to create a memorial for Em." The deep bass of his voice is heavy with unspoken questions. Questions that leave me curious about what's in the box.

He opens it and lifts out a stone angel statue in prayer. Long hair cascades over slim shoulders and intricately carved wings. She's serenely, stunningly, heartbreakingly beautiful.

"She's perfect," I whisper past the hot grief wedged in my throat. "Emily would've loved it." If she could see it from heaven, I know she would be smiling.

Garrett positions the angel among the purple asters in the flower bed, next to where Emily's life was tragically stolen.

He returns to my side and wraps me in a hug, pulling me to him, my back pressed to his chest. And I rest my head on his shoulder, absorbing the strength of this amazingly sweet man. *My* amazingly sweet and wonderful man.

The birds in the trees cheerfully chirp a tune Emily would approve of...and we say our silent, final goodbyes to our friend.

EPILOGUE
GARRETT

Two Years Later

Peony walks down the grassy aisle in time to the string quartet's version of "With You in My Arms."

With each step she takes, dropping rose petals from her basket, the hem of her pale-pink flower-girl dress swishes against her legs.

I can't get over how my little girl is almost four years old.

She reaches the front row, where Zara and I are seated. Flashing us her trademark sassy grin, she waves and blows a kiss for her baby brother asleep in my arms.

Her adorable gesture is greeted with a light chorus of "Awww" from those seated around us. She gives her audience a big silly smile and a wave, then skips down the row to join us.

Zara puts Peony's small basket on the ground by her chair and hugs our daughter. She says something in Peony's ear that has our little girl nodding excitedly.

My beautiful wife of sixteen months straightens, beams at

me, and leans in for a kiss. I happily oblige. I never turn down the chance to kiss her—whether it be in public or behind closed doors.

Kenan stirs in my arms at the movement, but his little eyelids remain shut. Long black lashes fan against golden-brown skin. He's the perfect combination of Zara and me.

Zara kisses our two-month-old small-miracle's cheek. And like magic, he settles back to sleep.

I missed out on Peony being this age. I'm glad I won't miss out on Kenan's early years. My publisher agreed to slow my release schedule to a book a year for the time being so I can focus on the things that matter—my career, yes, but mostly my friends, my wife, and my beautiful children.

The last few months were crazy enough as it was, what with two book releases six months apart and a movie premiere. There's talk of turning one of my earlier books into a limited-series TV show.

And after my daughter and Zara were kidnapped, there were no more issues with stalkers or overzealous fans sending me unwanted letters. The FBI tracked down and arrested the person who had sent me the previous messages.

Our lives have been relatively peaceful.

Peony whispers to Zoe, who's standing next to her. The pair giggle at whatever Peony said, and Lucas has to press his finger to his lips, a smile sneaking behind it, to remind them not to get too silly. For now.

They grab hold of each other's hands. I can only imagine what kind of trouble the two best friends will get into together as they get older. The idea of that makes me smile.

Next up are the two maids of honor in light-green, knee-length dresses. They walk down the aisle and take their position on either side of the ordained minister.

The music switches to the "Wedding March," and everyone seated under the white canopy stands.

Lauren walks down the aisle first, her father by her side. She's wearing an off-white silk jumpsuit, her black hair twisted up in a French knot, and she's carrying a bouquet of pink roses.

Her father kisses her cheek and walks to where her mother is sitting, smiling and dabbing her wet cheeks with a handkerchief.

Lauren stands next to her maid of honor, her eager gaze fixed in the direction she just came from.

And then Athena walks down the aisle in a sleeveless white gown that is as simple as it is pretty. She's beautiful, but nowhere near as gorgeous as Zara was on our wedding day.

No one is as gorgeous as the mother of my children—my best friend, my lover, my wife.

Lauren's cousin is by Athena's side. Charles beams proudly at the woman who is not only Peony's and Kenan's nanny, but who is also a children's book author. Her debut picture book, which she wrote and illustrated, released last week to great fanfare.

Athena and Charles stop at the altar, and he kisses her on the cheek. He gives his cousin a hug and a kiss and joins his husband sitting at the end of the front row.

All this love has me thinking of Zara and of our wedding. I loop my free arm around her waist and pull her to me, marveling at her strength, her passion, her drive, and her love. Her love for me, for our children, for her friends and family, for the community. Despite the chronic pain that is part of her everyday reality, she still shines bright like a star.

"In case I haven't told you lately," I murmur against her ear, "I love you."

Her soft laugh vibrates through my chest from where her body touches mine. "You did mention that this morning. After you made me come." Her whispered words are for my ears only.

Once the vows are exchanged, the wedding photos taken,

and the happy couple have danced their first dance together, I take Zara in my arms, and we sway to Ed Sheeran's "Perfect."

Peony and Zoe are also dancing, but they're moving to a much faster beat, heard only in *their* heads, which makes me chuckle.

Kenan is asleep in his infant car seat, his two grandmothers keeping an eye on him at their table while Zara and I dance.

I trace my thumb over the scars peeking from under the thin strap of Zara's dress. A delicate tattoo of pink carnations weaves and twists around the thick scars—the beautiful artwork a permanent memorial to Kenda and Emily.

And a reminder of how close I came to losing my daughter and the woman I love.

When Zara walked with me on the red carpet four months ago for the movie premiere of *Untold Mercy*, people knew she was the woman who had been kidnapped with my daughter. There was no way she could avoid them knowing. She had testified in court two months before that.

But none of those things are what the reporters asked us about.

They focused on how she was the muse for my hero's love interest, and on how she is best known for the work she's doing to bring awareness to spondyloarthritis, especially in women.

"In case I haven't told *you* lately," Zara says, "I love you too."

I brush a soft kiss on her lips, branding her with my love.

Branding her with our forever.

Forty minutes later, I wrap my arms around Zara from behind. "How much longer before I get to make love to my wife?" I murmur in her ear.

Zara nods at Peony and Kenan, who are enjoying their grandmothers' attention. "As soon as we get them settled in bed...you're mine." The smoky promise of her voice goes straight to my cock, and I almost groan in response. She lightly strokes her thumb along my wrist.

At home, I help Peony into her pajamas and read her a story while Zara nurses Kenan. He's practically in a breast-milk coma by the time they're finished. She lays him down in his crib.

Zara goes to say good night to Peony, and I watch my sleeping son for a few minutes.

"Sweet dreams, little man," I tell him. He doesn't stir.

I turn on the baby monitor and walk to Zara's and my bedroom. Zara is in the bathroom, so I shuck off my clothes and climb under the covers. I'm checking my socials when she walks into the bedroom wearing lacy panties and a see-through fuchsia slip that barely brushes the tops of her thighs.

And damn, my wife is even sexier than normal, and normally she's sexy as hell.

I put my phone on the nightstand, almost missing it because I can't take my eyes off Zara. "I haven't seen that outfit before."

"It's new. You like?" She does a little twirl, the skirt flaring around her hips, and I'm rewarded with a glimpse of her smooth stomach.

"I do. I love you naked too." The corner of my mouth slips up to one side, the thoughts of getting my hands on my wife making my cock excited. It presses into the loose sheet, tenting the cotton.

I toss the sheet aside and stride over to the most gorgeous woman in the world. The ends of her multiple braids rest on top of her breasts. I sweep the braids aside, revealing the thin strap holding up her slip.

Zara's rose-brown nipples tempt me through the purple gauze. I slide the strap over her shoulder and nudge it down her arm. I do the same with the other strap, and the slip falls and pools around her ankles.

I trace my finger along the fullness of her breasts and circle her nipple. Zara's breath hitches, and I can't help the smile that curves on my lips. She never fails to respond to my touches, to let me know how much she craves them.

She knots her fingers in my hair and lightly tugs, sending a rush of desire between my legs. "God, Garrett. I want you so badly inside me."

I also want that—in a moment.

I thread my fingers with hers and lead her to the bed. "Sit." I point where I want her.

Zara grins. "Always so bossy."

She sits on the edge of the bed, and I kneel in front of her. I hook my fingers on the waistband of her panties and peel them down her legs.

Eager to taste her, I toss the panties to the side and lift her leg onto my shoulder, opening her up to me. I lick along her pussy and flick her clit with my tongue.

"Oh, Garrett..." she moans, her head falling back, lengthening her neck. Her very kissable neck.

"Enjoying that, Golden Girl?" I grin at the woman who is squirming on the bed, clearly desperate for sweet relief. I know that sign only too well.

She lifts her head, her eyes bright, a sexy one-sided smile on her face. "Definitely."

I push a finger inside her and curve it how I know she likes it. I'm rewarded with a groan, and I withdraw my finger part way. I thrust it in and out, in and out, and add a second one, stretching her soft heat. My tongue continues to tease her clit, pushing her closer and closer to the edge.

She writhes under my touch, bucking against my mouth, her needy moans wanton. Her soft heat grips me tightly, begs me to not remove my fingers from inside her.

"Oh. God. Garrett." Her voice is quiet so not to wake up the kids, and she bites on her bottom lip as if trying to keep from crying out loud.

Her heat convulses around my fingers as she falls apart

under me. An endless wave of aftershocks tells me I hit the right spot as always with her. She flops back on the bed, looking dazed and happy and thoroughly satiated.

I unhook her leg from my shoulder and give her a moment to recover. Then we scoot farther up the mattress.

I lie next to her, and a sly smile lifts my mouth.

She pushes me onto my back and shifts down so her mouth is at the tip of my cock. She opens those sweet, lush lips of hers and takes my tip into her mouth. Her fingers lightly squeeze my balls.

I run my fingers along her cheek, appreciating the view of my wife consuming me this way, of her performing her magic. I watch her until I can't keep it together any longer. My thread of control is rapidly stretching just short of the point of no return.

"I need to be inside you. Now." My words ride on a stuttering breath.

Zara releases me, and before she can move or say anything, I have her on her back, my body positioned between her legs. I take a second to absorb the beauty in front of me.

Her ripe lips part, begging for me to kiss her. So, I do. Thoroughly.

I position my cock at her entrance and ease my way in.

Then I make slow, soul-shattering love to my beautiful wife. Telling her without words she is my forever. Today. Tomorrow.

And for all eternity.

ACKNOWLEDGMENTS

Athena's story came to be when I attended the Sexual Exploitation & Trafficking Awareness conference in Calgary a few years ago. It involved numerous presentations and keynote addresses, including with the FBI and several survivors of exploitation. I then attended a three-day workshop on the topic hosted by RESET Society of Calgary. Both the conference and the workshop were eye-opening and heartbreaking. I knew after attending them that I wanted to create a character who was not only a survivor, her story would be a combination of several real-life stories shared at the conference. Athena's drawings of girls were inspired by an exercise we did in the workshop. We were then shown the artwork created by some of the survivors who RESET Society of Calgary had helped over the past several years. A few of the pictures were the inspiration for Athena's breathtaking drawings described in the book.

Thank you to my brilliant developmental editor, Lauren Clarke. Your suggestions always help my stories reach their full potential. I couldn't imagine writing a book without your guiding hand. Thank you to my sensitivity reader, Livi, and to Margie Lawson, Erin, and Tracey for your support and suggestions for making my words shine. Erin and Tracey, I can't wait for the world to read your books.

To the readers and book creatives who share about my stories and cheer for my characters, the world is a better place because of the love you share for romances. You make us smile and eager to read the stories that you couldn't imagine life without. Thank you for finding a place in your heart for my books.

And lastly, I want to give a huge *Thank you* to my family. To my husband, Ralph. While you might not have ever read my books, you have always supported my decision to write and have been an amazing cheerleader. You were my real-life book boyfriend. I just wish I'd had so much more time with you—like we were supposed to have together. I love you so very, very much. Anton, Stefanie, and Anja, the past ten months have been some of the worst of our lives after losing your father in a tragic pedestrian-vehicle accident. You three were the reason I got up each morning when I could barely find the strength to face each day without your dad. You gave me a reason to smile and laugh when none of us had a reason to believe we could ever be happy again. Your dad might not be around to see all the amazing things you will go on to achieve, but I will be there being doubly proud of everything you accomplish. I love you three to the moon and back.

ABOUT THE AUTHOR

Born in Brighton England, Stina Lindenblatt has lived in a number of countries, including England, the U.S., Finland, and Canada. This would explain her mixed up accent. She has a kinesiology degree and a MSc in sports biological sciences.

In addition to writing fiction, she loves photography, and currently lives in Calgary, Canada, with her cat, three kids, and the memories of her cherished late husband.

For news about her books and to sign up for her newsletter, check out her website at stinalindenblattauthor.com.